If WAR Should Come

A Paul Muller Novel of Political Intrigue

WILLIAM N. WALKER

William N. Walker

If WAR Should Come is a work of fiction and a product of the author's imagination. While the story endeavors to recapture historical events accurately and to portray real places and institutions, it does so in an entirely fictitious manner reflecting the author's opinions and conjectures.

The novel refers to many historical figures, but they are characterized as the author imagines them. Dialogues and descriptions are fictional and are not intended to depict actual events or to alter the entirely fictional nature of the story.

Any resemblance to actual persons or events is entirely coincidental.

If War Should Come

DEDICATION

For

My wife

Janet Smith Walker

with deep thanks for her love and support

and for my children,

Gilbert, Helen and Joanna,

who mean the world to me.

CONTENTS

ACKNOWLEDGMENTS

I extend thanks to my editors, Rhonda Dossett and Marian Borden for their efficient and helpful work.

I am once again indebted to Colonel Ernst M. Felberbauer, Austrian Defense Academy, Vienna, for his encouragement and assistance as I wrote the novel. He has worked to keep the narrative historically accurate, so any perceived errors are entirely my responsibility. Having an expertly-informed advisor is very welcome presence in the creative process of writing the Paul Muller novels.

Mr. and Mrs. Henry Schacht provided very welcome encouragement and support–especially during the long pandemic shutdown.

Cover photo used with permission. www.goodfreephotos.com.

"Most believed that [even after the defeat of Poland] invasion of France would never happen, for Hitler would be economically strangled by then. This was not the Great War with its chaos and horror, it was "the phony war", it was "the bore war", or "la drôle de guerre", or the new German word "Sitzkreig". It was a twilight war, a time when all people could do was wait, a time of nothingness, a time of boredom born of the need not to think, a time of mordant expectancy that stifled enjoyment, excitement, and the wish for life. The phony war was a still and ugly calm at the center of the storm, a vacuum into which seeped the fears and frustrations of societies which knew and did not want to know that disaster was imminent."

The Phony War 1939-1940, Tom Schachtman, Harper & Row 1982. P. 113.

PREFACE

In our collective memories, World War II began in early September 1939 when Hitler invaded Poland and Britain and France responded by declaring war on Germany. But then not much happened until May 1940, when Hitler unleashed the German *Blitzkrieg* attack that conquered France in only a matter of weeks.

We think of that intervening period as 'the Phony War.'

And, certainly, the conventional wisdom is that the Phony War was simply a boring interlude.

But as the reader is about to be reminded, the reality was different.

There was *a lot* going on.

Paul Muller will find himself engulfed both by war and by frantic maneuvers by governments to avoid it: to change the alignment of forces in ways that offered the prospect that, if conflict should come, with its all its baggage of death and destruction, it would arise somewhere else.

In Russia, say, or Scandinavia; anywhere but the historic killing fields of Northern France where the Great War had come to its bloody close less than a generation earlier.

It was also a time of deep uncertainty. People didn't know what was going to happen or how their lives would be upended.

From our perspective eighty plus years later, we know all too well what lies in store.

But Paul Muller and the other characters in this novel do not. My effort will be to invite readers to put themselves in Muller's shoes as he navigates the confused and frenzied events that unfolded when war did come.

CHAPTER 1

It was the next to last day of August 1939, still warm and sunny; ordinarily–at least in summers past–the kind of weather inviting Swiss citizens to leave their offices early, or even skip work entirely, for the last picnic of summer. But this year was different; people were speaking to one another, not about picnics, but about news that war was imminent and their fears about what would happen to them if it did.

Newspaper headlines and radio bulletins were reporting strident threats by Hitler to invade Poland and Britain and France were beginning to mobilize troops to oppose him. If war were to break out, Switzerland would, once again, be caught in the middle and would need to defend itself. Only a day earlier, the Swiss Federal Council had called up 100,000 Frontier Guards and imposed restrictions on frontier crossings, and had issued orders banning overflights of Swiss territory by foreign aircraft.

So, nerves were already on edge that day when the Council announced that it would convene the Parliament to invoke emergency powers. Upon hearing the news, people quietly began to gather in the Bundesplatz, the wide plaza in front of the Federal Palace in Bern, the Swiss capital.

Paul Muller was among them and he was able to gain entrance to the Palace and squeeze into the public gallery that was situated above the Parliament chamber as both houses convened in Emergency Session. From his perch, he gazed down at the semi-circle of desks where delegates were finding their places and watched the members of the Federal Council stride forward to take their seats in the raised dais facing the delegates.

The Swiss Constitution provides that in a national emergency, Parliament has the authority to elect a General to be commander-in-chief of the nation's armed forces and take charge of the nation's defense. In this last week of August 1939, the Federal Council had met almost daily to assess the mounting threat of war, and now, at 5 PM on Wednesday August 30, 1939, it had convened the Parliament to declare a state of emergency and appoint a General.

It was a solemn occasion and Muller could feel the tension in the room. There was an air of resolve and a sense of confidence in the procedures that were being invoked to defend the nation at this parlous moment. But there was also an undercurrent of fear–Muller couldn't find a better word for it; fear of the unknown and fear of the harm a new war might bring–not just to the Swiss nation, but to individual citizens and their families.

The low buzz of conversation on the floor and in the gallery subsided and the great chamber grew quiet. The President of the

Federal Council, Marcel Pilet-Golaz, stood and struck a gavel on the desktop before him, the sharp sound echoing in the silence of the chamber.

"Upon direction of the Federal Council, I call this special session of the Parliament to order and direct the clerk to read the resolution inviting the Parliament to reaffirm Switzerland's assertion of neutrality and to declare a state of emergency in light of current political events that threaten the security of the Swiss state."

Pilet-Golaz had the reputation of being a weak leader, timid in the face of foreign provocation–especially threats by Nazi Germany to undermine press freedoms in Switzerland and compromise its neutrality. He also had the misfortune of physically resembling Adolf Hitler, a small black mustache above his mouth and black hair combed to one side; Muller had in fact ridiculed his appearance at a garden party not long ago. But he had to admit that in this parliamentary role, Pilet-Golaz appeared presidential and dignified.

The Parliamentary clerk, a slender, elderly man with wispy gray hair, stood and mumbled inaudibly the language of the emergency declaration, which had been distributed to the parliamentarians in advance. Pilet-Golaz moved immediately to the vote, without inviting discussion from the floor. The resolution was adopted with only two dissents.

Pilet-Golaz then immediately moved the nomination of Henri Guisan, the Colonel commanding the First Corps, to become the

General of the Swiss Armed Forces. Once again, there was no debate and Guisan was elected by another resounding majority. After Pilet-Golaz announced the tally, the chamber fell silent, and all eyes turned toward the doorway at the head of the center aisle.

After what seemed several long minutes to Muller, the door opened and General Guisan stepped briskly into the chamber.

He was in full uniform, shiny black riding boots below neatly pressed jodhpurs with narrow vertical stripes up each leg, and a tailored khaki uniform jacket, with a leather strap running crisply from his right shoulder to his left hip. He stood at attention, then carefully removed his uniform cap and pressed it against his heart. He then began to walk at a deliberate pace down the aisle toward the well of the chamber and as he did so, delegates rose to their feet and stood in silence, watching him stride past. There was no applause, and no one spoke; it seemed to Muller as if the entire assembly had decided to absorb the moment and no one could bring themselves to break the spell.

Upon reaching the well, Guisan again drew himself to attention and saluted the members of the Federal Council on the dais. He looked surprisingly fit and energetic for a sixty-five year old man and he conveyed an aura of confidence.

Guisan raised his right hand as President Pilet-Golaz administered the oath "faithfully to ensure the independence and neutrality of the Federal Republic," and he responded, "Je le jure," I swear, in a firm voice. At this point, the delegates broke into warm applause, a young woman in peasant costume appeared from the wings to hand the new General a bouquet of red and white lilies and the ceremony concluded.

Muller joined the crowd that exited to the Bundesplatz where people were stopping to mingle and exchange words. Military parades were a regular occurrence–very often here on the Bundesplatz itself–and Muller had often seen Guisan, on horseback, skillfully commanding cavalry maneuvers. As he made his way back to the Ministry of Military Affairs, Muller felt a surge of relief that the government had acted to install a fresh leader as war threatened, and he sensed that others in the crowd also came away reassured.

Time would tell, he told himself; but the government's response to the gathering crisis seemed to have gotten off to a good start.

CHAPTER 2

At dinner that evening, Hans Haussamann clinked glasses with Muller as they sampled a chilled Fendant from the Valais before turning their attention to the menu before them.

Haussamann was the Chief of Büro Ha, a shadowy private intelligence organization that Haussamann had assembled, and which served as the informal intelligence arm of the woefully understaffed Ministry of Military Affairs. Paul Muller had become a part of the Büro, working for Haussamann, since early 1938, when he had undertaken a mission to try to thwart Hitler's takeover of neighboring Austria and safeguard Austrian gold reserves. He had narrowly escaped the eventual Nazi *Anschluss* and over the past sixth months had become the Büro's economic section chief, seeking to defend Switzerland against economic threats not just from Nazi Germany, which Switzerland depended upon for vital supplies of coal and other commodities, but from both France and Britain as well, both of which also controlled exports vital to the survival of the Swiss economy.

"Selecting Guisan was Minger's plan," Haussamann said, referring to Rudolf Minger, who was Chief of the Swiss Ministry of Military Affairs and arguably the most powerful member of the Federal Council, the body elected by Parliament which comprised the leadership of the Swiss government.

"We're on the brink of war, and he was determined to establish a chain of command that sidelines the Council and can respond to the threats we'll surely face. He was at his wit's end over the Council's feckless behavior over the past week or so when it was unable to even to recognize the risk of a war that's staring us in the face."

Haussamann accepted Muller's proffer of a Gitane from his cigarette case and waved away the smoke as he exhaled.

"The Council met last Sunday, and he tried to explain to them that the Nazi-Soviet Nonaggression Pact, which Ribbentrop and Molotov cooked up in Moscow last week, laid out the welcome mat for Hitler to invade Poland, knowing that the Soviets won't interfere or align themselves with the British and French if they declare war, as they've threatened to do."

Haussamann leaned across the table, speaking intensely.

"But instead of reacting, the Council deferred to Motta, the Foreign Minister, who reported that our ambassador in Berlin–that hapless Hans Froelicher–reported that he'd met with Ribbentrop's deputy, who told him there was no threat of war. So, Motta proceeded to tell the press that there will be no war, pointing out that trains were still arriving punctually from Germany and France and that Swiss Air was maintaining its normal schedule of flights to Berlin.

"Minger was furious and forced another meeting of the Council the next day. I furnished him with an update from my German sources that told a very different story: Panzers massed at the Polish border, nearly a thousand Luftwaffe aircraft positioned on airfields bordering Poland in what used to be Czechoslovakia and reports of armed clashes at several frontier stations that the Germans were calling Polish provocations. By that time, the French had begun mobilizing three million reservists and the British had begun evacuating women and children from London to the countryside, fearful of German bombing attacks.

"Minger laid out the facts and delivered an ultimatum: either the Council would convene Parliament to declare an Emergency or he would resign and accuse the Council of betraying its obligation to protect the nation. Well, they all folded, and here we are, an emergency formally declared and Guisan installed as the General."

Haussamann stubbed out his butt in the glass ashtray and poured them each another glass of Fendant.

"And where does Büro Ha fit into this new arrangement?" asked Muller

"Minger persuaded Guisan to leave things as they've been," Haussmann replied quickly. "Being outside the Ministry structure offers us operational flexibility–and deniability–if that becomes necessary. Minger wants us to continue reporting directly to him;

Guisan decided he had a very full plate already and said he was comfortable with that arrangement."

"So, I'm to continue preparing to defend us against whatever acts of economic warfare might ensue if and when war is actually declared."

Muller didn't phrase his statement as a question.

As he expected, Haussamann nodded.

"You've already been told by the British that they're ready to mount an all-out campaign of economic warfare against Germany and warned that they may have to destroy the Swiss economy to accomplish their goals. We have to assume that the French have a similar strategy. We haven't been targeted yet by the Germans, but I'm afraid we won't have long to wait. Just a British naval embargo will shut down German overseas imports of vital raw materials almost immediately; along with other steps they're talking about, Germany will be faced with supply shortages very quickly, and they'll almost certainly try to force us to help them out more than we want to and in ways that we won't like.

"Yes, I think you'll have a very full agenda on your hands, Muller, and soon, too."

They clinked glasses and finished the wine.

Haussamann signaled for the bill, then glanced at Muller enigmatically.

"Of course, if war does come, you may have more than economic disputes on your hands."

CHAPTER 3

On the morning of September 1, 1939, as Paul Muller made his way toward the Ministry, he observed clusters of men gathered in storefronts and in café doorways. It had become his custom to take a cup of black tea and a croissant at the Café Friederich, which was situated close to the Ministry offices. In the summertime, he usually went inside to get served, then sit at a small table on the terrace with his *petit déjeuner* and the newspaper and that had been his intent this morning. But the doorway was crowded, and he had to elbow his way to the bar. Once inside, he heard the radio delivering announcements of some kind.

"What's going on?" he inquired.

"The Germans are invading Poland," one of the men closest to him said.

"Quiet," said another man. "We're listening."

"*...German radio is reporting that units had returned fire from Polish invaders and were taking steps to punish the Polish Army*," said the announcer, who then paused. "*This just in, the German* *battleship Schleswig-Holstein opened fire at Polish targets at 5 AM this morning in the Free City of Danzig. Polish radio is claiming that its forces are offering stiff resistance to this assault."* The announcer paused again. *"Danzig is a City protected by a League of Nations mandate, but it's surrounded by Polish territory and apparently this report is referring to fighting on Polish territory....Sorry; I take that back, there are also reports of a direct attack on the Polish Post office which is situated within the so-called Free City."* Another pause. *"We are receiving wire service reports from Warsaw claiming that the city is under attack from German bombers. Yes, we now have two separate reports to that effect...."*

Muller felt the ground beneath him shift. He had spent two years of his life in Danzig–the Free City of Danzig, which was indeed a mandate of the League of Nations pursuant to explicit provisions in the Treaty of Versailles.

Danzig itself was under attack? And Warsaw was being bombed?

He took a large gulp from his mug of tea, stuffed his croissant in his suit jacket pocket, shoved his way out the doorway of the Café and began running toward the Ministry.

Inside, people were milling about, many in full uniform whom he'd never seen before–evidently reservists called up with Guisan's appointment. He began frantically searching for a radio somewhere in the building and ultimately found that the only set was in the basement office of the Ministry's communications unit–and it wasn't even turned on. He introduced himself to the official in charge and politely explained that the local Swiss station in Bern was broadcasting information about what appeared to be a German invasion of Poland–an event that could have profound importance for Switzerland. It took a little coaxing, but eventually he persuaded the official–Edgar Fromm was his name, he said–to assign someone to monitor the broadcast, take notes and give him regular updates.

"Oh, these reports will go directly to you for the Minister himself?" Fromm asked, biting his lip in confusion about how to do what was being asked–apparently by the Minister.

"Well, I'll ask our senior stenographer if she can do something.

"Miss Brenner?" He beckoned to a tall, spare, middle aged woman dressed in the grey business frock favored by the women in the typing pool.

"This is Mr. Muller, a senior Ministry intelligence officer," Fromm said to her as she hurried forward in response to his summons.

"He needs a running report on the news bulletins being broadcast on the radio concerning an apparent German invasion of–what was it, Mr. Muller, Poland?–Right, Poland." Fromm hesitated, "You said it was for the Minister?"

"Yes, the Minister," Muller said, turning back to Miss Brenner.

"Yvonne Brenner, Mr. Muller," she said shaking his hand.

"I heard the news before leaving home this morning. I was actually a little surprised to find that we weren't monitoring it when I got to the office. But certainly, I can take that in hand."

"Mr. Fromm, you'll permit me to move both my typewriter and the radio into the conference room and assign Mrs. Laurent to be the courier?"

"Yes, yes," Fromm replied, obviously relieved to have someone else take over the job. He edged away and then hurried to the other side of the office.

Muller was amused at the byplay–Fromm's evident confusion and the stenographer calmly taking charge.

Yvonne Brenner smiled at Muller as if they shared a secret together.

"How about hourly reports, Mr. Muller, and right away if something important happens. I can also have Mrs. Laurent monitor transmissions we receive through our own system. What's your room number for her to deliver the information?"

Muller told her and smiled to himself as he made his way back upstairs to his office. He began to draft in his head a short memorandum for Minister Minger recommending that he establish a full-time Ministry newsroom monitoring and information distribution system; he had in mind the name of the woman whom he would propose to organize it.

The hourly updates that the women delivered didn't clarify the confusion. Hitler had addressed the German Reichstag–clad in a special field-grey Army uniform instead of his customary Brown

Shirt party regalia, it was reported–but his remarks were brief and consisted mainly of insults aimed at Polish provocateurs and familiar boasts of Germany's indomitable strength; no assertion that he had ordered an invasion. Radio Warsaw and stations in other Polish cities remained on the air, and the updates contained excerpts of broadcasts from them reporting German bombing raids and Polish resistance to German tank attacks. Reports about fighting in Danzig were repeated several times.

Muller passed the meager information he'd gathered to the Minister; Haussamann was nowhere to be found–probably seeking information from his sources within the German military, Muller guessed. There had been no official reactions from London or Paris and Muller thought their silence was ominous, given the pledges both nations had made to come to Poland's aid if it were attacked. The broadcasts indicated that mobilization was fully underway in France and that conscripts were being recruited in Britain.

So why weren't the two governments saying anything?

Late in the afternoon, when Muller delivered another news update, Minger scanned the typewritten report, then told Muller he was convening a senior staff meeting in an hour.

"I want you to brief the staff on what we know–which isn't definitive, but certainly points to the likelihood that we're witnessing the first stages of a German invasion," he said. "Maybe Haussamann will have more by that time, but we need to make some rapid decisions."

When the meeting convened, Minger sat at one end of the conference table and General Guisan at the other as Minger rapped the tabletop to begin the meeting. Roger Masson, Minger's Deputy, was in attendance along with several uniformed officers whom Muller had seen before, but didn't really know. Haussamann entered the room and took a chair opposite Muller as Minger began to speak.

"Gentlemen, as you all know, there are multiple reports of fighting in and around Poland. The information is incomplete and confusing, but certainly indicative of the German invasion of Poland that Hitler has been threatening for months. Mr. Muller, kindly tell us what you've been able to glean from the radio news bulletins that we've been monitoring."

Muller stood and summarized the information he'd delivered during the day to Minger.

Haussamann then stood. Minger nodded at him to proceed.

"I believe I can inform this meeting definitively that in fact a full-scale German invasion of Poland commenced this morning– starting with the shelling of Danzig by the German battleship *Schleswig-Holstein* around 5AM, as Mr. Muller has reported." Haussamann spoke quietly, but with an air of authority. "German Army Group South launched a three-pronged attack in overwhelming strength from German Silesia on the Polish Western frontier and on the South from what used to be the border with Moravia and Slovakia. No declaration of war has been issued and communications are deliberately being suppressed to foster the kind of confusion that Mr. Muller has described.

"But I'm afraid, Minister Minger, that the invasion to which you referred has in fact begun and that we must operate on that assumption."

Haussamann sat down and the room was still for several moments.

General Guisan then stood, one hand resting on the military cap he had removed and placed before him on the table. Muller noted that it now bore the gold leaf insignia of his office.

"With the first reports of fighting in Poland this morning, Swiss frontier units were alerted to report any indications of threats to Swiss borders from Germany, and also from France," Guisan said. "I am pleased to advise you, Minister Minger that no threats have been detected so far. But if what Mr. Haussamann has just told us is accurate–and I have assumed the likelihood of German invasion since the first reports of fighting began trickling in–war is almost certain to be declared against Germany by Britain and France and the threat to our nation is therefore immediate and acute. Accordingly, I shall issue an order tonight mobilizing the Swiss Army and instructing all Army reservists to report to their units immediately, according to plans that are in place for such a contingency."

Guisan paused.

"This is a solemn moment," he added, "and all Swiss citizens must assume their responsibilities."

Guisan took his seat.

Minger remained seated. "Hear, hear," he said quietly. "And it is also a moment to reassert our status as a neutral nation and to remind others of our neutrality" he added.

"General, kindly remind the Frontier units that while we are on alert, we are not at war and the frontier is not closed. Normal civilian passage into and out of Switzerland must continue and commercial traffic in goods and services remains essential. If war is declared, we may expect the belligerents to close their borders to one another and these actions may affect our economy and access to goods. We are not unmindful of these threats and Mr. Muller's economic section is actively addressing these threats.

"So, as we look to our responsibilities, the Ministry will lend its support to the military measures that General Guisan and the Army invoke to secure our borders and will equally take steps to protect our economic security.

Minger stood. "Gentlemen, that concludes our meeting."

He gestured for Haussamann and Muller to remain behind. Roger Masson, pipe tightly clenched in his teeth as usual also stayed.

"I assume your information came from reliable German sources," Minger said, looking at Haussamann, who simply nodded. He didn't need to say anything more. Haussamann had cultivated very well-informed sources in German military and intelligence circles–which he never revealed and which no one inquired about.

"Do we know what the British and French are doing? Muller, you reported that they seem to be mobilizing, but no statements at all?"

Muller shook his head. "Nothing. Mr. Minger you'll remember that I called your attention some time ago to the peculiar language of the British declaration of support for Poland issued in the spring. It came right after Hitler took over the rest of Czechoslovakia in March—a total abdication of all the promises he'd made in the wake of Munich about no more territorial ambitions. The British public was furious at Hitler's actions and the Parliament was in revolt; Chamberlain realized he had to assume a harder line or he'd be sacked as Prime Minister. So, he issued his declaration that said—I can even quote it, actually, because it irritated me so much. It said that if Hitler were to threaten Poland, England would 'feel themselves bound to lend the Polish Government all the support in their power.'

"That was it. He apparently couldn't bring himself to utter the word 'war.'

Muller paused and drew a deep breath.

"I'm very much the cynic about the British, as I think you know, sir," he said. "I'd be very surprised if at this very moment, Chamberlain and Halifax—with the French probably in tow—weren't trying to cut still another deal with Hitler that would permit them to wiggle out of that mealy-mouthed 'Declaration' and any commitment to Poland."

Masson rapped his pipe noisily in the glass ashtray knocking out the ashes; it was an annoying habit, Muller thought. But Masson was a smart and knowledgeable officer.

"I ran into the French Minister, Alphand, on my way to attend this meeting," Masson said. "Alphand is such a windbag–always prattling on about how France should be fighting the Soviets instead of sparring with the Germans.

"Anyway, he said he's learned from the Quai d'Orsay that Foreign Minister Bonnet is proposing to ask Mussolini to intervene as a mediator on the Polish affair and apparently the British have agreed."

He turned to Muller with a smile.

"Bonnet is another one who can't bring himself to use the word 'war'," he said. "Forget the Soviets, he doesn't want to fight anyone; no spine in him at all," Masson finished, shrugging.

"But you'd think they could at least say *something* with an invasion apparently underway."

As if on cue, a Secretary opened the conference room door and handed Muller a type-written page which he hastily scanned, then turned toward Minger.

"Our news monitors report that the British and French Ambassadors in Berlin have been instructed to deliver what's described as 'a stiff note' to the Germans this evening," he said. "We don't have the text except that it's said to be 'in the nature of a warning.' Apparently, the French Chamber of Deputies can't meet until tomorrow and the British decided to wait for them before acting. The broadcast that we monitored did say that both countries are mobilizing, so that's something."

Muller laid the paper he'd been given on the table.

Minger grunted.

"And it could be a cover to gain time for Mussolini to try and intervene," he said, then sighed deeply and stood, signaling the end of the meeting.

"We'll simply have to wait and see what happens. Our own mobilization order will tell everyone where we stand–which is to say, avowedly neutral and armed to defend ourselves to stay that way."

As they filed out of the conference room Minger spoke quietly to Muller. "I like this news monitoring system you've organized; please take steps to make it permanent and as efficient as possible."

CHAPTER 4

But the next day yielded no declaration of war or any other official statement from the French and British governments.

Muller had taken steps that morning to establish a News Distribution Section within the Ministry Division and to install Yvonne Brenner as the Section Chief, and the regular updates she delivered confirmed widespread reports of heavy fighting in Poland–as well as the conspicuous silence from Britain and France.

"Something's going on," Muller said to Haussamann as he shared the latest bulletin with him. "The German invasion is clearly underway, and they're keeping quiet for a reason."

Haussamann nodded. "Why don't you slip down to Geneva and see what you can learn from your British friends there," he said. "They promised their new Ministry of Economic Warfare was going to unleash a full economic assault on Germany and told you they wouldn't hesitate to attack us too if we got in their way.

"See if you can find out what they're up to."

Muller left a phone message with the British legation in Geneva for Air Attaché West–Jimmy, as he insisted upon being called–to meet that evening and proposing the Hotel des Bergues as the venue.

As Muller exited the Ministry and strode toward the railroad station, he saw that mobilization was on full display. Units of Swiss soldiers were marching in the streets, rifles on their shoulders and packs on their backs, while others were busily filling and stacking sandbags around public buildings. Regular train schedules had been suspended as trains were re-routed to support troop deployments, but he was able to secure a seat on a Geneva-bound train carrying troops to reinforce the Geneva border with France.

The train was packed, and soldiers spilled out of compartments, crowding the corridors; the men were generally quiet, seemingly subdued by the uncertainty of what lay ahead and there was an edginess to the atmosphere as the train sped South. Muller shared the moodiness of the moment, reflecting on how long he had labored, futilely it now appeared, to stave off the war that had now seemingly begun, even if belligerents were trying to obscure it; grim reality would soon set in, he was certain.

He reflected on Danzig in particular and the irony that this new war had apparently begun there. He had spent two years in that beleaguered small enclave as Secretary to the High Commissioner of the League of Nations, trying to fend off Nazi aggression and protect the Constitution that Danzigers had adopted and that the League was responsible for defending.

Muller sighed deeply. Sean Lester, the League's High Commissioner, had waged a valiant, but ultimately fruitless, effort to persuade the League and its member states to assert their diplomatic authority to preserve the freedoms that were under siege by the Nazis. Repeatedly undercut by League procrastination and the feckless British policy of Appeasement, Lester had been finally obliged to surrender his post, leaving behind only what amounted to a fig leaf of League authority. Now even that residual façade had apparently been violently overturned. Muller felt deeply saddened at the policy failure and apprehensive about the fate of the friends and acquaintances he'd left behind, when he'd been forced to leave too.

His mood wasn't improved by recollections of his last journey to Geneva to confront Jimmy West and his threat of British economic warfare against Switzerland as a 'regrettable but necessary' companion to Britain's plan to launch a full-scale attack on the German economy. West had blithely informed Muller that the British had concluded that Germany was vulnerable to economic attack and viewed their global economic power as a weapon they could brandish to bring down Hitler and his regime.

He did smile to himself remembering that he had been accompanied on that last trip by Hildegarde Magandanz–the Ministry's expert on the German economy with whom he'd fallen in love. She had ripped into West in that last meeting nearly as fiercely as Muller himself had done, though she hadn't been the one to threaten to punch him.

And they had spent that night after the meeting at his apartment, locked in each other's arms.

Hilde–he thought; what would become of them now, with war apparently at their doorstep? They had scarcely had time to see one another and steal a quick embrace since they'd returned from Grindelwald a week earlier in the wake of the announcement of the Ribbentrop-Molotov Non-Aggression Pact. Could they even think about the prospect of marrying one another in the face of such uncertainty?

He desperately missed her and the warmth of her presence. But he pushed the thought aside; there were too many questions.

Geneva's Cornavin Station was a beehive of activity in the wake of the mobilization order, but he was able to catch a tram down toward the lake and disembark at the Mont Blanc bridge where the Rhône River began its long descent to the Mediterranean Sea.

He strode along the embankment to the Hotel des Bergues, but unlike the last visit, he didn't spy Jimmy West awaiting him at a table on the narrow hotel plaza alongside the river. He took a seat and decided to wait, confident that West would show up. A white-jacketed waiter appeared through the revolving door to take his order.

"Mr. Muller, by chance?" he asked.

"Yes," replied Muller.

"Mr. West asked me if I would invite you to join him just up the Quai in the bar at the Hotel d'Angleterre; he said you'd know where it was."

Muller smiled and nodded, passing a coin to the waiter as he stood.

"I do indeed," he said.

The Hotel d'Angleterre, was a handsome four-story structure topped by an angular slate roof with a sweeping view across Lac Leman toward the distant Alps. The British had commandeered the hotel when the League was launched in 1920 and had occupied it ever since. They had transformed the interior into a little corner of England, with a reception resembling a London gentlemen's club, a pub featuring dart boards, Guinness on draft, virtually every kind of British whisky, and elevators manned by attendants costumed as Beefeaters.

Muller had spent considerable time there earlier, in the mid-30's, dealing with the British delegation during League debates over the fate of the Free City of Danzig. The lobby had always been loud and crowded, officials, clerks and hangers-on hurrying to and fro, and demanding service at the bar. But the last time he'd been there, it had seemed deserted as the British had downgraded their League presence and even evacuated their files from their basement vaults–as a precaution against a German invasion, he'd been told. So, he was surprised that Jimmy West wanted to meet him there.

But there he was, big as life and sitting at the bar, as Muller pushed through the revolving door at the hotel's entrance. West jumped up and came to greet him effusively.

"Sorry to make you hoof it up here from the des Bergues, old boy," he said, "but good exercise, don't you think?" He pumped Muller's hand and playfully punched his elbow. "Not much going on here compared to the old days," he continued, "but we've still got a top-notch communications system, and it's the best way to keep in touch with London–especially these days when people are being tight-lipped and it's hard to get information.

"So, I'm camping out," he said, grinning. "Not a lot of competition, but the bar's still open and the Comms office is only one floor up. What could be better, eh?

"Two double whiskies neat," he said to the bartender, steering Muller toward a table at the back of the bar. "Water on the side."

"Well, Mr. Muller," he said jovially. "I'm betting you've come all the way from Bern to find Jimmy West to see if he knows what the Hell's going on. Right?"

West clinked his glass against Muller's as the waiter retreated.

"Well, you've come to the right place," he said, swallowing a large gulp of his drink.

Muller grinned back at West. The man could be arrogant and annoying, but Muller had come to accept the fact that, for all his bluster, West was a competent professional and a well-informed source when he chose to share his knowledge–which he was now apparently preparing to do.

So, he took a deep draught of his own drink and decided to listen.

"Chamberlain's not one to be rushed," West began, his eyes sparkling merrily, clearly enjoying his role, "especially by something like a German invasion, even after the reality of what was going on had been confirmed by British diplomats in Poland and reports from MI-6. He wanted the French to be on board, of course, but he was looking for alternatives."

"Ways out, you mean," Muller interjected, then immediately regretted it.

West's eyes narrowed, and he started to make a retort, but thought better of it and instead picked up his narrative.

"The French wanted two days," he went on. "General Gamelin is concerned about the risk of attack by German bombers during their mobilization. And Bonnet, the Foreign Minister–now Muller *there* is a man looking for ways out–offered to invite Mussolini to try to mediate some kind of solution short of war. So, Chamberlain agreed. There were calls in Parliament and even in the cabinet for Chamberlain to declare war, so he had to appear to be doing something, and he got the French to agree to delivering a note to Ribbentrop last night–a 'stiff note' was how it was described."

West shrugged.

"I came over here to monitor communications earlier today, trying to get a read on what was really going on; there's a lot of confusion, I can tell you. Somewhere around mid-day, if I'm rightly informed, Mussolini agreed to approach Hitler, but by this time, public anger in Britain over the government's delay had mounted and there was the beginning of a revolt even within the Tory majority, so Chamberlain felt he had to go back to Bonnet and tell him that he would only consent to Mussolini's intervention if Hitler would first call a halt to his invasion and withdraw to the German border. So, as it stands now–or at least an hour or so ago, when I last checked, we're waiting for Bonnet who's waiting on Mussolini."

West gestured for two more drinks and stood.

"I'll run up to the Comms center to see if anything's changed."

Muller watched Jimmy West lope over to the elevator bank. He thought about what he'd been told and wasn't surprised. Chamberlain would surely search for any alternative to a declaration of war. Would the British public or his own party force him to act? Muller wasn't sure. But he glanced at his watch and saw it was after 6 in the evening–so, more than 36 hours since the invasion had begun–and counting.

He sipped his whiskey and munched a few Turkish pistachios from the plate the waiter had delivered with their second round.

Twenty minutes later West returned.

"Apparently it's bedlam in London," he said speaking in a low voice even though the bar was empty except for the bartender, idly polishing glasses behind the bar on the other side of the room.

"Members have been hanging around all afternoon waiting for Parliament to be called into session to issue an ultimatum and there seems to be a revolt underway. I just got through to Stevenson–he sends greetings, by the way–on what I was informed was a secure line. He told me that one of the Laborites stood up on the bar in the Commons Smoking Room and proceeded to harangue the members, declaring that the nation's honor was in tatters and calling for Chamberlain to step down–and he was wildly cheered. Sir John Simon is leading a group of cabinet members that are demanding action.

"Oh, and Mussolini has now apparently refused even to approach Hitler, so that plan's not on any longer. But the French are continuing to dither, so Chamberlain's delayed acting yet again–at least to this point."

West swallowed most of his drink.

"Who knows what'll happen tonight?" he added, then finished the last of his whiskey. "I'll bet it's going to be a busy one at Downing Street.

"But I'm afraid we'll have to wait till tomorrow to find out, old boy," he said rising to his feet. "Our comms team is shutting down for the night–and I have a very intimate dinner date planned, so–" he gestured toward the doorway.

"Jimmy," said Muller in a testy way, "War and peace are hanging in the balance–and no one's staying around to find out which one will prevail?"

West fixed Muller with a broad smile as he turned to depart.

"You're welcome to come back for breakfast and schnapps tomorrow morning to learn what happened. Toodle-oo old boy."

Muller finished his drink and exited the hotel, then, seeing an oncoming tram approaching, he hurried to the nearby tram stop and swung himself aboard.

He found a seat and his mind whirled as the tram descended the Quai Wilson with its familiar view of the Jet d'Eau in Lac Leman, its spray sparkling in the late afternoon sun, and the Salève, rising steeply behind it–ordinarily a vista that Muller relished; but he paid little attention as he tried to make sense of what he'd learned from West.

Chamberlain clearly was trying to avoid declaring war on Germany and God knows, he was a determined and powerful leader who had bucked public opinion many times in the past. But would he really abandon his pledge–however hedged he may have tried to word it?

And John Simon–now Sir John and Chancellor of the Exchequer–was heading a Cabinet Minister revolt over the prospect? Muller remembered interacting briefly with Simon over the Danzig issue several years ago, when Simon held the Ministerial portfolio for the League. He'd come away with the impression of a man who toed the line, not one likely to rock the boat.

The tram had crossed the Mont Blanc Bridge and glided to a stop to board passengers from the lake steamers, which docked nearby. On a whim, Muller disembarked and began striding up the embankment toward the Restaurant Parc des Eaux Vives, which commanded a striking view of Lac Leman and the Jura Mountains to the West. He'd sit at the bar, enjoy the summerlike evening and try to make sense of the unfolding events.

The tables on the grassy embankment were strangely empty, but Muller was engrossed in his thoughts and paid it no mind until he saw the restaurant entrance was chained off; a white sheet of paper affixed to it read:

CLOSED DUE TO MOBILIZATION

Well, Muller thought to himself, lighting a Gitâne.

He was deciding what to do next when a black, four-door Peugeot drove up to the restaurant entrance and out stepped Alexandru Munteneau, the Romanian Chargé d'Affaires and another man he didn't recognize.

"Muller," exclaimed Munteneau, "What a nice surprise," and he hurried over to shake Muller's hand, a broad smile on his round face. Munteneau was a short, heavy-set, balding man; he had an engaging manner, a quick wit and was and one of Muller's favorites in the local diplomatic community.

"You must be acquainted with Timur Sadek, the Turkish envoy to the League," Munteneau said. "No? Well, Ambassador Sadek, meet the intrepid Paul Muller, Swiss diplomat extraordinaire." Muller shook the other man's hand; he was tall, with thick black hair and an athletic bearing. They exchanged greetings and Sadek's French accent was impeccable.

"You must join us," said Munteneau, gesturing for Muller to accompany them as he stepped toward the entrance, then saw the sign.

"Merde. That's an annoyance," he said.

"I expect most other restaurants will be closed too," said Muller; "I was just trying to figure out what to do next when you drove up."

Sadek smiled. "Easy answer, gentlemen; we drive to Scimitar, a Turkish restaurant on the Annemasse side of town," he said. "The staff is Turkish, not Swiss, so they're not being mobilized and I'm sure it'll be open."

Sadek proved correct. Munteneau's driver followed his directions and within five minutes they pulled up in front of a brightly lit storefront on a narrow cobble-stoned side street with a green sign above the doorway bearing the symbol of a large, gold, curved scimitar. They were shown to a table in the small courtyard beneath a leafy plane tree. Sadek was obviously well-known there and the proprietor–Emin, he was called, said Sadek–welcomed them, clicking his fingers to hurry Turkish-garbed waiters wearing red fezzes, who delivered plates bearing Turkish appetizers. Emin placed glasses before them and opened a bottle of raki, pouring a generous portion for each of them.

"I'm sure you know raki," said Sadek, who took the pitcher of water on the table and added some to each glass.

"See it turn milky-white?" he said, "We call it 'aslan sütü'–lion's milk–the touch of absinthe." He clinked their glasses and toasted.

"Serefe–to your health."

They drank; Muller decided it had an anise flavor, much like Greek ouzo. He smacked his lips; it was good.

"The favorite of our great founder Ataturk," Emin said, pointing through the doorway to a large photo of a formally dressed man hanging on the wall, who Muller took to be the famous Mustafa Kemal Ataturk.

The men passed the *mezé* appetizers back and forth, helping themselves, before they were able to sit back and begin to converse.

"Well, Muller," said Munteneau with a sly smile, "has the war begun?"

"The fighting has certainly begun," replied Muller, smiling back agreeably, "but to my knowledge, it hasn't been favored yet with a formal declaration of war."

"Mmmm," replied Munteneau, removing from his mouth the seeds of the black olives he'd been chewing. "That's what I was afraid you'd say," he finally added, wiping his mouth with a white napkin.

"You'll remember, Muller, that the French persuaded the British to extend Chamberlain's threat of war to any German aggression against Romania too. But if they haven't even honored their original pledge to declare war when Germany attacked Poland, how much reliance do you think we Romanians ought to place on his word about protecting us?

"It's been a day and a half–even more now–since they launched their attack; German Stukas are dive bombing Polish cities and German Panzers are slicing up Polish Army units. What are they waiting for?"

"There's been no attack on Romania, has there?" asked Muller. "Is there something I don't know?" He looked at Munteneau in alarm.

"No, no; I'm not saying that," Munteneau replied hastily. "I'm talking only about the guarantees that were made to Poland if they were invaded. That's now happened–and all we're hearing is silence."

Munteneau took a deep breath.

"Think of the map, Muller," he said. "We share a border with Poland–their Southernmost border and our Northern border. We're already seeing Polish refugees trying to flee into Romania and it'll probably only get worse in the days ahead. I don't know if we're going to let them in, but we can't stop everyone, even if we wanted to. And what about Polish soldiers who may try to escape capture? If the Germans were to conquer Poland–which is a pretty good bet, I'm afraid–will they claim the right to pursue them into Romania– and how far will they push that line? We all know they desperately want access to our oil fields at Ploesti," he went on. "Would they simply keep going and occupy us too?"

They paused while the waiters replaced the *mezé* with dishes of fish and meats. Emin delivered another bottle of raki then, with a flourish, pressed a switch on the trunk of the plane tree, illuminating the terrace with dozens of tiny lights strung in the branches overhead.

"Enlightening your conversation," he said–an obviously well-rehearsed line, thought Muller–but they did enhance the ambiance.

Munteneau gestured to the lights.

"They've instituted strict blackout rules in London," he said. "I have a daughter working there and she actually put through a call to me this morning. A staticky line," he said, "but she told me about the blackout–and also, that families are evacuating children to the countryside out of fear of German bombing attacks."

He paused and played pensively with a fork.

"She asked me if she should leave too," he said, pausing again. "It's one thing hearing that other people's children are being sent away; it's different when it's your own daughter asking."

"What did you tell her?" asked Muller quietly; he could see that Munteneau was uncomfortable.

Munteneau finally looked up. "I told her to stay for now–but to make sure she kept her gas mask handy and knew where the closest air raid shelters were."

"I hope I did the right thing," he added.

Muller and Sadek both clinked glasses with Munteneau and offered reassuring nods.

Muller broke the ensuing silence.

"In answer to your earlier question, Munteneau, my guess is that soon–maybe as soon as tomorrow–war will be declared," he said. He summarized what he'd learned from West–but without identifying his source.

"Chamberlain's devious and I'm sure he's looking for ways out. But it's hard to see how he can renege on his commitment and still remain Prime Minister; so, I'm persuaded that he'll hold his nose and do what he has to do to stay in power–which means declaring war on the Germans."

"That doesn't sound like you believe he's ready to do much for the Poles even if he declares war," said Sadek.

Muller sighed, then nodded.

"I asked one of my British contacts not long ago what the military plan was to protect Poland in the event of war. His reply was to 'forget Poland', that it was just a sideshow; the real action, he said, would come in the form of an all-out British and French assault on the German economy.

"So, yes," he continued, "if I were Polish, I wouldn't hold my breath for any real military support from either Britain or France even after a declaration of war."

They paused and lit up, awaiting the next course.

"Let me relate a story," Muller went on.

"My brother-in-law is a Captain in the French Army. He arranged for me to attend the massive military parade the French put on–with full participation of the British, I should add–back in July, to celebrate the Sesquicentennial Anniversary of the fall of the Bastille. It was an absolutely massive show of strength; soldiers, sailors cannons, tanks, airplanes–everything you could imagine."

Muller tapped his ash into the glass ashtray.

"It went on for hours, soldiers or every description marching down the Champs Elysèes and across the Seine."

Muller paused again, then went on.

"Paris was jubilant; you could feel it in the air. They felt *safe*! The planes and troops and all the rest–especially the Maginot Line–would protect them.

But–and here's my point–there was no call to arms; no boasts about chasing the Boches to Berlin if war came–just a palpable sense of relief that they were safe.

"The French are playing defense, not offense," he said.

The three men stubbed their cigarette butts in the ashtray as the waiters delivered plates of grilled loup de mer and green salad and they attacked their meal.

Timur Sadek paused to remove a sliver of fish bone from his mouth and gestured toward Muller with his fork.

"Mr. Muller, there was a reason Mr. Munteneau and I were planning to dine together this evening, and I see no reason not to share it with you–unless you object"–he glanced quickly at Munteneau who shook his head.

"You see, Romania and Turkey are Black Sea neighbors and, consequently, we share a certain wariness of the Soviet Union, which occupies the entire northern shore of the Black Sea and which has asserted territorial claims against both of our countries. For Turkey, the threat comes from Russian demands for control of the Dardenelles Straits–the waterway connecting the Black Sea to the Mediterranean. For Romania, the threat is Russian claims to

Bessarabia, a bitterly contested strip of territory which forms the border between Romania and the USSR–just to the East of Romania's border with Poland that Mr. Munteneau referred to a moment ago."

Sadek deftly served himself from the green salad bowl as he continued to speak.

"Both are long-standing disputes. Russia has coveted control over the Dardenelles for centuries–and the new Soviet rulers are just like their Czarist predecessors in that regard. Bessarabia has been a flashpoint of tensions between Romania and the Soviets for years.

"And everything just got turned completely topsy-turvy"–Sadek used the English term–"with the announcement of the Molotov-Ribbentrop Non-Aggression Pact," he said.

Munteneau took up the conversation.

"There are those of us who are skeptical that this is a 'Non-Aggression Pact' the way they're describing it," he said. "It looks to us more like an alliance, in fact if not in language. Hitler gets to play a free hand in Poland; where does Stalin get to play a free hand? In the Balkans? Bessarabia, for starters? In Turkey? License to force the Dardenelles?"

"And what about the Baltics?" Sadek chimed in. "That's not our neighborhood, but how secure would you feel sitting tonight in, say, Estonia, or Latvia or Finland? Not very, I suspect," he added, his face grim. "We don't believe for a second that Stalin handed Hitler a free pass just out of the goodness of his heart.

There are quid pro quos for sure; we just don't know what–or where–they are."

Munteneau nodded and then chimed in again.

"For the past year–ever since the Munich sell-out–we've tried to create some kind of Balkan alliance to resist German–and Italian, for that matter–attempts to destabilize our region…," he began.

"Who's 'we'?" Muller interrupted him.

"My country, Romania, plus Albania, Yugoslavia, and Greece, together with Turkey supporting us at the margin," he replied. "Bulgaria and Hungary wouldn't play; they're still consumed by resentments stemming from the Versailles settlement. But we are all situated in the Balkan peninsular–all of us created by the Great Powers at Versailles from the ruins of Austro-Hungarian Empire– and we remain vulnerable to the Great Power rivalries playing out now, twenty years later.

We're all grasping for lifelines–and we're persuaded that mutual cooperation among ourselves offers some–not much, mind you, but *some*–added protection."

Muller proffered his Gitanes and they lit up as Munteneau continued.

"So, imagine how upsetting it was to us when Hitler marched into Prague in March and swallowed the remainder of Czechoslovakia–also a state created at Versailles; Chamberlain proceeded to issue his so-called Declaration on behalf of Poland without consulting any of us–and then, just two weeks later,

Mussolini invaded Albania. An incompetent performance for sure; but a takeover nonetheless–and," he snapped his fingers, "a Balkan pawn swept off the board.

"The Great Powers may have shrugged, Mr. Muller" Munteneau said. "But we trembled."

Sadek again took up the argument.

"The Republic of Turkey was built on the ashes of the Ottoman Empire, not Austro-Hungary," he said. "And not at Versailles but by the Treaty of Lausanne, after the Allies tried to occupy us and we drove them into the sea–at the point of a bayonet, in fact, led by Ataturk," he added, gesturing toward the photo Muller had noted earlier.

"So, our nation was founded upon revolution, not Great Power diplomacy like our Balkan neighbors.

"But, again, look at the map, Mr. Muller," Sadek spoke slowly. "We are at the hinge of the Eastern Mediterranean; strategically situated–but also very exposed–including exposure to the same risks as our Balkan neighbors."

They clinked the small glasses of brandy that had been placed before them.

"Serife," said Sadek before resuming.

"The Czechs supplied a huge share of Turkish military requirements from their Skoda works," he said. "After Munich, when they were swallowed up by Germany, we began discussions with Britain and France about replacing them; we were even toying with an agreement to align ourselves with them against Germany.

But then they issued that unilateral Declaration in favor of Poland–leaving us out in the cold–and their indifference to Mussolini's aggression in Albania…." Sadek paused and shook his head.

"Right now, we're trying to pretend we're Switzerland," he finished with a wan smile; "trying to be as neutral as we can be."

But then he leaned forward. "Except, now we don't just have to fear the Germans," he said. "We have to fear the Russians too, Germany's new, putative–if undeclared–ally.

"Does anyone seriously question the possibility–the likelihood–that Stalin and Hitler have agreed to swallow us all up and divide the spoils?" Sadek's statement–it was a statement, not a question–hung above the table, along with the smoke, as they ground out their cigarettes.

"Oh, and by the way," Sadek added, "There's a British vessel sitting off Istanbul waiting for permission to join the queue to transit the Bosphorus. It's loaded with Hawker Hurricanes and Fairey Battles–even a couple of Spitfires–along with Browning Automatic Rifles, machine guns, ammunition; it's a floating arms bazaar, Mr. Muller.

"The equipment is all supposedly destined for Poland by way of the Romanian port of Constanta and Romanian rail connections North to Krakow. Maybe this is part of some secret British plan to reinforce the Poles," Sadek said, shrugging in indifference.

"But for both my Turkish government and Mr. Munteneau's Romania, allowing this arms shipment to transit the Bosphorus and connect to Poland via Romania poses a serious risk of reprisals–

and not just from the Germans, as we might have assumed two weeks ago; now we face the risk of reprisals by Germany's new *de facto* ally, the Soviet Union, as well."

"See the dilemma we face, Mr. Muller," Munteneau added quietly.

"If you plan on communicating with your British friends tomorrow, you might want to remind them that unless they provide tangible support for our two governments, we're not prepared to take steps that are likely to irritate either Berlin or Moscow."

"That vessel faces a long stay in the Sea of Marmara," said Sadek with a grin, as they tossed off the last of the brandy.

CHAPTER 5

Muller awoke the next morning in his apartment with a headache and a lingering taste of licorice from the raki. Brushing his teeth and gulping two aspirins seemed to help.

He was disappointed, but not surprised that his corner Café was shuttered by the mobilization. Happily, the boulangerie next door had a few fresh baguettes left and he grabbed one as he descended the hill toward his tram stop on La Rue Gustav Ador, that ran along the lakeside. There was a large crowd already waiting; service was evidently severely reduced. So, he set off on foot along the Quai and over the Mont Blanc Bridge, turning right to join other pedestrians strolling along the broad esplanade that turned North toward the Palais Wilson.

The Hotel d'Angleterre sparkled in the morning sunshine as Muller approached it, then pushed his way into the lobby. Dust motes danced in the bright shafts of sunlight from the tall windows, filtered through gauzy white curtains, and brightening even the bar area.

Jimmy West was nowhere to be seen, but the same bartender–Muller wished he remembered his name–was behind the bar, still absently polishing glasses. He smiled at Muller and motioned to a seat near where he stood.

Muller sat down, then laid the baguette on the bar.

"This is to share," he said. "Any chance you've got some jams available?"

The words were hardly out of his mouth when the bartender reached back to a shelf behind him and produced a half dozen small marmalade and jam containers.

"The wife made me some nice fried eggs for breakfast this morning," he said, declining Muller's offer. "Good thing we have the chicken coop and our garden," he added. "It's likely there'll be shortages before long."

He poured Muller a large mug of black tea.

"Lieutenant Fraser in Comms upstairs might want some of that baguette. Shall I ask him to come down?"

Muller nodded vigorously. "By all means."

Duncan Fraser soon exited the lifts and approached the bar with a file of papers under his arm; he and Muller shook hands.

"Bread for news?" Muller said with a smile, pulling off a chunk of the baguette and handing it to Fraser.

Fraser took a seat, laying his file on the bar and began addressing the lineup of jams the bartender had assembled, quickly selecting the marmalade.

"Sure," he replied as he unscrewed the top of the jar.

"Air Attaché West–Jimmy–said I should expect you and share what I can, so I've got a few current clips for you to look over.

"The most recent news, though, just arrived over the ticker," he added, spooning the marmalade on a piece of the baguette. "At 9 AM this morning, Britain and France delivered a message–an ultimatum, I guess you'd call it–to the Wilhelmstrasse in Berlin. It gave Germany a deadline of 11:00AM. to announce that it was prepared to withdraw its troops from Poland or else a state of war would exist between Britain and Germany."

Fraser began chewing the baguette.

Muller put his elbows on the bar and drew a deep breath.

So, it had finally happened; Chamberlain had put aside his reservations and acted, almost certainly alongside the French.

He turned back toward Fraser.

"Wait, is that what it said? That 'a state of war would exist?'" he asked. "No direct statement that Britain and France are formally declaring war to oppose Germany's unlawful invasion of Poland? Just that 'a state of war would exist?'"

"That's what it said," Fraser replied, nodding. "Not a very belligerent choice of words, was it?"

"Pffh!" replied Muller rolling his eyes disdainfully. "You can almost see him holding his nose."

"Anyway, Chamberlain will deliver a radio address sometime after 11:00," said Fraser. "I'm setting up a wireless here in the bar for anyone who wants to listen. I know Jimmy will be coming, and you're welcome to stay."

Fraser stood to leave and return to his post, the remainder of his baguette firmly in hand with a liberal coating of marmalade. He slid the file of news clips along the bar to Muller.

"This is all public information, Mr. Muller; feel free to have a look."

"Thanks, Lieutenant," Muller replied.

"Wait, before you go," Muller paused, then plunged on. "If I were to pass you a confidential message for RCS Stevenson in London–Eden's advisor–do you have a way to send it to him?"

"Stevenson? Certainly, sir," Fraser replied. "He's been here many times, so we know how to reach him."

"Oh, incidentally," Fraser added, "in those clippings you'll see an announcement about a cabinet shakeup that was apparently made as part of the decision to issue the ultimatum to Germany. Winston Churchill has been brought in as First Lord of the Admiralty–and, pertinent to your question–Eden's been made Minister for the Dominions."

Fraser waved as he stepped toward the lifts.

Muller swallowed the last of his baguette, then took his mug of tea, along with the file folder of news clips, and retreated to a table toward the back of the bar with a comfortable wicker chair.

Minister for the Dominions? Was Eden being sidelined? Somehow, he doubted it.

He opened the folder Lieutenant Fraser had given him, looking for the announcement of the Cabinet appointments, and stopped at the very first item. There in the folder sat a newspaper photo of Franz von Papen, the newly appointed German Ambassador to Turkey, boarding the train in Berlin for Istanbul, accompanied by his very attractive wife, whom the photo caught wearing a winsome smile.

Muller stared at the photo. Marte von Papen. His mind conjured up the memory of that night in Vienna when he had rescued Marte from a Nazi street brawl. She had taken him to bed–well it wasn't as if he'd been reluctant to accept the invitation–and she'd shared with him her hatred for Hitler and contempt for the Nazis. She'd tried to help him resist Hitler's Austrian takeover–the *Anschluss*–and when it came, she'd warned him to flee.

Now Marte was accompanying her husband–whom she held in disdain–to become Germany's Ambassador to the Sublime Porte–as the Turkish Foreign Ministry was still referred to–in Istanbul.

He thought back to Ambassador Sadek's comments last evening describing Turkey's precarious balancing act among competing pressures from Germany, the Soviets and the Allies and filed away in the back of his head the information about von Papen's appointment–and Marte's presence–in Istanbul.

He continued to flick though the news clips in the folder. For some reason, Fraser had included a story, with photos, about a recent gala at the New York World's Fair where a collection of big bands–Tommy Dorsey, Guy Lombardo, Artie Shaw–had all performed to an overflow crowd in the pavilion of the Aquacade. It looked like fun, Muller mused, glancing at the photos–a whole world away from the crisis enveloping Europe. He wished he'd been able to visit the Fair; secretly he'd always wanted to watch Frank Buck taming his wild beasts. That was the Pavilion he'd have visited first.

Ah, there it was. A short wire story reporting on Cabinet changes. Churchill had been appointed First Sea Lord and a few other portfolios had changed, Eden's appointment as the Minister for Dominions among them. But there was no commentary or explanation.

Muller placed the folder on the table before him and lit a Gitane, exhaling a long trail of smoke that caught the sunlight, shapes and shadows dancing before disappearing.

What the Hell, he thought to himself. If war came, Britain would surely try to impose restrictions on Switzerland as part of its assault upon the German economy–Jimmy West and that lugubrious British Consul General in Geneva, what was his name? Ah, Hansen, he remembered–had gone so far as to threaten to destroy the Swiss economy too. if it were necessary to bring down Germany.

Ordinarily, he didn't like volunteering information, but this might be a smart moment to curry some favor in London.

So, he removed the World's Fair article from the folder, turned it face down, then took out his fountain pen and began to write on the clean reverse side.

Stevenson: Turkish support for Allied cause on hold because of perceived failure to offer reassurances and deliver needed arms. Also, your SS Lassell carrying arms for

Poland is under informal internship off Istanbul and will not be released to enter the Black Sea. Turkey and Romania both fear reprisals from Berlin-and from USSR, which they now view as Germany's de facto ally. Non-Aggression Pact is seen as cover for an Agreement by Germany and USSR to conquer and divide up the Balkans and Turkey. You have work to do. Muller.

P.S. Hitler just sent von Papen to Ankara; can mischief be far behind?

Lacking a blotter, Muller waved the piece of paper back and forth to dry the ink. Then he folded it in quarters, handed it to the bartender along with a ten-franc coin and asked him to pass it to Duncan Fraser.

A round clock on the wall showed the time as only minutes before the 11:00 AM deadline when the ultimatum to Germany was supposed to expire.

At that moment, Jimmy West pushed his way through the revolving door into the lobby and bounded toward Muller, his face wreathed in a smile.

"Well, old boy," he said cheerfully extending his hand. "Here we are together at the witching hour. One more tick of that clock on the wall"–he gestured toward it and at the same time drew out his pocket watch and ostentatiously checked the time–"there it is: we're at war," he said triumphantly.

"In the passive tense," replied Muller sourly.

West looked at him inquiringly.

"The ultimatum said that if Hitler didn't back down 'a state of war would exist.' That's the passive tense–no forthright statement that 'we are declaring war', let alone a commitment to achieving victory," replied Muller. "Just a passive event–a little like catching influenza," he added; "one doesn't actually *do* it, it just *happens.*"

"Ah, Muller you're a sourpuss," said West waving him away. He turned to the bartender. "Digby, my man, war calls for two double whiskies! Chop Chop!"

In spite himself, Muller smiled; West was undeniably upbeat. And what better excuse than a declaration of war–even if accomplished in the passive tense–for a double whiskey at eleven o'clock in the morning?

They clinked glasses.

A corporal from the Comms section was setting up a wireless over near the bar where Digby could operate it, so Muller and West drew closer to hear better; Muller saw members of the hotel staff–even including the imperious front desk clerk–beginning to gather as well.

Digby turned on the set and adjusted the dial to the hiss of static, then the BBC Home Service announcer could be heard saying that the Prime Minister would soon be addressing the nation from the Cabinet Room.

"...As we await the Prime Minister this morning, silver barrage balloons float above London, glinting in the bright sunshine after the fierce storms of last night, and people are in the *streets–a large crowd has gathered outside Downing Street–aware that a historic moment is at hand....*

"And now, the Prime Minister."

Silence and static. Then a thin, reedy, voice began to speak, softly; Digby tried unsuccessfully to increase the volume.

"I am speaking to you from the Cabinet Room at 10, Downing Street.

"This morning the British Ambassador in Berlin handed the German Government a final note stating that unless we heard from them by 11 o'clock that they were prepared at once to withdraw their troops from Poland, a state of war would exist between us. I have to tell you now that no such undertaking has been received, and that consequently this country is at war with Germany."

There was a long silence.

Is that all? Muller said to himself. Then the soft voice continued.

"You can imagine what a bitter blow it is to me that my long struggle to win peace has failed. Yet I cannot believe that there is anything more or anything different that I could have done and that would have been more successful."

A burst of static interrupted the broadcast and the men in the hotel bar shifted in their seats with impatience. Then the signal returned.

"Everything that I have worked for, everything I have hoped for, everything I have believed in during my public life, has crashed into ruins."

More static, then the signal again.

"We have done all that any country could do to establish peace, but a situation in which no word given by Germany's ruler could be trusted and no people or country could feel themselves safe, had become intolerable. And now that we have resolved to finish it, I know that you will all play your part with calmness and courage."

The balance of the speech, less than a minute, was again swallowed by static. Then the announcer returned to the air and the signal cleared, apparently stronger in the BBC studio than it had been in the Cabinet room of 10 Downing Street.

"You have just heard an address by Neville Chamberlain, the Prime Minister, announcing that Great Britain is at war with Germany. Please stay tuned for important announcements..."

The bar was silent, each man apparently lost in his own thoughts.

Muller sat back. He found himself shocked at Chamberlain's delivery; he had never heard the man speak in public before, but reading his remarks over the years he'd conjured up the image of a forceful leader, imperiously hurling demands, and forcefully demanding allegiance from both Parliament and the people. What he'd heard today, by contrast, was a timid and quavering voice that inspired little confidence. Maybe it was the airwaves that made him sound so timorous; but whatever it was, Muller concluded, Chamberlain sounded tired and hesitant.

And where was the clarion call to arms; the challenge to rise up as a nation and defeat the German enemy? Why wasn't there even any mention of prevailing and being victorious in the struggle ahead?

Muller glanced at West and saw him staring, unseeing into the distance, one hand on the small table gripping his glass so tightly that his knuckles were white. He sighed audibly and, as if speaking to himself, said in a low voice.

"That was the sound of a man lamenting his failures, not a leader commanding a call to arms."

West sighed again and shook his head sadly.

The announcer was delivering instructions on caring for gas masks and observing blackout restrictions when, suddenly in the background, there was an unfamiliar growling sound that rose to a howl and filled the signal.

"*London is now under threat of attack*," the announcer said, his tone suddenly sounding anxious. *That sound you hear is an air raid warning.* There was a pause, then the announcer stated quickly, *"The BBC Home Service is now leaving the air so personnel can seek safety. We shall resume broadcasting as soon as it is safe to do so."*

And the wireless sound went dead.

The men in the bar glanced at one another in disbelief.

London under attack from German bombers? Only minutes after declaring war?

"What the Hell?" said West, shaking his head, his expression querulous.

"What the Hell?" He repeated, more loudly this time. Then downed the balance of his drink, smacking the glass down loudly on the table.

"Digby," he said in a commanding voice, "a round for everyone."

The room was silent as Digby retreated to the bar and began distributing whiskies.

When he'd finished, West stood and offered his glass to the assembled men.

"Shoot the bastards down!"

The others stood. "Shoot the bastards down," they repeated, and each took a large swallow.

They had hardly taken their seats when the wireless lit up.

"*This is the BBC Home Service in London*", the now familiar voice returned, sounding authoritative. "*We can now announce that the air raid warning was a false alarm. Londoners are now exiting the shelters and resuming their normal business.*

The men in the hotel bar seemed to breathe a collective sigh of relief and began to speak animatedly.

"Good job, Jimmy," said one man loudly; "Your toast scared them away."

Everyone laughed and toasted Jimmy West, finishing their drinks and drifting out of the bar, back to their stations.

West clinked glasses with Muller.

"What a cock up, Muller," he said with a grim smile. "Not a harbinger of things to come, I hope."

Then he leaned forward toward Muller and spoke in a quiet tone.

"I'm assuming the economic attack on Germany will begin almost immediately," he said. "I don't have any instructions yet about restrictions we'll place on Switzerland, but we'll be in touch.

"Oh, by the way, Muller, we appreciated that mobilization waivers were granted to the Oerlikon workforce so they could continue filling that big order for cannons for the Royal Navy.

"Notice was taken of what you and that pretty lady told us last month about that.

"Please pass on my regards."

West stood and clapped Muller on the shoulder as they departed the hotel bar.

"We'll be in touch, old boy," he said.

Muller smiled to himself; he was now on 'old boy' terms with West?

As Muller reflected during the train ride back to Bern, he especially looked forward to conveying West's compliments to 'the pretty lady.' Hilde had firmly, yet ever so politely, kicked both West and his colleague Hanson, the British Consul General in Geneva, squarely in the seats of their pompous fannies with an unvarnished threat to terminate Swiss delivery of crucial military components if West's and Hanson's real employer—the new British

Ministry of Economic Warfare–followed through on its threat to attack the Swiss economy.

They'd leveled the threat at Muller in a raucous bar in Geneva weeks earlier–even before the outbreak of war. 'We're going to destroy the German economy and bring it down,' they'd said; 'we may have to destroy the Swiss economy in the process. Sorry; but we expect you to cooperate fully.'

While Muller and the Ministry groped for a response, Hilde had pointedly reminded both men that the Royal Navy was depending upon delivery of Oerlikon antiaircraft cannons to protect the fleet, and the RAF needed Swiss-made altimeters to keep their aircraft aloft–oh, and those Swiss-made fuses used by every howitzer in the British Army; those would stop too.

It was called retaliation.

She'd smiled, as the two British agents paled.

And he'd proceeded to fall in love with her.

They'd returned from a visit to his parents' chalet in Grindelwald upon learning of the signing Ribbentrop-Molotov Non-Aggression Pact–a stunning development that had accelerated the rush to war.

He'd introduced her to his parents, who were immediately smitten too, and they'd had a night of passionate lovemaking before making a hasty departure to resume their posts at the Swiss Ministry of Military Affairs in the sudden crisis that the Pact had unleashed.

Muller sighed; they'd barely seen one another in the intervening few days since then, and they had no proper quarters in Bern to meet romantically. He hoped she'd be around the Ministry so they could at least meet for dinner and laugh about Jimmy West.

But when he returned, she was nowhere to be found.

CHAPTER 6

Two weeks passed in a whirlwind of confused meetings as the Ministry began to adjust to a war footing. After a few days, the initial mobilization order was loosened and reservists began returning to their jobs, an essential step to keep the economy functioning. But lessons were being absorbed, trying to learn from mistakes that had been made and the Ministry's staff began expanding as new defensive measures began to take shape.

A new Ministry Security Service was established that began the arduous process of creating a workable secure domestic cipher system; a signals corps began organizing a radio intercept system, both along the borders and internally to monitor foreign nationals and possible subversives; a counter-intelligence office sprang up and began systematically interviewing both foreign travelers to Switzerland and Swiss citizens returning to the country.

There was a palpable sense of urgency to the process–and not a little use of sharp bureaucratic elbows, as government officials established new programs and maneuvered for influence and authority. Muller's role was mainly one of monitoring the process; Büro Ha remained outside the government, protected –at least informally–by Haussamann's relationship with Minister Minger. But the structure of the Ministry was plainly changing and, as Muller weighed the process, he instinctively braced for the possibility of internal interference in what had so far been a free-form Ministry role.

That wasn't necessarily a bad thing, he decided; just different.

But the unseasonably warm summery weather had continued, and on this especially nice day Muller had decided to take his lunch on the terrace of one of the nearby cafés when, suddenly, he was summoned urgently to the Minister's office. He was quickly waved into the conference room where he found the Minister, his boss Hans Haussamann, and three other men, one of whom, he realized with a start, was Nicolas Odier, President of the Bank of International Settlements in Basle. Odier and his family had long been close friends of Muller's family; Nicolas and Muller's father had been classmates at university; his family, like Muller's, owned a private bank and the families had socialized in Zurich and skied together in the Alps for as long as he could remember.

"Nicolas," he exclaimed, deciding this was not the place to use the familiar 'Uncle Nicolas' appellation, which was how he'd addressed Odier since boyhood. They embraced and clapped one another on the shoulder. Recovering from his surprise, he then turned to the other two men, offering a hearty handshake to Alexandru Munteneau, the Romanian Chargè d'Affaires, with whom he'd dined only two weeks earlier, and found himself introduced to Franciszek Rachwalski, whom he recalled had served both as the Polish Minister in Bern and its representative to the League of Nations in Geneva.

"We met some time ago during the Danzig matter," Rachwalski said; "I assisted Minister Beck when he was rapporteur for the League for the Danzig issue and you were Secretary to Commissioner Lester."

Muller nodded in acknowledgement and they shook hands.

God, the man looked terrible, Muller thought to himself as they took seats at the conference table. His face was lined with fatigue, dark pouches under both eyes, and his suit and shirt looked like they hadn't been changed in days. His hand shook as he scratched at a match to light a cigarette and he coughed loudly as he exhaled. But he tried to pull himself together as he glanced around the table at the others, squaring his shoulders and adopting the role of petitioner.

"Thank you all for agreeing to meet on such short notice," he said, coughing again and gripping the table for support.

"You are all aware of the predicament Poland finds itself in," he said, drawing a deep breath and stifling another cough. "More than 50 German divisions have attacked my nation and I'm obliged to report they are overwhelming the Polish Army. Our air forces were destroyed at the outset of the invasion and we find ourselves defenseless against repeated bombing attacks on most of our major cities. Casualties are very high and civilians are trying to flee, resulting in catastrophic conditions.

"You also have probably heard that, early this morning, Soviet troops invaded us from the East. Frankly, I don't know much more than that, but I guess we have to assume Hitler and Stalin have decided to divide us up somehow."

Rachwalski paused to light another cigarette from the butt of the last one and coughed again.

"My country is in a state of collapse," he went on. "The Government has taken the decision to flee Warsaw and go into exile–I suppose somewhere in France or Britain," he paused again and shrugged. "I don't know how or when....I guess I just have to have faith that somehow it'll happen."

Muller thought Rachwalski was close to breaking into tears; he was clearly at the end of his rope. But drawing on some inner reserve, the man straightened in his chair, stubbed out his butt and resumed his remarks, his voice acquiring a stronger tone.

"We are obliged to improvise gentlemen," he said, "and we have set plans in motion to preserve the wealth of the Polish Nation. To that end, stocks, bonds and other securities held in the Central bank were put aboard a high-speed vessel at Gydinia and sent to Stockholm and our foreign exchange holdings, along with Polish Zlotys from the vaults, were flown safely to Copenhagen.

"That leads us to the matter of safeguarding Poland's gold reserves–which is the subject of this meeting."

Rachwalski paused and even smiled thinly. The men sitting around the table gazed at him intently.

"Like most nations, Poland maintains gold reserves in London, in the vaults beneath the Bank of England. Gold is heavy; it's expensive and risky to move, so nations have agreed for years to use the Bank of England as a common depositary for most of their gold–but not all of it. In our case, gold worth $11,400,000, in 5-pound ingots, was held in the Central Bank in Warsaw."

"With Warsaw under attack, we had to move it quickly so it would not fall into the hands of the Germans–or maybe now the Soviets," he added, almost as an afterthought. "We started the evacuation two nights ago," Rachwalski said, "and it's been successful so far. But we need to finish the job and that's why I'm here."

Minister Rudolph Minger had a roundish face with a beard that made him appear the Vaudois farmer he had been until being elected to office a decade earlier and becoming the dominant figure in the Swiss Federal Council. His appearance masked a keen, well-informed mind.

He looked gravely at Rachwalski.

"What assistance are you seeking from Switzerland, Mr. Rachwalski?" he said evenly. "I would remind you that Switzerland has a policy of strict neutrality in the current conflict."

"Sir, it is exactly because of that policy of neutrality that I– we"–he gestured to the other two men seated alongside him "have come to seek your help."

Minger shifted uneasily in his seat.

"Please go on, Mr. Rachwalski," he said.

Rachwalski glanced about the room, checking to see that the door was firmly closed.

"You will understand that what I am about to tell you is highly confidential," he said, pausing only a moment for emphasis before continuing.

"My government requested Romania's help to permit a Polish train to transport the gold across the Polish-Romanian border, then transit Romania to the Port of Constanta where it could be loaded aboard a chartered vessel and shipped across the Black Sea and through the Dardenelles to Beirut. Romanian authorities agreed, so, very secretly, we loaded a Polish train with 8,906 gold ingots hidden in the ten-inch space below the floorboards of six freight cars and four passenger cars and that train departed Warsaw two days ago for the Polish border with Romania."

"Somehow, the train evaded German aircraft attacks and made it to the town of Sniatyn where it crossed the border into Romania. But it's stuck there and can't go any further. We're trying to find a way to rescue it and we need your help."

Rachwalski's shoulders sagged and he coughed heavily again. Haussamann stepped to the sideboard where he filled a glass of water from a carafe and handed it to Rachwalski, who took several deep swallows.

"Thank you," he said, drawing the back of his hand across his mouth before resuming.

"Our Polish train was directed to a siding on the Romanian side of the border and the crates containing the gold ingots were physically transferred from our train to a Romanian one, drawn up alongside. So far, so good.

"But now Romanian authorities have refused to permit the Romanian train to leave the siding and travel to Constanta. They are telling us that they fear retaliation by the Germans or the Soviets–or both–if a Romanian train were used to transfer the gold reserves of Poland, a nation with which both countries are now at war. That would be seen by them as actively aiding their enemy."

Munteneau interrupted, speaking forcefully.

"Romania is a weak state, gentlemen; we're vulnerable." Munteneau glanced around the table. "We are being pressured by Germany to avoid taking any actions which can be construed as aiding Poland–or face the prospect of being invaded ourselves.

"If Germany–or the Soviets, for that matter–decide they're going to invade us too, there's not much we can do to stop them. My government is obliged to proceed very cautiously in the face of these threats, and it is determined to avoid any provocations.

"So, yes, we gave our assent to moving Poland's gold through Romania to the Black Sea where they could find somewhere safe to ship it. But that was before Poland's military collapse–and before this new Soviet incursion–which has all the earmarks of a German-Soviet deal to divide up Poland–and maybe swallow us too."

"We don't know, and frankly we're…" Munteneau hesitated, "frightened," he said finally. "That's not a diplomatic word of art, but we're *frightened*."

Munteneau paused, letting his words sink in.

"At the same time, we're sympathetic to the plight of Poland and mindful of the importance of the gold to a future Polish government-in-exile–if one can be established. And, frankly, we don't want the gold to fall into the hands of either the Germans or the Soviets.

"So, what to do?" Munteneau looked inquiringly around the table. "The gold's not going to disappear," he went on, "but maybe–just maybe–we can do the next best thing and convert the *Polish* gold into *neutral* gold. That way, if this business were to become known to the Germans and Soviets–and we have to assume they'll find out about it; trains packed with gold ingots don't materialize every day, after all–we can plausibly claim that we weren't transporting contraband or enemy gold–but instead the shipment was gold belonging to the Bank of International Settlements, a non-belligerent international organization.

"And voila!" Munteneau snapped his fingers. "We have an acceptable solution allowing us to send the gold on its way to Constanta and the Black Sea beyond."

Minister Minger turned to Nicolas Odier.

"So that's why you're here, Mr. Odier," he said.

Odier nodded.

"I am prepared to involve the Bank in this matter, provided the procedures that are followed are proper and in accord with both law and practice," he said, then added with a glance at both Rachwalski and Munteneau, "and that means formally conveying possession of the gold from the Polish Central Bank to the Bank of International Settlements. It can be done and I have the documents right here," he said, pointing to the briefcase at his feet.

The he looked directly at Minister Minger.

"But we need Swiss help to do it.

"The documents require a signature and stamp by the Polish official who has charge of the shipment–and who Mr. Rachwalski advises me is in Romania with the train–together with the signature of a witness–someone we know and trust–who will represent the Bank.

"The Bank has a small staff. We do not have anyone who has the kind of field experience that will be required to carry the official documents to Romania, obtain the requisite signature and official stamp and co-sign the documents as a witness."

Odier paused and turned his gaze toward Paul Muller.

Then he addressed Minger directly.

"Minister Minger, on behalf of the Bank of International Settlements, I'm requesting that your Ministry second Mr. Muller to the staff of the Bank as our Official Representative to carry out these responsibilities."

Muller reacted with shock and his head snapped up to look at Nicolas Odier. What was he saying?

"Excuse me?" he said, still looking at Odier.

"Just a minute," Minger interrupted. "You are asking a Swiss Ministry to assign one of our officials to the Bank of International Settlements to oversee the transfer of Poland's gold reserves–currently sitting on a train somewhere on the Romanian border–to the gold reserves of the Bank of International Settlements? Is that what you're proposing?"

"That's it exactly," said Odier, his face unsmiling.

The room was silent for a moment as Minger sat back in his chair and digested what Odier had said.

Then Odier leaned forward and broke into a tight smile.

"I'm perfectly aware that this is a highly unusual proposition to put to you, Minister Minger. But let me explain my reasoning.

"First, the concept of adding Polish gold to the books of the Bank's gold reserves account is quite consistent with practices regularly undertaken by the Bank. We're a Central Bank for central banks," he said disarmingly. "Accepting and holding national gold reserves is part of our basic charter. Transactions in gold reserves occur daily and are recorded on our books.

"So the basic premise of transferring Polish gold reserves to the books of the Bank is quite normal."

Odier took a cigarette case from his suit jacket, extracted a cigarette–a Gitane, Muller noted with approval–and quickly lit it, exhaling a plume of smoke.

"Transferring Polish gold that is sitting on a train at the Romanian border, fleeing an invasion and trying to find safety aboard ship in the Black Sea is–of course–not an ordinary event. Accordingly, to be done properly, the transfer must be accomplished by the measures I have described: the signature and official stamp of the transferor–the Polish official who currently has the gold in his possession–and the signature of a witness on behalf of the Bank to accept the transfer.

"We don't have anyone remotely capable of carrying out those duties. Mr. Muller, whom I have known since childhood–and whom I trust–has the two attributes we need: He is a citizen of a neutral party–Switzerland–and he has experience operating in highly-charged and dangerous environments, as witness his previous assignments as Secretary of the High Commissioner of the Free City of Danzig and as Commissioner General of Austria before the German *Anschluss.*

"I would have confidence appointing him a Special Representative of the Bank of International Settlements."

Minger scowled at him. Then he turned to Rachwalski and Munteneau.

"This plan has your support?" he said, eyes narrowed and his lips tight.

"Yes." They spoke in unison.

"The Romanian Foreign Ministry will appoint an official to accompany and assist Mr. Muller when he arrives in country," Munteneau said.

"And I have prepared written instructions for the Polish official on the train to cooperate fully," Rachwalski added.

"Mr. Muller would have to deliver those too, I assume?" Minger spoke gruffly.

Rachwalski nodded. "That's correct."

He then coughed again, obviously nervous, but plunged on.

"It was clearly presumptuous, Minister Minger, but since time is short, I've also taken the liberty of booking a seat for Mr. Muller on a flight for Rome that leaves Geneva this evening. If connections are on time from Rome through Athens, Mr. Muller would arrive in Bucharest tomorrow afternoon."

CHAPTER 7

The plane lunged, then dropped precipitously, and Muller retched again into the airsick bag that was now filling with vomit. The cabin of the DC 3 aircraft stank as the plane jack-knifed through the unstable air above the Greek mountains; most of the dozen or so passengers–even the stewardess–had been sick and the trolley used to serve refreshments lay askew in the aisle toward the front, where one of its four struts had crumpled during an especially violent episode. Broken crockery and spilled food lay in heaps on the stained rug.

God, what a flight. The connection in Athens from his Rome flight had been close–he had simply walked across the asphalt taxiway from the Ala Littoria plane to board the waiting TAE aircraft–this miserable DC 3-for the final leg to Bucharest. He had been assigned a single seat on the left side of the aircraft and he'd slumped into it, feeling utterly drained by the long overnight flight, his mouth dry and leathery from the pressurized cabins. Before takeoff, the TAE stewardess had served a glass of juice and Greek pastries for breakfast, along with some strong and welcome black coffee. From his window seat, he could look down at the green countryside as the aircraft flew north toward Bucharest. Then the Greek mountains came into view and the plane began to gyrate wildly in the unstable air and clouds.

He had been sick repeatedly over the last hour and felt utterly miserable. With one hand, he gripped the rubbery arm of the seat, trying carefully to avoid spilling the bag clutched in his other hand. Eyes shut, he willed himself to overcome the nausea and, when the flight began to become smoother, he ventured a peek out the window to see blue sky, and below them a wide river. The Danube, he realized; they'd finally passed over the mountains and reached the plains of Southern Romania, where the great river continued to flow East, curving North around the Dobruja Plateau until it finally emptied into the Black Sea. His spirits lifted and he decided he would survive the ordeal after all.

He heaved a sigh of relief and dared to put the smelly bag on the floor–still close enough to grab if needed, but maybe, just maybe, he was finished with it. Moments later, the pilot came on the intercom and said something in a language Muller couldn't understand, but included the word Bucharest, so he figured they'd be coming in for a landing soon.

What kind of reception awaited him in Bucharest, Muller wondered.

It was admittedly a bizarre mission. He'd agreed to accept it mainly because he trusted Nicholas Odier, but also the prospect of another opportunity to keep gold reserves out of Hitler's clutches had appealed to him.

When the three visitors had left the conference room, they had discussed the proposal among themselves and decided the plan was plausible. Minger had been encouraging.
"The Romanians are not belligerents," he'd said, "and the Bank is a neutral institution. The fact that you'll be acting as the Bank's representative gives us diplomatic cover; the Germans may not like it, but this arrangement doesn't jeopardize our neutral stance.

. And The plan sounded plausible, and Minger had been encouraging.

"In fact," he'd continued, stroking his beard as he thought further, "assisting other neutrals to stay that way–in this case, helping Romania get rid of a gold shipment on its territory that two belligerents lay claim to–seems entirely consistent with our role as a neutral state.

"We'll appoint you as Swiss Ambassador to serve as the Bank's Special Representative for acquiring the Polish gold and taking it out of play.

"Yes," he'd added, mostly to himself, "that has a nice sound to it."

Minger had smiled broadly, then turned to Muller.

"Well, Ambassador Muller, you've got a plane to catch tonight in Geneva; you'd best get packed and on your way."

Now, only a day and a half later, and half a continent away, Muller sat back in his seat and tried to gather his thoughts, gazing out the plane's window at the broad dark river below him, sparkling in the afternoon sunshine.

Suddenly he saw a shiny silver Messerschmitt-109 fighter plane dive out of nowhere and begin flying alongside.

What?

He leaned forward in his seat with a start, face pressed to the windowpane. The plane had blue, red and gold markings which he took to be Romanian. He could plainly see the fighter pilot gesturing–he assumed to the pilot of his DC-3. The gestures seemed to be saying keep on straight to your destination and don't make changes. The pilot of his plane must have agreed, as Muller saw the fighter pilot give the thumbs-up signal before arcing gracefully away and disappearing from Muller's sight.

What was that about?

Muller shook his head. He glanced back at the stewardess; she had her head in her hands staring at the floor and obviously hadn't seen anything. The pilot didn't get back on the intercom with any information. Very strange. But by now they had begun descending to land, so he tried to put the incident out of his mind.

Munteneau had told him that he would be met at the airport by an official of the Foreign Affairs Ministry who would brief him and make arrangements to get him to the train with the Polish gold in Northern Romania.

The DC-3 landed smoothly, and Muller began preparing to disembark. Then, looking out of his passenger's window, he saw several military vehicles, with armed soldiers aboard, speeding alongside the plane on the runway, an officer in the lead car gesturing to the pilot to turn away from the terminal which was visible on the left. The pilot brought the plane to a halt and must have opened his cockpit window because he could see the officer yelling something and continuing to point to a destination away from the terminal. Apparently, the pilot agreed and turned the aircraft, so it taxied in the direction the officer had ordered.

Finally, the pilot spun the plane to a stop and shut down the engines.

The stewardess moved to open the passenger doorway behind Muller's seat, and he descended the small flight of stairs, breathing in the fresh air–humid, but welcome after the rancid smell in the plane. Then he looked up and came to an abrupt halt. A half dozen soldiers with rifles at the ready stood facing him. The same officer who had directed the plane now pointed at him and the other passengers who were disembarking and, in a language Muller didn't understand–Romanian, he assumed–made it plain they were to line up toward the rear of the aircraft. Muller did as he was told and stood in a line with the other passengers, gripping his briefcase tightly in his left hand.

What the Hell was this? And where was his Foreign Ministry greeter?

The plane was parked on the very edge of the airport tarmac, the terminal visible, but a mile or so away. Passengers began muttering to one another, but the officer barked at them and they fell silent. The pilot and stewardess now de-planed and were ordered to move under the wing.

No one said anything, but looking around, Muller saw two cars speeding in their direction, trailed by a passenger bus. The two cars pulled up sharply; one was painted in military camouflage, the other, a shiny Skoda sedan, displayed Romanian flags in holders on both fenders. A military official with a gold braided collar epaulet and brimmed cap with red piping stepped out of the camouflaged vehicle. He and the officer heading the contingent exchanged salutes and began speaking in what Muller supposed was Romanian. The Skoda door opened and a tall, formally dressed, dark-haired man stepped out, carefully placing a black homburg hat on his head as he strode deliberately toward them.

Both officers deferred to him.

"Ambassador Muller please identify yourself," he said.

Muller raised his hand slightly and stepped forward.

"I'm Muller," he said.

The man stepped forward and offered his hand with a dignified smile.

"Welcome, sir," he said gravely in French.

"Fetch his bag and put it directly in the boot," he said to the junior officer, who looked at him blankly, then leapt to the plane's baggage compartment when the senior officer spoke sharply to him in Romanian.

"My name is Marius Danita, Third Secretary of the Foreign Ministry" said the diplomat, directing Muller toward the Skoda, where a liveried driver stood holding the back door open for him.

"You must excuse the unusual circumstances of your arrival," Danita said, as they settled into the car. "Our Prime Minister was assassinated just a few hours ago–while you were en route, in fact. Things here are in an uproar as you might imagine".

Muller shook his head in disbelief.

"Prime Minister Câlinescu? Murdered? Today?"

Danita nodded. "Ambushed and shot in his big Cadillac, nearly in front of the Residence. Iron Guard killers–probably with help from the Nazis."

He shook his head, his face grim. "Bastards!" He fairly spit the word.

Muller drew a deep breath.

Well, that probably explained the fighter plane–and diversion of his flight to this remote taxiway.

As his bag was loaded into the boot and the trunk lid slammed shut, Muller saw the soldiers grabbing one of the other passengers, a short burly man, and dragging him away.

Danita, watching too, shrugged.

"No idea," he said, "but retaliation is underway and will be merciless."

He spoke in Romanian to the driver who gunned the car away from the aircraft.

"I'm taking you to a remote hanger where I've organized a plane to fly you up to the border and get you to the train."

"I hope you mean to fly *us* up to the border," Muller replied, suddenly wary of being shuffled aside by the Foreign Ministry.

"No, you'll be met there," Danita said airily,

Muller didn't reply and pondered his options.

Moments later, the Skoda pulled up in front of a large hangar with a semi-circular roof atop two-story walls. The front and back of the building were open and, peering inside, Muller could see several aircraft were parked.

They got out and Danita led the way toward the doorway of the office complex attached to the hanger. Inside was a large, cluttered room with desks and scattered over-stuffed sofas; evidently part office and part holding room for the pilots and crews.

Danita began speaking rapidly to one of the men—a pilot, Muller assumed, since he was wearing a light flight jacket and a pilot cap with goggles was on the seat cushion next to him. The conversation quickly became animated and the two men began arguing, each pointing at the other.

Finally, Danita turned to Muller.

"He won't fly," he said in French, pointing to the Pilot. "He said they've declared an emergency, grounded all planes until further notice and issued orders to the Air Force to shoot down any violators."

"I'm not taking the risk," the pilot said in heavily accented French. "Not worth it. These guys are serious." He glared at Danita.

Danita stood above the pilot, hands on his hips and glared back.

Then he turned and looked around the room.

"Where's an office with a phone?"

The pilot pointed to a doorway to the rear and Danita strode toward it.

"Wait here," he ordered Muller.

The pilot offered a raised third finger toward Danita's retreating back.

"Sorry to disappoint you, sir," he said, turning to Muller and continuing to speak in French, "but I'm not going to disobey a no-fly order for anyone–especially that self-important prick."

Muller nodded and smiled.

"The idea of getting shot down doesn't appeal much to me either," he said.

Tiring of waiting for Danita to return, Muller went back outside, stood by the car, and lit up a Gitane, his mind trying to grasp what this latest development might mean.

In their last conversation before he'd left Switzerland, Munteneau had described Prime Minister Armand Câlinescu as the power behind King Carol II, and the undisputed leader of Romania.

"He's no democrat," Munteneau had said, "but he's a fervent anti-Communist and very wary of Hitler. He's a product of St. Cyr, the French military academy, and has close ties to the French government. He signaled he'd support moving the Polish gold across Romania to the Black Sea, but he faces strong local opposition from the Iron Guard–Green Shirt street brawlers that want to set up their own isolationist dictatorship, cut ties to France and chase all the foreigners out of Romania. The Nazis are backing them because they're a de-stabilizing influence. But so far, Câlinescu has held them at bay."

Well, maybe not anymore, Muller thought to himself. Did the assassination mean the Iron Guard had seized power? Would Germany now be pulling the strings? Was his mission at risk?

Muller ground out his butt with a shoe as Danita began striding toward him from the office.

"They've ordered the CFR to take charge of the train issue," he said, getting into the car and gesturing for Muller to join him. He issued orders to the driver in Romanian.

"What's the CFR?" asked Muller.

"Sorry, Căile Ferate Române is the Romanian rail company," Danita replied. "I just spoke to the Deputy General Manager, and he's instructed us to meet him at the Gara Cotroceni; that's the Royal train station located in Eroilor near the Residence. Apparently, your gold train is causing serious issues for CFR operations and he wants to see how you can help solve their problems."

Danita lapsed into silence, then grew animated as a police checkpoint slowed traffic.

He yelled at the driver, clearly ordering him to go around the barriers.

"That's why I put the flags on our fenders," he growled in French.

Policemen barred their way, then waved them through, saluting as the car went by.

Danita gravely lifted his hand in recognition and turned back to Muller with a smirk.

"Works every time," he said.

"So, am I to understand that the Foreign Ministry is now washing its hands of this issue and turning it over to the railroad?"

Muller allowed his annoyance to show.

"Ambassador Muller, you should be very happy," Danita said. "Căile Ferate Române is one of the most powerful organizations in the country. It manufactures rail equipment for nations across Europe as well as our own; it operates our vast national railroad system; it employs thousands of workers; and, most important, it has bought every Romanian politician in the country worth owning. Believe me, in terms of influence over domestic affairs, my Ministry can't hold a candle to CFR.

"So, yes, we're handing both you and your mission over to them." He looked over at Muller and smiled sardonically. "You'll have to see what you can make of it."

They had turned off the highway into a neighborhood of tall, leafy trees and large, imposing homes.

"Embassy Row in Bucharest, Ambassador Muller," Danita said, "now heavily guarded against the Iron Guard, as you can see." And it was true, as Muller saw armed policemen on street corners as they drove past, before the car entered a broad plaza that fronted a tall, ornate building with large columns and an imposing high portico.

"Cotroceni Palace," said Danita; "the Residence."

Tanks and armored cars were parked along the perimeter of the plaza and armed soldiers were stationed at intervals within it, forming a corridor toward the right of the Residence and Policemen no longer cowed by the car's flags directed them to pull over and stop.

Danita rolled down his window and began arguing with a police officer who was clearly ordering them out of the car. Finally, the policeman yanked open Danita's door and poked him in the chest with a leather truncheon.

Danita shouted what sounded like obscenities but began to get out of the car, gesturing to Muller to do the same thing. A group of policemen, clearly angered by Danita, began shoving them both toward the center of the plaza, yelling and gesturing at them to move along.

Muller tried to stay a step or two ahead of the policemen until they reached the corridor formed by two cordons of uniformed guards and they were pushed into a crowd of other civilians being herded along the corridor's path on the plaza.

"What the Hell's going on?" he asked Danita.

"They say we have to see how traitors are treated," Danita said out of the side of his mouth as he tried to avoid being pushed again, clutching his Homberg.

He glanced ahead, then stopped and crossed himself.

"Oh, God," he said in a soft voice.

Muller looked and blanched.

There before them were five mutilated bodies strung up on lampposts, half naked, bloody genitals hanging down, their faces frozen in hideous expressions. Hand-lettered signs hung from each one which Muller couldn't read, but he supposed said something like 'Death to Traitors.'

The crowd was pushed along by the police, so they had to file past the bodies. Black crows, uncowed by the pedestrians below, were pecking away at them, cawing and fighting with one another and causing the bodies to sway.

Muller gagged and thought he might be sick again, and in fact, people in the crowd bolted to the edges and vomited, hastily wiping their mouths, and trying to hurry past the grisly spectacle.

He and Danita moved along as quickly as they could, and finally got past the end of the corridor, only to be confronted by a black Cadillac, its fenders dented, and its body pierced by dozens of bullet holes. Bouquets of flowers had been placed on the car and

Muller heard a low sound of lament from women, kneeling next to it.

"Călinescu's car?" whispered Muller.

Danita nodded.

They hurried past the vehicle until finally the crowd dispersed, and they were permitted to return to their car. The driver had been forced into the crowd as well and had not yet reappeared.

Christ! Muller lit a Gitane and leaned on the car. The assassination was certainly a terrible deed, but this reaction was barbaric. Danita stood on the other side of the car, arms crossed, Homburg pulled down on his forehead, his face a mask, staring into the distance. Neither spoke and when the driver returned, they got back in the car. This time, the police waved them around a growing crowd that was being funneled into the corridor leading to the bodies.

"They're going to force everyone in Bucharest to see this," Danita said quietly. "File past the bodies; as if that would change anything."

He sighed.

"At least it tells us that the government remains in charge," he added. "They'll decapitate the Iron Guard leadership–whatever's left of it."

Danita paused again.

"I suppose that's something, right?"

Several minutes later, they pulled up in front of a small, one story building with a coat of tan-colored paint next to a train platform visible above tracks and a railhead.

"It doesn't look very 'royal' does it?" said Danita. "Well, at one time it was very grand, but it burned to the ground and this is all the government would do to replace it."

A uniformed railroad agent with a large white mustache strode from the platform to the doorway of the building, opened the door and gestured for Muller and Danita to enter. To Muller's surprise, the interior was elegantly appointed. A sitting area with comfortable chairs and a sofa surmounted a plush Persian rug; a small dining area with a table and chairs was set with China and two tall candles.

The agent said something in Romanian that seemed welcoming; they were clearly expected. He and Danita exchanged words.

"The CFR Deputy Manager is expected soon," Danita said. "There's a bedroom through that door and he's going to put out some food for us. You might want to take the opportunity to clean up."

Muller carried his suitcase into the bedroom suite and found it had a full bath—with a stall shower. He quickly stripped, showered and shaved, luxuriating in the warm water, and donned clean clothes. Then he removed the false bottom of the suitcase and took out the money belt Odier had given him, unbuttoned his clean shirt and fixed it around his waist.

'Ten thousand dollars in U.S.one hundred dollar bills," Odier had said. 'You're likely to need cash for...incidentals." He hadn't smiled.

Muller decided not to remove the brass knuckles that he'd begun regularly carrying, or the snub-nosed pistol in the ankle holster that Odier had insisted he take. Then he replaced the false bottom of the suitcase, repacked it and returned to the station sitting room feeling re-energized. As he did so, he heard the unmistakable sound of an approaching locomotive presumably carrying the CFR official.

"Ludovic Cozma," said the CFR Deputy General Manager, entering the room and extending his hand in greeting. He was a sturdily built man with wide shoulders and close-cropped hair that was turning gray. He had black eyes below heavy brows, a broad forehead and a wide mouth. He radiated energy and had a take-charge bearing.

"I wish this were a social occasion, Ambassador Muller," he said as they shook hands, "but I'm afraid we are meeting at a moment of crisis for my country, so we'd best get to it." Cozma's French was fluent and his manner friendly, but business-like.

"The rail system is on high alert for acts of sabotage in the wake of the assassination," he said. "So, there are frequent stoppages and schedules have been drastically altered.

"But there's another problem too; conditions along our Northern border with Poland have fallen into complete chaos. Thousands of Polish soldiers and refugees are pouring over the border to escape the German invasion. And that Polish gold train has apparently been taken over by Polish fighters who have surrounded it and refuse to allow any traffic on the mainline of my railroad to move until their demands have been met."

"What are the demands?" asked Muller.

Cozma turned to Danita.

"Your ministry has taken charge of the gold issue. They won't tell us anything. My orders are to run my train up to the border as fast as I can and sort things out." Cozma pointed out the window to the locomotive and cars standing on the platform. "We need to restore the system. Getting that gold train out of the way is going be necessary to clear the tracks."

He pointed to the desk and telephone on the far side of the room. "I suggest you call your superiors and tell them we need instructions."

Danita gave a startled look at Cozma.

"I'm just supposed to hand Ambassador Muller over to you," he said defensively, "then I'm finished with this business."

"Like Hell, you are, Mr. Third Secretary," retorted Cozma, taking a step toward him and grabbing his lapels, his face inches from Danita's. "You're not doing any Goddam disappearing act," he said, forcing Danita backwards. "You'll do as I say, or I'll toss you into the locomotive boiler along with the fuel."

He shoved Danita toward the phone.

"Make the call. Now!"

Danita, clearly cowed, walked to the phone, picked up the receiver and began to dial.

Cozma took Muller's shoulder and led them to the doorway. They stepped outside on the platform and Cozma offered Muller a cigarette, flaring his lighter.

"He'll wet his pants if I'm standing over him," Cozma said with a sardonic smile. "I know his type; mostly bluster. But he knows his ass is on the line; so, let's let him try to find out what's happening."

Then he turned to face Muller.

"How much authority do you have over the Poles?" he asked. "Someone's got to take charge of what seems to be a chaotic situation."

Muller shook his head. "I'm a Swiss diplomat representing the Bank of International Settlements," said Muller. "My authority only extends to safeguarding the gold."

He decided to leave it at that and not elaborate on the plan to transfer ownership of the gold from Poland to the BIS. He didn't know Cozma or what *his* agenda was for the gold shipment.

Cozma dragged on his cigarette and exhaled a plume of smoke, eyeing Muller with a faintly amused gaze.

"A mysterious Swiss diplomat who just suddenly happens to drop into our country at this pivotal moment," he said quietly, almost as if speaking to himself.

"Well, at least you're Swiss and the Swiss are neutral; that's something. The Bank of International Settlements?" he shook his head. "Never heard of it. So, I'll not inquire too deeply–at least not now" he said.

"But we appear to have a real mess on our hands with the train, and the gold that's apparently attracting even more flies than shit does."

There was no longer any amusement in the gaze he fixed on Muller.

"You'd better be worth the trouble we're going through to bring you into this business."

Cozma dropped his butt and ground it out with his heel.

Returning inside, they found Danita standing at the desk staring down at the black telephone, receiver now returned to its cradle.

He straightened up, lifting his head to face them directly.

"It's gotten even worse," he said, then sighed deeply. "Our people believe Hitler ordered Câlinescu's assassination and that Gestapo infiltrators recruited the Iron Guard to ambush him. They also fear that the Germans are mounting an operation to take the train by force."

Danita began tapping the table before him with his fingers, trying to control himself.

"Apparently, the German Ambassador called on the Prime Minister yesterday and delivered a note from Hitler demanding that Romania seize the Polish gold and turn it over to the Reichsbank. Câlinescu refused and they had a terrible row. The

Ambassador stormed out of the Residence threatening immediate reprisals."

Danita paused.

"They carried out the assassination," he said; "no one knows if they'll attack us too."

Cozma interrupted, eyes blazing and fists clenched. "Have they mobilized the Romanian Army to oppose a German attack?"

Danita shook his head. "The Cabinet can't decide what to do. They haven't been able to elect a new Prime Minister and they're totally split on how to respond.

"Apparently, after the row with the Ambassador, Câlinescu ordered plans drawn up to immediately transport the gold to the Port at Constanta where the Poles could ship it off to wherever they decide. He also directed the Finance Ministry to assume all the expenses–including the costs of taking care of the Polish soldiers and refugees too. That caused a fracture in the Cabinet, so nothing was done to carry out his orders before he was murdered.

"But now he's dead, no one's taken charge and no decisions have been taken one way or the other. The government's paralyzed."

"So, what are your orders?" Cozma's tone was sharp.

Danita looked at him with a blank face and took a deep breath before responding.

"I am to accompany you to the North and together we are to fix the problem," he said quietly.

The room was silent as the message sank in.

Muller watched as the two men faced one another.

"Just 'fix the problem'," Danita repeated.

Now it was Cozma's turn to take a deep breath. Then, he straightened and fixed his gaze on Muller.

"Ambassador Muller, whatever it is Mr. Danita and I decide to do, you're going to be a part of it too."

Muller couldn't think of anything to say in reply, so he just nodded.

Cozma pointed a finger at Danita.

"Mr. Danita, call your Ministry back and tell them to get a message to whoever's in charge of the train; tell them to expect us later tonight and that we have full Cabinet authority to act on the government's behalf."

CHAPTER 8

They departed immediately.

Cozma's train had only two cars attached to a diesel locomotive. The first was a well-appointed parlor car that had been turned into a combination office and living space which Cozma was obviously accustomed to using. The second was an upgraded military wagon that housed a dozen well-armed soldiers, a radio compartment and a work-space with counters that could be used for typing and other office tasks. Reversible seats could be converted to bunks and a table at the back apparently served as a mess, with a small cooking stove and sink nearby.

Cozma strode to a map of the Romanian rails system that had been mounted on a panel affixed to one wall of the railcar.

"This is a nearly 600 kilometer trip we're making, gentlemen," he said. "It will take us all night unless we encounter delays–which I hope can be avoided."

Cozma took a pencil from a nearby desk and used it as a pointer.

"We're here in Bucharest," he said pointing, "very far South. We have to travel all the way up here," his pencil traced a line up through Ploesti, then arcing North. "This is Cernâuti, right on the border with Poland. That's where we're going. The gold train is there–somewhere. Fortunately, we're running on our main North-South rail link. This whole area to the West," his pencil pointed, "is mountainous–the Carpathians–difficult terrain. You can see the line runs East of them.

"Now, look here," he said pointing to the region surrounding Cernâuti. "You can see the Polish border is only this wide; maybe a hundred kilometers. Here to the West is Czechoslovakia–or used to be; it's now Germany, of course. Then on the East is the Soviet Union–hardly a friendly destination if you're a Pole fleeing the Germans.

"So, you can see, it's almost like a syphon. All of Southern Poland points down to this narrow border with Romania. It's the only escape route. And that's why so many refugees are crossing over in this region.

"If that damned train with the gold is blocking the mainline–and it sounds like it is–that's going to clog up the whole system; so, once we get up there, our first job is going to have to be to find the train and figure out what to do with the goddam gold so we can move it out of the way."

Cozma turned to Muller.

"That's when you'll have to perform your magic, Ambassador Muller."

Cozma looked at his watch.

"Nearly 8 PM. Let's get a good meal under our belt tonight," and he pointed to a table that had been setup for them with plates heaped with meat and stuffed rolls of some kind.

"My chef prepares a mean mâmâligâ," Cozma said. You'd probably call it Polenta, Ambassador Muller. And everyone loves our sarmales–cabbage rolls."

He poured them each a large glass of red wine from a carafe on the table.

"Bon Appetit." They clinked glasses. "And eat up; I suspect food will be scarce on the border."

Danita seemed content to follow Cozma's lead, but he had apparently recovered his confidence, and he gestured toward the map with his fork.

"I actually spent several summers camping in that border area as a young man," he said between mouthfuls. "The region was–is–called Bukovina, depending upon whom you speak to," he said. "It was Ukrainian for centuries, then part of the Austro-Hungarian Empire, before Romania took it over 30 years ago, after the War– the last war," he corrected himself. "And it's full of restive minorities including Ruthenians, Moldovans and who knows how many others. The Soviets have been eying it for years; they think of it as part of the Russian Empire that they lost in the War and want it back. And the Hungarians to the West are still furious that it became Romanian, not Hungarian."

"Filling up that region with refugees–and finding ways to feed and house them–that'll be an enormous challenge, and it's likely to create more unrest, too. The last thing we need is some kind of insurrection there."

"It probably has its share of Nazi sympathizers too," added Cozma, nodding.

"What's the topography like?" asked Muller. "Could the Germans send a tank column over the border to attack the train?"

Danita shook his head. "Not a chance. It's very rugged country. No, they'd have to mount a serious campaign to do that. Mr. Cozma's right; using local Nazis is probably their best bet if they really decide to take the train."

"Or sabotage it en route if we finally get it moving," said Cozma, refilling their wine glasses.

They ate in silence lost in thought.

"If Polish fighters have taken control of the train, we're going to have to get rid of them, somehow if we're going to get it moving," said Cozma.

Muller sipped his wine before speaking.

"Or somehow co-opt them into helping us," he said.

"Look, what are their choices? They have to move the train to get the gold somewhere safe–presumably to your Port of Constanta and aboard a ship. They may be our strongest allies if we can offer them a way out of this impasse."

"Or they could decide to act unilaterally somehow, and trigger a fight," said Cozma.

Muller was tired of arguing. He finished the last of the polenta on his plate, and felt his head begin to droop; he hadn't really slept since leaving Geneva nearly 48 hours ago.

Cozma pointed to the bunks in the rear of the car.

"Take one of those," he said.

CHAPTER 9

Muller was awoken by someone shaking his shoulder. He struggled to sit up, nodding his head groggily, and saw the grey light of early morning out the window. Cozma handed him a large cup of black coffee and he took a draught, then spluttered.

Cozma smiled.

"A little brandy never hurts in the morning."

Muller rubbed his eyes then ran his hands through his hair trying to get his bearings.

"We're nearing the border?"

"We're approaching Râdâuti," Cozma replied. "That's where the backup of stalled trains begins. We passed through Suceava twenty minutes ago and the station chief told me nothing's been able to get past Râdâuti going North for the last 24 hours and there's no southbound traffic either. So the train is somewhere up there and it's blocking everything. We're going to have to commandeer a truck in Râdâuti to go find it."

Muller finished his coffee and idly munched on the remains of a sarmale that he found on a nearby plate. Minutes later, he felt their train slowing down, then, suddenly come to a complete stop. Outside the window, he could see nothing but forest.

Cozma went to the doorway and had to jump to the ground.

"Mr. Danita, come with me please," he said. "Ambassador Muller kindly wait while we sort things out." Muller decided to jump down too. Ahead, a long line of trains was stopped, and Muller could see passengers sitting and standing alongside the tracks. Next to where they'd stopped was a copse of trees and Muller stepped in to take a piss. Finished, he looked around and heard the gurgle of a stream off to one side. He clambered down a bank and found a rock where he could kneel and splash himself with the cool water and take a few mouthfuls.

Returning to the train, he sat alongside and lit a Gitane, shaking his head with a wan smile at the predicament he found himself in. This was exactly how they'd planned it in the Minister's office 48 hours ago, right?

Hah!

Cozma and Danita were striding back toward him.

"It's a real mess up there," said Cozma. "Trains stopped, no more food, water running out; passengers ready to revolt.

"Get your things, Mr. Ambassador. We're hoofing it into town and finding ourselves a truck."

Muller firmly gripped his suitcase in one hand, briefcase in the other, as they strode along the rail lines, with six of the soldiers accompanying them, rifles over their shoulders. They passed along the trains and Muller could hear moans and angry exchanges. Passengers eyed them suspiciously as they walked past. Muller felt uncomfortable and avoided eye contact, but there were no incidents and, a few minutes later, they entered a small leafy village with neat homes situated on either side of a dusty dirt road.

Ten minutes later they found themselves in the village center where attractive two-story buildings surrounded a cobble-stoned plaza. Cozma mounted the steps to what Muller took to be the Mayor's office. He tried the door, but it was locked; too early in the morning for the Mayor, apparently. A café at one of the corners was open and Cozma began speaking with the proprietor, who pointed to his right. Cozma gestured them to move along in that direction and they followed him, stopping at the entrance to what seemed to be a freight warehouse with several trucks parked in front. None of the trucks had keys, but one of the soldiers mounted the fender of the biggest truck, opened the hood and fiddled with the wiring for a moment.

"Vroom." The engine sprung to life. The soldier smirked and jumped back down.

Muller vaulted into the open back of the truck with the soldiers while Cozma took the wheel and Danita took the passenger's seat.

A tourist road sign directly in front of them advised that Cernâuti was 24 kilometers ahead. Cozma gunned the engine and they began speeding in that direction.

Not five minutes later, they mounted a hill, and, in the distance, they could see the smoke rising from dozens of campfires ahead. Polish Army units? Was the train there?

As they began their descent, soldiers leaped from ravines on both sides, surrounding them, rifles pointed at them. Cozma braked to a halt and they raised their hands. The soldiers began yelling at them. Muller recognized they were speaking Polish; he only knew a smattering of Polish words from his time in Danzig, but he was able to shout "przyjaciel" "'friend." He shouted it again and again.

The soldier who seemed to be in charge of the detachment approached the truck and began speaking loudly to Muller in Polish.

"No mowic" Muller repeated. "Don't speak."

"Przyjaciel," he said again.

The soldier ordered Muller down from the truck where he was quickly surrounded by members of the detachment, rifles pointed at him. The leader gestured that he was to stay, then sent two of his men running down the hill toward the campfires.

Everyone seemed frozen as the minutes slowly ticked by. No one said a word. Finally, a motorcycle with a sidecar came into view, racing up the hill toward them. It pulled up in front of Muller and a man in an officer's uniform stepped out of the sidecar.

He asked a question in Polish, and Muller replied in French.

"We are officials representing the Romanian Government on a mission to help Polish interests."

The officer replied in heavily accented French.

"Show me your credentials."

Muller reached in the pocket of his jacket for his passport.

One of the soldiers raised his rifle menacingly, but the officer spoke to him sharply and he lowered his weapon.

Muller handed the officer his passport and the Bank of International Settlements document certifying him as a special representative for the Polish gold reserves.

The officer studied the documents. He was clearly confused by them.

Finally, he looked up, eying Muller uncertainly.

"You're a Swiss diplomat and a representative of this Bank, whatever it is, to deal with our gold reserves?"

Muller nodded and reached for his papers. Then he pointed to the cab of the truck.

"This is Mr. Cozma, who runs the Romanian railroads and Minister Danita of the Romanian Ministry of Foreign Affairs. They are part of my mission.

"And who are you?" Muller asked, turning back to the officer in a commanding way.

"Captain Jurzyk, Sir," he replied, coming to attention.

"Well Captain," said Muller, "the Germans are at your back and we're your only way forward, so you'd better get on that motorcycle and lead us to whoever's in command here."

Muller turned and began striding confidently back to the truck; the officer, after hesitating a moment, said something to the detachment of soldiers, who began backing away. Then, he folded himself into the motorcycle sidecar and the vehicle turned around, driving rapidly back down the hill.

Muller climbed aboard and Cozma put the truck in gear and followed the motorcycle.

Crossing a bridge guarded by dozens of sentries, the road curved up a steep escarpment. As Muller looked off to one side, a valley materialized below them and, as they climbed, he could clearly see a huge encampment with tents, fires and clusters of people–a lot of them; there weren't just hundreds–thousands. The road then leveled out ahead of them and he saw train tracks leading into a tunnel, where a train was parked; ours, he wondered?

The road took them around a bend on the other side of the escarpment. He could see an entire valley laid out below them– with still more camps and people. But most important, next to the road, was the other end of the tunnel where two trains were lined up, side-by-side on the two tracks, the cars covered by camouflage netting that had been strung above them.

There was a clearing next to the trains and a large tent had been erected, also covered by camouflage, and guarded by machine gun emplacements and rows of trenches. A heavily armed checkpoint blocked their path and soldiers quickly surrounded the truck.

Captain Jurzyk spoke sharply to an officer who appeared to be in command of the checkpoint. The barrier blocking the road was lifted and Jurzyk led them to one side of the clearing where Cozma parked the truck.

Jurzyk dismounted from the sidecar and strode toward the tent, gesturing for them to wait.

He returned in a moment, flanked by a senior officer from the look of his uniform, who walked directly toward them with a welcoming smile.

"Minister Danita?" he said.

Danita lifted his Homburg and stepped forward.

"I am Danita."

The officer stood to attention and saluted.

"General Pletzki, Commander of this Polish Army detachment," he said. "You are expected. Welcome."

Pletzki led them into the large tent where clusters of tables and chairs were occupied by soldiers and some men in civilian clothes, all seemingly hard at work with files and typewriters. On the far side, closest to the trains, an assortment of couches and tired-looking overstuffed chairs were occupied by men speaking in groups and poring over documents on low tables.

To Muller's astonishment, as they approached the seating area, he spied none other than Jozef Beck, the Polish Foreign Minister, seated in one of the chairs and apparently engaged in heated argument with men on either side of him.

General Pletzki approached the seated men and announced, loudly enough for all of them to hear, that the Romanian delegation had arrived. Conversation stopped and the men all turned to gaze at them. Several of them rose in apparent welcome.

A short, pudgy man offered his hand.

"May we address you in French, gentlemen?"

"Please do," said Danita, removing his Homburg, placing it on one of the tables, then straightening and assuming a commanding stance, chest out, feet apart and hands clasped behind him. He looked every inch the part of the senior diplomat.

"I am Marius Danita, Secretary of the Foreign Ministry," he announced in stentorian tones, "and I speak for the government of the Kingdom of Romania. May I know whom I am addressing?"

Beck rose from his chair.

"We are the government-in-exile of the Polish Republic," he said. "I am Jozef Beck, the Foreign Minister and provisional head of this group of government leaders. We have been driven from our country by German invaders, but we have not surrendered and, together with colleagues in Paris and London, we are in the process of forming a fully sovereign Polish government-in-exile to oppose and ultimately defeat our enemies."

He paused.

"We are in need of assistance in this current state of disorder and we therefore greatly value this opportunity to cooperate with the leadership of the Kingdom of Romania."

Beck bowed in Danita's direction.

You have to give Beck credit for the dignity he was able to muster, thought Muller to himself, even though he's a nasty and untrustworthy prick. And, as if on cue, Beck put on display the overbearing attitude that Muller remembered so well from dealings with him in Geneva.

"I can assure you that, as the new government of the Polish Republic, we will consider very seriously any proposals that the Kingdom of Romania may wish to offer us."

Then he sat down with a faint condescending smile, as if indulging supplicants.

Danita, smiling in return, began to reply in a contrite, engaging tone when Cozma loudly interrupted him.

"Enough! Both of you. Cut the crap!"

He stepped forward, black eyes blazing beneath his heavy brow, veins pulsing in his forehead, his hands clenched in fists.

"I am Cozma; I run the Romanian Rail system. Right now, those fucking trains," he pointed to where they stood on the tracks, "have shut down my main trunk line and fouled up the entire system. So, we're going to move them—one way or another."

Cozma pointed at Beck.

"You're visitors on our soil—and, for the moment at least, you're welcome. But we make the rules here. The Germans have driven you out of Poland and now they're threatening to attack us too—mainly because of the gold you've got stashed on that train." He pointed again. "So, we've got decisions to make. I need someone to brief me—NOW—about what's going on so I can figure out what to do."

Cozma stood, hands on his hips and looked around the semi-circle of seated men.

General Pletzki strode to a map that was hanging from what looked like a coat stand.

"Let me show you what we know, Mr. Cozma," he said. Using a fountain pen, he pointed.

"Here you can see the border, and here we are, on the Romanian side, just South of Cernâuti.

"Up here is Lwow, the largest town in Southeast Poland; it's about 80 kilometers North of the border. Our military planners refer to the area here, between Lwow and the border, as 'the Romanian Bridgehead." He pointed and made a sweeping motion to show the large swath of territory he was referring to.

"This is where our forces were preparing to dig in and make a stand if we were facing defeat by the Germans. It's ideal defensive territory, with steep hills and deep ravines that we could use to advantage to resist German attacks. Tank traps and trenches had been dug in preparation and large storage facilities were pre-positioned, stocked with food and ammunition. We were confident of holding this area and resist the Germans, through the winter if necessary, until the French mount their offensive to defeat Germany in the West."

Pletzki paused and looked directly at Cozma.

"Our Commander, General Rydz-Smigly, issued orders for Polish forces to retire to this Bridgehead, two days ago."

He paused again.

"That's the same day the Soviets invaded Poland from the East. They sent forces flooding into the region, captured Lwow on the first day and forced our troops away from the Bridgehead into this narrow valley," again he pointed, "running along the Southern

Polish border from Kolomyia and Sniatyn to Cernâuti. That's where we escaped over the border."

Pletzki turned back to the map.

"Then yesterday, German and Soviet forces linked up and," WHACK! Pletzki angrily slapped the map, nearly knocking it over. "They've completely occupied the Bridgehead and sealed off the border. Any Polish forces left behind will be crushed.

"The Soviets totally fucked us."

Pletzki stepped away from the map and returned the fountain pen to the breast pocket of his uniform. His face bore a look of angry resignation.

"The men camped down there, are the Polish forces that escaped over the border?" asked Cozma.

"Only some of them," Pletzki replied. "More troops are scattered all over Northern Romania and even West into Hungary. There are tens of thousands of them," he added, "and civilian refugees that fled too."

"What are you doing for provisions?" asked Cozma.

"Barely scraping by," replied Pletzki. "Most of our stockpiles in the Bridgehead have been lost to the Soviets, so we're using whatever provisions we were able to salvage–along with supplies your government made available when we arrived. But we're nearly out and we're already short of medical supplies for the wounded."

Cozma nodded, his face grim. He shoved his hands into his pockets and began to pace.

"Tell me about the gold train and how you came to park it here," he said.

The short pudgy man who had greeted them in French stepped forward.

"My name is Krakowski," he said. "I'm Deputy General Manager of the Bank of Poland and I accompanied the train from Warsaw. The journey to the Polish border was under the command of a Polish intelligence officer appointed by the Interior Ministry. He got us safely to the border–and that was no easy thing, by the way. But once we crossed over into Romania and the gold was loaded onto one of your trains," Krakowski nodded to Cozma, "the intelligence officer shook hands with everyone and headed back to Poland."

Cozma nodded impatiently.

"Go on,"

"Once the gold was safely transferred, your railroad officials were ready to take over and send the train along," said Krakowski, "but they were over-ruled by Romanian Customs and Border officials. They said the government had ordered them to hold the train because the Prime Minister had been murdered and all plans were on hold.

"Who in the government issued that order?" Cozma asked.

Krakowski shrugged.

"They didn't say. They just blocked us from leaving.

"The situation was complete chaos, Mr. Cozma. It was the middle of the night; we couldn't risk turning on overhead lights for fear of German planes, so it was pitch dark and hard to see what we were doing. Gold is very heavy, and we had to recruit retreating Polish soldiers to help us move it over to your train. It was hard work.

"When we finally finished and the Romanian officials refused to give the orders to send it off to Constanta, as agreed, all of us–including the soldiers and their officers–became very angry. We sure as Hell weren't going to let that gold be sent back to Poland or captured by the Germans sitting just across the border. So, we took matters into our own hands and commandeered the train.

"We forced your engineer–Iulio was his name–to fire up the locomotive, and we started moving South, away from the border, even though the Romanians officials objected. Polish soldiers got aboard with their rifles ready and told them to get the Hell out of the way.

"When we got to this tunnel, Iulio said that was as far as he was willing to go. That seemed okay to us; we didn't know how to get to Constanta anyway, and the tunnel seemed to offer some protection. So, here we are," Krakowski said.

"That's a pretty accurate account," added General Pletzki, interrupting him.

"I've questioned the Polish officers who were in charge. Our people–including Mr. Krakowski," Pletzki gestured toward him–"were furious at the Romanians; they thought the delay put our Polish gold reserves at risk–and by that time, everyone knew that's what we were transporting–so they took matters into their own hands.

"Separately, my command had been ordered to continue retreating away from the border so as not to attract German–or Soviet–pursuit, and we decided to set up our headquarters here too. I directed our people to halt the next North-bound train in order to shut down your rail artery and get someone's attention."

Pletzki turned to face Cozma.

"So that's all we know, Mr. Cozma. We succeeded in getting your attention; so now that you're here, we're ready to help solve our mutual problem."

Cozma smiled thinly and walked over to Pletzki, shaking his hand.

"Fair enough, General," he said. "Let's find someplace we can sit together and figure things out."

Muller pulled his passport and BIS credentials out of his suit pocket and approached Krakowski.

"May we speak privately?" he said quietly, handing Krakowski his papers.

Krakowski looked at them, then lifted his eyes toward Muller with a look of bewilderment.

"A Swiss diplomat?" he said querulously, "representing the Bank of International Settlements?" He looked at the papers again before handing them back to Muller. "What the Hell is this about, Mr. Muller?"

"The gold reserves," Muller answered. "We need to have a quiet word together."

Krakowski drew a breath, then nodded and began striding to the edge of the tent, turning his back on the other leaders.

"What do you have for me?" he said.

"A possible solution for shipping the gold," replied Muller.

Krakowski eyed him suspiciously, but Muller took him by the elbow and began leading him toward the train, out of earshot from the others.

"The Romanian Prime Minister was assassinated yesterday because he refused to turn the gold over to the Germans."

"What?" Krakowski blinked in disbelief. "Our gold? You mean this train?"

"Precisely," Muller nodded. "That's why the authorities in Cernâuti refused to send the train South to Constanta after the gold was transferred. No one was willing to take responsibility for deciding what to do, so they just said 'stop.' I think you were certainly right to take charge of the train yourselves. Germany's insistence on seizing the gold is still very real–maybe even more so than before. So, the immediate issue is how to get the gold from here to Constanta and aboard ship."

"You have a plan?" asked Krakowski gazing intently at Muller.

"Actually, it's not my plan; it's your government's plan. But I'm part of it."

Muller returned Krakowski's gaze; he spoke quietly, but forcefully.

"The idea is to transfer ownership of the gold from Poland to the Bank of International Settlement. That way, it's no longer Polish gold the Romanians are transporting; it's BIS gold–and they can tell that to the Germans. Once transfer of the ownership is accomplished the train can be released and resume its journey to Constanta–where the Romanians will be happy to see it loaded aboard ship and sail away–to anywhere, so long it's no longer Romania's problem."

Krakowski continued to stare at Muller as he absorbed the information.

"You have documents describing this transaction?" he said finally, looking around him apprehensively for eavesdroppers.

Muller nodded and tapped the briefcase in his left hand.

"Come with me." Krakowski strode toward the train, saying something in Polish to a soldier guarding the entrance. With no platform, they had to jump and pull themselves aboard. Krakowski opened a compartment door, and they took seats across from one another.

"Show me," he commanded.

Muller unlocked the briefcase and slid out the document folder, handing it to Krakowski, who opened it, lay the papers on the table between them and read them carefully. Then he sat back and stared at Muller.

"This is very clever; how did it come about?"

Muller related what he had been told at the meeting in Geneva, which now–only a few days later–seemed almost a distant memory.

"Of course, no one anticipated that that Prime Minister would be murdered–apparently because of this very issue. But even before that, the Romanian Foreign Ministry was having cold feet about transporting the gold for fear of German retaliation. Your minister in Switzerland, Rachwalski, and Munteneau , the Romanian Chargé d'Affaires, designed this plan to overcome the ministry's objections, and they got Odier, the head of the BIS to buy in."

"I know Rachwalski only slightly," Krakowski said; "but I know Nicholas Odier rather well. The Bank of International Settlements is a central bank for central banks–and as one of Poland's most senior central bankers, I was in their offices in Basle on a regular basis."

Krakowski picked up the documents and scanned them again before placing them back on the table, lips pursed in a straight line, his face frowning in concentration.

Finally, he straightened his shoulder and turned to Muller.

"Odier has signed this conveyance document," he said, pointing to where it lay on the table between them. "But it is expressly conditioned upon two additional signatures: that of a Polish bank official who can affix the formal bank stamp–which is in my possession; he patted a pocket–and yours, with a Bank stamp.

"You have it, I presume?"

Muller pointed to where the stamp lay in his open briefcase.

"So, Mr. Muller, who are you?" Krakowski said.

"I'm a Swiss diplomat and Odier selected me to be the Bank's special representative for this transaction," Muller replied. He wasn't going to give Krakowski a lot of detail. But he decided to add, "It might interest you to know that I served as the Secretary to Sean Lester, High Commissioner for the League of Nations in the Free City of Danzig several years ago."

He was not going to tell him that Jozef Beck, who held the League of Nations chair for Danzig at the end, had betrayed the League over Danzig and nearly cost both Lester and Muller their lives.

"Ah," said Krakowski, "Lester; the High Commissioner. Yes," he said; "Lester enjoyed a good reputation for a time. You were his Secretary?

"Ummm.

"Well, I need to consider this proposal with my colleagues, Mr. Muller," he said, standing, passing the folder back to Muller and leading the way off the train toward the headquarters tent.

CHAPTER 10

As Muller and Krakowski walked the few meters from the train to the cover of the camouflaged tent, they heard the sound of a plane in the distance. Others in the tent heard it too and conversation abruptly stopped as people listened and searched the horizon for the aircraft.

"There," someone said, pointing to the other side of the valley.

A man with binoculars began tracking it.

"Got it" he said. "BV 141; a reconnaissance plane."

The aircraft lazily circled above them, almost as if thumbing its nose at them in its high-altitude cocoon.

"Sonofabitch," the men muttered.

"Are the Heinkels on their way?" one asked.

There was an undertone of fear; Muller could almost feel it. These were men who had endured weeks of combat and been bombed and strafed by German aircraft directed by reconnaissance planes just like the one above them.

But then the buzz of conversations began again, and Muller realized the men were resigned to facing whatever would come and able to get back to what they were doing. He watched as Krakowski gathered several other men around Beck and began speaking intently. At one point, he gestured toward Muller and the group turned to observe him before resuming what rapidly became an animated discussion.

Muller saw that Cozma and General Pretzki were seated at a table off to the side, surrounded by aides and drawing up lists. Danita was standing alongside them, but not involved, and was looking around impatiently.

He's angry, Muller realized. After preening himself in his opening remarks as 'speaking for the government', he'd been sidelined, first by Cozma, who'd taken over the initial discussion, and then by Muller himself, whose talk with Krakowski had generated the intense discussion among the Polish leadership that was taking place out of their earshot.

Would an irate Danita be a problem?

"Mr. Muller, please join us." Krakowski was standing and waving at him.

"Is this what's required to move our gold to Constanta and get it aboard ship? What assurances do we have that the Romanian government will accept this scheme you've proposed?" Beck asked him peremptorily.

"Well, they sent me up here to present it to you," Muller replied. "But ask Secretary Danita, if you like; he's speaking for the government."

Danita, unbidden, had walked over when Muller had been summoned.

"It's only a start," he responded, as faces turned to him.

"What do you mean?" asked Beck.

"The Romanian government will be incurring extraordinary expenses to deal with this whole mess," he said. "So, you're going to have to pay us."

"What?" Anxious faces glared at him.

Danita glared back, resolutely.

"General Pretzki and Mr. Cozma are making plans to move your soldiers to internment camps away from the border and find a way to feed them," he retorted. "It's going to be a major undertaking and very costly. So, we need *your government*"–he pointed a finger at Beck–to hand over $4 million of your gold ingots to reimburse us for our expenses."

The Poles reacted indignantly.

"Absolutely not!"

"That's an outrage."

Danita faced them, his face grim and unsmiling, standing his ground as they argued back and forth.

"Your Prime Minister himself promised that the government would transport our gold without charge." Beck's face was red as he shouted at Danita.

"Well, the Prime Minister's dead," snapped Danita, "murdered on account of your goddam gold. And he certainly didn't expect tens of thousands of defeated Polish soldiers would come pouring over our border seeking our shelter.

"You've got the money," he said pointing to the train. "It's right there; you can damned well pay."

He's relishing this, Muller said to himself; he's the center of attention now and the one dictating terms. He finally had the stage on which he could play his role as spokesman for the Romanian government. And, as Muller knew, he was making it up; he had been instructed 'to fix it,' but he had no idea if the government would support what he decided to do.

Muller ground out a cigarette butt with the heel of his shoe and strolled slowly to where Cozma was impatiently watching the proceedings.

"Christ almighty," Cozma said angrily. "These goddam politicians arguing like we've got all day and this is some kind of debating society. I've got to get my rail system back in operation. And now Danita's playing the role of big shot."

Cozma kicked at some gravel in his annoyance.

"Maybe you should warn him not to overplay his hand," Muller said quietly. "You and I both know he's making this up as he goes along. He's got a point about the Poles paying at least something for the rescue mission; but it's time to back off a bit and lower his demands.

"If I suggest that, he'll throw me to the wolves back in Bucharest," said Cozma, shaking his head. "'I had them eating out of my hand until Cozma stepped in,' he'll say. 'You don't like the deal? Blame him, not me'." Cozma pursed his lips.

"I know how his type play the game."

Muller shrugged. "But you can't move the train until there's some kind of deal," he said. "You may not like waiting, but your hands are tied until everyone's on the same page. And that includes me," Muller said quietly. "Because that gold is going to be mine, when the documents are signed." He tapped his briefcase.

Cozma stared at Muller a moment, then a slow smile spread across his face and he shook his head.

Now I get it," he said. "The 'magic' you're dispensing is to transfer the gold to the Bank of what's it called...?"

"Bank of International Settlements," said Muller.

"Right," continued Cozma. "What was Polish gold will instead belong to the Bank of International Settlement; and you're the representative of the Bank of International Settlements..."

"...With a crucial stake in seeing to it that the gold gets safely aboard ship at Constanta," Muller said, finishing the sentence and gazing intently at Cozma.

Cozma responded with a broad smile.

"Very clever; but how do you suggest doing that, Mr. Magician?" Cozma asked, with a cock of his head and a half salute. "What kind of leeway will I have to begin getting my system working again? The gold train is only one issue–a big one and risky too–but I've also got to ferry all these damned soldiers to camps farther South. They can't stay here; that'd just be inviting a German invasion."

"I think you're going to be the one dictating the terms," Muller replied. He pointed to the group, still huddled and speaking intently to one another, Danita now very involved too and, Muller noticed, General Pretzki was participating as well.

"Those guys are going to make a deal," Muller continued. "They're going to agree to transfer the gold to the Bank, except for a sum to be paid to Romania to cover their costs. I don't know what that number is, but they'll come to agreement on a figure below what Danita demanded, but big enough to be respectable. And they'll agree that, in return for the payment, Romania commits to moving the gold to Constanta and to moving the Army away from the frontier."

Muller paused, looking around him, to be sure he wasn't being overheard and continued, as Cozma listened intently.

"What's going to happen then? You know as well as I do that no one in Bucharest is going to be consulted about how to implement the deal that Danita's making–they're all going to look to Danita for a solution.

"'Just fix it' right?" Muller fixed Cozma with a wan smile.

"And Danita won't have any idea what to do," Muller continued. "He's going to turn to you and say something like–'And Mr. Cozma, here, will take charge of the details.'

"You're going to be the man in charge, Mr. Cozma. So, I recommend that you decide pretty quickly what you want to do, because once those guys–and I–sign those documents, we're going to be looking to you to get started right away."

Moments later, watching the group, they saw Beck walk over to Danita and offer his hand. There were smiles all around, as the two men shook hands.

"Ambassador Muller," said Krakowski, beckoning him to join them. "Bring your documents. We're ready to sign."

Muller did as he was told, but he kept a firm grip on his briefcase.

"All of the gold on the train is to be conveyed to the Bank, as provided in the papers I showed you?" he asked.

"All but $1.5 million," Krakowski said. "We've agreed to pay the Romanians for their expenses."

"And is there a commitment to deliver the gold aboard ship in Constanta?"

"Yes, yes," said Krakowski, turning to Danita who nodded. "That's right," he said; "all agreed."

"May I see the agreement?" Muller asked. "My documents don't say anything about conveying any of the gold to Romania. I need express direction from Polish authorities to do that. And Mr. Danita, I need a written commitment from your government that whatever gold is conveyed to the Bank will be safely delivered aboard ship in Constanta."

Danita looked at Muller blankly.

"What the HELL?" Cozma exploded. "We're sitting ducks here, and you want some kind of gift-wrapped document?"

Muller placed his free arm around Danita's shoulder and began pulling him away, hissing in his ear, "They're setting you up, Danita; listen to me!"

"Give us a moment to confer, gentlemen," Danita said over his shoulder to the rest, moving away with Muller and motioning Cozma to join them.

Muller led them to the side of the train, gesturing to the guard to move away.

"If you don't get this in writing, they'll screw you." Muller said, hands on hips, facing Danita. "They'll blame you–personally– for blackmailing them to hand over precious Polish gold reserves and your government will be only too happy to disown you and throw you to the dogs–and you too," he added, turning to Cozma.

"'Rogue diplomat, acting without authority, undermines Romanian solidarity with Poland in her hour of distress.'–that's your headline, Mr. Danita," he said. "And railway official is complicit in a major diplomatic scandal."

Both men looked at him angrily. Cozma, veins pulsing in his forehead, pushed his face toward Muller's.

"What the Hell are you talking about?" he said. "Why would they do that if we get them out of this pickle?"

Muller stood his ground.

"Because someone's going to have to take the blame for giving away *any* of the Polish gold reserve that was heroically transported to the Romanian border on its way to safety. Do you think for a moment that Jozef Beck is going to step up and say, 'yes, we believed it was only fair to give some of our gold reserve to the Romanians in return for their help?'

"No! He'll blame you and probably claim you stole some too. 'A Romanian diplomat and railway official forced us to pay–and by the way, they helped themselves to some of our gold to too.'

"They'll say you're crooks."

Muller paused a moment.

"Without a written agreement, it will be his word against yours, Mr. Danita: the word of the beleaguered Foreign Minister of the new Polish government-in-exile–still bravely resisting the Nazi invaders–against a third secretary of the Romanian Foreign Ministry whom no one's ever heard of.

"Think about it," Muller said, his voice low but intense.

Muller watched as Danita and Cozma looked at one another, both of them pursing their lips and beginning to shift their weight back and forth as they stood.

"What the fuck?" Cozma shook his head.

"Look," said Muller, "You've made a deal that you can sell to your government–to the world, for that matter. *But you've got to finish the job.*"

He turned to Danita.

"You can wire your Ministry and claim–legitimately–that you negotiated with the Poles and won two huge concessions: a way to fend off German threats by conveying the gold to the Bank, and an agreement forcing the Poles to use some of the gold to reimburse Romania for its expenses. *AND that they agreed to the deal–in writing*."

"How much have they agreed to pay?"

"$1.5 million," Danita said. "Not as much as I wanted…."

"It doesn't matter," Muller interrupted; "no one's going to know or care.

"But you've got to get the Poles to sign a document confirming that they not only agreed to pay $1.5 million to the Romanian government–and that sounds like a lot of money, by the way–but that they authorized the Bank of International Settlements to physically hand over that sum in gold ingots directly to you– Marius Danita, the representative of the Kingdom of Romania.

"You'll look like a hero in Bucharest, Mr. Danita," Muller said excitedly, poking Danita with his finger.

"Not only will you deliver a deal that takes your government off the hook, but you've even gotten the Poles to agree to pay for it–and you have it in writing–an agreement which the Poles can't deny and which your government will happily trumpet as a resounding success.

"It's all perfect," Muller said.

"*But you've got to get it in writing.*"

"And, frankly, I need it in writing too, as the Bank's representative."

Danita heaved a big sigh and nodded.

"He's right," he said to Cozma. "Who knows what they'd say later, even if we save their asses".

Danita turned and stalked back to the Polish group.

"Minister Beck, I need a stenographer and a typewriter from your staff to formalize our agreement in writing."

"Ah," said Beck, waving him away with a big grin, "no need for that. We've made our deal together; let's just get started."

"Right," said Danita, "we've made our deal; and since you and I are representing our governments, we have an obligation to record what we've decided–we don't want any junior clerks to second guess us, do we? No; as the two leaders, you and I can do this in only a few minutes."

He began striding toward one of the tables, looking around for a typewriter to use.

Beck turned, angrily hissed something in Polish to his colleagues, and they began to argue. Then Beck strode over to where Danita was standing.

"My colleagues and I see no need for a written text," he said. "We understand one another, Secretary Danita; that's sufficient."

"No, I'm afraid it's not," Danita replied, drawing himself to his full height–a full head taller than Beck. "Ambassador Muller requires written authorization as the representative of the Bank of International Settlements, and I believe my government would insist upon a written record too, if I am to instruct Mr. Cozma to set our agreement in motion.

Beck reacted angrily.

"I am the Foreign Minister of Poland;" he said. "I have given my solemn word and that will suffice."

"Then I shall have to return to Bucharest," Danita retorted, "and explain to my government why you refuse to perform the duties of a government minister and make a record of what we've agreed to."

"Gentlemen," he said, turning to Muller and Cozma and beckoning them to follow him, "our mission here seems to be finished."

"Wait! Stop. You can't just leave the train here with our gold," exclaimed Krakowski. "It's our most vital government asset and it's at high risk," he said.

"Tell that to Minister Beck," said Danita as he began striding toward their truck parked nearby.

Krakowski began speaking to Beck and was joined by others, urging him to change his mind.

Beck shook his head, then disentangled himself for the group that had surrounded him.

"Secretary Danita," he said, loudly enough for Danita to hear and turn back to face him. "There's no need to rush off in a huff. If you had told us earlier that *you* would *personally* take responsibility for implementing the agreement *immediately* if we reduce it to writing, then we could have avoided all this unpleasantness. Now that you've explained yourself, why of course we shall have a written agreement."

He smiled and bowed slightly in Danita's direction, then turned and said something sharply in Polish before once again facing Danita.

"These two members of my staff will take responsibility for preparing it," he said.

Danita stopped and returned Beck's smile.

"I shall be pleased to have their assistance, Minister Beck," he said striding back toward the table and motioning the two men to join him.

"We have work to do, gentlemen," he said.

Muller did a double take; had Danita just winked at him as he walked by?

Forty-five minutes later, Danita strode back to where Cozma and Muller were seated.

"They're typing the final version," he said, pointing to Beck's staff members seated in front of their typewriters at the table. "You were right, Ambassador Muller," he added; "they kept trying to water down the text. But I've got it right now, and they'll sign it.

"So, Mr. Cozma, what do we do now?" Danita asked. "How do we implement this 'fix' that they've agreed to?"

Cozma stifled a smile and glanced at Muller before responding.

"I've got a plan," he said.

They strode over to the conference table and Muller examined the text that had been typed.

"It's satisfactory," he said and opened his briefcase, passing the Bank of International Settlements documents to Krakowski to sign and stamp, then doing so himself. Beck silently signed the text before passing the pen to Danita, who paused before sitting to sign.

"Before I commit the government of the Kingdom of Romania to this document, I want it agreed that the representatives of the government-in-exile of the Polish Republic will accompany the gold train to Constanta and leave the Kingdom aboard the vessel transporting the gold."

"What?" spluttered Beck; "we are no longer welcome in Romania?"

"Minister Beck," Danita retorted, "Romania has been threatened by Germany–which now has a victorious army situated on our border–and by the Soviet Union, which has claims on our territory and also has an army at our border. We are under threat, and you, sir, are targets. We have sufficiently deflected the gold issue by the conveyance to the Bank of International Settlements. But your presence here–and that of your defeated army–represent continued risks."

He pointed toward the valley where the Polish soldiers were encamped.

"We can't just make them disappear overnight," he said. "We'll disperse them to the South and try to send them off to countries that want them. But that'll take time. General Pletzski can remain to help coordinate the effort–which we've committed to pursue in good faith.

"But you and your colleagues, Mr. Beck, must conduct your business elsewhere. So, you will leave with the gold."

"Then our ministers must be allowed to have a detachment of armed Polish soldiers to accompany them on that train," General Pletzski interjected. "They are entitled to protection by our forces as they depart."

Cozma stepped forward.

"I will accept fifty solders with rifles and sidearms only," he said. "No heavy equipment."

"No more delay," Cozma said emphatically; "get ready to move out on my signal in 30 minutes."

CHAPTER 11

The trip to Constanta turned out to be uneventful. Cozma shifted trains along the parallel tracks, shunting one, then another, onto switches and sidings so no one could tell which of the swiftly moving trains was the one carrying the gold.

"Ever play three-card monte, Ambassador Muller?" Cozma said. "That's what I'm doing here, and potential saboteurs aren't any more likely to pick the right train than you are to pick the right card."

The process took time, though, and it was after midnight when their train–the one carrying both the gold and the Polish government-in-exile–arrived at the Constanta rail complex. Cozma had alerted the stationmaster to have personnel on hand to shunt the train through a maze of switches in the sprawling Black Sea port.

Bright overhead lights illuminated their progress, initially blinding them, as they had run blacked out since darkness had fallen. Constanta had been a port facility since Roman times, and

Muller caught glimpses of rotting old wooden pilings alongside modern cranes and winches. There was a stench of fuel oil in the air, along with an aroma of salt water as they crawled through a shadowy landscape revealing piles of coal and other commodities, stacked burlap bags, hulking pieces of machinery, abandoned rail cars and other shapes that Muller couldn't begin to identify. Occasionally, groups of cloth-capped men could be seen pushing or pulling at objects, or sitting around barrels with low fires, even though it was warm and humid.

There was something eerie about the scene, he thought.

Krakowski had said the *SS Eocene* had been chartered by the British agent in Constanta that the Polish government used for purchasing arms and other sensitive supplies that, in normal times, were unloaded at the port and shipped North by rail to Poland. Tonight, the vessel was said to be berthed at H Quai. Cozma had used a locomotive turntable to switch the engine to the rear of the train, so when they reached a chain link fence marked with an 'H', the cars would be the first to enter the pier alongside the vessel.

Muller could see a dozen or more men standing near the pier entrance. Longshoremen? No, something else. He was in the rear of the train and heard shouts but couldn't make out what was being said. Then he saw some pushing and shoving as the men were apparently trying to force their way through the narrow fence entryway onto the pier.

Then he clearly heard Captain Jurzyk, who was in command of the detachment of Polish soldiers, direct his men forward with their rifles to take charge of the entrance and push away the intruders. The train crept onto the pier and the fence behind was locked. Cozma directed his detachment of soldiers to stand guard against someone trying to force the fence or climb over it, and Jurzyk organized the Polish soldiers to begin unloading the gold.

Muller accompanied Krakowski up the gangplank and they were escorted to the bridge of the *Eocene* where a short muscular man in uniform greeted them.

"Welcome aboard the *Eocene*, gentlemen" he said in a thick Australian accent. "Robert Meers, Captain of this vessel. English all right? My Polish isn't so good."

When Muller translated in French for Krakowski, Meers turned to them and, in heavily accented French, said "Bonjour messieurs; Français ça va."

Two other men were standing alongside Meers on the narrow bridge. A sallow man with greasy dark hair over his ears, said, "Phillips; Hornbeck & Co., agents for the shipper," and offered his hand. The other man was stout and balding with a grey stubble and a faint odor of whiskey on his breath. "British Consul General James Bottomley. You were expected earlier," he said disapprovingly. "But now you're here, so let's get to it. His Majesty's Government has instructed me to facilitate this transaction."

Meers gestured to the table behind the ship's tall, round, spoked wheel. "Someone has the manifest and the other documents?"

Krakowski was carrying a thick envelope which he opened, placing a sheaf of documents on the table, which Meers and Phillips began examining.

Meers then looked up and turned to Krakowski.

"I have been told that my vessel is to transport the gold reserves of the Republic of Poland to Beirut in Lebanon. That is a highly unusual and, frankly, rather risky assignment," he said gravely. "Are you the shipper? And what safeguards have you arranged for this shipment?"

Krakowski nodded to Muller that he had understood Meers' fractured French.

"The Republic of Poland is the shipper of record, Captain Meers," he said. "Payment for the journey has been provided by our agent Hornbeck & Co, as described in the shipping documents." He pointed.

"However, the actual owner of the gold is the Bank of International Settlements, Basle, Switzerland, represented by Ambassador Muller here."

Muller nodded in Meers' direction.

"As for safeguards, we have a detachment of fifty armed Polish soldiers who will accompany the shipment and there are a dozen Romanian soldiers sent by their government who are guarding the gate." He pointed back toward the chain link fence. "And, by the way, why do we have intruders trying to get onto the pier?" he asked.

"Why to steal the gold, of course," answered Meers, without smiling. "And if we are not quick about it, there'll be a lot more of them to contend with."

"This shipment was supposed to be a closely guarded secret," said Phillips, glancing up from the papers. "What the Hell happened? Christ! We'll have claims for higher rates from the vessel owners and increased insurance premiums. Who'll pay for those?"

"Some secret," sneered Meers, ignoring Phillips question. "We were on our way to Baku to pick up coal when we were suddenly diverted here to load the Polish gold reserve. By the time we berthed, everyone seemed to know what was going on. My crew went to the bars and were threatened by other sailors unless they agreed to help steal the gold."

Meers continued peering at Krakowski.

"Your soldier-boys won't be of much help once we get underway," he said. "What I meant was, what safeguards have been arranged in the way of a naval escort to protect us against attack from a submarine or surface vessel?"

He turned to Bottomley, the British consul.

"Is the Royal Navy offering support?"

Bottomley shook his head and began to recite limitations in the Montreux Convention that barred British warships from the Black Sea, when, suddenly, Danita appeared on the bridge, out of breath and perspiring heavily.

"More people are trying to storm the fence," he said loudly to Meers, not bothering with introductions.

"I need your radioman to put me in touch with the Romanian police immediately. And your crew have just informed us they've quit loading and they're going on strike."

Meers strode rapidly back to the bridge and looked down at the pier where, sure enough, he could see his crew members standing off to one side while soldiers tried to maneuver the heavy crates of gold into position to be winched aboard.

"Sonofabitch," he said in English, taking the stairs down to the deck two at a time and racing down the gangplank toward his crew. Muller watched from above as the crew members shook their heads and walked up the gangplank toward their quarters, leaving Meers on the pier shouting at them.

Muller stood with Danita and Krakowski on the bridge as they watched the scene unfold before them.

Then he turned and strode into the command center and the corridor at the rear, opening doors, first finding the captain's quarters then, next to it, the radio room, unattended, but with the lights showing it was fully operational.

"Danita," he said, pointing, "can you operate that?"

Danita took a glance at the equipment and nodded.

"Basic diplomatic training," he said as he pulled out the operator's chair and took his seat at the radio set. "I'll get reinforcements."

Muller stepped into the captain's quarters, tore off his shirt and untied the money belt around his belt. He pulled out a thick wad of crisp new $100 bills, then pulled his shirt back on and descended the bridge stairway. He made his way across the deck to the doorway of the crew's quarters where he stood for a moment, hearing loud voices quarreling inside. He drew a deep breath and opened the door.

Ten swarthy men were seated and standing around what appeared to be a mess table in the center of the small room, and they all stopped speaking to stare at him.

Then several began shouting at him in a language he didn't understand—Greek maybe?

"Who speaks English, Deutsch, Français?" He asked, speaking loudly.

A dark-haired man standing on the other side of the room wearing a dirty, sweaty shirt, responded.

"Most of us speak English," he said. "What the Hell do you want?"

"I want you to go back to work," Muller said, steeling himself and looking around the room.

"Fuck you," said a muscular man seated to his right, "all that gold makes us a target—either for that mob at the fence or an attack when we're seaborne. None of us signed up for that, so go to Hell."

Other men in the room grunted assent and nodded.

"Get out."

Muller pulled the wad of bills out of his pocket and elbowed his way to the table.

He began laying the $100 bills in a stack, counting them one-by-one.

The room grew silent and the men watched him.

Muller counted to eighty, laying the last of the bill on the stack. Then he picked up the stack and began laying the bills out again, this time stopping at forty.

Muller stood back and pointed. "That's yours now if you go to back to work," he said. "The rest," and he put the remainder of the bills back in his pocket, "is yours when you get this vessel to its destination."

The men began speaking to one another loudly and urgently, but the quarrelling was also leavened by smiles.

Finally, the first man who'd spoken crashed his fist on the table, and the men obediently quieted.

"All right, mister," he said in a loud voice, "we'll play your game. Put down another $500 now and we'll go back to work. But you give that stack of bills to the captain to hold. We don't know who the Hell you are, but if the captain agrees to hold our money and pay us off when we get to port, we're good with that."

Muller nodded his head.

"Agreed, he said.

"All right then," the apparent leader said, turning to the men; "let's get to work and get this tub ready to sail."

It took nearly another hour. Jurzyk had to organize the Polish soldiers into a bucket brigade to carry the last heavy crates of gold onto the vessel after the winch broke. The ship's crew energetically assisted in the process, suddenly finding sturdy carts which could be used to stack the crates and wheel them from the train to the vessel's side and directing storage once the crates were aboard.

Watching the process alongside the train, Cozma spoke quietly to Muller.

"So, you bribed them to go back to work."

Muller shrugged, continuing to eye the loading process.

"Well, you're a pretty popular guy right now," Cozma continued. "I know enough Greek to hear them telling one another they're going to earn an extra year's salary and talking about how they're going to spend it.

"Ha!" He clapped Muller on the shoulder. Then he angled his head toward Muller and spoke quietly out of the side of his mouth

"Got something for your train person too?"

Cozma's expression suggested he was only half kidding.

During the long train ride to Constanta, Krakowski and Danita had undertaken to calculate the amount of gold that should be turned over to the Romanians.

"How do I figure out how many 5-pound gold ingots add up to the $1.5 million we agreed upon?" asked Danita, his brow furrowed. "What's the value of an ingot?"

Krakowski took a pad of paper and made a quick calculation.

"586 ingots," he said. "Well, actually, 586.8 ingots, but I rounded the number."

Danita looked puzzled.

"How do you figure that?"

"Easy," replied Krakowski. "The price of gold is $34.42 per troy ounce. There are 14,583 troy ounces per pound. So, it's simple arithmetic."

He handed Danita his pad.

"How do you know there are 14,583 troy ounces per pound?" Danita asked suspiciously.

Krakowski shrugged. "I'm a central banker, Mr. Danita," he replied. "I calculate gold values for a living. Every mathematician knows the value of pi is whatever it is; I frankly don't remember pi. But every central banker knows that a troy ounce is 1.1034 grams, which converts to 14,583 troy ounces per pound."

Danita sighed and handed back the pad with a look of resignation.

"Have it your way," he said. "But the number is rounded up to 587 ingots."

Krakowski pursed his lips but held out his hand with a tight smile. "Done."

Krakowski had returned to the compartments of the train occupied by the government officials, and he'd gotten a staff person to type an agreement in triplicate for signature when the actual transfer took place later, when they got to the ship: by

Danita, for Romania; Muller for the Bank of International Settlements; and himself for Poland.

Now, standing on the pier in Constanta, with the first light of dawn brightening the horizon, the three men stood next to stacks of crates holding exactly 587 5-pound gold ingots which were to be conveyed to Romania. Krakowski placed the three copies of the agreement on the topmost crate of the nearest stack and handed his pen to Danita, who signed each page with a flourish. Muller then signed for the Bank and added his stamp, and Krakowski did the same. They solemnly shook hands.

"Too bad there's no champagne," said Danita brightly. He had recovered his swagger since Romanian police had arrived in force to clear away the attackers and secure the pier entrance.

"I told them there was $1.5 million in Romanian gold at risk," he'd said, smiling as the reinforcements rapidly cleared the area.

"That got their attention, so they sent me a full detachment."

He was in an almost jubilant mood.

"Not so shabby, Ambassador Muller," he said, grinning. "We got the gold aboard ship without any new German attack, and I've got $1.5 million to spend on clearing out the Polish Army.

"I'll bet they'll hold a parade for me in Bucharest–and probably put up a monument too!

"Ha!" He clapped his hands in satisfaction and waved as Krakowski and Muller mounted the gangplank and Captain Meers ordered the crew to cast off from the dock without further delay.

CHAPTER 12

Once they were aboard, Krakowski walked across the deck to the vessel's wardroom where Beck and the rest of the Polish government contingent were being housed after boarding the *Eocene*. Muller headed back up to the bridge.

Meers was standing next to the helmsman, giving him orders and peering ahead in the early morning light as they followed the curving harbor channel, slowly steaming past wharves and warehouses and ships tied up on both sides. Finally, the vessel reached the harbor entrance, rounded the mole and headed out into the Black Sea. Meers relaxed, stepped to the bridge galley and poured two cups of coffee, handing one to Muller.

"At least we've got Constanta in our wake," he said. "That place is crawling with informers of every stripe–including Nazis. I'm told they were behind the murder of the Prime Minister–and because of this goddam gold too. When I heard that, I thought for sure they'd mount some kind of attack against us on the pier–even try to hijack the ship.

"That guy Danita may be a blowhard but give him credit for getting a full detachment of police to clear the area.

"There's still some risk of attack even though we're underway," he continued. "That shipping agent–Phillips, I think– was nervous about it and kept urging me to hug the coastline off Bulgaria and Turkey and avoid open water." He walked to the chart on the navigation table and pointed.

"I think that would be a mistake; a couple of heavily armed small boats could attack us if we're close to shore. No, I think we go full throttle across the Black Sea direct to Turkey.

"Here's the Bosphorous," again he pointed at the chart. "That's our target. It's about 190 nautical miles; if we run at top speed, say 10-12 knots, we should reach the entrance shortly after midnight tonight. We'll likely have to queue up and the Turks will put a pilot aboard to steer us through, then we can lay over at the Istanbul port before heading down to the Dardenelles and the Mediterranean.

"Damned if I'm going to sneak along that coastline like some contraband runner."

"The crew was frightened of a submarine attack," Muller offered.

"Argh," Meers waved his comment away. "The only submarines in the Black Sea are Russian," he said dismissively. "There are no German U Boats. They'd be a genuine threat; but the Russians?" He shook his head.

"The Russians would probably love to steal the gold if they could; but sink it? I don't think so.

"No, I'm going to steam like Hell for the Bosphorous, keep total radio silence and bet we can outrun anyone who's after us."

Meers offered Muller a cigarette and flashed his lighter for both of them.

He exhaled and turned to Muller with a curious look.

"I've put that cash you offered the crew in the safe. Are you serious about paying them? It's a lot of money for a bunch of swabs."

Muller nodded. "There'll be some for you too, captain."

Meers smiled in agreement.

Mid-afternoon, a vessel on the horizon approached them, closing as they steamed toward the Bosphorous. Meers pulled out binoculars, looked quickly and handed them to Muller, smiling thinly.

"It's a Turkish cutter," he said. "I'm assuming they're coming to help."

The sleek warship came alongside the *Eocene* and, by hand signals and barely audible shouts from one bridge to another, made clear it was assigned to escort the *Eocene*. Captain Meers and the Turkish vessel's commander exchanged salutes and the cutter hauled off leading the way, first to one side of the Eocene's path, then the other side.

"Well, maybe that British consul wasn't so drunk after all," said Meer. "I told him that if the British government couldn't summon the Royal Navy, maybe he could message his counterpart in Istanbul to get the Turks to give us a hand."

Muller felt a sense of relief as he watched the cutter carve a path ahead of them and he proceeded to nod off.

Night fell early, but the cutter kept its running lights on, and the *Eocene* had no trouble following its lead. Meers was carefully charting their progress and shortly before midnight, he beckoned Muller back to the bridge.

"We've made excellent time," he said, "favorable wind and current. We should be arriving at the queue any time now,"

And, as Meer predicted, ten minutes later, running lights of several vessels came into view. They were either anchored or running in neutral, as they didn't seem to be moving. The cutter closed toward the *Eocene*, and flashed its semaphore light, then heeled and began passing the waiting ships.

"He wants us to follow," said Meers, taking control of the wheel and plowing ahead in the darkness, closely following in the cutter's wake. Then the cutter signaled stop and Meers pushed the engine room controls to dead slow and swung the wheel sharply to stop their progress.

The lights of a pilot ship appeared in the darkness, its searchlight finding the *Eocene*'s bridge. It signaled a request to board and quickly maneuvered alongside, as Meers ordered the crew to hang a boarding ladder from the rail.

A man in dark coveralls and a black knit cap nimbly climbed aboard and mounted the stairway to the *Eocene*'s bridge.

Meers relinquished the wheel to a crewmember and strode to meet the pilot.

"Welcome aboard," he said in a loud voice, crisply saluting the pilot, who was removing his cap and shrugging out of his coveralls.

The man returned the salute casually, then, shaking a full head of black hair, he smiled broadly at Meers and extended his hand for a hearty handshake.

"Welcome to the Bosphorous," he said, "I'll get you through in no time, sir," he said in heavily accented English. "My authorities want a speedy transit, so let's get to it."

"We've gone to the head of the queue?" asked Meers.

"Right to the front of the line," the pilot relied with a smile. "You must be pretty important, Captain."

He strode toward the wheel to take control of the vessel, then stopped and pulled an envelope from a pocket and handed it to Meers.

"This is a message I was told to deliver upon boarding, Captain," he said. "You have a passenger aboard named Ambassador Muller who is being directed to disembark with me when we reach the Golden Horn.

"May I take control of the vessel, Captain?"

"Permission granted," said Meers, taking the envelope.

Muller was standing to one side watching and could clearly hear the conversation.

What was this, he thought to himself? Disembark? Here in Istanbul?

Meers moved toward Muller and handed him the envelope.

"It's addressed to you."

Muller took the envelope and stepped toward the Captain's quarters, where the light was better. Using a finger, he broke the seal and removed a single page.

There was no letterhead; the document was a flimsy taken from a telex machine.

"AMB P MULLER   YOU ARE DIRECTED TO DISEMBARK ISTANBUL STOP TURKISH MINISTRY WILL EXPLAIN   N ODIER PRESIDENT BIS"

Muller blinked, reading it again. Odier's name and title; there was no doubt about his instructions. Short and sweet.

But what did it mean?

Muller stepped back to the bridge and nodded to Meers.

"I'm instructed to disembark," he said. "No explanation, but very clear. I'll get my things. How long before we arrive?"

"Roughly thirty minutes," Meers answered, his eyes staying focused on the entrance to the Bosphorous, barely visible on both sides, as the *Eocene* began its passage through the narrow waterway.

Muller unlocked the suitcase he'd left in the Captain's cabin. He removed the money belt and returned it to the secret compartment, taking care to extract a crisp one-hundred-dollar bill for Meers. He weighed whether or not to tell Krakowski and the Poles that he'd been ordered to leave the ship and decided against it; they'd ask questions he couldn't answer. He'd gotten them this far; they could fend for themselves the rest of the way.

He returned to the bridge and stood quietly, gazing at the shadowy shoreline that was passing by, barely visible at nighttime, lit only by the occasional building or window light and the pilot beacons along the waterline. He wished he could see it; Asia on his left, Europe on his right.

Finally, he made out what had to be Topkapi Palace atop a high hill, the walls brightly lit by spotlights; a kind of defiant statement of longevity, Muller thought to himself.

As the *Eocene* emerged from the Bosphorous, Muller could see the Galata Bridge and nearby ferry terminal, also brightly lit and still evidently busy, even at this early hour of the morning. This was the famed Golden Horn, he realized, again wishing it were daylight so he could see it better.

A pilot barge appeared on the starboard side of the *Eocene* and the pilot turned the wheel back over to a member of the crew. Muller picked up his suitcase and followed him down the staircase from the bridge, stopping only to shake hands with Meers and palm him with the money, before being helped down the side and successfully boarding the waiting barge.

CHAPTER 13

As promised, there was a car waiting to take him to the Turkish Foreign Ministry promptly at 11:00 AM the next morning.

When Muller had disembarked from the pilot's barge, wet and cold, a young ministry official had driven him to a nearby hotel along the Golden Horn and, after handing over his passport to the front desk clerk and being shown to his room, Muller had mustered just enough energy to remove his clothing and hang his things in the closet before collapsing on the bed, instantly sound asleep. Now in the bright light of a sunny morning, refreshed by the first solid night's sleep in what seemed like a week, and a good breakfast, he felt ready to face whatever lay ahead.

It was a very short drive; Muller wished he'd been able to walk the quarter of a mile or so from the hotel entrance back toward the Galata Bridge, then past it, and up a short rise to the Ministry. Looking to his right, he'd caught sight of what had to be the entrance to the famed Istanbul Bazaar and was that the spice market? His driver wasn't offering any tourist commentary.

The car pulled into a courtyard in front of a low, sand-colored building and a uniformed guard with high black boots and a tall, plumed helmet stepped forward to open the car door and gesture him toward the wide doorway.

Well, here I am at 'the Sublime Port', Muller thought to himself, the exotic and faintly mysterious term used to describe the Turkish Foreign Ministry. Muller had always thought it invoked images of plush carpeting and voluptuous, scantily clad harem dwellers. But nothing exceptional was presenting itself; just a polished wood and glass entry to what, once inside, resembled rather standard government office décor.

He was met by a slender well-dressed young man who greeted him by name and directed him down a long corridor, with a slightly worn-looking carpet-runner underfoot rather than Turkish carpeting, Muller noted. At the end of the corridor, his guide opened a tall door and motioned him to proceed him inside.

Muller was met with a sun-bathed, bright interior with –there they were–the plush, colorful, rugs underfoot he'd been expecting, the affecting appearance further enhanced by esoteric wall hangings and large floor-to-ceiling windows facing the Bosphorous. From behind a large wooden desk, a tall, nearly bald man, rose from his seat with a welcoming smile and an outstretched hand. He was a large and imposing figure with broad shoulders and narrow hips; like the Number 8 in a rugby scrum, Muller thought fleetingly.

"Emin Unsal, Ambassador Muller" said the man, pumping Muller's hand. "Welcome to Istanbul. I'm the Second Deputy Minister of Foreign Affairs of the Republic of Turkey and we're pleased to have you in our midst after what must have been an adventurous journey."

Unsal motioned for Muller to join him in a cluster of green upholstered chairs to one side of his desk.

"Please take that chair with the best view of the Bosphorous," he said gesturing. "Even those of us who've grown up gazing at it find ourselves endlessly enamored; for our guests, it's always a revelation."

Unsal's French was fluent, and he seemed both at ease and genuinely pleased at Muller's presence.

"The Minister's in Moscow," he continued, "and his Deputy is even now, as we speak, entertaining the arrival of the German Ambassador who, I'm quite certain, is here to demand–or at least to insist–that the Turkish government intercept and impound the Polish gold reserves that you shepherded this far and which, by now, are well out of Turkish waters and merrily sailing to their destination on the Mediterranean Sea.

"So, the happy opportunity to greet you falls to me, rather than the tiresome duty to inform Ambassador von Papen that his visit to us is in vain.

"Ha!" Unsal chuckled and pulled a silver case out of his jacket, offering Muller a cigarette and a light with a small lighter, also silver.

"Von Papen?" Muller said in surprise. "He's here now? Seeking the gold?"

Unsal nodded and exhaled smoke with a broad smile.

"He can be insistent sometimes," he added; "but unhappily for him, the matter is now well out of our hands."

Unsal then leaned toward Muller.

"But you, sir, are owed an explanation about why you were directed to disembark here instead of continuing on with the vessel to its destination. In addition to the message that I received and had the pilot deliver to you aboard ship, I received this." He reached for an envelope on his desk and handed it to Muller.

Muller unsealed the envelope and read the message.

P MULLER WELL DONE GETTING GOLD TO TURKEY STOP CHAIRMAN POLISH CENTRAL BANK ESCAPED POLAND AND CAME TO ME STOP APPROVED TRANSACTION BUT WE SIGNED INSTRUMENTS HERE CONVEYING OWNERSHIP BACK TO POLAND EFFECTIVE UPON VESSEL DEPARTING TURKEY AND ENTERING INTERNATIONAL WATERS AFTER EXITING DARDENELLES. REQUEST YOUR RETURN VIA AIR STOP BEST N. ODIER

He folded the message and slipped it in his breast pocket.

"You know the contents?" he asked Unsal, who nodded.

"We wanted to be certain that ownership of the gold remained with the Bank until the vessel had departed Turkish waters," he said. "Like Romania, Turkey has been pressured by Germany to avoid aiding Poland and to seize their gold reserves. Von Papen's presence here, at this very moment, is clear testament to that," he added with a smile.

"We felt ourselves on solid diplomatic and legal grounds to permit passage of gold owned by the Bank of International Settlements through the Straits to the Mediterranean. Still, we wished to get it accomplished without any delays, so passage of the vessel was expedited, as you probably noticed."

It was Muller's turn to nod.

"The pilot said we must be somebody important to jump the queue and transit the Bosphorous so quickly," he said.

"Turkey has no desire to reward Germany by seizing the gold," Unsal went on. "Their invasion of Poland has been a brutal, full-scale assault, which we have roundly condemned–and then to have the Soviets jump in and invade from the East…." Unsal drew a deep breath and shrugged. "It's a deeply unsettling series of events.

"So, while we can sit here and have a bit of fun at von Papen's expense–which I have to say, I'm rather enjoying–the reality is that we find ourselves facing a threat that can't be lightly dismissed. I'm telling you this, Ambassador Muller, in part because of the role we've learned you played in encouraging the British government to repair relations with us, but also, in part because Switzerland, even as a neutral nation, is not immune to the same risks we face."

"I assume you're referring to implications of the Ribbentrop-Molotov Agreement," Muller replied.

"Correct," Unsal continued, "an agreement that has all the earmarks of a strategic alliance between Hitler's Nazis and Stalin's Communists to conquer and divide up–well, who knows what, exactly–but certainly parts of our neighborhood and maybe even Turkey itself.

"Come," Unsal stood, "I need to show you something that was delivered to us a day or so ago by von Papen's German embassy. It's a film being distributed courtesy of Minister Goebbels' Propaganda Ministry."

Unsal led the way back along the corridor.

"We have it set up in a room along here which we can darken."

He opened a door and led Muller into a windowless conference room where a movie projector was set up on a table facing a blank, white-washed wall, with an operator seated behind it.

"Please begin," Unsal said, closing the door behind them.

"Yes, Emin-bey," the operator responded, flicking a switch that turned on the machine, then striding to the door and dousing the lights.

A flourish of trumpets sounded on the soundtrack and a giant Nazi flag appeared on the wall, rippling in the breeze as a strong, deep voice began speaking in German, and what Muller took to be subtitles in Turkish appeared at the bottom of the screen.

"Today in the City of Brest, the victorious armies of the German Reich and Soviet Union greet one another to celebrate the destruction of the Polish nation and the subjugation of its citizens. Poland was a product of the hated Treaty of Versailles that was forcibly imposed upon the German and Soviet peoples. Today we

show the world how, together, armed forces of the German Reich and the Soviet Union have crushed this verminous state.

The German Reich and the Soviet Union stand together, victorious and proud to link arms in a common commitment to remake the world and defeat the minions of the decadent, capitalist West."

The announcer continued his florid account of events, his voice rising as martial music swelled in the background.

The movie began focusing in on a platform, draped with both German and Soviet flags, erected in front of a columned structure which Muller took to be a government building in Brest. Was it the Mayor's office? In the background, German soldiers in their distinctive helmets could be seen mingling with the oval helmets of Russian soldiers, smiling, smoking and waving at the camera. In the foreground, on the platform, stood what had to be the two commanders, Panzer General Heinz Guderian in a well-tailored German Army greatcoat, wearing shiny jackboots, and Russian Tank Brigade Commander General Semyon Krivoshein in a dark leather belted coat, collar up, and matching leather boots. Guderian appeared taller, but Krivoshein was broad-shouldered and powerfully built.

The two men were shown speaking together in animated fashion, smiling and gesticulating.

"I've been doing some lip-reading," said the movie operator, "and I think they're both speaking French."

Then, as if on cue, the two commanders turned to face the camera and came to attention as a military band broke into a march and began striding, in step, past the platform, accompanied by German and Soviet flags, which the two Generals saluted. There followed another ten minutes of film showing German and Russian troops parading before the platform, again to salutes from both Generals. There were German motorcycles with sidecars followed by tanks and half-tracks laden with soldiers towing artillery. Soviet tanks clanked along too, though they appeared primitive by comparison to the sleek German Panzers. Soviet soldiers marched on foot and their artillery was towed by unsightly but powerful workhorses.

The movie concluded with the massed troops doffing hats and helmets as the band played the German national anthem and the Soviet *Internationale.*

The operator turned the lights back on.

Unsal shook his head.

"Until a month ago, those two countries took every opportunity to insult and abuse one another–they were the bitterest of enemies for years; Nazis versus Communists. And now? A love fest. Linking arms–literally–to remake the world.

"That was no 'Non-Aggression Agreement' they signed," he said. "That film shows their true colors. And, frankly, it frightens us," he added.

Unsal guided Muller to a terrace overlooking the Galata Bridge and the busy terminal with ferries crossing the Bosphorous.

A table had been set for lunch with a chilled bottle of white wine alongside in a cooler.

"It's a little early in the day for raki," Unsal said, almost apologetically; "but some wine with lunch seems appropriate."

A white-jacketed waiter seated them, poured each a glass of wine and supervised the delivery of the plates of *mezé*.

"Serefe," Unsal said, toasting Muller.

"I told you our Foreign Minister was in Moscow," Unsal said. "We hadn't yet seen that film, of course; but we'd already concluded that the Germans and Soviets had cooked up some kind of alliance together. The Soviet invasion of Poland from the East confirmed our worst suspicions. So, the minister decided to pay a visit to the bear's lair."

Unsal gestured with his fork to a dish with small pieces of something pink and moist.

"Be sure to try our lakerda," he said. "It's a delicacy."

Muller took a bite; it was tender and melted in his mouth.

"Very tasty," he said nodding and reaching for another.

"Freshly caught today in the Sea of Marmara," said Unsal with a smile gesturing to his right where the Bosphorous widened into the Sea of Marmara.

Raw fish? Thought Muller. Really? Well, no matter; it was delicious.

"So how are the Moscow meetings going?" he asked.

Unsal's face tightened.

"They're giving him the cold shoulder. Literally. Nice rooms at the Hotel National with a view of the Kremlin and Red Square, but no meetings. 'Please to wait', is what they're saying."

Muller raised his eyebrows. Bad manners, even for Soviets, he thought to himself.

"It seems their new best friend von Ribbentrop is back in town," said Unsal. "They're apparently formalizing the division of Poland and wrapping it into what we're being told is a 'Boundary and Friendship Treaty.'

"That's not doing much to ease our deep suspicions about what the two of them are up to," he added.

Fresh grilled fish appeared along with a green salad. Muller decided he would happily become a gourmet of Turkish cuisine if given the opportunity.

"But you indicated earlier that you had repaired relations with the British" he said. "Your Minister in Geneva, Ambassador Sadek, had alerted me to an issue there when we dined together early in the month."

Unsal nodded, "And we greatly appreciate what we're told was your intervention with an official at Whitehall that restarted British talks with my government. But it's never easy with them."

Unsal continued speaking as he deftly took spoons in hand to transfer lettuce from the bowl onto their plates.

"In assessing the growing risk of war, we concluded fairly early on that the advantage lay with the West. Britain and France, especially when they're aligned with America and the Soviet Union as happened in the Great War, are a lot stronger than Germany–to be sure, it was Russia in 1914, but no matter; the Soviets didn't seem that much different as we weighed the comparative strengths of the rivalry that was emerging. So, we began talks, especially with the British, about formally aligning ourselves with them, to make sure we're on the right side this time.

"Then, when Hitler took over the Sudetenland in the wake of the Munich Agreement, we also needed Britain to sell us armaments, because the Skoda works, which was our traditional supplier, suddenly began to supply the *Wehrmacht* instead of us.

So, we thought of ourselves on friendly terms with Britain, though we were certainly rattled at Chamberlain's unilateral decision to issue his famous Declaration and the fact that they simply shrugged at Mussolini's conquest of Albania right afterwards. There always seemed to be excuses for the delays in delivering the arms that we'd bought from them too. And you will appreciate that our concerns increased in the wake of that Ribbentrop-Molotov Agreement."

He paused and gazed directly at Muller.

"A German-Soviet alliance is not such a total mismatch against the British and French, Ambassador Muller, especially as America is still firmly on the sidelines."

Unsal drew his silver cigarette case from the breast pocket of his jacket as the waiters cleared the table and brought bowls of fruit. Muller accepted a Turkish cigarette and Unsal's light.

He was content to keep listening and see what he could learn.

"When war was ultimately declared, after a nearly three-day delay—which I can tell you was duly noted here—the Turkish government publicly sided with Britain and France; President Inönü even made a speech to that effect in Parliament. But the British continued dragging their feet on delivering the arms we'd purchased. Now, three weeks into the war, we see that—despite the famous Declaration boasting that they'd come to Poland's aid in the event the Germans invaded—the British, and the French too, have effectively hung Poland out to dry. They haven't really lifted a finger to help the poor Poles, have they?"

It was a rhetorical question and Unsal continued, not expecting Muller to answer.

"So here in Turkey, we've begun looking at one another and asking ourselves whether relying upon the British is actually such a good idea."

Muller ground out his cigarette in the glass ashtray on the table.

"So that's why your minister decided to visit Moscow," he said.

Unsal nodded.

"We've got to cover our bets," he said.

"Look," he went on, "The Soviet Union and Turkey occupy the same neighborhood. We share a border in the East and they're directly across the Black Sea from us. If they've all of a sudden made an alliance with Germany, that's something we need to pay attention to."

Unsal paused, then added, "And it also makes getting the British to deliver the armaments we need even more important.

"It's a complicated time," he said, standing, indicating the lunch meeting was over.

"We've booked your flights back to Switzerland," he said "You'll depart our Yesilkoy Aerodrome on a Turkish Air flight to Athens at midnight tonight. The tickets will be in your box at the hotel.

"Oh, and when you return to your hotel, you'll also find an invitation from the British Consul for dinner tonight. He's booked a nice restaurant along the city walls that's on the way to the aerodrome and they'll have a car for you, so it's really on your way. I'm going to try to join too, though I may be delayed.

"You should accept," he said. "The consul suffers from an impossibly stuffy name, Hughe Knatchbull-Hugesson–why do the British do that to themselves do you think?–but he's actually a rather nice fellow and an effective diplomat."

"I'll accept," Muller responded. "My only plan has been to visit your bazaar and do a little shopping."

"Ah, said Unsalm taking one of his cards and quickly penning a message on the back. "Show this to one of the boys at the entrance and they'll direct you to my friend's store; he has the best gold jewelry and he's honest–but bring your Swiss bargaining skills along."

Muller pocketed the card.

"Thank you," he said, "But before I leave, a question about von Papen. Isn't the German embassy in Ankara? Why would he be making the rounds here in Istanbul instead of Ankara?"

"Apparently his wife finds Ankara boring," Unsal replied with a smile. "So, he's taken a large suite here to placate her–in fact it's actually in your hotel.

"Maybe you and Franz should meet for drinks."

Unsal laughed and clapped Muller on the shoulder playfully.

"Until this evening, then," he said, waving as Muller followed a young officer down the corridor toward the entrance.

Muller released the car when it deposited him back at the hotel a few minutes later. The room clerk handed him his key along with two sealed envelopes.

"These items were delivered while you were out, Mr. Ambassador," he said deferentially.

"Thank you, Muller replied.

"Incidentally, can you tell me if Frau von Papen is currently present in the German Embassy suite?"

"Yes, I believe so, Mr. Ambassador,"

"Can you deliver a message to her?" Muller asked.

"Of course, sir," the clerk replied.

Muller strode to the desk on the far side of the lobby where stationery and the house phones were situated.

He sat down and wrote a note on a piece of hotel stationery.

Please meet me between 4:00 and 4:30 PM this afternoon at the café on the far end of Galata Bridge.

Your Commissioner General, Charles Boyer.

Sealing the note in an envelope, he handed it to the desk clerk along with a coin and asked it to be delivered directly to Frau von Papen immediately.

CHAPTER 14

Muller put the two envelopes–he assumed they were the airplane tickets and the invitation to dinner–in his room, then set out on foot toward the Galata Bridge a few hundred meters to his right. He crossed to the Golden Horn side of the broad tree-lined street, then turned left on the bridge. Fishermen had stationed themselves along the railings and Muller was wary of a stray cast as he walked, carefully avoiding the buckets of bait and spills along the sidewalk. There was a traffic light at the far end of the span, and he crossed to the Bosphorous side. He found himself at the edge of the busy ferry terminal and was briefly caught up in a crowd of passengers boarding and disembarking from the cross-Bosphorous ferries. But not fifty meters ahead, he could see the red-tile roofed, two story building he'd spied during lunch from the ministry's terrace, with a bright neon sign reading 'Café' hanging in front.

He walked inside and found himself in an airy space with tall windows open to the nice weather. Dozens of wooden tables and chairs with rattan seats, most of which weren't occupied at this time of the afternoon filled the space. Toward the back, he spied a small nook, protected by a large potted plant which offered a hint of privacy. He walked toward it and took a seat. When the waiter came, he asked in French if the plant could be moved to offer even more of a screen from the rest of the café. The waiter didn't speak, but must have understood, as he began pushing the pot in the direction Muller was pointing. Muller smiled at him and touched his heart, mimicked an embrace.

The waiter smiled conspiratorially.

"Kadin," he said, approvingly–"femme."

Muller nodded and ordered a coffee, then sat down to wait.

He was certain Marte von Papen would understand the note. They had met–well, they had had their encounter was a better way to describe it–in Vienna two years earlier after having–separately– gone to a movie theater to watch Charles Boyer starring as Pepe Le Moko in the hit film *Algiers*. They had gotten caught in a street riot as they exited the theater. Muller had rescued her–and himself as well. The rioters weren't being discriminatory about whom they attacked.

Muller lit a Gitane and remembered.

Charles Boyer was her heart throb, she'd told him later, when at last they'd escaped the mob. That was before they'd had a fierce, impulsive bout of love-making; and afterwards, she'd told him how she hated Hitler and detested the Nazis, notwithstanding her husband's station in the government.

Peering through the fronds of the potted plant, he had a view of the end of the bridge–and suddenly he saw her, wearing a bright blue blouse, her hair gleaming in the sunshine. Then she turned toward the ferry terminal and he lost sight of her. He almost didn't recognize her when she reappeared, walking slowly toward the café entrance, but now with a modest kerchief covering her hair and a shapeless brown shawl drawn over her blouse.

Being cautious. Good, Muller thought to himself.

He sprang to his feet, went to the doorway, and approached Marte with his finger to his lips. When she saw him, her eyes widened and she missed a step, but, seeing his gesture, she proceeded to take his arm without a word, and they entered the café. He led her to the secluded niche in the back and turned to face her. Marte yanked off the kerchief, then threw her arms around him, kissing him warmly on the lips.

They sat in adjoining chairs, still holding hands and gazing at one another.

"My God Paul," Marte whispered. "I couldn't believe your note. What in the world are you doing here in Istanbul?"

"Protecting Poland's gold reserve from being stolen by Hitler," Muller replied with a disarming grin.

Marte stared at him uncomprehending, then, absorbing what he'd said, she drew a big breath and began laughing uproariously, covering her mouth to muffle the sound, doubling over and stamping both feet lightly. She then paused, looked away, then resumed gazing at him and began laughing again, but more quietly.

"Is that really true?" She whispered, "Franz just returned from the Ministry, angry as he could be, cursing the Turks for having allowed the Polish gold to get away."

She leaned forward and gave Muller a smooch on his mouth.

"You were the one who saved the gold? Really? That is too funny; I absolutely love it."

She resumed chuckling, then pulled a hanky from her sleeve to dry her eyes.

"I didn't act alone," Muller replied, still smiling, "but, yes, I was one of them. The gold is now on the Mediterranean Sea and safely out of Hitler's grasp."

"Well, he'll certainly be furious when he learns about *that*," Marte said, smiling back at him. "Franz was under enormous pressure–from Hitler himself, in fact–to somehow seize the gold. Now that it's gone, I hope he doesn't order Franz back to Berlin and shoot him or put him in one of those awful camps.

"I suppose he might," she added, then shrugged.

She took his hand, gazing at him.

"So, you come to me in yet another moment of triumph," she said, "and arouse me all over again. Pffff. Too bad I don't have time to smuggle you into bed," she said with a grin. "How long are you here?"

"I fly out tonight," said Muller, with what the hoped was a suitably crestfallen look.

Marte sighed.

"Well, you have a really good tumble in my credit ledger."

She laughed again.

"Any other favors I can offer?"

"Actually, yes," said Muller, pausing as the waiter set two small coffees on the table beside them.

"What can you tell me about the Ribbentrop-Molotov Agreement?"

He looked at her over the top of the demi-tasse coffee cup.

"Many of those I speak to see it more as an alliance than a non-aggression pact."

Marte paused and sipped her coffee, gently placing the cup back on its saucer.

"I don't know," she said finally. "Franz hasn't seen a copy of the whole document– actually, no one seems to have seen the secret parts, except Hitler and Ribbentrop. So, he's not privy to the terms and hasn't been given any inside information."

"Well, they certainly agreed to divide up Poland," Muller said. "I was shown a German propaganda film by the Turks hailing their joint victory, have you seen it?

Marte nodded.

"The parade in Brest with Guderian and that Soviet General strutting around and saluting one another? They made everyone in the embassy watch it. Can you imagine, Paul; a month ago, saluting the Soviet flag would have earned anyone a one-way trip to Dachau. Now they're our victorious comrades-in-arms."

Marte fingered her demitasse.

"I can understand how people would be suspicious," she concluded.

"What's Franz's mission here, Marte?" Muller asked. "Do you know if he's coordinating with the Soviets on some kind of plan to take over Turkey or the Balkans?"

"No," she replied. "Franz is certainly a trouble-maker; but he's not clever enough to try that. He keeps saying his job is to keep Turkey out of the clutches of Britain and France and he's finding that hard enough to do–witness the fact that you seem to have slipped the Polish gold right past him."

Marte smiled conspiratorially, then her face turned serious and she laid her hand on Muller's arm.

"No, I don't have an answer to your question," she said, speaking quietly.

"But I do know Adolf Hitler, and he's not a man who builds alliances. Look at the trail of bloodshed and betrayal that follows in his wake," she added. "You may think that you're his friend today, but tomorrow you're likely to find a bullet in your head."

Marte took a deep breath and shook her brown curls.

"Hitler trusts no one but himself," she said. "The Soviets may provide him an advantage now, but if I were Stalin, I wouldn't turn my back on him."

Marte finished the last of her coffee, then leaned forward to kiss Muller again..

"I must get back before I'm missed," she said, re-tying the kerchief under her chin.

"I'm looking forward to our next meeting," she said, and winked.

She stood to leave, then leaned back, putting her mouth close to Muller's ear.

"By the way," she whispered, "you should tell the British Consul here that his landline to London runs through Germany and Berlin is listening to every word."

She straightened, blew Muller a kiss and strode out of the restaurant toward the bridge, where she was quickly lost in a throng of disembarking ferry passengers.

CHAPTER 15

Muller strolled back across the Galata Bridge, once again having a care for the fishermen and their paraphernalia at the rail. It was a crowded span, a tram line down the center, traffic inching along in both directions and people hurrying to and from the ferry terminals. Gulls swooped and squawked at one another and deep horns sounded from vessels on the Bosphorous to his left, all contributing to a vibrant atmosphere that added to his good mood.

He'd enjoyed seeing Marte von Papen again and he smiled, recollecting her outburst of glee in learning that he'd snatched the Polish gold out of Franz's grasp. He had full confidence that she'd keep his role secret; their entire relationship was clandestine after all.

But the encounter served to reinforce his determination to formalize his relations with Hilde. He'd pondered their situation on the long train ride to Constanta. They hadn't known each other that long–not even six months; clearly too short for a proper courtship. But now that war had come, who knew what lay in store for them?

How much time could they expect to be with one another? The war wasn't even a month old and already she'd been stationed in Speiz to assist General Guisan, and he'd been dispatched to Romania. What other unexpected separations might they face? He thought he loved her, and that she loved him too, and they both desperately wanted to be in one another's arms.

But there wasn't really any place to do that in Bern; he was in an all-male barracks and her tiny dormitory room wasn't much better. They couldn't just rent an apartment and live together; the only way to do that was to get married.

So that's what he'd decided they should do. But what would she say, he wondered; would she agree? He intended to find out when he returned. But first, he was determined to take advantage of this opportunity to buy her a gift that would be a proper sign of his affection.

At the entrance to the Grand Bazaar, Muller stopped to peer inside. He saw a vaulted, tile ceiling soaring high above rows of shops and stalls lining both sides of a walkway which led to a shadowy interior, seemingly lit only by the bright lights that spilled out of displays in the shop windows. He decided the Bazaar did indeed look as romantic as he'd imagined it, so he summoned his courage and strode in, walking slowly and gazing at the vast expanse that unfolded before him. The walkway extended as far as he could see; the place looked huge, and it was crowded.

He hadn't gotten far inside when he was surrounded by a group of a half dozen boys, all about ten years old, clamoring for attention.

"Mister!" "Monsieur!" "Gold!" "We help".

Muller stopped and raised his hands to his waist, hoping to calm them. One of the boys, just at his right hand, stood still, dark eyes imploring him, a lock of black hair falling on his forehead.

"Please mister," he said several times, but quietly.

"What's your name?" said Muller to the boy bending in his direction.

"Tolga," the boy replied, looking up at him. "I take you to best shops," he said smiling confidently.

Muller pulled the card Unsal had given him from his pocket and showed it to the boy.

"Yes, yes," the boy said nodding, "I take you there" and he began pulling at Muller's suit jacket, pushing the other boys aside. "We go there now."

Muller surrendered to the moment and began to follow Tolga. The other boys quickly disappeared in search of other marks.

Tolga wanted to hurry Muller along, but instead, he slowed to a stroll, absorbing the moment. He walked past shops with glass cases displaying dozens–hundreds–of gold bracelets, necklaces, brooches and other items of jewelry. There were stalls with bright colored pashminas, shawls, and other textile items, and others stacked with tins of coffee and tea and bins filled with spices. Muller found it all quite exotic and a little overwhelming.

They came to an intersection and Tolga led him to turn right and, again, this new walkway extended as far as he could see, lined with still more shops and stalls on either side.

Goodness, Muller said to himself, this is a shopping maze; he was sure he could easily get lost in here.

After another right turn at another intersection–also leading to still more stalls and shops–Tolga stopped at a glass-enclosed store-front, gesturing that Muller should enter.

The space was small, but brightly lit, and it displayed gold and other jewelry in seemingly every nook and cranny. A well-dressed man pulled aside a curtain at the back of the store and approached Muller with a welcoming smile, addressing him in flawless French, seeming to intuit that Muller was a French speaker. He probably speaks a half dozen languages, Muller thought to himself.

Muller explained what he was looking for, and the man, who introduced himself as Cihan, showed him a variety of gold jewelry choices, recommending especially a gold necklace, with interlocking links and small metal clasp at the back–what Muller thought of a choker, though he was sure that wasn't the proper term. But he liked it and asked the price.

"Only for a guest introduced by Minister Unsal, the price is $3,000," he said, "not less; this piece was handmade probably two hundred years ago, perhaps in Mesopotamia. It is unique and nearly priceless. We shall hate to have it leave our collection, but it will surely grace your fiancée's neck and become part of your life together."

Muller smiled to himself. He had seen the same necklace prominently displayed in the windows of other gold shops they'd walked past, and he was pretty confident it had been cast less than a month ago in a factory somewhere near Istanbul by a goldsmith skilled at producing attractive items that could be breathlessly offered as unique and life-changing.

Well, he decided that he should play along too, and adopted the role of the penniless civil servant for whom this would be the most expensive investment of his life, finally, reluctantly, persuading himself to offer a price of $500.

After ten minutes of role-playing, they settled on a price of $1,200.

"Oh, and I'd like that bracelet too," Muller said, pointing to a slender and delicate piece displayed on the counter next to them.

"Excellent choice," Cihan exclaimed enthusiastically.

"That will be a total of $2,200."

Muller had had enough. He straightened to face Cihan, spread his hands and set his face.

"I will pay you $1,500 in new US one-hundred-dollar bids, Cihan. No more; take it or leave it–oh, and you'll kindly pay Tolga here," he pointed to the boy who was standing silently by the door, "for leading me to your shop–and for guiding me out when we leave."

Cihan reacted by smiling and putting out his hand to seal the deal.

Muller stepped behind the curtain and removed his money belt, extracting the money; he'd repay Nicholas Odier when he returned to Switzerland.

Later, when the car sent by his British hosts picked him up in front of his hotel at 7 PM, he debated whether to permit his suitcase, with the gold jewelry safely tucked away in the secret compartment, to be placed in the boot, or whether he should keep it with him, ultimately deciding that the boot was probably safe enough.

The route the driver took followed the shoreline, curving East, then South, as the Bosphorous gradually widened into the Sea of Marmara. On his left, Muller could see the wharves and warehouses of the Port of Istanbul and scores of vessels tied up or riding at anchor just offshore, some of them, he supposed, awaiting clearance to enter the Bosphorous and head North for the Black Sea. But what really captured his imagination was the view on his right, of the vast stone wall that the Ottomans had constructed centuries earlier to protect Constantinople. It was still light enough for him to see clearly the vastness of the structure which towered some ten meters or more in height, topped by battlements and angled promontories. It remained a formidable edifice even all these years later, crumbling and in ruins is some places, but still mainly intact and forbidding.

His driver finally slowed and turned into a vaulted, stone-clad opening in the wall, entering a cobble-stoned courtyard which was surrounded by the wall on one side and low buildings on the other, and appeared to be a busy neighborhood, with brightly lit storefronts at street level and what seemed to be residences above.

The driver pulled the car around the courtyard, parking it against the wall and opened Muller's passenger door, gesturing him to mount a stone staircase next to the wall. Muller did so and found himself at the entrance to a restaurant built along the top of the wall with a dozen or so white-clad tables on a terrace overlooking the Sea of Marmara. He gave his name to the maître d'hotel who nodded and led him to a table right at the wall, where a slightly built, clean-shaven man with black hair parted in the middle stood to greet him. He was in his fifties, Muller estimated, with high eyebrows above dark eyes and a prominent chin.

"Ambassador Muller," he said, extending his hand, "Hughe Knatchbull-Hugesson, His Majesty's Consul in Istanbul. Welcome." The complicated name rolled effortlessly off his lips and betrayed a strong upper-class British accent that Muller was very familiar with.

"Welcome and my thanks for accepting the invitation to dine together this evening. Our mutual friend Stevenson speaks well of you, so I'm pleased to have this opportunity to meet you–and to offer my congratulations for your success in rescuing the Polish gold. My colleague in Constanta, Jim Bottomley sent along a message with the details."

"Please," he said, gesturing for Muller to be seated.

"I chose to have wine this evening rather than traditional raki, will you join me?"

"Gladly," Muller replied. Raki ahead of a long flight might not be the best idea.

Knatchbull-Hugesson offered a cigarette–British Churchman's–and a light; a Dunhill, Muller noted approvingly.

"I want to hear all about what must have been a real adventure with the gold," Knatchbull-Hugesson said, "but I also want to seek your assessment of what's going on in Europe. Worldly as it is, Istanbul is a little insular and I don't often get the chance to exchange views with a well-informed traveler like yourself."

Muller smiled. He recalled his own long stints in Danzig–also a busy port city and worldly in that sense–but bereft of informed outside insight.

"I'd enjoy that, Consul," he replied, choosing to use the man's title rather than risking mis-pronouncing his name, "especially when we find ourselves in a time of war, but where the even the identity of the warring parties remains unclear."

"Serefe–Cheers". They clinked glasses.

"Well, to that point, Mr. Ambassador," Knatchbull-Hugesson said, "I greatly appreciated you nudging Stevenson to get Whitehall's attention in delivering armaments to Turkey–whom we'd be happy to get onside in this conflict. Having a genuine ally here in the Near East would have great strategic value for us," he went on, "but somehow the Cabinet's attention gets diverted to other subjects, closer to home."

Waiters were now delivering the familiar plates of the *mezé.*

"Do you suppose we could order a plate of lakerda?" Muller asked, seeing none.

Knatchbull-Hugesson chuckled.

"You're a fast learner: I was about to say the same thing." He signaled for the waiter and made the request, passing the plate first to Muller when it quickly arrived.

"Pity we can't get something as nice and fresh as this in England, despite being an island surrounded by water–and fish," he said, helping himself, before continuing.

"Whitehall accepts in principle the Turks' insistence on acquiring more weaponry. But our armed forces are loath to part with the tanks, the motorized artillery and the fighter planes they've ordered, because we're short of the same equipment ourselves. There's just not enough to go around.

"We were able to divert the arms on that ship that was bound for Poland, but was effectively interned here. The Poles collapsed so quickly that we couldn't deliver it, so we handed it over to the Turks.

"As the expert in Polish gold, you'll be amused to learn that we reimbursed the Poles in gold–we moved some ingots from our stack to their stack in the vaults beneath the Bank of England."

Muller smiled as he stubbed out his cigarette in the colorful porcelain ashtray.

"That's a less risky point of transfer than at the Polish-Romanian border," he said.

"But are you confident that you'll be able to get the Turks 'onside', as you put it?" Muller asked. "They tell me they're fearful that they're facing a German-Soviet alliance that threatens not just the Balkans but Turkey itself."

Knatchbull-Hugesson nodded.

"And their minister's been forced to cool his heels in Moscow for three days while Ribbentrop is there again, negotiating who knows what, this time. Carving up Poland, for sure, but what else?

"We don't know," he added, refilling their wine glasses.

"Our French allies are hinting they may be ready to declare war on the Soviet Union. As you're doubtless aware, there a big slice of the French public that would much prefer fighting the Communists than the Nazis. I'm being told that Churchill, now that he's in Cabinet, is urging a pre-emptive invasion of the Balkans– maybe a new Gallipoli," Knatchbull-Hugesson chuckled mirthlessly. "That's what General Weygand, the French Middle East commander wants to do too."

"But neither government seems willing to even talk about attacking Germany while its entire army and air force are a thousand miles East, busy fighting in Poland, and the French could march straight to Berlin from their Maginot Line fortifications." Muller spoke quietly, but forcefully, and eyed Knatchbull-Hugesson.

The Consul used his napkin to wipe his lips before answering.

"No," he replied, "they won't talk about that, let alone do it."

He paused again.

"No one wants to re-start the battles of the Great War."

The two men sat without speaking for several minutes. Muller broke the silence.

"The British government informed my government this summer that its new Ministry of Economic Warfare intended to mount a full-scale economic attack against Germany that it believed would cause the German economy to collapse and lead to the downfall of Hitler.

"They also told us that the campaign would be so severe that it might destroy the Swiss economy too," he added. "You will appreciate, Consul, that a threat like that–coming from your government–was decidedly unwelcome."

Knatchbull-Hugesson didn't react.

"Switzerland is a neutral nation, Consul, as you are well aware," Muller went on, "and we're prepared to defend that status. We didn't expect to be threatened by Britain, and we'll retaliate against your government if we need to. Somehow, we'd gained the impression that Britain's enemy was *Germany*, and that Britain would be threatening *Germany*–not far-off nations in the Balkans or a neutral like Switzerland–or even Turkey, for that matter.

"Is this whole thing just a charade to extend British influence in the world, using a war that you've declared, but don't seem willing to fight, as an excuse?

"You'll forgive me Consul," Muller went on leveling his gaze at Knatchbull-Hugesson, "but I have too much experience being pushed aside by your government when it suits their fancy. You don't do alliances very well, sir."

Muller helped himself to another cigarette from the cigarette case Knatchbull-Hugesson had left on the table. He was annoyed. Britain had, for years, championed a policy of Appeasement, cheerfully giving Hitler nearly everything he wanted; then, disillusioned, it declared a war it hadn't begun to fight–but even so proceeded to issue threats against other nations. And still, it expected those other nations to kowtow to it.

He exhaled a cloud of smoke, waving it away impatiently.

Knatchbull-Hugesson returned Muller's gaze with a thin smile.

"Touché," he replied.

"I sometimes speculate about how difficult it must be for other nations to be on the receiving end of the changing policies that His Majesty's government so forcefully advocates."

Knatchbull-Hugesson took another cigarette as well.

"For example, how confident can anyone be that now, with Poland having effectively disappeared from the map–again–my government and the French won't cobble together a new agreement with Germany that will foreclose the bloody prospect of actual warfare between them?

"You didn't hear it from me of course," he added, "and in truth I have absolutely no basis in fact to predict something that would happen. But…." He shrugged and toasted Muller as he drained his wine glass.

"Of course," he said with a grin, "if the Soviets have in fact changed sides and aligned themselves with Germany, that *would* change the equation, wouldn't it."

They paused as waiters arrived with their next course and rearranged the table.

Muller had begun carefully removing some bones from his grilled loup de mer and placing them on the side of his plate when he caught sight of Emin Unsal approaching their table–a little unsteadily.

"Flash!" Unsal said, stopping before them and mimicking a photographer. "Secret diplomatic démarche exposed. Smile!" He mimicked a flashbulb exploding.

Unsal pulled up a chair from an adjoining table and sat down heavily.

The maître d'hotel scurried to the table.

"Whiskey," said Unsal, a bit too loudly. "Double. And neat," he added.

"I hope I'm not interrupting," he said turning first to Muller then to Knatchbull-Hugesson. "Ha! I'll bet you two are cooking up some scheme or other," he said, then looked around. "Where's that whiskey?"

A waiter placed the drink before him and he lifted it, taking a large swallow, then coughing.

The man is drunk, Muller said to himself, and glanced at Knatchbull-Hugesson who was staring disapprovingly at Unsal, having evidently come to the same conclusion.

Unsal belched, then took another, smaller, swallow of his whiskey and smiled at them both.

"Yes, yes, I know,' he said," shouldn't make a spectacle of yourself when you're drinking." He belched again, then drew a deep breath, attempting to gather himself.

"But when you discover your nearest neighbor is now formally allied with that madman Adolf Hitler and is almost surely aiming to destroy you, there are only two choices: flee or get drunk; I chose the latter."

Unsal reached into his breast pocket and pulled out a yellow flimsy, evidently pulled from a teletype machine, and handed it to Knatchbull-Hugesson who read it, then handed it to Muller.

It was an International News Service story datelined Moscow, that very day.

"Joint Statement Accompanying signature of German-Soviet Boundary and Friendship Treaty Signed by Molotov and Ribbentrop.

As Foreign Ministers of our respective nations, we mutually express our conviction that it would serve the interests of all peoples to put an end to the state of war that exists at present between Germany on the one side and England and France on the other.

Should, however, the efforts of our two governments toward this goal remain fruitless, this would demonstrate that England and France are responsible for the continuation of the war, in which case, the Governments of Germany and the USSR shall engage in mutual consultations with regard to necessary measures."

"Hot off the ticker, gentlemen," said Unsal. "About as clear a statement as ministers are capable of mustering," he went on.

"'Either England and France surrender, or Germany and the USSR are free to divide up the rest of the world'" he said, using his hands to mimic quotation marks. "Well, maybe not China," he added. "But certainly Turkey." He belched again.

"Molotov has finally deigned to meet our minister tomorrow at the Kremlin, now that his new best friend von Ribbentrop has returned to Berlin," he said. "Do you suppose our minister should keep a straight face when Molotov utters expressions of eternal friendship and comity with its esteemed neighbor, Turkey?" he asked mockingly.

"Or, instead, should he ask when the two of them have agreed to invade us?"

Unsal looked around for another whiskey, but Knatchbull-Hugesson put a hand on his arm.

"Maybe not such a good idea, Emin."

Unsal looked at him and grunted.

"I'll leave you two to your own devices, then," he said, rising from his seat and steadying himself. The maître d'hotel scurried forward and took Unsal's arm, leading him away.

When he'd left, Muller returned to his fish; it had gotten cold but was still moist and flavorful–and he was hungry.

"Has Unsal read too much into that statement?" he asked between mouthfuls.

Knatchbull-Hugesson sighed. He was only picking at his meal.

"It's pretty damning language," he replied. "If Unsal's right and they really have agreed to conquer this part of the world and divide it up between them, that certainly alters the equation of opposing forces that we talked about earlier."

He reached for the flimsy that lay between them.

May I take this? I'm afraid that I should leave and report to London," he said, rising. "I'll take care of the bill. Please finish your meal; you won't find much to eat at that aerodrome."

As Knatchbull-Hugesson turned to leave, Muller motioned him to resume his seat and leaned toward him, speaking quietly.

"I probably should have said something earlier when I arrived, but you should know, Consul, that your land line to London passes through German territory and has been tapped. Berlin knows every word you're reporting to London."

Knatchbull-Hugesson's head jerked quickly and his lips pursed into a narrow line.

"What…?" he began to say something, then looked at Muller who continued gazing levelly at him, his face grim, saying nothing more.

Knatchbull-Hugesson sat back in this seat and drew a deep breath. Then he stood.

"Thank you," he said, "it's been an eventful evening," and he strode away.

Later, when his driver deposited Muller at Yelsilkoy Aerodrome and he was shown to the threadbare VIP Departure Lounge to await his flight, he was glad he'd stayed and finished dinner.

If War Should Come

CHAPTER 16

It was an exhausting return trip; dense fog in Rome and Milan had closed both airports, so his Ala Littoria flight from Athens to Rome had been forced to divert to Ravenna where, upon landing, he counted eight other aircraft parked on the grassy aerodrome, also apparently awaiting a break in the weather. The small terminal itself was crowded and seemingly overwhelmed. All the seating was occupied, and passengers were sprawled on the hard linoleum floor; a small canteen was serving a long line of passengers, many of whom argued with the servers at the skimpy rations they received.

"Christ, they're out of nearly everything," said a balding man balancing a small plate of pasta and a half bottle of chianti as he edged past Muller toward the door, apparently electing to look for somewhere outside to deposit himself.

"It'll all be gone by the time you get there," he said.

The lone clerk manning the Ala Littoria gate was angrily parrying passengers' questions.

"Look, I don't know when any flight's going to be released.

"It's the weather," he said, impatiently. "I can't do anything about it; just find a place to wait. No, there's no hotel, out here. Just WAIT!"

The man slammed his fist on the wooden stand in front of him and stormed back into an interior office, slamming the door behind him to the howls of the passengers.

"Sonofabitch!"

Muller took a deep breath. It was the end of September. Northern Italy regularly experienced days of grey lingering fog and mist; so did Geneva. It just happened; and seemed to decide for itself when it would clear–or not. This could be a very long wait indeed, he decided. So, he strode back outside to where his aircraft was parked. The pilots were seated in the cockpit smoking; apparently the terminal's crew quarters were no better than the passengers' side.

Muller strode toward the cockpit.

"Can I get my bag out of the back?" he said loudly enough for the co-pilot to open the window and stick his head out.

"The bag you checked?" he said.

"Yes," Muller replied. "I'm going to find a train in town. I'd rather take a chance on that than wait here."

The co-pilot flicked his cigarette butt out the cockpit window and levered himself out of his seat. Emerging in the doorway at the rear of the aircraft, he pulled a lever that opened the small cargo door and stood aside.

"Which one is it?"

Muller spotted his suitcase toward the back of the space. Using both hands, he managed to pull himself far enough into the cargo bay to grab the handle and maneuver the suitcase to the door, where he gave it one final yank and set it down next to him.

"Here's the tag," he said, handing the yellow ticket stub to the co-pilot. "Thanks."

He gave a mock salute and headed toward the front of the terminal where cars were standing, confident he could hire a driver to take him to the Ravenna train station.

He lost count of the number of connections, but about eighteen hours later, he'd finally reached the familiar confines of Geneva's Cornavin railroad station and easily connected to Bern where, for the first time since he'd departed the Ravenna Aerodrome, he encountered bright sunshine as the train approached the Bernese Oberland.

Hilde was nowhere to be found; still assigned in Spiez, he was told. He made a call to Army headquarters there, trying to find her, with no success, finally leaving her a message that he had no confidence would ever be delivered.

During the long train trip, he'd handwritten a detailed report on the Romanian mission. He'd run out of ink in his fountain pen, but a sympathetic dining car attendant had refilled it, so he had been able to complete the report without resorting to a stubby pencil. After the unsuccessful telephone attempt to reach Hilde, he'd taken the document to the Ministry's typing pool and asked that it be prepared for the Minister's attention the next morning.

It was evening, by then, so he went to a café near his quarters, ate an indifferent meal with a bottle of local Dôle red wine, and went straight to bed.

When he reached the office the next morning, Minger summoned him, standing and coming around his desk to shake his hand and guide him to a seat by the window overlooking the Aare River where they could sit together without the large desk separating them.

"It was good work, Mr. Muller," Minger said with a smile offering his cigarette case; Muller took an Ambassador and lit for them both.

Minger exhaled.

"I'd gotten the gist of it earlier," he said, "but your report confirms that we made the right decision to help the Romanians.

"We have messages of appreciation from both Bucharest and Istanbul," Minger said. "They're struggling to stay neutral just like we are; we have to help each other out when we can. So, we've booked a little goodwill that may, one day, come in handy," he said.

"But we're not going to crow about it publicly; in fact, I've ordered the files to be sealed and I'm admonishing people in the Ministry–and that includes you especially Mr. Muller–to keep the story to themselves. There's no point in provoking the Germans by bragging about how we outfoxed them. But equally important, we don't want to offer our critics here in Switzerland a bone to chew on."

Minger smiled.

"We've sidelined them so far, but the Ministry has adversaries that we need to keep at a distance.

"So, keep it to yourself.

"But I found the parts of your report about the apparent alliance between Germany and the Soviets to be especially troubling," he went on. "The German Minister here in Bern–that odious Otto Köcher–delivered a copy of their propaganda film to our foreign ministry last week. I haven't seen it yet, but I'll take your word for it that it's pretty damning."

Minger tapped his ash and gestured to a neat stack of papers closest to them on the nearby desk.

"You probably haven't had the opportunity since you're returned to read the daily news summaries that –what's her name? Ah. Miss Brenner–has been distributing. That's turned into a very valuable tool, and she's become very good at pulling information off the radio and teletype and organizing it for us.

"Anyway, when you read them, you'll see stories reporting that, right after the Soviets invaded Poland and divided it up with the Germans, they also began moving to take over the Baltic states. They started with Estonia, insisted on stationing troops there, and according to a report yesterday, they're doing the same thing now to Latvia.

"No direct invasion, mind you; just a friendly occupation," Minger pursed his lips.

"Is there a pattern here, Mr. Muller?" he asked rhetorically. "Do you suppose Lithuania and Finland might be next? While the Germans simply look the other way?

Minger looked levelly at Muller.

"It certainly has the appearance of an agreement between them to divide up at least that region–alongside Poland–as your report suggests.

"Meanwhile, closer to home, Köcher is crowing that the French and British–and by implication, we here in Switzerland– can expect no help from the Soviet Union in resisting German demands; They're now on our side, he tells us–all the while becoming increasingly aggressive in demanding that we stop supplying arms and components to British and French customers and reminding us that we buy all of our coal–and a lot of other things we need too–from Germany. The threat that Germany will retaliate against us–even invade us–is never very far beneath the surface of his demands."

Muller was listening carefully. This was more time than he'd ever spent alone with the Minister; he got the sense that Minger was confiding in him and, by implication conferring a promotion on him–no longer just as the Büro Ha subordinate to Hans Haussamann; now more as an advisor in his own right.

"I'm convening a special meeting this evening on that subject, and I want you to attend," Minger went on. "I have a new role in mind for you. Be here promptly at 8 PM but be sure to dine before you come; I don't want any food servers or staff to be present."

"Yes, Mr. Minger," Muller replied.

Minger stood and Muller followed suit; the meeting was over, but Muller hesitated before leaving the office.

"Sir, may I inquire if Miss Magandanz will be reassigned back here in Bern anytime soon?"

Minger turned to Muller and smiled broadly.

"Ah, yes, Mr. Muller," he said. "The fair Hildegarde, with whom you are said to have formed a relationship." Minger put up both hands. "No reason to deny it, Mr. Muller, nor is anything wrong with it; she's smart and pretty too, so why not?

"The problem, Mr. Muller is that she's too competent to remain here as a mere staff director for German research. Our army mobilization exercise earlier this month was not a success on many fronts; mobilizing the women's army was a particular disaster.

"General Guisan realized he had a problem. He and his adjutant and I all speak Vaudoise; we were sitting around that conference table discussing the problem, and I suddenly thought to myself, I have on my staff a woman who's shown herself to be especially competent–and who also speaks Vaudoise. So, I called her in and the four of us began talking about the issue."

"In Vaudoise," Muller said, interrupting in his annoyance.

"Why yes," Minger replied evenly.

"And within ten minutes of hearing her respond to the problems, the General decided to hire her and take her to Spiez to sort the whole thing out. For now, she's working for Guisan's Adjutant; they apparently knew of one another when they lived in the Jura Mountains of Vaud. But I think Guisan aims to make her a captain and run the program."

Muller interrupted again. "You mean take command the women's Swiss Army?"

Minger shrugged.

"The Army commanders will retain their authority, of course. But they've proven pretty helpless in trying to organize things and they seem happy to defer to her–at least most of the time," he added.

"It's Guisan's call, but I could tell the Adjutant was very taken with her too."

"And who's this Adjutant?"

Minger frowned a moment in thought.

"Thibault was his name," Minger said; "yes, Colonel Thibault. Nice looking fellow, Mr. Muller. Actually, he'll be attending the meeting this evening, so you'll get to meet him."

Minger turned to his desk and Muller strode back down the corridor to his office.

Hilde had become the de facto commander of the women's division of the Swiss Army?

He sat at his desk and tried to absorb the information–and what it might portend for their romance and the prospects for an early wedding. It didn't sound very promising. And this Adjutant? Who was 'taken with her'? What was that supposed to mean?

Shit!

He tried without much success to concentrate on the documents that had piled up in his absence. He did find the daily news reports compiled by Yvonne Brenner to be informative. She had carefully stacked them in a separate pile on his desk and had highlighted with green ink items that she'd thought he'd find especially interesting, among them, the stories the Minister had just mentioned, reporting Soviet advances against the Baltic States.

As Muller read the reports, he concluded that Soviet behavior had the look of a classic provocation. The campaign against Estonia appeared to have begun with Molotov issuing a statement condemning Estonia for 'permitting' the escape of a Polish submarine from Tallinn Harbor. Over the next few days, the Soviets proceeded to mass troops on the border and began Red Air Force overflights into Estonian airspace. A few days later, when a Soviet merchant vessel was sunk in the Baltic, the Soviet press asserted it had been torpedoed by the same Polish submarine–and pressure on Estonia mounted. When the Estonian Foreign Minister hurried to Moscow to defuse the crisis, Molotov had presented him with an ultimatum demanding that Estonia submit to Soviet authority; the government capitulated and within days, 35,000 Soviet troops had occupied the country and seized the Estonian naval base at Tallinn, on the Baltic.

And, again as Minger had told him, yesterday's news summary reported that a garrison of 30,000 Soviet troops was in the process of occupying Latvia and seizing Latvian naval bases at Liepaja, Pitras and Ventspils, also on the Baltic.

Muller sat back, lit a Gitane, and reflected.

These aggressive Soviet actions certainly suggested an understanding–an alliance–with Germany, giving the USSR a free hand in the Baltic states–even new ports on the Baltic Sea. Lithuania and Finland were almost certainly next in line.

And an emboldened German Ambassador in Bern was trying to tighten the screws on Switzerland.

There did seem to be a pattern, he decided.

CHAPTER 17

Muller reported to Minger's office at the Ministry a few minutes before 8 PM that night. He arrived at the same time as Hans Haussamann and Roger Masson. General Guisan had preceded them and stood at the far end of the conference table in conversation with two Swiss Army officers whom Muller didn't recognize, but from their insignia, he saw that one was a Colonel, the other a Major.

The Colonel had to be Thibault, and Muller eyed the man as he entered the room. He was wide-shouldered, with an athletic build, and he had a mop of dark hair worn long and combed back; his thin mustache was trimmed and straight beneath an aquiline nose and dark eyes. Muller thought he resembled someone.

Christ, the guy looked like Clark Gable!

Really?

But it was true.

Sonofabitch!

The two officers approached them.

"Major Olivier Charlet," said the first, extending his hand. He was a slim man with wavy fair hair and a cluster of broken veins high up on each cheekbone.

"Colonel Phillipe Thibault," said the other, and as Muller grasped his hand, he clapped Muller on the shoulder.

"Very nice to meet you, Mr. Muller. I bring you greetings from Hildegarde in Speitz," he said genially. "She is essentially running the Swiss women's army these days," he added; "we work well together, and she is doing an excellent job."

Muller mumbled that she was a very well-organized person.

'We work well together'?

I'll bet you do.

Even the creases of his smile were Gable's; vertical, just so, on both cheeks above that square jaw.

Shit!

Muller had never had the occasion to meet General Guisan; before his appointment as General, he had only seen him from a distance performing official duties, which he did with a quiet sense of dignity. But in the short space of just over a month since assuming command, Guisan had become a national folk hero; a reassuring symbol of Swiss resolve. His official portrait, smiling warmly beneath his round, braided uniform cap, had become ubiquitous, hanging, as one commentator had put it, next to the crucifix, over the radio or next to the mirror at the hairdressers. During the mobilization, he was seen and photographed daily and shown in news reels, lending a hand with a shovel to dig a trench or sharing a meal with the troops, his face and demeanor engaging and encouraging.

Guisan had flinty blue eyes, but they seemed welcoming and crinkled around the edges when he smiled, as he was now doing.

"Mr. Muller," he said. "It's a pleasure to meet you, after having heard about your exploits from the Minister.

"Among other things, I'm told it was you that had the good sense to extract Miss Magandanz from the basement of the Swiss National Bank; well done." Guisan smiled broadly. "She's proving to be an invaluable asset to the Army. I'm sure the Ministry will miss her being here, but she's become a fixture in Spiez and keeps finding inventive ways to shift women into jobs that free up men for me to deploy as soldiers. It's very helpful."

Minger entered the office and waved everyone to seats around the table and Guisan, as he had in the earlier meeting, took the seat at the far end of the table, opposite Minger. Muller seated himself on Guisan's right.

Minger began the meeting without engaging in any small talk.

"I have asked you gentlemen to come this evening to address what I can only describe as a solemn turning point in the defense of Swiss neutrality," he said.

"Briefly put, General Guisan has reluctantly been forced to conclude that no coherent military plan currently exists to defend our border with Germany. As a result, we have determined that extraordinary measures must be taken to reduce the very real risk of a German invasion. It is therefore our intention to enter into an agreement with the French Army to plan a coordinated defense of Switzerland in the event of a German attack upon us across the Rhine."

Minger paused and glanced around the table.

"This is an unprecedented step and is being undertaken in strictest secrecy. I have invited you to this meeting because each of you has a vital role to play in implementing this plan. No one else in Switzerland must learn of it. May I have your consent to participate on that basis?"

Masson was seated at Minger's right.

"I agree" he said and looked to Haussamann next to him, who said the same, and each of them around the table followed suit.

"Thank you," said Minger.

"Switzerland is a neutral nation," he said. "We have consistently maintained our neutrality, and this step of allying ourselves with France in the event of a German invasion is not intended to change that policy. The new agreement would come into effect only in the event that we are invaded by Germany–in which case, our neutrality will already have been violated, by Germany; so, under international law, as a neutral, we would then be entitled to seek help from third parties–like the French–to help defend ourselves."

Minger then paused again.

"However, the reality is that adversaries–both here at home and, say, in Germany–might seize upon the fact of this new agreement to assert that we have violated our status as a neutral nation, and use it as a weapon against us politically–or, in the case of Germany, even as an excuse to invade us.

"It is a risk we are compelled to take," he said. "But it underscores why even the existence of the new agreement must not be revealed–to anyone, including the Swiss government–so they may truthfully say that they know nothing of any such agreement and can therefore deny it.

"Secrecy is essential," he concluded.

Minger leaned back in his chair, withdrew a cigarette from a silver holder that he placed on the table, lighting up and inviting others to do the same, which each did, save Masson, who lit his pipe, and Thibault, who waved off the offer of a cigarette from Haussamann, seated next to him.

Christ, he doesn't even smoke, Muller thought to himself.

Thibault was seated nearly opposite Muller on the other side of the table, and he stole glances at the man.

He really *did* resemble Clark Gable.

Muller willed himself to concentrate on remarks by General Guisan, who'd begun to speak at Minger's invitation.

"In the wake of the mobilization last month, my staff and I," General Guisan gestured to Thibault and Charlet, "conducted a review of our fortifications, our troop deployments and the plans that had been prepared to defend Switzerland against invasion. We discovered that the entire strategy is premised upon plans that were drawn up nearly twenty years ago in the immediate aftermath of the Great War and have scarcely been altered since.

"They don't take account of today's weapons of mechanized warfare–tanks, motorized infantry and artillery or the capabilities of modern military aircraft–to cite just the most obvious examples. They are, largely, useless."

Guisan paused.

"For practical purposes, therefore, Switzerland is undefended," he said.

"Moreover, many of the defenses that *do* exist are aimed at repelling an invasion by France, not Germany. I understand the reason for this legacy–our policy of neutrality encouraged treating Germany and France the same way. But from a military perspective, the prospect of France invading Switzerland is nonsense.

"The only conceivable rationale for such an attack would be a French decision to invade Germany by first attacking us, then crossing the Rhine to invade Southern Germany. But that's a wholly unrealistic scenario. The German region that lies across the Rhine from us is the Black Forest; it's heavily wooded forestland with narrow roads, steep hills and valleys; it could be easily defended. It's entirely unsuitable for an invasion.

"The French military fully understands that; so, there's been no French planning or preparation for such an attack. It's not even on the table. The French have lots of military issues facing them; attacking Germany through Switzerland isn't one of them."

Guisan paused a moment, then continued.

"By contrast, however," he went on, "the reverse scenario–a Germany attack on France using Switzerland as an invasion route– is very high on their current list of concerns. If the Germans were to attack us and force the Rhine, they would arrive on our Gempen Plateau. You've all been there, gentlemen; you know what it's like: open, rolling countryside that offers a very inviting corridor for a German invasion that could bypass Basle and the Maginot Line and allow the Germans to head West, straight to Paris."

Muller saw heads nodding around the table.

What Guisan was saying was something that every knowledgeable Swiss knew was true; a German attack on Switzerland, aimed at invading France, offered Germany important potential strategic military advantages, and, consequently, it was a danger to Swiss sovereignty. But it was a subject that, by common consent, just wasn't discussed.

Among other things, there was a vocal minority within Switzerland that was sympathetic to Hitler and the Nazis; no one wanted to stir them up. And there was no stomach among the leaders of the elected Swiss Federal Council leaders to confront Germany on the issue. Hitler's bitter denunciation of criticism of his regime–and of him, personally–in the Swiss press had led him to threaten invasion on more than one occasion. No one in Swiss leadership circles wanted to risk further escalation by warning that a German invasion was a realistic threat; instead, both the Swiss government and Swiss citizens fell back on asserting their long-standing policy of neutrality, hoping that would keep Hitler at bay.

But now the issue had been placed squarely on the table; Minger and Guisan were aiming to address the German threat by making an alliance with the French. This indeed was, as Minger had stated at the start of the meeting, a solemn moment in Swiss history, and Muller felt tension around the table as the other participants all grappled with it.

Guisan broke the tension.

"Rudolph," he said playfully, smiling at Minger and addressing him by his first name, "without in any way diminishing the seriousness of our discussion this evening, I don't think it would be out of order to break out some of that nice brandy I know you keep nearby.

"This is a common endeavor we're embarked upon," he added, smiling at the other faces around the table. "Major Charlet, did you bring the small wheel of vacherin de Mont d'Or as I requested?"

"Yes, General," Major Charlet responded, standing and retrieving a sack from behind him which he opened, extracting a round brown wooden box which he opened, removing the cheese, and, using a sharp knife, expertly sliced off the rind, disposing of it in the sack and placed the cheese in a small wicker basket with chunks of bread. He then handed napkins around the table and offered the basket first to Guisan, who cut off several pieces of cheese, placed them on his napkin and added some bread.

Minger had produced a bottle of Courvoisier XO and cutglass snifters, which he distributed around the table.

They filled their snifters and toasted.

"Santé" Minger said, smiling, "and continued neutrality."

They drank and began to share the cheese.

"Tastes like first Vacherin of the season," Guisan said. "From one of your Vaudoise fromageries, Colonel?"

Thibault reached to pick up the round wooden container and looked at it quickly, then nodded.

"Saint Ursanne, one of the smallest, but oldest of our fromageries; a good selection," he said, glancing at Charlet.

Christ, Muller thought to himself; Clark Gable was also the proprietor of fromageries in the Jura? He sighed quietly.

But as Guisan had doubtless intended, the tension in the room receded as the men began helping themselves.

"I tend to have a more relaxed view of neutrality than the Minister does," Guisan said, resuming the discussion, but in a conversational tone.

"I think the Germans assume that–if they were to attack us, we'd turn to the French for help; it's normal," he said. "So, I don't see the new defensive initiative we're considering with the French as being quite so ground-breaking as he does."

"Well, the Germans might think so," Masson interjected, characteristically and noisily tapping ashes out of his pipe into the ash tray before him.

"At the very least it would give the Germans grounds to work themselves into high dudgeon–that's something Herr Hitler specializes in–and offer a fresh excuse for attacking us verbally– maybe even invading us."

"Does he really need an excuse to do that?" Thibault sat forward in his chair.

"There are two different issues at stake here," Masson continued, his voice intense. "The first is whether Germany sees any advantage in invading Switzerland just to occupy and loot us. I would argue that's a very different calculation than invading us as a means to attack France from the East. I can make the case that the first scenario–invading us to conquer us–would be a very hard decision for Hitler to make. Switzerland would not be an easy target the way Poland has proven to be. I think we have the means at hand to resist and at least make Hitler think twice–or more, even–before doing that.

"By contrast, attacking us to use us as–what did the Minister call it?–'a corridor' to attack France?–is all too likely.

"Think what Germany would gain from doing that," Masson went on. "They'd flank the Maginot Line–they could even attack it from the rear and stand a pretty good chance of destroying it. They could certainly head for Paris and avoid the French and British forces that are deployed to defend the World War I venues in Flanders and Northern France.

"It is a strategy that would upset nearly everyone's calculations–which is why Hitler's likely to choose it," he concluded, reaching for a square of Vacherin and popping it into his mouth.

"It will never be the main thrust of a German invasion of France," Hans Haussamann snorted. "Hitler's generals are all still looking at the traditional battlegrounds of Northern France. This is a sideshow, he went on; my German intelligence sources report no imminent threat to invade us."

"I still want to know what it would look like," Minger said. "Even as a sideshow it could be devastating for us, so Major Charlet tell us what we should expect if the Germans decide to attack."

Charlet glanced at General Guisan, who nodded.

"Minister, any attack upon us by Germany would have to begin with crossing the Rhine," Charlet began. "At the first sign of such an attack, we'd blow the bridges; they're all wired with explosives and the Swiss frontier guards have been trained to do that. So, the Germans would have to build pontoon bridges across the Rhine to get at us. That's no mean feat, sir," Charlet added, "the Rhine is a real obstacle. But we have to assume German forces are capable of successfully doing that, if they set their minds to it.

"Still, they'd be vulnerable during the crossing. Again, our Swiss frontier guards are trained to resist a river crossing; they have artillery and emplacements for just that purpose. But the Germans know that, of course, so they'd pick advantageous crossing sites where we're weakest.

"Most important, though, we assume they'd initiate an attack by dropping a couple of divisions of paratroopers on our side of the river; a surprise airborne assault that would sow confusion and chaos–and greatly hamper our ability to resist."

Guisan leaned forward to interject.

"Think of it Minger," he said. A couple of thousand German paratroopers descend on our Gempen Plateau; they attack our frontier guards along the Rhine from the rear and set up check points to intercept reinforcements that we try to send. I issue a new General Mobilization order but, before our army reservists can even assemble in the battle zone, they're at the mercy of marauding German paratroopers. Our ability to resist would be deeply–maybe fatally–compromised."

Guisan gestured with his hands to emphasize his point.

"As Major Charlet correctly asserts, that kind of assault would create chaos on our side–and we really don't have either the resources or a plan to defend against it.

"And that's why we need the French," he concluded.

Roger Masson interrupted again, this time without banging his pipe, Muller noted, suspecting the habit would reappear shortly.

"And what is it that we expect the French to do if they come? Masson paused, then banging his pipe on the ashtray, continued; "and maybe more important, what will the French *agree* to do if we do ask them to come to our aid now, before any invasion?"

Minger smiled, looking around the room.

"Those are the precise questions we need answered–and that's why each of you is present around this table, right Henri?" Minger gestured to the General.

Guisan nodded.

"Minister Minger and I have agreed that any agreement we reach with the French is to be only a *military* agreement; that is to say, it is to be signed only by General Gamelin for the French Army and me for the Swiss Army; no civilian government officials are to be signatories…"

"Or to be involved or informed," added Minger. "Strictly an agreement between the two military commanders".

Again, Guisan nodded.

"But Minister Minger and I have agreed that both he and I must agree to the language of the agreement before I sign it on behalf of the Swiss Army.

"You are to be a silent partner, Rudolf," he said, gesturing back at Minger, who nodded with a smile.

"Precisely."

"To that end," Guisan said, "I am appointing Colonel Thibault to represent me in the negotiations with the French and Mr. Minger has appointed Mr. Muller to represent him. The two of you will be responsible for getting the French to agree to something we can both accept," he said, glancing at each of them.

Muller heart sank and he shot a stricken look in Minger's direction.

"Sir," he said, "I have no military background…"

Minger held up his palm.

"Mr. Muller, you are not expected to evaluate the military decisions reached in this agreement. You'll be there for one reason only: to ensure that the Swiss state is not compromised. I want to ensure that our status as a neutral state is protected as much as possible; that's your assignment.

"Frankly," he said, "just the fact that you're at the table will serve as a reminder to the military–theirs as well as ours–" and here he nodded at both Thibault and Charlet, "that this is no carte blanche we're agreeing to. It is to be as limited a commitment as we can manage–consistent with getting the French military support we need."

Minger smiled at Muller.

"A simple diplomatic assignment Mr. Muller."

Muller gazed back at Minger, then took a deep breath and sat back in his chair, his mind spinning. He'd just been tossed the proverbial hot potato and couldn't pass it along. Instinctively, though, he understood that the role Minger had just described had elevated him to becoming the most important participant in these upcoming negotiations; in the end, they had to satisfy Minger– which meant satisfying *him.*

Well, he said to himself, if that's the case, it wouldn't hurt to exercise a little of that authority right now.

Masson had begun to speak, but Muller interrupted.

"General Guisan," he said, turning to face the General directly. "Since I am to serve as Minister Minger's representative, perhaps you can begin by advising me where and when these negotiations are to take place."

Guisan returned Muller's gaze levelly.

"In two days at the Ministry of War in Paris," he responded.

Muller thought for a moment.

"With all due deference, sir, I think that venue should be changed," he said. "It has the appearance that either France summoned the Swiss to Paris, or that the Swiss sought out French help by visiting Paris. Neither impression is in keeping with what I understand to be Minister Minger's objective–which is to downplay the significance of what we are embarking upon–to present it as a small-bore military tactical step.

"To my thinking, that implies that the negotiations should take place neither in Paris, nor in Bern; rather they should be in the field, preferably somewhere close to where the actual effects will be felt. That suggests in Basle, or somewhere nearby. In addition to being where the Swiss Gempen Plateau region connects to the French countryside; it's where the German, French and Swiss borders all converge."

Muller paused a moment, then went on.

"If I'm not mistaken, there's been an informal stipulation among all three nations not to build defense installations in Huningue, the actual point of intersection of the three borders, just outside Basle; that's why the Maginot Line ends there.

"It's also where any French Army advance into Switzerland to engage a German attack would start. That strikes me as a better place to hold these negotiations."

Muller sat back in his chair. He hoped he hadn't over-reached; but if so, better to find out now.

Guisan had been looking down at his hands on the table as Muller spoke.

He didn't speak for a moment, then looked at Colonel Thibault.

"Colonel, you've organized the talks. Can the venue be changed, as Mr. Muller has proposed?"

Thibault pursed his lips, frowning and looking displeased.

"It's a little late in the day, General," he responded. "The arrangements have been made."

The room was silent, then Guisan, smiling down the table at Minger, spoke up.

"Then I guess they'll have to be re-arranged, Colonel," Guisan said; "Mr. Muller has made a valid point–a subject we should have thought of ourselves, actually.

"Well, no matter," Guisan went on briskly. "The French 8th Army is headquartered at Colmar; that's close to Basle and they shouldn't object to shifting locations to one of their command centers. Will that do the job, Mr. Muller?"

His tone was genial, but his eyes were serious.

Muller turned to Minger for guidance.

"What a good idea, Henri," said Minger smiling, and slapping the table softly, enjoying the byplay.

"I can see what a resourceful delegation we've assembled for these negotiations."

The meeting didn't last much longer, but at one point, Minger and Masson questioned Major Charlet about the types of emplacements the Army was currently building in the Gempen Plateau. Charlet responded with descriptions of tank traps and antiaircraft batteries. Muller listened; this was not a subject he knew much about.

But suddenly he had an idea.

"Major," he said, "this is your expertise, not mine. Could you arrange a briefing for me at Speitz before the negotiations? Just the basics, you understand; so I don't inadvertently say anything that might conflict with your plans."

Guisan nodded and Charlet said he'd find time the very next afternoon.

"If you take the lunchtime shuttle bus from the Ministry to Speitz, I'll leave a pass at the gate and have you escorted to our offices; there are late shuttles back here that you can take when we're finished."

Muller thanked him. A briefing would be informative.

And somehow, he thought, once at Speitz, he'd find a way to locate the offices of the women's division of the Swiss Army and at least catch a glimpse of Hilde, however fleeting.

He smiled to himself.

When the meeting broke up, General Guisan shook hands all around, including words wishing Muller good luck in the upcoming negotiations. Muller had found the General to be more garrulous and engaging than he'd expected. Charlet had also come around the table to reiterate his invitation to visit the next day. But Thibault left without a word; he'd retrieved his uniform cap from a nearby shelf, put it firmly on his head and, unsmiling, walked rapidly out of the Minister's office.

When the Army contingent had departed, Minger poured each of them a small shot of brandy, finishing off the bottle.

"Well, that was successful," he said, tipping his glass to the others.

"Mr. Muller, your suggestion was excellent; the General understood it at once. That's what I hope you'll do in these negotiations."

"Colonel Thibault was less impressed," said Haussaman with a chuckle. "He thinks this is his show and didn't appreciate Muller's intervention at all. Did you see him stalk out just now?"

Muller shrugged.

"Well, Colmar's not that far from the Jura Mountains; maybe his Fromageries can cater the Vacherin for the negotiations."

"Ha!" Minger finished his brandy and clapped Muller on the shoulder.

"Nothing like a little rivalry to keep things interesting, right?"

Muller decided against revealing that one of the reasons he'd accepted General Guisan's suggestion of holding the negotiations at Colmar was that his brother-in-law, Christian Francin, a Captain in the French Army, was stationed there. Ideally, he'd have liked to have the negotiations conducted in a Basle hotel out of everyone's sight; but when the General had proffered Colmar as the site, he'd immediately decided to agree. Francin was smart and reliable; he might be a useful resource in the negotiations.

Striding out of the Ministry into the cool October evening, Muller decided this new assignment would be a challenge, but that he would go in holding a few important cards.

Also, he was pleased he'd wangled an invitation to Spiez, and the opportunity–finally–to see Hilde again.

CHAPTER 18

Spiez was situated about an hour East of Bern along the shores of Lake Thun in the Bernese Oberland. Muller had never visited the town before and found himself struck by the stunning view of the Bernese Alps towering above the lake. The large autobus had been nearly empty on the journey from the Ministry and Muller had been able to change seats to get the best view as they approached the town.

The day was sunny, and the mountains were on full view, which, Charlet later told him, wasn't always the case. "We get a lot of misty days with moisture rising from the lake to obscure the peaks," he'd said, "but you're in luck today."

The Army had taken over Spiez Castle itself, a large, stone-clad structure topped by a five-story tower situated on a small peninsular jutting out into the lake. A steepled, Calvinist church occupied the tip of the peninsular. Rolls of barbed wire topped by concertina wire encircled the entire grounds establishing large semi-circular perimeter along the lakefront, and when the shuttle pulled up to a heavily guarded entrance at the wire, Muller could see they were disembarking nearly a kilometer from the Castle itself. The enclosed grounds were a beehive of activity as crews were at work constructing wooden-sided buildings amidst a sea of large tents that had been pitched. Soldiers were scurrying about, and the large complex had the air of barely suppressed chaos.

Muller gave his name to one of the guards and he was directed to a nearby tent outside the wire to await an escort.

He took out a Gitane, offering to one of the guards, who was stationed nearby. The soldier shook his head.

"No smoking on duty," he said with a grin, "but thanks anyway."

Muller lit up.

"Too bad. But tell me soldier, is one of the big tents here for the women's Army unit?"

"You bet, sir," replied the guard. "Two of them, actually–they seem to keep growing–some pretty good-looking girls too," he added, grinning. "It's all hands-off for us soldier boys, though; look don't touch. You'll see their tents when you get closer to the Castle."

The guard leaned toward Muller and added with a wink, "the laundry they have hanging out to dry gives them away."

Muller smiled and, following a young corporal who led him through the grounds to the Castle entrance, he was amused to in fact see female bloomers and other women's paraphernalia hanging on lines strung from one of the tents; the tent sides were tied down and secured, so he couldn't see inside, but at least he knew where he wanted to go before he departed back to Bern.

A guard at the Castle entrance checked Muller's papers before gesturing for them to mount the steps and they pushed open two tall wooden doors to enter. Temporary office warrens had been constructed in the vast entry hall and, with the press of mostly uniformed personnel hurriedly coming and going, the space radiated the same high energy level as the grounds had done.

Muller was led back along a corridor to a suite of offices where the corporal motioned him to enter. Another corporal rose from his desk at the entry and led Muller into a large room with a table and chairs in the center. Glass walls on two sides showed busy offices, while the wall facing him was dominated by two tall windows facing the lake and the mountains beyond.

A group of a half dozen uniformed officers was gathered around the table. Major Charlet rose to greet him, excusing several of the officers.

"Welcome, Mr. Muller," he said, introducing his colleagues who remained and gesturing to a seat at the table with the best view.

"Even as a native Swiss and accustomed to our mountains, this is an especially arresting vista, when the mist doesn't shut it off," Charlet smiled and sat down to begin the briefing.

There followed a lengthy presentation describing tank traps, how to arrange steel girders to protect meadows against gliders, and the characteristics of pill boxes and other military engineering projects. Major Charlet and his colleagues were friendly and informative, but Muller's mind wandered from time to time and he occasionally glanced into the offices on either side of them. One of them, he realized, was occupied by Colonel Thibault, who was ostentatiously ignoring Muller's presence, even though they were clearly visible to one another through the glass walls. At one point, they locked eyes, but Thibault looked away immediately.

After a suitable length of time for the briefing, Muller called a recess, and asked to speak alone to Major Charlet.

They stood at one of the windows overlooking the lake, sharing cigarettes.

"Major, you haven't told me what your command wants the French to do if they enter Switzerland to help us oppose a German invasion. Is there something I'm missing?"

Charlet took a deep drag on his cigarette before responding.

"You weren't supposed to notice that little omission," he finally said, with a wan smile. "You'll have seen that Colonel Thibault has studiously ignored us in here speaking together," he added, inclining his head toward the glass wall where Thibault was working.

"In fact, I did notice," Muller replied. "Is he still annoyed at my comments last evening in Bern?"

"Well, that too," said Charlet, "but mainly he's annoyed at anyone–including me and my staff–who is trying to influence the tactics of a French advance. Thibault spent a year at St. Cyr, the French military academy, and he's decided to defer to whatever the

French propose for their campaign. Not to display our dirty laundry, Mr. Muller, but there are some among us–including most especially me–who find him too much in thrall to the legend of French military infallibility."

Muller smiled. Tactical military disagreements; who'd ever heard of that before? Ha!

"What's your solution, Major Charlet?"

Charlet drew a deep breath before responding.

"I'm under orders not to reveal that, Mr. Muller," he said.

"Well, consider that I'm speaking as the Minister," Muller replied, still smiling. "I'm his representative; would Thibault like me to ask the Minister to put the question to you?"

Charlet eyed Muller suspiciously, then began to grin and motioned Muller toward the chair he'd vacated and sat down next to him.

"Since you put it that way, sir," he said, "I guess I'm obliged to respond–though I hope you'll protect me," he added.

Charlet folded his hands in front of him and began to speak, seemingly relieved at being able, finally, to say what had clearly been on his mind.

"I want the French to commit a motorized battalion to this mission, including a company of their Char B1 tanks," he said. "That's seventeen tanks and about a thousand infantrymen; enough to stall a German cross-Rhine invasion for days; certainly long enough for the French to reinforce them following that first incursion.

"Those Char B1 tanks are monsters, Mr. Muller," Charlet continued, "they weigh over 30 tons each, they're heavily armored and they're armed with both a 75 mm cannon and a 48 mm turret gun–and they're fast, over 28 km/hr; they're really fearsome weapons.

"Think of it, sir," Charlet leaned forward, speaking quietly but urgently. "They could reach the Rhine from the border in no more than four hours. Those 75 mm cannons could cripple the German pontoon bridges and they could engage armor dropped in support of German paratroopers.

"I know you're no military expert, Mr. Muller, but it should be obvious to anyone that a mobile French offensive backed by that kind of firepower would constitute a huge deterrent to the Germans and a major boost to our own resistance."

"Colonel Thibault opposes this idea?" Muller asked.

"He doesn't want us to try to dictate any French tactical deployment ahead of time," Charlet replied. "Let them decide' is his answer–to everything." Charlet pursed his lips, not hiding his annoyance.

"Sir, the whole idea of this new agreement is to coordinate a military response with the French if the Germans attack us; deferring decisions until the attack occurs defeats the whole purpose of the exercise. It's completely the wrong approach."

Charlet pursed his lips, glancing for a moment toward Thibault's office, then he straightened in his seat, clearly regretting his candor.

"Sorry, sir," he said quietly, his voice suddenly reproachful. "I'm speaking out of turn; kindly pay no heed to those remarks."

Muller waved his hand, dismissing Charlet's comment.

"What does the General say?" he asked.

Charlet paused before responding.

"General Guisan has largely kept his own counsel," he said, then paused again before turning to face Muller.

"I think General Guisan and General Gamelin, the French Commander in Chief, have reached an understanding between themselves on what to do," he said quietly. "I don't know what they've decided, but in my opinion, the exercise we're going through is largely ceremonial.

"I think they've both concluded that it's important to get the two sides committed in some more formal way–even if it's in secret. But I think it's meant to serve as a ratification of the understanding the two of them have come to."

"And what would that 'understanding' consist of, Major?" said Muller eyeing the man, who was now plainly uncomfortable and nervously pulled a new cigarette from a crumpled pack, lighting it quickly.

Charlet exhaled a billow of smoke and waved it away.

"That's a question, I can't answer," he said, smiling wanly again.

"Can't or won't?" Muller countered quickly.

"Can't," Charlet replied. "I simply don't know."

Drawing on his cigarette then tapping an ash into the ashtray, he suddenly grinned at Muller.

"I've already told you things I wasn't supposed to," he said lightly. "But that's a question I don't know the answer to."

Muller's gaze was drawn to the tall windows where a sudden breeze off the lake sent the curtains into a dance and scattered papers at the far side of the table where they were seated.

"Is there anything else you weren't supposed to tell me Major Charlet?" he asked returning his smile.

Charlet, chuckled.

"Well, Colonel Thibault told me to block you from any attempt to contact Hildegarde Magandanz while you're here."

The smile on Muller's face suddenly changed to a look of annoyance.

"And why would he do that, Major?"

Charlet shrugged.

"Protecting a special relationship, I suppose," he replied neutrally.

"She's become his right hand in organizing the women's Army program," he added. They spend a lot of time together and seem to get on well."

Charlet paused, then raised his eyebrows in mock surprise.

"Could there be a hint of romance in the air?" he said. "Why else would he tell me to keep you away from her?"

"I don't know, Muller replied quickly, "but I hope that's another order you're prepared to disobey."

Charlet's smile returned.

"Leave it to me," he said, standing and extending his hand.

"I won't ask you why you want to see her," he said. "But I don't think making that happen will jeopardize any state secrets."

Moments later, Muller's escort guided him out of the castle, past the heavily guarded entrance and down the steps, before pointing him to a tent adjoining the one with the hanging laundry that he'd noticed earlier.

"I'm instructed to await you here, sir," the escort said, stepping to one side.

As Muller strode toward the tent, he saw Hilde open the flap and step outside, a perplexed look on her face. He scarcely recognized her, in full grey uniform, her hair in a tight bun beneath a regulation cap.

Suddenly seeing Muller, Hilde's face lit up in a wide smile of surprise and she ran toward him, arms wide and met his embrace, kissing him warmly on the lips, before catching her breath and stepping back, glancing over her shoulder.

"On duty," she muttered before retreating several steps, then taking his hand.

"Oh my," she breathed. "Paul, I can't believe it's really you. It's been so long. Oh my, oh my," she repeated, squeezing his hand and gazing at him. "You're all right; safely back from Romania? I heard about that and was so worried–and there's no place to call you.

"Oh my!"

She squeezed his hand.

"Come," she said, "we can at least grab a quick coffee at the canteen."

"I've been back in Switzerland for ten days," Muller said, "I've tried calling you and left messages. I'm just fine, but I've missed you."

"It's the Army system," Hilde said. "There are no public phones, and the switchboard operators are instructed not to pass along personal messages. We're on active duty here, all day every day–and night too; it's never ending."

"And you're running the women's Army unit?" Muller asked.

Hilde took a deep breath.

"Essentially, yes," she said; "I don't formally have the rank, but yes, I'm running it–albeit under the watchful eyes of the men that have the command responsibility, but no idea about what to do."

They'd entered a tent with tables and chairs scattered around, most of which were vacant. They poured themselves coffees at a counter, then found a table off to the side. They sat close to one another and held hands under the table.

"Oh my," she said again, gazing at Muller and squeezing his hand. "It's been so long, and so much has happened."

Hilde took a deep breath.

"It all began with the mobilization. They'd been planning it for years, of course, but they'd never actually tried to do it before and when the order came down on August 31, it was a mess; units separated, transportation fouled up, assignments fumbled–you name it. But the worst was the women's mobilization.

"They'd never even tried small-scale women's mobilization drills before, and no one had planned for what missions the women were meant to perform once they were called up. There was no real women's command structure and the Army commanders–that is, the men, with all the other problems they were experiencing– simply ordered the women to the kitchens to feed the men and wash the dishes–all fifteen thousand of them. You can imagine how well that worked," she added, shaking her head. "Talk about too many cooks.

"Not only that, there weren't separate women's latrines or changing or sleeping accommodations. Well, it was chaotic and you can imagine all the 'stuff' that went on," she said, smiling ruefully.

"I was exempt from the call up as a Ministry official, so I played no part in it. But a day or so after it began, Minister Minger summoned me to his office–and sitting there with him were General Guisan and Colonel Thibault. They were frantic; they'd mobilized thousands of women, but they'd really never thought about what to do with them.

"Since my office was just down the hall, the Minister decided to call me in; maybe a woman would have some ideas.

"'How do we deal with so many women,' they asked. 'We don't need all these cooks and bottle-washers, but what else do we do with them? And they need separate facilities, or we'll have all kinds of scandals.'"

Hilde rolled her eyes.

"Well, having been pigeon-holed for so long at the Bank, as you well know, Paul, I have a pretty good idea of how to go about breaking shackles. So, I told them. Start by identifying jobs that women are obviously capable of performing as well as male soldiers; not just peeling potatoes, but becoming communications specialists and code writers, dispatchers, planners, supply clerks–Paul, do you know how many things have to be purchased and hauled around every day just to keep an army in the field? Well, the list goes on and on. I sketched this out and then pointed out how this arrangement would also free up men to do the soldiering kinds of jobs the General needed them to do.

"They'd never thought of it that way before," she added.

Muller smiled at Hilde's intensity.

"So, they said 'You do it, then', am I right?

Hilde sighed and nodded.

"And I haven't stopped even to catch my breath since. I've got multiple staffs of people–women–writing up new assignments we can take over, I've had to order engineers to build us facilities–first the tents you see and now actual buildings for us to work and live in–with our own facilities. And every day, I'm fighting with men who treat us like donkeys–or worse.

"But the General's all for it and Phillipe's been wonderful."

"Phillipe?" asked Muller.

"Sorry, I meant Colonel Thibault," Hilde said hastily; "We work very closely together and he's so helpful. You must meet him sometime; I'm sure you'd like him. He's so nice."

I'll bet he's 'so nice', Muller said to himself. Shit. He gritted his teeth.

"I'm sure," he said drily,

"Hilde," he said gazing at her, "when can you get away?"

When can we get married, he wanted to say, feeling giddy being at her side.

"Oh, Paul," she said, her face falling. "I can't leave; we may have to mobilize again soon and we–I–have so much more to do to get ready."

Hilde sighed deeply and leaned forward taking both of his hands in hers.

"I've loved being with you," she said softly, "in every way," she added with a mischievous smile. "But it seems almost like a lifetime ago; I've become consumed by this job–by an opportunity to be an actual *leader*. It's a huge responsibility–and I just can't even think about almost anything else.

"Of course, I miss you, Paul," she said, then took a deep breath. "But for now, this has to be my priority.

"Please don't be angry. This war is upending everything; including us, I'm afraid–at least for now."

Hilde dabbed at her eyes with a napkin, then finished the last of her coffee, and stood, drawing him to her and kissing him again on the lips. Then she he took his arm and smiled up at him as they made their way back toward her tent.

"This isn't what either of us signed up for, Paul," she said, "and I know it sounds trite, but these are the hands we've been dealt.

"We're going to have to get used to them."

Muller found one of the last available seats on the autobus shuttle back to the Ministry in Bern and slumped into it. He paid no attention to the soldier in the window seat next to him who had to shift his position and gave him a dirty look.

As Muller reacted to what Hilde had just told him he felt a profound sense of loneliness descend on him. He'd been so sure; confident that she loved him the way he believed he loved her. He'd missed her during his assignment in Romania and Turkey and she'd been in his mind, especially during the long train ride to Constanta. He'd even purchased the gold jewelry for her at the bazaar in Istanbul, relishing the prospect of an intimate moment to present the gift–and hopefully seal an engagement.

But instead, she'd given him, well, if not a cold shoulder, something very close to it.

We're apart; that's the reality, the hands we've been dealt by the war.

Shit!

And there was 'Phillipe;' bloody Clark Gable. Had he in fact stolen her heart?

It was a depressing bus ride back to Bern.

CHAPTER 19

Muller had booked a late afternoon train to Colmar. Changing at Basle, he'd made the long trek to the French SNCF system at the other side of the terminal, stopping for a quick dinner at a restaurant. As the French border was only a few kilometers off, Customs clearance took place on the Colmar departure platform, but it was perfunctory–surprisingly so with a war on, Muller thought to himself–and he easily found his compartment for the short journey.

De-training at Colmar less than an hour later, he'd been met by a French corporal, who drove him to the French Army Command Center, where a deferential lieutenant welcomed him. Muller's Ambassadorial rank had been restored and when he presented his papers, the lieutenant immediately sprang to attention and saluted him, then hurriedly checked his name off a list, and summoned his escort.

Muller fixed the lieutenant with a stern look,

"Lieutenant, my office dispatched a message requesting that Captain Francin be made available to confer with me this evening upon my arrival."

His office had done no such thing, of course, but Muller couldn't think of a better way to find Francin, so he decided to pull rank.

The lieutenant was disconcerted and began frantically searching the pages on his clipboard, then his logbook.

"Sir…ah… Mr. Ambassador, sir…I don't see any notation here."

He looked nervously at the escort then back to Muller, uncertain what to do.

"You have no record of such a message, Lieutenant?" Muller raised his voice.

"No sir…I don't see anything…"

"Call your superior officer, Lieutenant, and see that Captain Francin is notified and sent to my quarters right away.

"Yes sir," replied the Lieutenant, obviously relieved to find a solution.

"Right now, sir," he said as he reached for the phone.

Muller was led across what appeared to be the parade ground, now converted into a veritable sea of mud from the seemingly-incessant rain, and entered a low, stucco building with a brick entryway. His escort led him up a flight of stairs and opened the door to a large, well-appointed corner suite with overstuffed furniture and several Persian rugs tastefully adding color and warmth. Muller noticed what appeared to be a well-stocked bar in one corner.

"I hope you'll be comfortable here, sir," said his escort. "I'll come at 7 AM to escort you to the officer's mess for breakfast."

Muller strolled through the suite, smiling to himself.

Rank did have its privileges.

He had just poured himself a whiskey when there was a rap at his door. Opening it, Muller found Christian Francin standing before him with a perplexed smile on his face.

"Christ, Muller," he said, extending his hand, "what the Hell is this about?"

Muller drew him into the suite and gave him a quick hug.

"'Report at once to the VIP Suite at the request of the Swiss Ambassador,'" continued Francin. "Some young lieutenant called the BOQ frantically trying to reach me and order me over here. Ha!" Francin grinned and returned the hug.

"So, now you're now an Ambassador," he said, bowing deferentially, "and occupying the Generals' suite here on a French Army base. There must be serious business afoot, Muller, so pour me some of that whiskey you're holding and tell me what's going on."

Muller offered Francin a glass at the bar, poured a healthy slug, then picked up the bottle of Dewars and gestured to chairs where they could take a seat, putting the bottle down within easy reach.

"Santé,"

They clinked glasses.

"I can't do that," Muller said smiling.

"Or," he added, knowing Francin would understand, "as you told me last summer, 'if you don't already know, I can't tell you.'"

Francin, frowned, then smiling thinly, nodded his head.

"Fair enough, Muller," he said. "There is a war going on–or so they say," he added, pursing his lips–"so we each have secrets to keep, I guess."

"There *is* a war going on," Muller replied. "I've been working at propping up neutrals like Romania and Turkey–which I can't tell you much about either; but what about you, here at the frontlines, facing off daily against your German enemy on the other side of the Rhine?"

"Pfff," Francin replied with a disdainful exhale.

"I've been marching soldiers around our parade ground, making sure our guns are well-oiled, and enjoying the last of the fraises des bois for desserts. Which is another way of saying that I haven't been doing anything, and it's damned frustrating.

"You remember the big parade down the Champs Elysées last summer, Muller, showing off the most powerful military machine in the world; well, that machine hasn't done anything since then; it just sat on its ass while Hitler's army proceeded to crush Poland. We haven't lifted a finger."

Muller refilled their glasses.

"I did notice actually," he said lightly, "along with the rest of the world," he added provocatively. "Some of us thought that the

French Army could have marched straight to Berlin while Hitler's Army was a thousand miles away in the East."

"Don't even get me started, Muller," said Francin, angrily.

"Look," he said, "a week into the war, General Gamelin ordered an advance against Germany. But instead of a massive attack, it was just a small probe by a couple of divisions."

Francin paused long enough to accept one of Muller's Gitanes, exhaling a billow of smoke before continuing.

"The Germans immediately retreated, and our units advanced nearly 20 kilometers into Germany, right up to their Westwall defense–which is no Maginot Line, by the way. Anyway, they overran a couple of small towns that were booby-trapped and began taking casualties. German snipers and scattered machine gunners began taking potshots at them, which apparently unnerved some of the commanders. Then they encountered a minefield and halted for a full day to await a truckload of pigs to send out ahead of them and detonate the mines.

"But then they just stopped and began digging defensive trenches to hold the ground that they'd gained–against almost no resistance. And there they stayed, not trying to advance another kilometer for three whole weeks until, at the end of September, Gamelin, somehow convinced the Germans were planning to attack, ordered the entire force to abandon even that little bit of territory we'd conquered, and retreat back to the Maginot Line.

"We were back where we'd been when the war began a month ago–and with nothing to show for it."

Francin took a large swallow of his whiskey.

"As you can tell, my friend," he said with a sardonic smile, "I'm deeply ashamed of what we've done–or more accurately I suppose, what we *haven't* done–just sitting here on our fat asses."

Muller leaned forward to stub out his butt in the ashtray on the table between them.

"So how should a diplomat from a neighboring neutral state– that might need to depend upon a speedy French response to a German attack across the Rhine–react to what you've just said?"

Francin sat back in his seat, gazing at Muller."

"You know I can't answer that question, Paul," he replied softly, "not even for my brother-in-law."

"I'm not asking you to reveal your tactics," Muller replied; "I want your opinion about French nerve."

Muller leaned toward Francin, hands together, elbows on his knees.

"Everyone knows there's a risk the Germans will invade France from the East by attacking us, bypassing the Maginot Line and heading right for Paris. It's a subject polite people avoid dwelling on because it raises uncomfortable issues that they'd rather not talk about. But it's there, in plain sight, and everyone knows it. I assume that the French military has a plan to deal with that contingency; I don't claim to know what that plan is and I'm not asking you to reveal it–if you even know, which you may not.

"No," Muller went on, his voice low and his gaze intense, "my question is different; it's whether the French command and the

French government have the *nerve* to react aggressively to a threatened–or even an actual–attack on Switzerland that would place a German Army on a path to invade France."

Muller paused.

"Will that powerful military machine you described a moment ago–and which we both saw on display when it paraded down the Champs Elysée back in July–have the will to spring into action if that were to happen?"

Francin didn't respond. He gazed back at Muller and sighed, then he extracted Gitanes for both of them from Muller's pack and accepted Muller's light.

"I have no reason to think they won't," he said finally, speaking slowly, before pausing again and shaking his head, clearly groping for the right words.

"But I understand your question, Muller; our failure to come to the defense of Poland raises doubts about our resolve. So, your inquiry is fair–albeit a bit awkward."

Francin paused again, the leaned forward and began speaking more confidently.

"But Muller, of course our military is well aware of the risk you describe and of course they've prepared for how to respond to that 'contingency', as you put it."

Francin smiled at Muller.

"Still, I'm not revealing any secrets when I tell you that our plans are dependent upon the actual circumstances of any German attack that might be launched. Is it a surprise attack or will we see it coming? Can we gain control of the air over the battlefield? Is a German attack in Switzerland a feint to draw us away from the Western front? Is it in fact coordinated with a separate attack in the West? And so on; there are a whole host of obvious and wholly legitimate questions that would need to be evaluated when and if an attack were to occur.

"So, I repeat, I have no reason to think we won't respond to an attack; Switzerland is not Poland, Muller; it's not a thousand miles away. No, the risk that would arise for France from an attack on Switzerland would be immediate and compelling. So, I think you can safely assume that our military would respond nearly instantaneously to a German attack on you."

Muller replied sharply. "But even after you mobilized all the Army reserves when war was declared in September, we didn't see any maneuvers or exercises along our border to defend against that risk, or to send a message to the Germans that you were ready for it."

"Or did we miss something?" Muller added.

Muller had no idea if any defensive maneuvers had been taken or not, but he was determined to press Francin, whom he hoped would confide in him—at least within limits.

"Muller, you're being a pain," Francin replied. "Defending against a German attack on Switzerland was not exactly the highest priority for our General Mobilization. Come on; you know that; it wasn't the time for maneuvers or exercises, for Christ's sake."

Francin tone was impatient.

"Muller, you're sitting right now–right this minute–in the headquarters of the French 8th Army; the force with responsibility for defending the entire French border North of Grenoble– including our borders with both Germany across the Rhine from us, and with Switzerland to our South. You ought to have some confidence that my command is ready to do its job if circumstances should arise requiring us to react."

Muller smiled at Francin, as he refilled their drinks, and clinked their glasses companionably.

"Right," he said; "of course I do. You built Maginot fortifications along your entire Rhine frontier with Germany. But you stopped building at the border with Switzerland. So, to be fair; that sector presents a different set of military options, and one that might–just might–require some maneuvers and exercises by the forces you've got stationed here on the Rhine, in the event of an attack on us."

"That was my point, Francin," Muller grinned. "I'm not impugning your command; I'm just probing a bit to understand better how–what's the right word? *Aggressively*, I guess–how *aggressively* you sense your superiors would leap to our defense if the Germans attacked us."

"Ha!" Francin responded, lifting his glass to Muller's.

"They can't *wait*; I can hardly hold them *back*," Francin rolled his eyes and inclined his head in mimicry.

"Shit, Muller, I haven't the faintest idea," he added, his face now serious, "nor does anyone else; you know that, for Christ's sake."

Muller grinned, and sat back into his chair, acknowledging Francin's point, but then still grinning, leaned forward.

"I thought this is where you were going to tell me that the first reaction to any German attack on us would be for your command to unleash a company of your big Char1B tanks across the border to come to our rescue."

Francin guffawed.

"Paul Muller, who do you think you're kidding? You don't know a goddam thing about our Char 1B tanks, for goodness sake; what are you trying to tell me?"

"Well, I know they're 30-ton behemoths and they've got both a 75 mm cannon and a turret machine gun; they're heavily armored and they're fast–28 klics, right?

"Fearsome weapons, I'm told."

Muller grinned at Francin and they both laughed.

"So that's how the Swiss expect to be rescued from a German invasion, is that it, Muller? That's what you're looking for?"

They grinned again at one another.

Muller shrugged.

"You're right, Francin; I don't know any more about your Char 1B tanks than I've just told you. But someone in the Swiss Army thinks they'd be a very effective weapon to repel a German invasion; I have no idea if he's correct or not, and certainly I'm not in any position to demand–or even suggest–that's what the French should do."

Muller spread his hands and nodded in mock deference toward Francin

"But to a simple Ambassador," he added, "it does seem like a pretty appealing response."

"Pfff." Francin replied rolling his eyes.

Muller was amused. The French have an entire vocabulary of grunts, 'pffs', and other dismissive sounds and gestures that unmistakably convey scorn for something just said and with which they disagree. Even as a fluent, nearly native, French speaker, Muller had never mastered the skill to project disdain this way; but he certainly understood when it was being invoked–as it was here.

"Don't just 'pfff' me, Francin," he said, chuckling. "Come on, speak."

Francin smiled broadly.

"Muller, somebody's been watching too many movies," he said; "the cavalry's not always the answer."

"So, no tanks?" asked Muller in an innocent tone.

Francin smirked back at him.

"You want to talk about tanks, Muller?" Francin said. "All right then; let me tell you about a real issue that's got our tank people staying up at night worrying."

Muller looked at Francin quizzically.

"Is there any more whiskey?" Francin asked. "This subject requires another glass at least."

Muller strode to the bar and returned, this time with a bottle of Johnny Walker, and poured them each a large slug.

"Christ, Muller, we should have started with this stuff," Francin said, sniffing it, then taking a large sip and sighing contentedly.

"Much better," he said.

"All right, now, about those tanks, Muller." Francin sat forward on his seat.

"We got a retired French General assigned as an observer to the Polish command in Warsaw and he had a bird's eye view of what actually happened during the German invasion. He somehow escaped being captured, and since he got back here, he's been circulating a report describing *Wehrmacht* tactics that he says necessitates drastically changing our French Army rules of engagement–especially the way we deploy our tanks.

"It's caused a real uproar," Francin continued.

"Is this what people are calling 'Blitzkrieg?'" Muller asked, lighting their Gitanes. "I've seen that term used in recent news reports about the German attack, but I'm not sure what it really means."

Francin nodded, exhaling smoke and waving it away.

"It's become the new description people are using.

"*Blitzkrieg*" he repeated; "it even sounds scary doesn't it?"

"Well, Muller, what it refers to–and what this General of our is describing in his report–is the German tactic of using spearheads of massed armor–tanks mainly, with some motorized infantry and artillery–to slice through an enemy's line–and then just keep going. Instead of stopping to wait for the infantry to catch up, they proceed to wreak havoc behind the lines, attacking supply lines and undefended positions in the rear, and creating chaotic conditions that undermine the enemy's ability to resist the attack. That chaos enables the infantry following in the tanks' wake to exploit the breakthrough and deal with pockets of resistance that the tanks bypassed. Then, as the by-now confused and demoralized enemy tries to fall back and regroup, they proceed to attack their new position and repeat the whole process again.

"According to our General, the Germans used this tactic over and over against Polish forces with devastating effect. He describes it as a new form of mechanized warfare that capitalizes on tactical mobility and encourages frontline commanders to exploit opportunities on the spot instead of awaiting orders.

"And," Francin added, with a note of drama in his voice, "they coordinate the whole process by voice communication. Everyone can talk to one another via short wave radio systems *in every tank.*"

Francin paused long enough to take a large swallow of whiskey.

"That's not the way the French use their tanks?" Muller asked. This was new territory to him, but fascinating and, he thought to himself, maybe pertinent to the question of what kind of French support the Swiss might expect in the event of German attack. So, he refilled Francin's glass and listened closely.

"No," Francin shook his head; "it's very different.

255

"Our rules of engagement employ tanks mainly as armored support for our infantry, providing firepower and rallying points on the battlefield–a little like rooks on a chess board. The infantry is our main weapon–along with our fortifications, of course, especially the Maginot Line. We don't treat tanks as offensive weapons the way the Germans seems to be doing. And what is bothering some of us is that we couldn't do that even if we wanted to, because we don't have the right communications systems in place."

Francin eyed his drink, but then apparently thought better of it and instead leaned forward intently toward Muller.

"Those big Char 1B tanks you've fallen in love with don't have radios, Muller," he said, his eyes boring into Muller's; "they can't talk to one another. *They're fitted with radio telegraphy sets that use Morse Code.*" He hissed the words, then paused and decided to take a swallow of his whiskey after all.

"Think about trying to tap out messages on a telegraph key while you're careening around on a battlefield." Francin made a face.

"Oh, they've got pre-coded shortcut messages like, 'advance' or 'turn 100 meters left', things like that. In fact, the manual presupposes tanks will be directed to fixed locations to await orders as commanders in the rear manage the battle and deploy tanks to support the infantry as it trudges along or hunkers down to resist an enemy attack.

"It's not crazy; these are not stupid people. They've written a whole manual of tactical exercises maximizing use of tanks as pillars of strength to support French infantrymen–the centerpiece of French military strength.

"But Muller," he said, speaking intently, "it's a completely different concept of warfare; it assumes largely static battles–not necessarily the trench warfare of the Great War, mind you–but nothing like the fast-moving mobile tactics that this Blitzkrieg strategy seems to have introduced."

Francin pushed his drink away, but reached for another cigarette, this time flashing his own lighter for both of them.

"French tanks really can't talk to one another?" Muller asked.

"Tanks are noisy," Francin said; "the engines are loud and when they fire the cannon and machine gun it's even worse. Nobody can hear a thing. So, what's our solution? Use Morse Code; it has its own shortcomings, sure, but at least it doesn't get drowned out by the noise a tank makes. And anyway, our tanks are meant to be used as set pieces, not move around a lot on the battlefield; they're just meant to sit there and follow orders from headquarters. Morse Code transmissions can accomplish that."

"So what's the reaction of the French Command to this Blitzkrieg report by the General?" Muller asked.

"Apparently he's been awarded a medal and packed off to a minor post in the Army's Paris command," Francin replied.

"That's all?" Muller said. "Really?"

"General Gamelin is said to have sniffed at it," Francin replied, "much as I did a moment ago. 'Pffff.', he said–or something equally insightful."

"Meaning?"

"Meaning, Muller, that we are the French Army, not a pack of bloody Poles who panicked in the face of a German attack. We are the mightiest armed force in the world, trained and equipped to defend ourselves against any attack that *the Boche* can mount against us.

"Call it Blitzkrieg or whatever you want, Muller; Gamelin and his commanders are supremely confident of crushing it if given the opportunity."

"Ha!" he said, slapping the table with his open hand, then standing to leave.

"There you have it."

Francin stood and strode a little uncertainly to the door.

"That's my bedtime story about tanks, Muller" he said.

"Sweet dreams."

CHAPTER 20

The next morning, Muller was escorted to the officer's mess at the Base's BOQ, again trudging across the muddy parade ground, an army umbrella scarcely able to protect him from the downpour that seemed to have been going on for more than a week. He was directed to a private room and found Colonel Thibault and Major Charlet looking at menus, evidently just having arrived themselves. They greeted one another and shook hands perfunctorily. A uniformed waiter arrived and took their orders, Muller, seating himself and waving off the menu, ordered Croissants, with breakfast baguettes and cheese and a large café au lait.

Thibault eyed Muller from across the table.

"Major Charlet and I arrived a little late at the BOQ last evening, and we intended to invite you for a drink and a short discussion, but we were informed you had been assigned a VIP General's suite and were conferring with a French Army Captain."

Thibault's tone was civil but distant–and, Muller decided, deliberately condescending; not exactly the way to begin a day when they would be expected to conduct important joint negotiations with the French.

Well, screw you Clark Gable, he thought to himself.

"Colonel, you arranged for me to travel here separately, and I had no indication that we were to meet last evening; had I known, I certainly would have accommodated you. And, actually, I thought my quarters were appropriate since, as you well know, being the Swiss ambassador, I out-rank even senior military officers."

He didn't add, 'including you Colonel.'

Instead, he merely shrugged.

"Captain Francin is my brother-in-law and a good friend. Since nothing else was on the agenda for last evening, I invited him to my quarters to catch up on family and relax ahead of our negotiations today.

"Is there some problem with that Colonel?"

Thibault grunted, and paid close attention to cracking the soft-boiled egg he'd ordered.

"Well, it was just curious," he said, still attending to his egg.

Major Charlet stole a conspiratorial smile at Muller before returning his attention to spooning jam on a croissant.

At that moment, after a brisk knock on the door, two uniformed French officers entered the room, and strode smiling, toward Colonel Thibault, with hands outstretched and claps on the shoulder; they were clearly well-acquainted.

They stood, and after greeting one another, Thibault turned toward Muller.

"Colonel Garteiser and Captain de Longvilliers, let me introduce Ambassador Muller, whom I believe you know will join us today."

The two Frenchmen bowed toward Muller, who smiled and inclined his head in acknowledgement.

"Please accompany us to the meeting room," said Garteiser; "there is ample breakfast and coffee for us, and we can begin our discussions even more promptly."

Garteiser was a slender man with a few dark strands of hair pulled over his nearly bald head. His smile seemed to come easily below dark eyes and arched eyebrows, his sharp cheekbones softened by a round, clean-shaven chin. He fell into step with Muller as they strode back across the parade ground to the stucco VIP building, skirting puddles, this time entering a large, windowless ground floor conference room with a sideboard heaped with baguettes, pastries, and cheeses.

After helping themselves to pastries on china plates and filling large, sturdy mugs with dark coffee, Garteiser guided Muller to a seat at the conference table. The others took seats on the other side of the table and began eating and chatting among themselves. Muller sensed this was not by accident and that it offered Garteiser an opportunity to speak more privately to Muller.

Muller found him an easy conversationalist and they chatted easily and comfortably with one another.

After a pause, Garteiser inclined his head toward Muller and, even though smiling, fixed him with a direct gaze that announced, without his saying so, that they were getting down to business.

"You will note, Ambassador Muller, that there is no one on our French delegation who is not in uniform," he said quietly. "That is by direction of General Gamelin himself," he added. "The French Government is not to be involved in these discussions.

"Can you advise us about the role you, as a civilian–albeit with Ambassadorial rank–will play in the discussions we are to have with your military representatives today?"

Muller decided not to glance in the direction of Colonel Thibault, and, instead, replied directly, speaking quietly but firmly.

"Colonel, I assume you have been notified that I am appointed to participate today as the representative of the Swiss Ministry of Military Affairs, in support of its mission to defend the Swiss nation."

"But you are a civilian, Ambassador Muller," Garteiser said. "Our negotiations deal with military issues–and highly sensitive ones too; I'm not sure what perspective you would bring to the table."

Garteiser took a deep breath, evidently uneasy.

"I don't mean to be rude, Mr. Ambassador, but I believe I'm bound to inquire."

Muller smiled. He'd bet that Thibault had put Garteiser up to this 'inquiry.'

"Actually, I'm pleased that you asked, Colonel Garteiser," Muller said easily, noting that the other men across the table had stopped speaking and were listening closely to what he and Garteiser were saying.

"As you well know Colonel, Switzerland is a neutral state in the current conflict; preserving our neutrality–both in form and in substance–is the highest priority of both General Guisan and Minister Minger. My role here is to ensure that our neutral status is protected in the defensive agreement we are both proposing to enter.

"The military tactics that are to be considered by you and the Swiss military officials accompanying me today are of course important and will be of considerable interest to us," he went on, still smiling. "Colonel Thibault will have charge of that subject for us.

"My role is to determine if the substance of any agreement is satisfactory in adequately preserving Swiss interests, or not–and hence, whether it will be acceptable to Minister Minger and to General Guisan–or not."

Then, just to turn the screws a little, he gestured toward Thibault across the table.

"I'm sure Colonel Thibault will readily confirm our respective roles; he will evaluate the military content of any potential agreement, while it is reserved to me to pass judgment on whether it is consistent with the Swiss national interest."

Eyes all turned to Thibault who pursed his lips and sat back in this chair.

Thibault paused a moment, then nodded.

"That's essentially correct, Colonel," he said "But…" his voice trailed off, obviously aware of the spot Muller had put him on.

"But yes," Thibault reluctantly added. "of course; we'll certainly… coordinate our roles, Colonel. As I had indicated earlier to you," he finished, lamely.

No one was fooled; Thibault had sought to undermine Muller, but he'd suddenly been firmly subordinated by Muller's response to Garteiser's seemingly innocent inquiry. Muller, not Thibault, would decide if an agreement was acceptable to the Swiss.

"Well, then," said Garteiser, "let's get started, shall we?"

At his signal, French Army staff suddenly appeared, placing manila folders before each of the participants, setting up a tripod stand with pulldown sheets alongside a blackboard with multi-colored chalk in the grooves beneath the slate. No one, Muller mused, could accuse the French Army of being unprepared–at least for efficient briefings.

Muller was assigned a seat, as head of the Swiss delegation, next to Garteiser for the French; Colonel Thibault and Major Charlet were seated to their left and Captain de Longvilliers and other French officers opposite them on the other side of the table.

There proceeded nearly three hours of intensive and–Muller was pleased to conclude–detailed exchanges of views on potential French responses to various German invasion scenarios. It was evident that the French had given the threat of German invasion through Switzerland serious and highly professional attention. Nine French infantry divisions populated the 8th Army positions along the Rhine, with a heavy concentration at Colmar on the Southern end that would be the first rapid response to a German threat to cross the Rhine and invade Switzerland; The French confirmed, for example, the prospect of being able to reach defensive positions in Switzerland within four hours after the start of hostilities along the Swiss border and the two delegations proceeded to exchanged in-depth commentary focusing on the element of surprise in any attack, prospects for establishing air cover, tactics for resisting German pontoon bridge maneuvers and a host of similar issues.

Muller noted that both Colone Thibault and Major Charlet engaged with their French counterparts knowledgably and forcefully; they clearly knew their briefs.

During breaks and when the others were deeply engaged in tactical discussions, Muller discreetly looked through his manila folder, finally coming across an actual draft of the proposed Swiss–French Agreement itself. He was annoyed that Thibault hadn't provided it sooner. Still, reading it he was pleased to see that it was short and understated. But he saw things he wanted to add, and penciled some notes to himself in the margins.

Shortly after noontime, Garteiser declared a recess for lunch and led them across the hall to a private dining room, where a table had been laid out for them, with a white linen tablecloth, starched white napkins, and places set for six, attended by shiny silverware and multiple wine glasses; low displays of autumn flowers and foliage completed an elegant presentation.

Place cards assigned seats in the same order as in the conference room, except there was a vacant seat between Garteiser and Muller at head of the table. Muller was just bending to read the name when the dining room door opened and a tall, uniformed French officer strode into the room, his chest bearing rows of medals, and a gleaming, round silver helmet on his head, bearing a General's insignia.

Everyone at the table stood quickly to attention and saluted, except Muller, who stood too, but clasped his hands in front of him.

"General Antoine Besson, Commander in Chief, French 8th Army." Garteiser announced. "Welcome sir."

General Besson returned the salutes, then removing his helmet he strode toward the table.

"At ease, gentlemen," he said, with a smile.

He had a large head, Muller noted, with a high forehead and lantern jaw, and a long, straight aquiline nose perched above a bushy white mustache. He carried himself with ease and had a confident bearing about him; a man accustomed to command, Muller thought.

Besson shook hands with Muller and Garteiser, then took his chair between them, conversing in friendly terms. When, finally, after multiple courses and three wines, cigars were offered. A bottle of brandy was placed on the table with snifters and the wait staff disappeared.

Besson took the brandy, pouring generous helpings in each snifter and passing them around the table.

"Santé," he offered. "Let us hope for a formal agreement with Switzerland that we are never going to have to invoke."

The men toasted and the General continued to speak.

"We do think it advisable to formally agree on terms governing our Army's operations in the event we find ourselves obliged to take actions against Germany that involve occupying Swiss territory," he said. "Forward planning to avoid misunderstandings is vital, especially given the proximity of the enemy and the potential that we might need to take pre-emptive action there in the event of a credible threat to our interests.

"So, I hope you gentlemen have progressed today in achieving those goals."

Besson turned his head, first toward Muller then to Garteiser and smiled.

"Well, sir," Garteiser hesitated, then continued. "We have had productive military discussions this morning, mainly at the tactical level."

Colonel Thibault then broke in, speaking in a deferential tone.

"From the Swiss Army's perspective, we've been reassured by the range of options the French command is considering in the event of a German attack,"

"We have great respect for the French Army's experience," he concluded, bowing in Besson's direction.

Garteiser then proceeded to summarize some of the tactical options that they'd discussed in the morning session and Besson nodded in apparent approval.

Muller became increasingly uncomfortable with this show of military bonhomie.

"General Besson," Muller broke into Garteiser's remarks, "I think there is considerably more to this negotiation than planning for potential French rules of engagement; that's certainly part of it. But more importantly, we must agree upon how to align Swiss and French decision-making in the event of an actual, or threatened, German invasion of Switzerland. If that were to happen, sir, vital Swiss as well as French interests must be taken into account. Any agreement between us must address those issues."

Besson turned to face Muller.

"And what are those issues, Ambassador Muller?"

Besson looked impatient and his tone was peremptory.

"First, sir, any agreement we reach must provide that it comes into effect only upon the order of General Guisan. There is to be no French deployment on Swiss territory except upon his direct order requesting French assistance under the agreement."

Muller could sense the tension in the room rise–a kind of collective sucking in of breath around the table. Speaking like that to a General?

"Second," Muller continued, "while any French troops deployed in Switzerland will remain under the command of French officers, overall strategic command of a Swiss front will remain in the hands of General Guisan. Among other things," he added, "that includes French agreement to withdraw from Swiss territory if ordered to do so by General Guisan."

Muller had intended to continue, adding a warning about the need for respecting Swiss neutrality. But he was pre-empted when Besson slammed his fist on the table.

"Enough," he fairly shouted the word.

"Out!" he ordered gesturing to the others around the table.

"Now! Leave us."

The men hurriedly stood and filed rapidly out the door without saying a word.

When the door closed behind them and they were alone, Besson's face softened into a smile and he pointed to Muller's cigarette case that lay on the table between them.

"May I?" Besson inquired. "I keep trying to quit, but I'm afraid it's hopeless."

Muller offered a Gitane and a light for them both.

Exhaling, Besson's smile grew wider.

"I really quite envy you, Ambassador Muller," he began. "Here you are, sitting in French Army headquarters, surrounded by a bunch of uniformed and self-styled experts in French military operations–including me, the senior commanding officer, and a General, no less–and you, the only civilian in the room, proceed to blurt out–and rather bluntly, I might say–the only issues that really matter.

"And you got them right, as well," he added.

Besson paused to tap his cigarette ash in a nearby ash tray.

"The agreement that General Gamelin, our Commander-in-Chief, will sign alongside General Guisan, your Swiss Commander-in-Chief, must contain precisely the language you just articulated. And I will see to it that the language is inserted," he continued.

"But as I suspect you very well understand, Ambassador Muller, what's written on a piece of paper–even one signed by such august officials as General Gamelin and General Guisan–may not necessarily determine what either side may, in the event, decide to do."

Besson sighed, tapped his cigarette again and with his other hand slid his brandy snifter toward him, gazing at it, as if seeking inspiration.

"There's a reason there's no French civilian in this negotiation playing a role equivalent to what you're doing for the Swiss side," he went on. "It's because, unlike the Swiss–where you seem confident of representing common interests of both your military leadership and your Ministry–we, on the French side, are unable to find common interests either in our military leadership or in our government, and hence are reduced to conducting this negotiation with you by a divided military and without even the knowledge–let alone the participation–of the French government."

Both men stubbed out their butts and each took a small sip of brandy.

Muller sat quietly, paying close attention, content to permit Besson to continue, as he then proceeded to do.

"I'm confident, Ambassador Muller, that you've been told that I assumed this command only in mid-October. My predecessor, as you doubtless also know, was General Georges, a distinguished senior officer in the French military hierarchy. But–and there's no reason you'd know this–General Georges and General Gamelin cannot abide one another. They're two scorpions in a bottle, if I can use that analogy; I'm afraid it fits, in this case.

"They came to loggerheads on a host of issues, so Gamelin kicked Georges upstairs to the role of Commander Eastern Front– whatever that means, he doesn't have anyone reporting to him anymore–and appointed me as Commander of the Eighth Army which, has full responsibility for this sector–including, most importantly for our purposes, the Franco-Swiss border.

"I'm junior to both Gamelin and Georges in the pecking order," Besson went on, "but I actually get along with both of them–often by just not telling them what I'm doing."

Besson smiled broadly.

"Which is what I'm proceeding to do here today, and in this agreement we're discussing," he said.

"Fortunately, Gamelin can keep it out of the hands of our government," he continued.

"I don't know how familiar you are with French politics, Mr. Ambassador, but we have two scorpions in a bottle there too: our Premier, Edouard Daladier, a corpulent Socialist who clawed his way to power from humble beginnings, and Paul Reynaud, our finance minister–and so much more, I should add–who is trim and lithe, enormously wealthy and staunchly conservative. They detest one another," Besson went on. "Oh, and each has a powerful and deeply ambitious mistress, and they detest one another too."

"You smile," he said to Muller. "But this is Paris, we're speaking of; these things matter."

"Anyway, if word of this negotiation were to leak, one of the two men would strongly support it and the other bitterly oppose it; that's what they do–oppose one another. So, the issue would immediately become a part of their political duel and any prospects for addressing it on the merits would go up in clouds of public recriminations.

"That's why Gamelin is keeping it from them; and he's actually rather good at doing that."

Besson's smile was a bit cynical, Muller thought.

"But Colonel Garteiser has Gamelin's confidence, Ambassador Muller," Besson added. "We'll make a deal today and he'll sell it to Gamelin. You can be confident that the agreement we reach will be signed by Gamelin and will become part of the French Army's rules of engagement."

Besson reached for his snifter, clinked it against Muller's, and downed the last of his brandy, wiping the back of his hand across his lips. It was evident he'd finished with what he'd wanted to say.

Muller took a moment before responding.

"But you're also telling me that, whatever the document says, the actual French reaction to a German attack on Switzerland–or even just the threat of attack–may not follow the script we agree on."

Besson shrugged.

"Ambassador Muller, I expect your General Guisan–and your Minister, as well–understand the situation quite well," he said, and leaned toward Muller.

"They've made the decision that, given the seriousness of the German threat, it's in Switzerland's interest to formally engage with the French–but only on the military plane; neither government to be involved in any way–and to limit that engagement in the ways you just articulated: a defensive alliance triggered only at the behest of General Guisan and one over which he retains strategic command.

"It's a smart move," he went on.

"But I'll wager they're also clever enough to understand that if the eventuality should ever in fact arise, it will likely do so in unexpected ways and spawn unforeseen reactions–on the part of both nations."

Besson sat back in his chair and grinned broadly at Muller.

"We'll do the best we can here today, Ambassador Muller," he said. "And hope for the best." He stood and offered his hand.

"Now, as we invite the others back in, please look suitably chastised."

CHAPTER 21

It didn't take long to complete the negotiations. General Besson took charge and led the French team in producing a document that was specific enough to commit the two nations to a defensive alliance in the event of a German invasion of Switzerland and incorporate Muller's demands for Swiss overall command over any Swiss battlefield, but still general enough to meet the French insistence on deferring tactical commitments until details of an actual attack were known.

After Muller declared himself satisfied, he exchanged handshakes with General Besson and Colonel Garteiser.

"I'm appointing Colonel Thibault to deliver the Swiss text to General Guisan," he said rather grandly, continuing to exercise de-facto chairmanship of the delegation and–deliberately–reducing Thibault to the role of delivery boy.

He relished Thibault's look of annoyance as he was obliged to agree.

To his surprise, when the meeting broke up, Colonel Garteiser offered to drive him to Basle to catch the train back to Bern and he readily accepted.

Thibault and Charlet would be left to fend for themselves; fine, he decided.

The short trip was uneventful, traffic was light in the wet weather, and he and Garteiser passed the time in easy conversation; Muller had assumed Garteiser had some message he wanted to convey privately, but he offered nothing out of the ordinary; Muller found him an engaging companion and decided that he liked the man.

Then, after driving into the large entry to the Basle station, Garteiser stopped the car and turned to Muller.

"These are dangerous times, Ambassador Muller," he said quietly, his face serious, and handed Muller his card. "It might become useful in the days ahead for us to be able to communicate with one another discreetly. Here are my coordinates; I have yours from our security people."

Muller took the card and returned Garteiser's businesslike glance.

"I expect you may be right, Colonel," he replied. Then he smiled and shook Garteiser's hand before exiting the car.

Arriving back in Bern, Muller went straight to the Ministry and found Minger and Haussaman awaiting him in the Minister's office. Muller could see the two men were deep in conversation, heads close to one another and speaking intently.

He hesitated, then rapped quietly on the door to announce his presence.

The two men looked up and Minger stood to welcome him.

"A successful negotiation?"

"Yes sir," Muller replied.

He took a seat and proceeded to describe the events that had transpired, including his tête-à-tête with General Besson.

"Colonel Thibault has the only copy of the document," he concluded. "But I'm confident that you'll find it satisfactory for General Guisan to sign for the Swiss side."

Then he added, "Oh, and all the drafts were destroyed in the interests of strict secrecy".

Minger sat back in his seat, taking an Ambassador from his cigarette case, and offering it to the others. Muller provided his lighter.

"All right," Minger concluded. "It's a step we needed to take. I hope it doesn't somehow backfire on us.

"And let's hope we never need to invoke it," he added, then turned to Muller with a quizzical look.

"But General Besson's willingness to air some of the French dirty laundry with you is intriguing. What message was he sending us do you think?"

Muller had pondered this question himself, staring out the rain-spattered window of his compartment on the train ride returning to Bern.

"I concluded that it was a mixed signal, Mr. Minger," he replied, tapping a cigarette ash in the ashtray.

"It was certainly an admission that the French decision-making arrangements are very fractured and messy–so we shouldn't assume we can pin down the French government's response to a German threat to Switzerland no matter what any signed document might say. But he was also saying, in effect, don't worry; we're in charge here and we know what we're doing, so relax.

"I think he wanted to communicate a sense of cavalier self-confidence.

"I think he was also implying that you and General Guisan probably understood all that going into this exercise–and that's why you'd instructed me to keep the agreement from becoming too specific."

Minger chuckled and exhaled the last of his cigarette, grinding the butt in the ash tray.

"General Guisan and I have both learned to be a little cynical when dealing with the French," he said, nodding. "We both view the agreement as more symbolic than operational; but nonetheless significant–for both nations.

"But despite Besson's remarks you said you came away with the conviction that the French have taken serious steps to anticipate a German attack on us."

"Yes sir," Muller replied. "Clearly Major Charlet and his French counterparts have reconnoitered our Gempen Plateau in great detail and developed plans to strengthen our position there. The French 8th Army has nine divisions available to respond to an attack; that's a lot of firepower."

Haussamann interrupted.

"But they haven't committed any of those troops," he said.

"Oh, I know," he added quickly, "they're keeping their options open–that's what the French do these days, it seems; while political mistresses manipulate their policies."

Haussamann's sarcasm was plain.

"The French–and the British too, for that matter–are sitting back behind their defensive lines, confident that they're stronger than Germany and playing a waiting game. Meanwhile Herr Hitler, fresh from his triumph in Poland, has moved his armies back to the West and–as I was just explaining to Minister Minger–has ordered an attack on France beginning before mid-November."

Minger nodded.

"We were discussing that risk when you arrived, Mr. Muller."

Haussamann leaned over to stub out his butt.

"I was also telling the Minister that the German High Command is dead set against mounting any attack at the moment," he said. "I'm told their resistance is so strong as to amount almost to a mutiny against Hitler; but he's still determined to proceed– within a matter of days, and whether the Army command likes it or not."

Haussamann sat back in his seat.

"The contrast in attitudes is striking, don't you think?" he continued. "Your report, Mr. Muller, seems to confirm that the leadership of France is still largely in denial about the fact that there's a war on, while my sources are telling me that Hitler is so determined to mount an offensive–and do it *now*– that he's pushed his military commanders almost to the point of revolt."

"Do the French know that an attack is imminent, as you've just told us?" Muller asked, a little more sharply than he intended. "I certainly didn't get any sense of urgency on the part of General Besson when we spoke today."

Would even a cocky French military conduct leisurely negotiations and serve a four-course luncheon for visiting diplomats in the face of a threatened attack that–if Haussamann's information was correct–would occur in only a matter of days?

Muller didn't think so; something just didn't add up.

Haussamann smiled and shrugged.

"That's what I was saying to the Minister," he said. "We've passed our intelligence along to Paris through the normal channels, but we don't see any reaction. Normally, you'd assume that their Deuxième Bureau would be alerted to these reports even before they were passed to me; but they're sitting on their hands."

Muller fingered the card Garteiser had given him in Basle. Should he call the man to deliver Haussamann's warning?

Minger stood, signaling the meeting was over.

"I'll communicate with General Guisan regarding the agreement you negotiated with the French, Mr. Muller," he said. "At least we seem to have that situation in hand."

Turning to Haussamann, Minger offered an enigmatic smile.

"I'm afraid we have no choice but to wait and see how your intelligence plays out, Haussamann. But let's be sure we don't take any action in the meantime to call attention to ourselves; maintaining strict neutrality is probably our best way of keeping a low profile in what sounds like a very unstable situation.

"Good night, gentlemen."

Was signing an agreement with the French military consistent with 'maintaining strict neutrality'? Muller wondered to himself. But he decided he should not contact Garteiser. Minger seemed resigned to waiting for events to unfold and, at least for now, to remain passive.

As they exited Minger's office together, Haussamann asked Muller to join him for dinner.

"The weather's too nasty," he said; "rather than trying to drive back to Lucerne I've decided to stay overnight."

Muller readily agreed and a few minutes later, they found themselves seated in Chez André, a small neighborhood restaurant, in a booth toward the back. Muller noted that the tables nearby were unoccupied, so they could converse without being overheard.

Haussmann remained tense, as he had seemed in Minger's office, clearly troubled by the intelligence he'd learned.

"It's curious, Muller, how our warring friends seem so willing to confide secrets to us," he said, sipping the Aigle Les Murailles wine from the Valais that they'd ordered along with dinner. "General Besson telling you about how screwed up French decision-making is, and Germans revealing the possibility of a coup to me," he went on; "it's almost as if they feel an obligation to confess their apprehensions about what they see happening around them.

"Somehow, they view us–neutral Swiss–as offering a kind of safe sanctuary to express their misgivings."

Haussamann accepted Muller's Gitane and light, pausing as he exhaled, blowing a smoke ring.

"You know, Muller, that I've been cultivating contacts with key German leaders for years and developed close ties with many of them," he continued. "They buy the high-end optical products my company offers, of course; I'm one of their most important suppliers. We regularly swap information on weapon applications and so on; but that's led to relationships where, for a handful of important German friends, I'm viewed as a trusted resource and sounding board.

"No more so than now," he added, and leaned forward toward Muller.

"They're frightened," he said quietly.

Haussamann glanced over his shoulder, instinctively making sure he would not be overheard.

"They're scared of Hitler's security apparatus if they should dare to disobey him–a bullet in the back of the head or, maybe even worse, being hauled off to one of those Gestapo basements– but they're also deathly afraid of being ordered to mount an attack on the French which–in their current state of disarray after the Polish invasion–they fear they'd lose, badly, with fatal consequences for Germany."

They paused as the waiter brought their meal, filet des perches with frites; perfect for a chilly, rainy night. When he'd finished fussing and left, Muller spoke.

"At the ministry, you said the German military leadership was on the brink of revolt," he said quietly cutting the filets into smaller, bite-sized portions. "Are you talking about the likelihood of a coup?"

Haussamann nodded imperceptibly, again glancing around the room.

"To overthrow Hitler? Get rid of him?" Muller's voice was a whisper.

Haussaman nodded again, silently, this time gazing down at his plate as he chewed the filet des perches.

The two men continued to eat, saying nothing to one another as they contemplated the consequences of what they were discussing.

Haussamann finally began to speak.

"The Generals are adamant that the Army needs to re-group after Poland," he said. "Too many units failed to perform, even against weak Polish opposition; the Generals insist on re-training them before facing off against the French. The Luftwaffe is short of bombs; German ammunition stocks are very low; they consumed bullets and artillery shells at a rate seven times the rate of production and they came close to running out. More than a quarter of their vaunted Panzers suffered breakdowns or were destroyed and their Mark I and Mark II models are no match for the French tanks.

"There's more," he added," but put yourself in Brauchitsch's position Muller; he's ordered to attack the combined armies of France and Britain, which have the strongest forces in the world, fresh and ready to fight. By contrast, the German Army is in disarray and short of basic weaponry. They fear it would be a mismatch."

"Like Schmeling versus Louis, match 2," he added, refilling their wine glasses. "Knocked out in the first round." He smiled thinly.

"Only after this fight, the crowd wouldn't go home; it would proceed to destroy Germany–and the Army would take the blame."

Haussamann pushed his plate aside and leaned toward Muller.

"Brauchitsch surely has to see an image of himself hung from a lamppost in Berlin in the wake of a German defeat."

Then, absently picking at his frites with a fork, he smiled again, this time more widely.

"A month ago, he was on the cover of *Time* magazine in America," he said, "full uniform, winning grin–the very embodiment of the victorious commanding general."

Haussamann lifted his wine glass and clinked it against Muller's.

"Here's to the General".

Then his smile vanished.

"But that was yesterday, Muller; today, he's in a very different position."

Muller was hesitant to interrupt; Haussaman's uneasiness at what he'd just described was evident. So he paused before speaking.

"There've been stories of conspiracies being mounted against Hitler by military leaders in the past, Haussamann," he said. "Occupation of the Rhineland, the Austria invasion and especially the assault planned against the Sudetenland in Czechoslovakia; military leaders opposed then all and, according to rumor, plotted to overthrow Hitler–then backed down every time.

"Is this so much different?" he asked. "Do you really think the military leadership is up to killing Hitler and trying to take over the government? These are men trained to obey orders not to overthrow their superiors."

Haussamann sighed, accepting Muller's light and exhaling.

"Well, you've certainly identified the issue," he said. "You're right; this is the German Officers Corps we're talking about, trained practically from infancy to obey commands without thought or reflection. Just obey; do what you're told, period.

"Will one of them–Brauchitsch, or Halder, or some subordinate–pull his pistol out of his holster and empty the magazine into Hitler–a man most of them detest and disdain, but who is their superior officer and of whom they're rightly afraid?

"Well, all I can tell you, Muller, is that it's gotten to the point where they're talking about doing just that."

He signaled for the bill.

"I can tell you, I'm happy not to be in Brauchitsch's shoes tonight."

When Muller finally got back to his quarters in the Ministry's barracks, he shook the rain off his umbrella, hung up his dripping raincoat and plopped down in the easy chair. He picked up the September 25, 1939 edition of Time Magazine that was sitting on the coffee table. He'd purchased it when it arrived on the local newsstand but hadn't gotten around to reading it. Now, he studied the handsome, smiling visage of Walther von Brauchitsch that graced the magazine's cover.

He remembered meeting the man four years earlier in Danzig, when he was Secretary to the High Commissioner. He'd acted as translator at a small dinner party given by the German Consul and Brauchitsch, who was then commander of the German forces in Prussia, had been a guest and was seated next to him, so they'd conversed together. Brauchitsch had been adamant in his condemnation of the separation of Germany created by the Polish

Corridor under the Treaty of Versailles; he'd fumed at what he viewed as the humiliation of having to pass through Polish customs just to travel between Konigsberg, the capital of Prussia, and Berlin, the capital of Germany, of which Prussia was a part. But he had been calm and civil and had seemed like a normal fellow–not the kind of man whom one would expect to be contemplating murdering the German Chancellor–even if that Chancellor was Adolf Hitler.

Muller tossed the magazine back on the coffee table.

As he went to bed, he wondered if Brauchitsch was doing so too, in a posh Army commander's quarters somewhere in Germany–fearing, as he pulled up the covers, that he might be awakened in the middle of the night by the sound of his door being kicked open and Gestapo thugs beating him, then spiriting him off, chained, in the back of a Black Maria.

Muller remembered very clearly when it had happened to him.

It was not a memory that was conducive to a good night's sleep.

If War Should Come

CHAPTER 22

A man who had become a regular patron at the Löwenbräukeller restaurant, mingled with other customers, mainly men, whom he'd gotten to know in his many visits since August. He was a slender man in his mid-30s with thick black hair and a friendly smile and no one had noticed when he became a regular customer in mid-August, taking his dinners there most nights and staying until the 10:30 close, nursing a coffee, or sometimes a beer.

The restaurant was situated in the Haidhausen section of Munich, and was adjacent to the Bürgerbräukeller, a cavernous beer hall which had become famous when Adolf Hitler, then a young and unknown right-wing political agitator, had selected it as the site to launch a failed coup d'état aimed at toppling the government of Bavaria. On the night of November 8, 1923, he had burst into the vast hall with a coterie of followers and fired his pistol into the ceiling as a signal to seize several Bavarian political leaders in the crowd as hostages. He had mounted a podium at one end of the hall and delivered a passionate address vilifying the widely despised Treaty of Versailles, heaping scorn on Jews, and declaring a National Socialist revolution.

Police rapidly put down the movement and arrested Hitler. He was tried, convicted of treason, and sentenced to five years in prison. But the event, little noted at the time, launched Hitler's meteoric rise to power, and the "Beer Hall Putsch", as it became known, ascended into cherished memory in Nazi mythology. Each year, Hitler and his most rabid early supporters returned to Bürgerbräukeller on November 8 for a night of speeches and celebrations; it was an annual reaffirmation of power and authority; a date sanctified by the Nazi faithful–a rally to rouse members to a frenzy; an annual commemoration not to be missed.

The new regular customer at the restaurant was named Georg Elser, a man who was determined to assassinate Hitler, and had decided that was where he would do it. Hitler was notorious for changing schedules, cancelling appearances, and abruptly making new plans. But Elser was confident that on November 8, 1939, Hitler would be in attendance at the annual Bürgerbräukeller Hall celebration and Elser could murder him there.

Having come to his decision, Elser had paid a visit to Bürgerbräukeller Hall and strolling the cavernous interior with a stein of beer, an idea began to form in his mind. Right behind the podium where Hitler always stood to deliver his speech to the rapt, cheering crowd, there stood a single large, wood clad pillar supporting a massive overhead balcony. What if, Elser thought to himself, I place a bomb in that pillar that would both blow up the podium where Hitler would be standing and bring the overhanging balcony crashing down on top of it to finish the job. He could kill Hitler and the Nazi leadership arrayed behind him on the stage all in one fell swoop.

The more he thought about the plan, the more he liked it.

He also reconnoitered an escape route. Taking the train South from Munich to the Swiss border at Konstanz, he saw how easy it would be to slip across the wooded border. There were hourly departures from Munich, so there would be no difficulties in boarding a train after the device was activated; he would slip away unnoticed.

So, it was decided.

Elser moved to Munich and took a job as a clerk in the Waldenmaier armaments factory situated nearby. With the fast pace of German rearmament, firms like Waldenmaier were desperate to hire additional staff to meet demands from the German Wehrmacht for weapons and ammunition. No one noticed when dozens of blasting caps and detonators went missing after Elser was hired. Nor did anyone at the nearby Vollmer Quarry pay any attention to the slender man who often appeared at the site on weekends, when work was suspended for maintenance, but bags of blasting powder were strewn about, and handfuls could be scooped up and hidden in small packets the man brought along.

On one of his earliest visits to the restaurant, the slender man quickly discovered a storeroom used by both the restaurant and the adjacent Bürgerbräukeller. A shared staircase gave access to both establishments and he found a small space beneath the eaves where he could hide a blanket to catch some sleep after preparing the column for the device he was constructing.

As the restaurant closed, Elser would simply slip up the stairway, lie down in his hideaway, and wait till Christian Weber, the fat owner, locked up and left the premises. Weber was a committed Hitler disciple who profited handsomely from other members of the faithful that paid visits to the famed hall to have a few rounds; he was the kind of man who saw no reason to pay much attention to security.

Upon hearing Weber depart, Elser would descend the stairway to the cavernous hall and begin his painstaking work, using special tools he'd acquired in flea markets, and with only a flashlight to illuminate his work. He cut out a section of the wood clad pillar, using a saw with a kerf so narrow as to leave hardly any visible trace of the cut. Then he took a sharp chisel and attacked the stone pillar, using a rubber hammer to avoid any sound. It took a long time to fashion a cave in the column; each flake of stone and dust had to be carefully wiped up and removed before replacing the wood pillar section to avoid detection.

Elser worked carefully. He was a master woodworker and also experienced in clockwork, having worked for a watchmaker, so he was familiar with the intricacies of setting a clock to ring an alarm–or, in this case, to trigger an explosion.

It took time; Elser counted 35 different nights he'd performed his clandestine work, always ensuring that he and his work went unnoticed. Then, finally, the cavern he'd constructed was just the right size. At his rooming house, he had collected clock springs and timers and assembled the timing mechanism. Taking an occasional job in a wood working shop, he'd been able to fashion the pieces that he then carefully glued together into a wood box that he lined with cork to deaden the sound of the clock ticking.

The next night, he brought the box with him, hiding it in his coat until slipping upstairs at the close. To his horror, he discovered the box was too big; he'd erred in his calculations. But undeterred, he worked extra late with this hammer and chisel to enlarge the stone receptacle, and when he was done, found the box fitted perfectly, with just enough room to pack extra gunpowder around it for maximum explosive effect.

As November 8 neared, the man's attention was focused entirely on slipping components of the bomb and the box that would house the device itself into his hiding place and preparing to assemble and arm it.

He didn't pay any attention to angry and panicked outbursts from Christian Weber who had sold tickets for a record sellout crowd to greet the Führer when he made his appearance; Hitler wasn't coming. Press of other engagements—we're at war, you know, he was told by officious Party officials.

Weber, furious, refused to be put off by strutting Party newcomers. He placed frantic calls to Himmler and Goebbels—and especially to Martin Bormann, who seemed more in control of Hitler's schedule than anyone else.

But he received no assurances and was beside himself.

On November 7, Elser arrived at the restaurant earlier than usual and strolled with the gathering throng into the Bürgerbräukeller, watching Nazi flags and banners being hung. He led a raucous group of Party members bedecked with red armbands over to the podium, daring them to mount the step, which they all did, grinning and flashing arm raised salutes. The diversion enabled him to lean against his column, press his ear to it—and hear the reassuring faint tick of the timebomb.

It was ready.

Then his stomach dropped. What were they saying? The Führer was cancelling? No; it wasn't possible.

Elser returned to the restaurant and shrank into a booth in the back, his mind a blur. All these months of work; what should he do? The bomb would go off at exactly 9:20 PM, the next night, almost exactly halfway through Hitler's peroration that was scheduled to begin at 8:30 and would certainly last at least until 10 PM as it always did.

Then Christian Weber made a grand entrance from his office with shouts of 'Seig Heil' and a grin from ear to ear!

"He will come!" Weber shouted to cheers. "He will speak! Our Great Führer once again returns to lead and inspire us."

Weber ordered a round for the entire gathering and accepted handshakes and slaps on the back from rapturous customers.

So, the plan was back on track, Elser thought to himself with a rush of relief. He uncharacteristically stepped up to the bar with others, accepted a stein of beer and toasted the Führer.

But doubts persisted, and back at his rooming house, Elser decided he would delay his escape to Konstanz until that afternoon. He would wait at the station with the throng sure to be here to welcome Hitler's arrival–just to be sure his intended victim would show up, as Elser had counted on him doing for so long.

So that's what he did.

He was not disappointed. Despite the rain and whatever issues of state may have weighed on him, Adolf Hitler, the Führer, arrived on his special train just after 6 PM waving and smiling at the crowd of supporters who cheered and chanted 'Sieg Heil.'

Elser smiled to himself, turned his back on the spectacle and began to stride toward a platform on the other end of the concourse, where the 6:25 Express to Munich was preparing to depart.

At the entrance to Bürgerbräukeller, Christian Weber stood beneath a large black umbrella, beaming in anticipation as Hitler's black Mercedes Benz limousine pulled to a stop and security guards leapt to station themselves around him. Weber found himself being shoved aside, but he used his bulk and placed himself squarely in Hitler's path.

"My Führer," he said, standing as straight as his girth would permit and raising his right arm.

"Weber," Hitler responded with a smile of recognition.

"Always a great event, isn't it? A lot's going on; we've got a war to win–and we will, by God; we'll crush them." Hitler leaned closer. "Our celebration will go on, Weber, even in the face of all our challenges."

Then he was gone, whisked away by his entourage, and disappearing into the back room of the restaurant that had been sealed off for him to rest, conduct pressing business and prepare for his 8:30 address.

Weber turned back into the Hall to join the revelers who were happily awaiting Hitler's appearance. They sang the Nazi songs, pounded one another on the back and tried to be sure to have full steins before Hitler took the stage, because, by law, no one was permitted to buy beer while the Führer spoke.

And Hitler did not disappoint. He ascended the podium on schedule at 8:30 and the crowd roared in welcome. He knew how to rouse the crowd to a frenzy of cheers and chants. 'German blood', 'German greatness', 'Death to the Jews and other subhuman vermin', always pointing the finger of blame at 'them'; the 'others' whom his faithful could vilify and hate. He didn't disappoint.

But then, suddenly, it was over.

Hitler led the crowd in a furious round of 'Seig Heil' arms raised salutes–and he was gone, the podium empty and the ranks of Nazi officials seated and standing beneath the balcony departing in his wake.

It was 9:07 PM when he finished speaking according to a later official report.

The crowd, still energized and enthusiastic, surged toward the doorways to wave farewell to their beloved leader, jostling one another to get a look as the Mercedes Benz disappeared around the corner.

The rain had finally stopped, and the cool November night felt good to sweaty patrons and they had begun to disperse when, at precisely 9;20 PM–right on time–a huge explosion rocked the hall. The force of the blast knocked many in the crowd-even those outside-to the ground, Christian Weber among them.

Smoke and screams enveloped the hall as the concussion echoed in the narrow streets and debris showered those closest to the doorways.

Pandemonium ensued as the huge crowd, stunned by the violence, reacted in terror.

Weber was among the first to recover. Regaining his feet and racing back inside, he saw that entire section where the podium had once stood had simply disappeared in the blast, the pillar behind was shattered and the overhanging balcony had crashed to the floor, crushing everything beneath it.

He stopped and simply stared at the destruction, unable to move.

Outside, on the street adjacent to Bürgerbräukeller, a police car pulled to a stop and surveyed the scene. A veteran officer calmy picked up the microphone of his mobile radio and alerted his precinct headquarters.

"A bomb has exploded at Bürgerbräukeller, and there are casualties. But the Führer is safe."

And within minutes, the news flashed across teletype machines, first in Germany and then around the world. Hitler's private train was flagged down as it prepared to roar through Nüremberg and a frightened official boarded the train to pass the news.

Arriving in Kostanz at about the same time as his time bomb went off in Munich, Georg Elser hired a taxi to take him to the edge of town. Then he pulled his hat down against the rain and began trudging along the pathway he'd identified in the spring. It was dark and muddy, but he'd rehearsed the short journey and he knew that, after a dip of a few hundred meters, the path rose to a section of woods that paralleled the border. He strode along confidently, then became aware of a barbed wire fence that had been erected where he'd intended to enter the woods and slip across into Switzerland. No fence had been there in the spring. Should he try to find a way over or through the barrier or continue along the path to find a gate or some other way around it?

He hesitated, then froze as he saw lights moving toward him and heard the sound of dogs.

A German Patrol; Good god! What had become of the unprotected border he'd carefully reconnoitered?

Taken into custody, Elser was herded into a cell with other prisoners who were suspected of smuggling. When he was finally hauled into a brightly lit interrogation room, he was told to empty his pockets. He complied and laid his things on a table. They included a sketch of the bomb design he'd carried with him to persuade Swiss authorities of his anti-Nazi sympathies, and a postcard of Bürgerbräukeller.

He was lamely trying to explain himself to an impatient policeman when a loud alarm went off in the building, signaling General Quarters; a message had been received reporting that a time bomb had exploded at Bürgerbräukeller only an hour earlier.

His interrogator returned moments later along with burly policemen who pinned him to the ground, strapped him in irons, kicked him up and down, then stopped and stared at the gift that had just fallen into their laps.

CHAPTER 23

The next morning, Yvonne Brenner personally delivered copies of news bulletins about the failed assassination attempt directly to Muller's office.

"Here are the news clips I've collected, sir and we're monitoring the radio for any new announcements," she said. "They're not releasing much real information, just repeated denunciations of the 'cowardly attack' and defiant statement about punishing their adversaries."

"Thank you, Miss Brenner," Muller said, taking the documents and idly scanning them; he'd come to rely upon Yvonne's evaluation of breaking news.

"From what I've been able to piece together, they're blaming the British for the attack," Yvonne said. "There's no information about any alleged perpetrators, so this may be just a propaganda line; it's always hard to interpret German releases. The BBC has denied British responsibility, if that means anything," she added with a shrug.

"But they'd hardly want to claim responsibility for a failed attack, would they?"

She smiled.

"Is there any news about troop movements or rumors of a German attack in the West?" Muller asked, thinking of Haussamann's warning about Hitler's apparent intent to launch an invasion on November 12th, now only days away.

"No, sir," she replied; "nothing so far."

"Let me know right away if that changes," Muller said. "I'll need to inform the Minister."

He went in search of Haussamann and was told he was traveling. Muller nodded to himself; Haussamann seemed to find ways to be in Germany to collect information when important developments occurred.

Was it worth taking the train to Geneva and probing Jimmy West for information? Or even contacting André Garteiser in Paris? He decided no; the only thing that really mattered was whether troop movements could be detected that would signal the attack that Hitler had threatened–now only three days hence–and which the German Army commanders had supposedly opposed.

Was the assassination attempt somehow connected to that? Muller finally decided there was nothing to do but wait–either until there was an invasion, or until Haussamann showed up with information. There was certainly plenty of work that he had to catch up on, so he put his head down and waited.

Two days later Minger sent for him and when he entered the office, he found Haussamann looking for a coat rack to hang up a soaking wet raincoat.

"Awful weather," he muttered; "it even delayed the Berlin Express."

"Bad enough to stop a German invasion tomorrow?" asked Minger, looking at Haussamann expectantly.

Haussamann nodded, seating himself at the conference table.

"Something led him to call it off," he said quietly; "but it's hard to know what, in all the confusion."

"The assassination attempt?"

"That too," Haussamann replied.

"'Secrets of Zossen,'" he added enigmatically.

"You'd better explain," Minger said.

Haussamann nodded again, but this time leaned forward, elbows on the conference room table.

"I was being entertained at the German Army command headquarters at Zossen, in that mammoth building they confiscated after the Olympics," he said. "I'd been there many times before, of course; it's really the one place where the Army still feels totally in control; no Party snoops listening in or peering over their shoulder. It's old school Army, and well-outfitted too, with ample bierstube for the ranks and a top of the line mess for the high command.

"It's a place they can relax and let their hair down," he went on, "and it's where, in the past, I've been able to gather useful intelligence."

Haussamann stood, strode to the sideboard and poured himself a glass of water from a pitcher, drinking thirstily, looking inquiringly at Minger and Muller, who both declined the offer.

Returning to his seat, Haussamann continued.

"When I visited on this last trip, I felt uneasiness in the building," he said. "There was a palpable sense of anxiety and people's behavior was changed. I couldn't grasp what was going on. Then I learned that before departing for Munich for his speech—the one where the bomb went off—Hitler had delivered an absolute tirade to both Brauchitsch and Halder accusing them of incompetence and disloyalty, and even threatening to put them in front of a Gestapo firing squad."

"These are the two highest ranking German Army officers," Haussamann went on, "the men who commanded the invasion of Poland only six weeks ago. He apparently criticized them unmercifully for resisting his demands to order the full-scale invasion of France and the Low Countries on November 12—and did so in a way that left them, literally, quaking in their boots.

"'I know all about your so-called 'secrets of Zossen,' he told them, 'your plots to kill me and overthrow the Reich. Don't think you're fooling me for one second, because you're *not*.'"

Haussmann leaned forward, accepting Muller's offer of a Gitane and a light.

"I shared with you both earlier the information I'd been given about the German High Command being at the point of mutiny in its opposition to Hitler's invasion demand, convinced that it would fail, and they would be held responsible. So, Hitler wasn't wrong when he accused them of plotting to kill him–because they were in fact thinking about actually doing that.

"But they'd hesitated; they're Army officers, born and bred to *obey* not *resist*."

Haussamann paused to tap his ash into the glass ash tray before him.

"And Hitler knew it," he added, pausing for effect. "They knew he knew it, and they panicked.

"Instead of confronting him and forcing what could have become a fatal showdown, they backed down, denied any disagreements and, as I was given to understand it, effectively threw themselves at his feet. Any thoughts of resistance vanished, and they abjectly pledged total loyalty."

Haussamann stubbed out his butt.

"Most of the German Army leaders detest Hitler and think he behaves like a madman–but he's the Führer; their commander–a man whom they fear and can't bring themselves to oppose."

Haussamann sat back.

"That was the atmosphere that pervaded Zossen when I visited there that night." Haussamann said. "The Army leadership feared that Hitler had uncovered their secrets–the, frankly, pretty amateurish steps they'd taken to mount a coup–and that he'd unleash the Gestapo on them. So, the order of business at Zossen when I arrived for dinner was to destroy any possible evidence of their plot in order to save their skins."

Minger was about to interrupt, but Haussamann held up his hand.

"That was the atmosphere *before* news broke of the explosion at the beer hall, which was obviously aimed at killing Hitler, and probably his entire entourage too."

"The news flash hit Zossen as if *it* were a bomb," Haussamann said with crooked smile.

"It dawned on everyone there that no German Army officers had been with Hitler in Munich. His retinue had consisted entirely of Nazi Party officials and hangers-on. *They* were the ones targeted by the bomb–and no Army officers had been among them.

Haussamann sighed, looking from Minger to Muller.

"You can imagine the consternation that ensued at that point," he said. "Was someone in the Army responsible for the attempted assassination? Surely the finger of suspicion would fall on the Army leadership–since only Hitler and Party bigwigs had been targeted by the bomb.

"And, sure enough, the Gestapo in fact showed up, just as the Army leadership feared, and they just shut down the entire place. Direct orders from Himmler. No one could enter or exit Zossen for the next 24 hours. You could cut the tension with a knife."

Haussamann held up his hand again, continuing to speak.

"And then, suddenly, it was over," he said, smiling; "it was as if the sun had reappeared after a storm. They found out who the bomber was–some lone wolf German tradesman, apparently. They caught him trying escape into Switzerland. So, no involvement by the Army; Zossen was in the clear.

"The Party propaganda machine went into high gear to blame the attack on the British. The Army command, feeling as if they'd dodged a bullet, were only too happy to play along and parrot the same line.

"So that's where it stands."

"And no invasion," Minger said.

"No," Haussamann said nodding. "Apparently on the train trip down to Munich for the speech, Hitler issued orders calling off the invasion. No one at Zossen knew why," he added. "Their best guess was that having brought Brauchitsch and Halder to heel, Hitler was satisfied. He could see as well as anyone that the weather was completely unsuited to an invasion; he'd been unable to fly to Munich for the speech, it was so bad. He apparently decided that he could order the cancellation without looking as if he'd caved to the Generals–so he proceeded to do so, just canceling the order, without even consulting them."

Minger sat back in his chair at the head of the conference table.

"That's a lot of information to ponder," he said quietly. "It certainly seems to confirm Hitler's total control over the machinery of the German state–and no early resolution to the conflict that we face."

"The Army is completely cowed," Haussamann added. "Any thoughts of a coup–or any resistance at all–has vanished. No

invasion order and no Gestapo crackdown; the Army's in the clear–
for the moment. But they paid a price."

CHAPTER 24

"A new spirit of Malmö?"

Muller looked quizzically at Roger Masson.

For once, Masson left his pipe in the ashtray and didn't bang it on the glass to remove the used tobacco, so he felt relieved that, whatever Masson had summoned him to speak about, he wasn't going to have to endure his irritating pipe-banging habit–at least not yet.

Muller had come to respect Masson's intellect and judgment. He had a reserved manner and often seemed to be a passive listener in meetings that Minister Minger convened, though he could be sarcastic and was prone to intervene abruptly and dismiss comments he found unpersuasive with cutting put-downs.

The two of them had not spent much time together alone; ordinarily they met at Minger's request and with others present too. But this afternoon, Masson had summoned Muller to his office, which adjoined Minger's, but which seemed to have taken on a separate life of its own.

Upon arriving punctually he'd been asked to wait in the anteroom. Masson's secretaries–he now had three of them, Muller noted–seemed nearly overwhelmed, answering constant phone calls and preparing documents, which they furiously pecked away at on their large typewriters. A very different, almost frenzied atmosphere than he had been accustomed to before the outbreak of war and the mobilization.

Seated on an uncomfortable upholstered couch, Muller could see that he was not the only visitor summoned to the office. Three uniformed officers were huddled on chairs across the room, conversing intently, referring to files spread on their laps. Other men were standing in small groups in the corridor outside. Muller saw new military aides to Masson seated at tables set up against one wall, busily dealing with stacks of paper, speaking in low tones and rising occasionally to step toward a row of grey file cabinets to extract still more documents.

Masson's office had become a command center, Muller realized. The beginnings of creating a wartime bureaucracy that he had witnessed before departing to Bucharest two months earlier had now matured into a busy operational structure that Masson apparently was running. No more just the thoughtful deputy to the Minister, Masson was now clearly exercising direct ministerial command authority.

Muller hadn't been obliged to concern himself with political rivalries in doing the various jobs he'd been assigned. Büro Ha was situated outside the bureaucratic structure and his boss, Hans Haussamann, operated more or less independently, as Minger clearly intended, so he'd been able to do so too.

But he had not been unaware of resentment expressed by some in the chain of command at precisely this informality and–in the view of some–the lack of command accountability. Minger had shrugged off these concerns, content to operate unconventionally and getting things done his own way. His crucial goal had been to secure the appointment of Guisan as General–and to do so in a manner ensuring that Guisan could exercise authority without being submissive to the Federal Council and the Ministers that comprised its membership, most of whom Minger deemed incompetent.

He'd effectively set up Guisan as a separate power center, confident that, as General and Commander of the Swiss armed forces, Guisan would seize the reins and take charge–as he had clearly proceeded to do, even in the few short months since his appointment.

Now Minger seemed content to step back and let the process he'd set in motion play out.

Of course, he'd understood that the government–the bureaucracy that ran things–would mobilize to protect the nation and he hadn't stood in the way of reorganization–even within his own ministry–that was being implemented to establish new functions and reported to Masson, his deputy.

Muller had always been bemused by the fact that Minger had been a farmer for his entire life–a role that he had continued to play even after becoming Minister and the most powerful figure in the Swiss government. Was it Minger, the farmer, who was now content to sit back and watch a burcaucracy even one that he hadn't seeded–take root and grow?

There were obvious risks that a new and aggressive government system would collide with the personal diplomacy that Minger prized. It explained his embrace of Büro Ha, Haussamann's private and highly idiosyncratic intelligence service, which operated outside of channels and was, in fact, accountable to no one but Minger.

Muller was musing about these newly apparent tensions in the Ministry's leadership structure–and what significance they held for him and his role–when he was suddenly directed into Masson's office. He was quite unprepared for Masson's unexpected, out of the blue question.

"Malmö?" he said, feeling suddenly unsure of his ground.

"Right," Masson replied with a tight smile, gesturing to Muller to a seat. "Malmö."

"Long forgotten now," he continued, "but in December 1914, the three Scandinavian Kings took it upon themselves to meet in Malmö, Sweden–just across the Strait from Copenhagen–and issue a ringing statement reaffirming their common policy of neutrality in the Great War and warning the belligerents to respect their status."

"I confess, I hadn't heard of it either, Muller, so don't feel left out.

"But the Prime Ministers of what are now four Scandinavian governments–not three anymore, there's Finland too, now–have announced they are convening a meeting of representatives of the nations of Europe that are now self-proclaimed neutrals in this new war to once again warn off the belligerents–and it's to be held– where do you suppose, Muller?"

"In Malmö," Muller responded, now smiling too.

"And we'd like you to attend as the Swiss representative," Masson continued. "The Foreign Ministry has an Ambassador stationed in Stockholm, who is responsible for all the Scandinavian countries and who–even our Foreign Minister here in Bern concedes–is well past his prime; indeed, often in his cups, actually; so, Minister Minger had no difficulty in securing permission to restore your Ambassadorial credentials and appoint you as the Swiss representative for the Malmö Conference."

"When is this conference to take place?" Muller asked.

"Next weekend," Masson replied. "Not much time, but apparently the ministers are feeling threatened, with the Soviets, the Germans and the British all eying aggressive actions in the region, so they issued the invitation just a few days ago.

"My recommendation is that you make a quick trip to Geneva and meet with the Scandinavian delegations to the League and see what you can learn before you depart. KLM has service through Amsterdam to Copenhagen and we're working on a booking that will get you there in time; the Swedes have promised to look after accommodations once you're there."

Masson's brisk description made it apparent that this was not a proposal for Muller to consider; it was his next assignment.

"Do I have instructions on what I'm to accomplish during this mission?"

Masson smiled.

"The truth is–no; we don't know much more about the agenda than I just told you. So, your assignment is to promote the policy of neutrality." He shrugged. "Mr. Minger assumes that you'll look after our interests, Muller. After all, we're Swiss; neutrality comes naturally."

Masson rose signaling the meeting was over, but Muller paused before departing.

"Am I to operate as a representative of Minister Minger and this Ministry, or as a representative of the Swiss nation?"

Masson waved him away with a dismissive gesture.

"You'll be Ambassador Plenipotentiary, Mr. Muller, with full authority to represent Switzerland and promote neutrality," Masson replied as he summoned the waiting military officers into his office, obviously dismissing Muller's question and turning to his next order of business.

Well, Muller said to himself, if that was going to be his title, he supposed he should assume he had the governmental authority that went with it.

Muller stepped across the hall to Minger's outer office–which was decidedly less frenzied– and enlisted the assistance of Minger's principal secretary to track down Sweden's delegate at the

League to set up a meeting the very next morning at the Palais in Geneva.

First, though, on his way back to his office, he stopped in the main ministry conference room where a map of Europe took up part of one wall. There it was. Malmö; literally across the straits from Copenhagen at the point where the North Sea connects into the Baltic. It was, very clearly, a strategic chokepoint for commercial and naval traffic in the entire region–and that was evidently why it had been selected in 1914, and now chosen again in 1939 to assert Scandinavian interests.

It turned out that the Swedish Ambassador in Geneva was named Baron Lars Berglund, and he readily agreed to meet; schedules at the League weren't so crowded these days. Muller didn't know any Barons and was quite certain they'd not met during the periods he'd been affiliated with the League, so he wasn't sure what to expect when he took the first train to Geneva the next morning and arrived at the stately league offices in the Palais des Nations for the 10 AM meeting that Minger's assistant had fixed.

The appearance of the Palais had continued to deteriorate as the role of the League diminished. Security was very light, so Muller rapidly found his way to the appointed 8th floor office meeting place. No secretary was stationed outside, and the door was open, so Muller rapped and entered, to find a tall, very thin, man, coatless, at his window, hands on his hips and doing squats. The man turned, smiling, and slipped his jacket back on before striding toward Muller with his right hand extended.

"Ah, Ambassador Muller," he said grinning a little sheepishly.

"Skiing season will be here soon," he said. "I need to get these elderly legs of mine ready for the first snowfall–which I hear is scheduled in a few days. No downhill this year with the lifts shut by rationing, so ski de fond it will be."

His hands mimicked cross country skiing movements.

Muller smiled back at the man.

With the arrival of cold weather he'd begun to think about ski season too, and had also realized he wouldn't be able to ride the new double chair lift that had been installed at Grindlewald, as the entire mountain resort had been ordered shut down to conserve fuel.

"I'm afraid that's what we'll be reduced to," Muller replied as they shook hands; "we'll have to work for our schnapps, I'm afraid.

"Should I address you as 'Baron' or as 'Ambassador,'" he asked.

"Oh, just Ambassador," Berglund responded with a laugh. "Sweden prides itself on being very progressive with our version of social democracy–but Barons abound, and we're not taken very seriously anymore."

Berglund gestured to seats facing the view up Lac Leman toward Montreux. He offered cigarettes from his case and Muller provided his lighter.

"You're here about Malmö," Berglund said, matter-of-factly, as he waved away the smoke he'd exhaled.

"I'm pleased to hear that at least someone's paying attention."

Muller looked at Berglund inquiringly.

"None of the Southern Europeans seem to have any interest–
the Italians and the Greeks; both Spain and Portugal have declined
to attend; even the Belgians have said no. We hope the Dutch will
come; Andorra and Lichtenstein don't much matter, of course."

He grinned.

"But we're pleased to have Swiss participation. You're our
kind of neutral."

Muller returned Berglund's smile.

"But, what's the goal of this conference, Ambassador
Berglund, and what's the historic 'spirit' you're trying to revive?"

Berglund sat back in his chair, spreading his arms in a gesture
of supplication.

"What's our goal? Survival," he said.

"What's our motive for this conference? Desperation."

They ground out their cigarettes.

"Consider the geography, Ambassador Muller," Berglund
went on. "Norway and Sweden occupy that enormous peninsula
above the Baltic Sea; Finland is both next door to us and borders
the Soviet Union–at one point less than 40 kms from Leningrad.
Little Denmark is across the Straits and borders on Germany. Our
four Scandinavian nations occupy an enormous and hotly-
contested territory that all the belligerents covet–each for their own
reasons.

"Scandinavia is becoming the battleground where the warring
belligerents will fight it out, Ambassador Muller: Britain and

France aligned against Germany and the Soviets–and yes, I count the Soviets as belligerents, even though they piously claim neutrality; I count them as German allies, not just bystanders."

Berglund's air of good cheer had given way to a grim expression.

"I'm sure you're a well-informed diplomat or you wouldn't be here, Ambassador Muller, but just look at the forces we confront, sir, and you'll understand our dilemma.

"Let's start with my country," he went on, "Sweden is the principal source of iron ore for Germany–an absolutely vital part of the German weapons production program; if the delivery of Swedish ore to German industry were somehow interrupted, the consequences for the German war effort would be… he paused.

"Fatal," he finally added, drawing a forefinger across his throat to underline his point.

"They won't let it happen," he added.

"And neither will we."

Berglund leaned forward toward Muller.

"Sweden depends upon coal imported from Germany to supply nearly all of our energy needs," he said, "to keep the lights on, to run our factories, to keep us warm in winter. We're as dependent upon them as they are upon us.

"So, when we hear rumors of British plans to cut off our ore supplies to Germany, we become very fearful indeed. And it's no secret; the same issues came into play in the Great War. Twenty years may have elapsed, Ambassador Muller, but basic interests haven't changed much. That potential conflict with the British motivated the Malmö Conference in 1914; we rolled the dice with it then, and governments have decided to try it again now."

Berglund shrugged.

"I guess we'll see if it works, won't we," he concluded with a wry smile.

"What happened in 1914?" Muller asked. "Is there a real precedent at work here?"

"Well, none of the Scandinavian nations were occupied in the Great War," Berglund replied, "and that's something, I suppose."

"Wait," he said, standing and walking to his desk, where he opened a drawer. Sorting through some documents, he finally withdrew one and brandished it triumphantly.

"This, Ambassador Muller is Malmö," he said handing Muller a photo of three very tall, slender and mustachioed men, awkwardly standing in a row, obviously posed for the camera. All three wore double-breasted frock coats, high white collars and dark ties, and they gazed straight ahead, expressionless.

"The three kings," said Berglund with mock gravity. "Haakon VII of Norway, Gustav V of Sweden and Christian X of Denmark.

"How's that for a pose conveying moral rectitude?"

Berglund laughed.

"Actually, the meeting was important at the time, he said. "Norway had separated from Sweden only in 1905, less than a decade earlier. Haakon was the newly-installed King and the kid brother to Kristian of Denmark, and they all had a common ancestor.

"How's that for a bit of dusty royal history, Muller?" he said. "Very *ancient regime,* don't you think, Kings and all that?

"Except they're all three still there, *today*," he went on, "sitting largely as figureheads on faintly irrelevant thrones, but alive and occasionally influential, despite having been pushed aside by Parliaments and political parties."

Muller looked at the photo. It did look very old-fashioned, the three tall, angular figures, posed and stiff in their dated costumes.

"Will the three Kings be at this new Malmö conference?" he asked.

Somehow that would be incongruous, he thought.

Berglund smiled genially.

"Not a chance," he replied. "Oh, I'm sure they'd like to–at least Gustav would, our Swedish King. He's cantankerous and despises the Bolshevik regime in Moscow, so I'm sure he'd revel in an opportunity to heap scorn on the Soviets; but it won't happen.

"Anyway, Finland's now a Scandinavian state too. Not only does it lack a King, it didn't even exist as a nation in 1914; it was still a principality of Czarist Russia. It didn't become an independent nation until 1917 and had to fight a bloody civil war to suppress Bolshevik sympathizers to keep the Soviets at bay.

"So Malmö had no meaning for Finland in 1914."

Berglund took the photo and returned it to his desk drawer.

"But today," he continued, resuming his seat, "Finland's probably the most vocal advocate of regional neutrality for all of Scandinavia. Stalin's pressing them to make territorial concessions to extend Soviet borders. They're resisting, but they're fearful of not just a Russian attack, but a military response from Britain and France, which would make them–and the rest of us too–a battlefield where the two sides would collide, at our expense."

Berglund paused, gazing out at the grey expanse of Lac Leman.

"That's why this new Malmö conference is so important to all of Scandinavia, Ambassador Muller. We want to stay out of this damned new war, but the belligerents seem determined to drag us into it."

As Muller was preparing to depart, Berglund held up a hand for him to stop a moment, and returned to his desk. He took out the photo, carefully folded it into an envelope and handed it to Muller with a grin.

"You can use this as a credential to attest to your deep knowledge of Malmö."

As they shook hands and Muller turned to leave, Berglund followed him a step or two into the corridor.

"By the way," he said, 'I'd bring along a couple of extra layers to keep warm. It's brutally cold there this winter."

CHAPTER 25

Muller shrugged into the heavy parka when the KLM Lockheed finally jerked to a halt on the snow-covered tarmac in Copenhagen and the crew flung open the back door for passengers to deplane. The coat was bulky and hard to get on in the cramped aisle, without room for him to stand upright.

He'd taken Ambassador Berglund's advice and brought along warm clothing, including the heavy coat that he hadn't worn since a cold winter in Danzig years earlier. He was glad he had it now, even for the short journey from the plane to the low terminal, as a bitterly cold wind blew loose snow along the pathway. After collecting his bag, he took a 30-minute taxi ride to the ferry terminal to cross the straits. Even with the heater working full blast, it was so cold in the back seat that he'd asked the driver to pull over and moved up to the front–which was only marginally warmer.

The ferry terminal was prepared for evenings like this, with a covered bridge that passengers could use to board the sturdy vessel. The waiting room was comfortable and even the ferry itself was well-heated. It was completely dark outside, but the terminal area was well lit, so apparently no blackout rules applied. Signs in Swedish, German and English announced that the channel across the Oresund straits was less than three nautical miles wide–the narrowest point between the Northern tip of Denmark and the Southernmost part of Sweden. The crossing was a little rough, but took only about twenty minutes. A bus was waiting on the other side to take the passengers into Malmö itself.

Despite street-lighting, it was hard to see much of the town from the bus windows. Loose snow swirled in the wind and Muller had only a faint impression of Scanian architecture, with its half-timbered building facades, alongside more modern structures befitting Sweden's third most populous city. At the terminal, he'd picked up a brochure left over from the Baltic Exhibition that had apparently been a big attraction the previous summer; it said Malmö's population was 100,000. Well, all of them seemed to be inside somewhere staying warm, Muller decided, descending from the bus into the cold, dark night and seeing no one on the snowy sidewalks.

His taxi pulled up moments later in front of the Hotel Kramer, ablaze with light, its broad white stone façade sparkling between two three-story towers at either end, topped with pointed steeples. The hotel lobby was busy, but at one end, he spied a table below a sign reading 'Malmö Conference.' Two young men in vested suits stood to greet him as Muller strode over and introduced himself.

One of them checked his list, then handed Muller a room key and a welcome packet along with murmured words in Swedish, which Muller assumed were welcoming.

The bellman carried his bag and preceded Muller into a small but well-appointed second floor suite, turning on lights and checking the private bath for towels before retreating. Muller was tired from the trip–at least no airsickness this time–but he found the constant racket of the twin engines in flight and the bustle of making airplane connections fatiguing. Still here he was, and he was hungry, so he combed his hair, straightened his tie, put the welcome packet under his arm and descended to find the restaurant.

The lobby was even busier than it had been when he arrived. The bar was crowded with men and not a few women, Muller noticed, everyone well-dressed and seeming to be enjoying themselves; it certainly didn't present the foreboding image of imminent crisis that Ambassador Berglund had described, and Muller felt his spirits rise.

He was shown to a small table along the wall of the high-ceilinged restaurant, which was also filling up. Ordering a Dewars and soda, Muller emptied the packet he'd been given on the white tablecloth before him. There was an identification pin, which he proceeded to affix to his lapel, a map of Malmö, a bag of cookies and two envelopes, which he opened. One contained a document headed Provisional Agenda. They would begin at 9 AM the next morning at the Wallenberg Bank Building in–where else, but "the

Three King's Rooms". Muller smiled to himself; he wondered if the Kings themselves would show up after all, to reprise their earlier meeting, which the conference organizers were obviously trying to emulate.

He made a mental note to bring along the photo Berglund had given him.

The other document listed the participants.

Muller studied it more carefully, sipping his drink and spearing sardines from a plate that had been placed alongside by the waiter.

Three Balkan states were listed, Italy was there too; apparently Mussolini had decided he didn't want to be left out after all, Muller thought. Both the Belgians and Dutch were there; his name was listed for Switzerland. Ten nations, in all, he counted, including the four Scandinavian hosts. Not a bad showing, he decided.

At the bottom there was a smaller list of what were called "Observer States", which included both Britain and France and–a little jarringly for Muller–Germany.

Where are the Soviets? Muller wondered.

He ordered the fish of the day–wondering idly if it had been caught in the Baltic or in the North Sea which came together at Malmö–and a bottle of Austrian Grüner Veltliner. As he sat back relaxing and waited to be served, he became aware of two men at the next table engaged in a tense discussion, speaking English–in distinctly upper class British accents–loudly enough to be overheard.

Glancing at them, Muller immediately recognized the man on the left–P. I Wilson, who had been Anthony Eden's secretary and whom he'd met in London when he'd tried and failed to secure British help to prevent Hitler from taking over Austria in the spring of 1938. What was he doing here, Muller wondered, and who was the other man?

"Winston's determined to proceed," he heard Wilson say. The other man objected forcefully–something about the straits being too shallow. "He'll modify the battleships enough to get through," Wilson hissed back loudly. "With this show of force, we'll easily persuade the Scandinavians to abandon their annoying neutrality."

Muller discovered he must have begun leaning toward the table because when he went to put his drink back down on his table it missed and crashed to the tile floor with a loud sound of splintered glass, leaving a puddle of unfinished whiskey between the two tables.

The restaurant fell silent, and Muller, embarrassed, drew back in his seat.

Shit, he said to himself; how dumb was that?

He began to rise, but waiters sped to the table with towels and quickly whisked away the mess.

Muller felt obliged to speak to the two Englishmen.

"My apologies, gentlemen," he said, inclining his head. "I hope I didn't cause any trouble to either of you."

"No, no," the two men said, nearly in unison.

"No casualties here," said Wilson, smiling.

Then he bent toward Muller.

"Wait," he said, "don't we know one another? Ah," he said, his memory kicking in, "Commissioner Muller from the League–and Austria; of course."

He stood and offered his hand.

"Jim Wilson, British Foreign Office."

Muller stood and grasped Wilson's outstretched hand, smiling.

"You have a good memory, Mr. Wilson; of course, I recognize you too. Very sorry to interrupt you, sir."

"Not at all, Mr. Muller, you must join us. This is my colleague, Ambassador John Snow, our envoy in Helsinki. Are you here for this Malmö meeting? Why of course you are; I see your lapel pin. Please take a seat with us; we're trying to get our bearings for the meeting tomorrow and we'd welcome your perspective."

The waiter quickly put the tables together and reorganized the silver and glassware.

After they were seated, Muller explained that he was the Swiss Representative to the conference; he made a joking comparison between the straightforward name 'John Snow' and that of the UK Ambassador in Istanbul, whom he'd met in the fall, but whose name was decidedly more complicated, and in fact he couldn't recall it.

"Ah, our friend and colleague Sir Hughe Knatchbull-Hugeson," laughed Wilson. "Yes, rather a mouthful, that one;

names are one of our more endearing British characteristics, don't you think?"

"I recall you telling me that your own name, 'Polonius Ignatius', somehow became 'Jim', Muller replied with a grin.

"Ha!" Wilson grinned back and clapped Muller on the shoulder.

"Good memory, old boy," he said. "I'll bet even you didn't know about *that*, Snow," he said gaily to the Ambassador.

"And Mr. Muller, you've now transmogrified from a League of Nations Commissioner General to a Swiss Ambassador; Well!

"To Aliases," he toasted, now in high spirits, and they clinked glasses.

"You know, when Eden returned to the Cabinet not long ago, we had a conversation where he told me he wished he'd followed your advice on Austria just as he earlier wished he'd done so on Danzig; you were on the right side of both issues.

"Oh yes," Wilson went on, "he remembers you very well, Ambassador Muller; you're likely to hear from him sometime."

Not wishing to change the mood or disclose what might be classified information, Muller chose not to tell Wilson that Eden had in fact already contacted him, earlier in the year–warning the Swiss to cooperate with the new British plan to wage economic war on Germany or face punishing British retaliation. It was not a message he'd been happy to receive; another example of what he viewed as British arrogance in its conduct of foreign policy. But that was a story for another night.

"It would be a pleasure," Muller answered brightly. "Eden's a formidable figure."

That much was true. Eden's serene self-confidence and poise–just the way he carried himself–made him a presence which Muller had always found a little intimidating.

"And are you still one of his advisers, Mr. Wilson?" Muller went on, trying to steer the conversation back in their direction.

"Only indirectly," Wilson replied, "Eden's Minister for the Dominions now, but he's joined forces with Churchill who's nominally First Sea Lord but seems to roam all over the policy map. Halifax is Foreign Affairs now, and I'm nominally here to represent the Foreign Office.

"And I'm here to twist his arm and influence those narrow-minded mandarins in Whitehall to take bold action and fight the right war," Snow interrupted with a broad smile.

"Really?" asked Muller. "I thought you already have a war on your hand–with Germany; though except for a few naval engagements, it's fair to say there hasn't been a lot of action," he added.

"Do you have a new war to propose, Ambassador Snow?"

Snow had a shock of sandy red hair and bright blue eyes. He seemed to be a bundle of energy and he replied without hesitation.

"Our most important enemy is the Soviet Union," he said, "and that is whom we must fight."

"You're giving Hitler and Germany a pass?" Muller asked, deciding to be deliberately provocative. They seem ready to talk, he thought; let's see what's on their minds.

"Not at all," Snow replied, "but of the two, the Soviets are the most dangerous. And there's no doubt they're in cahoots. 'Teutoslavia' is what they're being called in Whitehall," he added, turning to Wilson.

"By some people in Whitehall," Wilson confirmed with a nod, "but not all."

"There was serious agitation over the joint statement that von Ribbentrop and Molotov issued after their Treaty of–what did they call it? Ah; the Boundary and Friendship Treaty," Snow continued.

"Something to the effect that it was the French and ourselves that are responsible for continuing the war and, unless we bring it to an end, they–the Soviets and Germans–will take necessary measures; about as clear a statement of joint intentions as you could ask for."

"A nasty and threatening pronouncement in our estimation," Wilson added.

Muller decided not to relate that he'd actually learned of the joint statement in Istanbul while having dinner along the Bosphorous with the British Consul General in Turkey–Hughe Knatchbull-Hugeson–and that both of them had read the language in much the same way–along with the Turkish minister who feared it portended a Soviet invasion of Turkey and had proceeded to get very drunk.

"And what's your current assessment?" Muller asked.

"We're divided!" Snow snapped, "and using bureaucratic uncertainty as an excuse to do nothing when opportunity and necessity both demand bold action."

Snow leaned forward, elbows on the table, and spoke intently.

"The Soviets have already gobbled up the three Baltic states and they're putting unmerciful pressure on Finland. I don't know how well you know your Finnish geography, Ambassador Muller, so let me offer a quick lesson; Wilson, you should listen too."

Snow placed the salt-shaker in front of him.

"That's Helsinki," he said. Moving his knife up and to his right, he said, "That's the Russian border–off to the East." Moving his finger, he traced a line from below Helsinki up to the middle of the knife. "That's the Baltic Seacoast," he said. "It goes right up to here," his finger stopped at the midpoint on the right side of the knife. "That's Leningrad," he said, placing the pepper-shaker there. "And everything on this side of the knife," he ran his palm from the knife to the left "is Finland.

"That knife-edge is the Finnish-Soviet border," Snow continued, "and at one point it's only 40 kilometers or so from Leningrad. The Russians see that as a problem–a threat they need to erase.

"Now here, is Lake Lagoda." Snow picked up a butt from the ashtray and placed it on the Finnish side of the knife, but farther up from where he'd put the pepper-shaker for Leningrad. "It's a really big lake," he added. Then put his thumb on the Baltic coast and his forefinger on the cigarette butt for Lake Lagoda.

"This area here," he used his other finger to point at the area between his thumb and forefinger, waggling them, "is the Karelian Isthmus, squeezed between the Baltic on the South and Lake Lagoda on the North. At its widest, it's only 100 Kms; the narrowest only 45 Kms.

"It's the most important piece of real estate in the region," Snow went on, still gesturing. "It's the closest point to the Soviet border and Leningrad. It's also where the Finns have anchored their defense against a Soviet attack; the Mannerheim Line," he added. "and the Soviets are demanding that the Finns hand the whole thing over to them."

Snow drew a deep breath then shrugged.

"If they were to do that, they'd be effectively disarmed, and the rest of Finland would be ripe for the Soviets to take over.

"Now down here," Snow drew his left hand to the edge of the table below the Helsinki salt-shaker, "is Hankö," he said. "That's a Finnish naval base and a commercial port that commands the entrance to the Gulf of Finland, which is what that part of the Baltic is called. The Soviets are demanding that too. Plus they want some islands in the Gulf."

Snow and Wilson accepted a Gitane and light from Muller.

"The Finns have refused the Soviet's demands and there's a standoff. The situation is very tense, and the risk of a Soviet attack is high. Everyone supposes that's one of the primary reasons to convene this conference–to rally international support for Finnish neutrality and persuade the Soviets not to invade."

Snow had to re-arrange his tableware as the waiters served dinner.

"So, you're here to promote Finnish–and Scandinavian neutrality?" Muller asked, with feigned innocence.

"Well, I am–at least to a degree," Wilson answered. "Snow sees this as an opportunity to widen the war."

"We must immediately sever diplomatic relations with the Soviets and warn them that any attack on Finland would be grounds for war". Snow spoke up without hesitation. "We should also enter into an alliance with Imperial Japan–*now*, not later–and support a Japanese declaration of war on the Soviets if they attack Finland. *That* would get Comrade Stalin's attention and stay his hand. The Soviets would stand to lose the entire Far East– Vladivostok, Port Arthur, Kamchatka; just think of it, gentlemen," Snow said, gesticulating with his knife and fork.

"Snow, the Soviets just defeated a Japanese Army in the East," said Wilson sharply.

"Yes, but it was a near thing, and the Soviets know they're vulnerable to a serious attack by the Japs."

Muller could see the two men were re-hashing arguments within the British government and listened without interrupting.

Snow renewed his argument.

"Playing the Japanese card is only the opener," he said; "we have to take every possible step to force Stalin on the defensive."

"Think about it, gentlemen; if the Soviets were to attack Finland, what's to stop them from proceeding to take the whole Scandinavian peninsular–or at least key parts of it–like the Norwegian Coast, for example, where they'd threaten Great Britain directly.

"That's why we should bomb the Soviet oil fields in the Caucuses; that would get their attention. Look, Wilson," Snow leaned forward, his eyes focused intently on the man, "the Foreign Office is even worried that Stalin will threaten India. With our forces busy elsewhere, it's the first time in generations when they could plausibly renew the Great Game rivalry for Afghanistan and other Central Asian nations to attack India.

"You know that's what they're saying in Whitehall," he said accusingly.

"But they won't *act.*" Snow hissed the word. "They seem paralyzed even though they know the French would be happy to go along; there's certainly more French public support for fighting the Bolsheviks than the Germans," he added.

"That's what I meant when I said it's time to widen the war, Ambassador Muller."

When the waiter came to clear the table, they paused, then lit up, awaiting brandy, which appeared quickly.

Muller decided to break the silence.

"And what of the war with Germany, Ambassador Snow?" he said, exhaling smoke from his Gitane.

Snow waved a hand as if dismissing the question.

"Germany can't support its war machine without new imports from the Soviets," he said, "and if Stalin's facing war against us and the Japanese on multiple fronts, he won't be sending precious supplies to Hitler; he'll keep them for himself, and our blockade will cut off the rest. So eventually–and not so long, either in my estimation–the German economy will crater and take Herr Hitler with it."

Snow brushed his two hands together to mimic the end of Nazi Germany.

"And Britain will cut off shipments of Swedish iron ore to Germany?" Muller added, "despite Sweden's legal rights–as a neutral nation– to trade with Germany?"

Snow nodded.

"Right," he said, "that's a bit of an awkward subject–but yes, we'll have to find a way to do that."

"Awkward?" snorted Wilson derisively. "Snow we're here at a conference to promote Scandinavian *neutrality*. Don't you find it more than just *awkward* to advocate a plan that would shred one of the principal tenants of neutrality?"

Snow shrugged and took a large swig of his cognac–a little defiantly, Muller thought to himself.

Wilson signaled for the check and stood.

"Gentlemen, I think we should leave it there," he said. "Ambassador Muller thank you very much for joining us to witness the full flower of British consensus on how to prosecute the war we've embarked upon."

After the two Englishmen had left, Muller remained at the table, reflecting on the conversation that he'd just witnessed.

He found it depressing.

How many times had he witnessed British policy makers take matters into their own hands and leave the rest of the world to suffer the consequences: appeasement, the Austrian Anschluss, Munich, the declaration following Hitler's occupation of Prague. Poland had been left to fend for itself after war was finally declared and no offensive had been taken against Germany–not even bombing raids. And now, there's a move afoot to go to war with the Soviet Union? To ally Britain with Japan? A sudden need to defend India? And what was that bit about bombing Soviet oilfields? That was a new one.

Muller lit another Gitane and swirled his cognac snifter.

It was blind hypocrisy for Britain piously to insist upon Russia's responsibility to recognize Finnish neutrality and avoid attacking Finland–while obviously harboring their own intentions to block trade between Sweden and Germany–in clear violation of Swedish neutrality. He recalled with irritation the reference he'd overheard Wilson make about Scandinavia's 'annoying neutrality.'

Muller shook his head.

Britain was no friend to neutrality, he said to himself–a familiar refrain. And here he was, representing neutral Switzerland–as Ambassador Plenipotentiary, no less–at a conference ostensibly aimed at promoting neutrality. Was there a way to help achieve an outcome that might advance the policy?

Something that might go beyond the communiqué that presumably would be generated by the conference? He didn't have any good ideas, but he decided to explore possibilities that might offer themselves.

CHAPTER 26

The Three Kings Suite at the Wallenbach Bank was, as Muller had expected, elegantly appointed. It featured highly polished mahogany floors covered by thick Persian carpets that contrasted with soft velvet wall coverings; bright chandeliers lit the chambers and fine art hung conspicuously in gold-leaf frames. The setting seemed determined to present an image of dignity and continuity–a metaphor for maintaining the status quo in a tense world at war– and most important, a symbol of the benefits of preserving Swedish–and by extension, Scandinavian-neutrality.

The meeting room itself was not large and offered a hint of intimacy. It was laid out with conference tables on three sides with seats for the delegates, each with a nameplate and flag in front of it, and seating for translators and stenographers inside the large U formed by the tables. Seats along the walls were provided for observers–no flags for them, Muller noted–and delegates' staff.

People mingled in the outer rooms of the suite awaiting the signal to file into the meeting room to begin the proceedings.

Muller didn't recognize anyone, except the Englishmen, whom he greeted perfunctorily, but then he saw that four men were standing beneath a large portrait to one side, evidently the foreign ministers of the host nations. Muller approached them and each greeted him warmly, speaking diplomatic French. Other delegates discovered their hosts at about the same time, so a small and orderly crowd gathered around the men.

Stepping to one side, Muller moved to a table near the center of the room and helped himself to a large coffee and a very rich-looking Danish pastry.

Someone appeared next to him and inquired if the pastry was as good as it looked. The man spoke in German and when Muller turned to him, he saw a red Nazi armband.

"Horner," said the man, introducing himself, with a smile. "Germany."

"Umm." Responded Muller, his mouth full of pastry. Then swallowing, he introduced himself and they shook hands.

"I hope you're feeling outnumbered, Mr. Horner," he said, "by neutrals, that is."

Horner smiled. He was a large, balding man with deep set eyes that seemed to flicker over the gathering of diplomats.

"Poor Germany nearly always find herself outnumbered and surrounded," Horner replied, projecting a resigned sense of dignity.

Muller was about to respond sharply, then caught himself. There was no point in starting a quarrel and risking the addition of a new entry in the file Muller was certain German authorities maintained on him.

So, he took another bite of the pastry–and simply walked away.

Entering the meeting room, he found himself seated between representatives of Sweden and Yugoslavia. A claque of reporters had filed noisily into the back of the room–separated from the conference by a thick blue velvet cord. A Movietone News camera stand was set up along one wall to film the event–or at least parts of it.

Rickard Sandler was Sweden's Foreign Minister and not only the host for the Conference, but evidently among the prime-movers, a point he emphasized in his opening statement, as he stood and delivered a forceful defense of Scandinavian neutrality–"all of Scandinavia, the three Kingdoms but most assuredly also including Finland, which is being hard pressed by her large and aggressive neighbor."

Muller had learned from his days at the League that conferences like this one follow predictable patterns. Participants make statements expressing their sentiments on the issue at hand, followed by an exchange of views–generally closely supervised by the conference chair–and, finally, they agree to the language of a communiqué, usually prepared by the chair, circulated toward the end of proceedings, setting out the conclusions the delegates had agreed to.

There was a ritual to the process that was reassuring. Yes, it was a set piece kind of sequence, and the process could be manipulated to bury, or simply ignore, contentious issues, as Muller had witnessed Anthony Eden do repeatedly during League Council meetings on Danzig. But when there was a consensus among participants and a common desire to take a stand, the procedure worked–and created a kind of momentum toward strengthening commitments to a common goal.

That certainly seemed to be the case, here, Muller sensed from the start. The participants in the Conference were deeply invested in a narrative that both embraced neutrality and insisted that belligerents and others respect it.

There were, of course, only so many ways to articulate the same message, so as the opening statements droned on, there was duplication and repetition, which, Muller was pleased to note, served to amplify the uniform support for neutrality among the participants. The speakers were on diplomatic good behavior and there were no direct attacks on individual nations or policies; but by indirection and, obvious hints and nods, statements were all aimed at the direct belligerents–Britain, France and Germany–and, not so subtly, the Soviet Union–to keep their hands off the neutrality of Scandinavia–and especially of Finland, which seemed most immediately at risk.

When it came his turn, Muller spoke briefly from prepared remarks (which he could distribute later to the press) stressing Switzerland centuries-long commitment to neutrality, but also underlining the rights of neutrals to engage in commercial trade with other nations, in accordance with well-established legal norms.

Muller intended it as a reminder to the belligerent states and the Soviets, not to interfere in Swiss trade with those on both sides of the conflict. But he also meant it as a defense of the stance of the Scandinavian hosts whose neutrality also involved trade with all the belligerents. As he'd delivered the remarks, Muller wished he could have called out the hypocrisy of his British dinner companions from the evening before–ever so willing to criticize the Soviet Union for interfering in Finland while secretly plotting to block Swedish sales of iron ore to Germany.

During a break in proceedings later in the morning, the Finnish Minister of Foreign Affairs, Eljas Erkko, approached Muller and asked if they might have a word in private. Muller agreed and Erkko led them out of the Three King's Suite to a small conference room down the corridor.

Erkko was a heavy-set man with dark black hair and round, black-rimmed glasses that seemed too small for his large head. His face bore a serious expression and he looked tired; in fact, once they were seated across from one another Muller got the impression that the man was exhausted.

Erkko offered to light their cigarettes and he coughed as he exhaled, shaking his head and waving the smoke away.

"Thank you for joining us," he said, coughing again, and pausing to draw a deep breath.

"Sorry," he said with a wan smile. "It's a very tense time for us Finns; we're under severe Soviet pressure and I'm a bit overwhelmed trying to stave off disaster."

"Keeping a neutral stance and holding onto our territory are causes Switzerland strongly supports, Minister Erkko," Muller said, smiling back at the man. "So, we're pleased to participate and lend our voice in support of your efforts."

"Good," said Erkko, "because I'd like to propose that you take a step going beyond just participating in the conference." Erkko tapped his cigarette in the ash tray and fixed Muller with a tired grin.

"I'm inviting you to lead a group of other neutral delegates to visit Finland, inspect our borders and reassure the world–especially our nearest neighbor–that our stance is wholly defensive and that we are neutral both in fact and in deed.

"We're hoping that some of Switzerland's high standing as a neutral might rub off on us," he added.

Muller ground out his butt and fixed his gaze on Erkko.

"Have you discussed this with other delegates?" he asked.

"No," Erkko shook his head. "Frankly, the idea came to me only as I listened to your prepared remarks this morning–which were very good by the way.

"I thought, how can Finland associate itself with the kind of moral authority that Swiss neutrality conveys? What if Ambassador Muller were to pay us a visit and endorse what we're trying to do?"

Muller rubbed his chin in thought. What an interesting suggestion, he thought to himself. It offered a new platform from which to project the importance of protecting neutrals from schemes being hatched by the belligerents–the kind of gesture he'd been groping for last evening after jousting with the British.

He was confident that Minister Minger would concur in promoting public support for neutrality–that's what he'd been sent to Malmö to do, after all. And it was a way–small, perhaps, but at least something–to oppose the kind of mischief that the British– and others– were planning and which he found so annoying.

"That's an appealing proposal, Minister Erkko," he said. "It would be consistent with what we're trying to achieve here in this conference and would add another layer of support for neutral nations and their policies. So, yes, I'm interested. What do you propose?

Erkko smiled and squared his shoulders, his body language suddenly projecting new energy.

"Excellent," he said. "We can begin almost immediately," he said. "I have a DC 3 at my disposal to return to Helsinki. The conference will conclude late this afternoon, so once it's done, we can go straight to the aerodrome. It's a short flight to Helsinki, and we can get you on an evening train to Viipuri so you can begin your border inspection first thing tomorrow morning."

"Viipuri?" asked Muller.

"Ah, sorry," Erkko smiled. "Viipuri is the major city in the Karelian Peninsular–the area in Finland that's closest to

Leningrad–and the territory that the Soviets are demanding that we surrender to them. You can do an inspection of the border area there in a day, or at most two, then meet with our ministries in Helsinki and hold a press conference to make your pronouncement in support of our neutrality–even in the face of Soviet provocation."

Muller nodded as Erkko spoke. It sounded like a good plan– and he liked the fact that it would begin right away.

"Count me in," he said.

Erkko rose and they shook hands.

"I'll invite others and make the arrangements," he said, leading the way back to the Three King's Suite.

Muller watched as Erkko worked the delegates, taking individuals aside, holding intense conversations in low tones; the man obviously knew his business. But he also saw delegates shaking their heads, apparently declining to participate.

When the Yugoslav seated next to him returned to his seat after conferring with Erkko, he leaned over to Muller.

"Not going to go," he said in a gravelly whisper. He pointed to his flag. We're called Yugoslavia now, but we remain Serbs at heart, just like the Russians now call themselves the USSR, but remain Russians.

"Serbs don't criticize Russians; we support one another."

Muller pursed his lips and returned the man's gaze. He was about to say something to the effect that Orthodox Serbs didn't necessarily have to line up with a Communist regime that had banished the Orthodox Church, just to honor an old alliance with Czarist Russia.

The Yugoslav leaned closer.

"If it were just poking the bear, that would be one thing. But now the bear is in alliance with Berlin to gobble up–we're not sure what, but we fear it might include the Balkans."

The man looked at Muller, then shrugged.

"So, we'll take a pass instead of taking a chance on irritating these new allies."

Instead of a long, sumptuous, multi-course sit-down luncheon, their Swedish hosts offered lunch in a buffet format, with generous helpings of gravlax, poached fish and cold cuts so delegates could mingle, table hop and converse with one another. Muller had opted for a high-top table where he could stand to eat, and he found himself quickly joined by the Belgian delegate, an older, white-haired man with veins prominently displayed in a bulbous nose.

He introduced himself–Etienne Deboeuf–and wished Muller good luck on his visit to Finland.

"But my Dutch colleague and I are in no position to participate in anything that might be construed to criticize one of the belligerents," he said. "Frankly, we were even hesitant to attend this conference, but it was ultimately decided that we should participate only to make the case for neutrality as a just, moral and legal national policy that all nations should respect. You'll perhaps have noticed that, in our prepared remarks, neither of us hinted at any criticism of any other nation; we simply stated the case for neutrality.

"We've been instructed to go no further out on any limb," he added, "so standing up for Finland is beyond our brief."

A pretty, blonde server appeared at their elbow and placed two glasses of aquavit on the table.

"Skol," she said, smiling.

Muller and Deboeuf toasted one another and drank.

Muller was not inclined to offer much sympathy.

"Don't you think that's a little short-sighted, Ambassador Deboeuf?" he said. "Belgium and the Netherlands were invaded in the Great War and if Hitler decides to attack France now, you'd likely be attacked again. The geography of Northern Europe's not going to change–so why not assert your neutrality more boldly?

"Today, Finland; tomorrow, Belgium," he added.

Deboeuf smirked.

"Actually, it was Belgium–and the Netherlands–and not tomorrow, but just three weeks ago," he said ruefully, speaking quietly and looking around to be sure he was not overheard.

"Our governments discovered that Hitler had given the order to invade first us, then the French, on November 12, Mr. Muller. Were you aware of that?"

Muller replied only that he was aware of press hints to that effect.

"Well, it's true," Deboeuf said. "Upon learning of the threat, King Leopold made an emergency late-night trip to the Hague. He and Queen Wilhelmina met through the night trying to find a way to persuade Hitler to change his mind. Their frantic calls to the Chancellery were rebuffed, so, finally, they decided to send a joint letter offering their services to mediate between the French and the Germans–hoping to galvanize world opinion enough to force Hitler to back down."

Muller nodded.

"That much was widely reported in the news," he said, "and it must have worked, since there was no invasion."

Deboeuf gave a dismissive shake of his head.

"Hitler never even responded to the message," he said. "Fate intervened, Ambassador Muller–well, fate and bad weather."

Deboeuf leaned toward Muller and spoke in a low tone.

"The invitation to mediate was delivered to the Chancellery on November 7," he said. "Hitler had already departed for Munich to deliver a speech–the one he cut short and left before the bomb went off–the aborted assassination attempt!"

Deboeuf finished his aquavit in one gulp.

"When we saw the report of the attack the next morning, we panicked," Deboeuf went on. "We didn't have any idea what would happen. We were terrified that Hitler would react in anger and unleash his army on us even sooner than planned. But, as you just said, nothing happened. We were told later that that the invasion order was canceled because the weather was so bad the Luftwaffe couldn't fly, and the Wehrmacht was stuck in the rain-soaked mud."

Deboeuf, took a deep breath.

"We still don't know the whole story," he said, "but both my government and the Dutch remain very nervous–and, frankly, scared. Neither one wants to rock the boat, Ambassador Muller."

Muller gazed back at the man impatiently.

"Ambassador Deboeuf, does anyone in either of your two governments seriously believe that your refusal to stand up for Finland will deter Hitler from invading you later if he decides he wants to do that?"

Muller ostentatiously placed his utensils on his plate and wiped his mouth with his napkin, preparing to walk away.

"Or is this just another excuse–the kind of refusal to stand up to Hitler which he's exploited for the last decade?

"Forgive me for leaving this depressing conversation," he said, "I'm going to fetch a custard from the buffet table."

As he turned to walk away, Deboeuf lifted his empty aquavit glass in a mock toast.

"Touché" he said, smiling grimly.

When the delegates began gathering in the meeting room after lunch to begin the afternoon session, Erkko took Muller by the elbow and spoke to him quietly.

"The others have all declined to make the trip to Helsinki," he said glumly. "I'll understand if you decide to reconsider."

Muller shook his head.

"No, Minister Erkko," he said, "if anything it stiffens my resolve to go. It's clearly the right thing to do and I'll not let myself be cowed by these timid officials. I'll get my things from the hotel at the next break so I'll be ready to accompany you when the conference ends."

Erkko's face broke into a smile and he shook Muller's hand vigorously.

"I'm glad to hear it," he said; "you won't regret your decision."

CHAPTER 27

If anything, the weather had gotten even colder and when Muller clambered aboard the Finnish DC 3 aircraft, he could still see his breath inside and kept his heavy coat on. Erkko seated himself across the aisle and, once they were airborne, and the roar of the engines subsided to a noisy growl, permitting them to speak to one another and be heard, he put his papers aside and leaned toward Muller.

"You're coming at a crucial moment, Ambassador Muller," he said. "I didn't say anything about it at the Conference so as not to distract from the communiqué endorsing Scandinavian neutrality, but I was informed last night that the Soviets have terminated the non-aggression pact between our two nations. I was up most of the night on the telephone dealing with an uproar in the cabinet. Most of us continue to believe this is just another Russian bluff–an attempt to scare us into yielding to their demands. But there are others who are persuaded that they intend to attack. So, we've ordered a partial mobilization of reserves, either as a political response or as a military safeguard, depending on your point of view.

"But whichever, our policy of strict neutrality is now our principal line of defense. The communiqué adopted this afternoon by the conference, trumpeting international endorsement of Scandinavian neutrality, has been distributed by the press across the globe. Any military reaction by the Soviets would be greeted by universal condemnation and I cannot believe Stalin would risk that now."

Erkko leaned across the aisle, speaking intently.

"Stalin's a hard man, Ambassador Muller, as I can personally attest, having dealt with him now over these last months in very tense meetings; but he's neither stupid nor foolhardy. He's seen how tough and determined we are to hold on to our borders. Frankly, I think our refusal to capitulate to his demands the way the Baltic states did surprised both him and Molotov, who's another tough customer, by the way, and it's forced them to reconsider. I don't think they want to risk international condemnation by attacking us."

"We'll see," he said, "but I remain confident.

"Moreover, the crisis makes your visit even more timely and significant," he added genially, smiling across the aisle. "An important Swiss diplomat–the very face of neutrality itself–arrives in Finland to add still more international–and moral–weight to our refusal to bend to Soviet pressure."

Muller turned away, gazing at the darkness outside the airplane's small oval window as he considered Erkko's remarks. The man was obviously wholly invested in his policy of resisting Stalin's demands and determined to convey an upbeat sense of confidence that it would succeed.

Muller understood that he was about to assume a role in the contest that Erkko was waging; he hoped the man knew what he was doing and not just grasping at straws.

A stewardess passed canapés and beer from a cart in the aisle. They each helped themselves, then Erkko leaned toward Muller again.

"When we arrive at Helsinki, I've arranged for two escorts to accompany you on the train to Viipui and the inspection. They both speak French, which is important, since not many Finns speak anything but Finnish–or Russian," Erkko grinned.

"At Viipuri, they'll get you outfitted with warm clothing for the front and billeted with the military for an early morning start to your inspection tour. The weather's deteriorating, but a little snow shouldn't deter a Swiss–who's embarking on a vital mission to defend neutrality and keep the peace."

With that, Erkko smiled, returned to his papers, and almost immediately fell into a deep sleep, his mouth open, snoring lightly.

So much for additional information about what this 'vital' mission of his would entail, Muller thought to himself, shaking his head and ignoring any misgiving about what lay in store ahead. He'd overheard a comment in the terminal that the strong tailwind they were riding would cut flight time to less than 90 minutes; at least that sounded promising.

And it proved to be an accurate prediction. The DC 3 yawed from side to side, fighting the wind gusts, as it approached the Helsinki airport to land; Muller gripped the armrests and exhaled when the plane finally bumped hard onto what appeared to be an icy and snow-covered tarmac. He followed Erkko out the plane's small rear doorway and trotted behind him in the cold to the nearby terminal doorway.

Inside, a clutch of reporters was waiting to greet them, and flashbulbs popped unexpectedly. Muller felt a little disoriented, put an arm up to shield his eyes, letting Erkko stride ahead to the airline counter, where he began taking questions. Muller hung back, sidling away from the cold doorway, but careful to stay out of the press limelight.

After several exchanges with the journalists, all in Finnish, so Muller wasn't able to follow what was being discussed, Erkko paused in his remarks, and gestured toward Muller–to Muller's surprise and annoyance. It was apparent Erkko was introducing him and, presumably, announcing that he was visiting Finland as a follow up to the Malmö Neutrality Conference.

The journalists turned toward him and flashbulbs popped again, this time in his direction.

Erkko invited him to the makeshift podium, and Muller waved him off. But Erkko continued to beckon him forward and several of the journalists shouted questions at him in French.

"Is Switzerland aligning with Finland?"

"What assurances are you offering Finland?"

Shit, Muller said to himself; I should have seen this coming.

Squaring his shoulders, he stepped to the podium.

"Switzerland is a neutral nation and views neutrality as vital national policy," he said. "The nations gathered at Malmö earlier today reaffirmed broad international support for neutrality and demanded that other nations respect it. I am here, at the invitation of Minister Erkko, as the Swiss representative to Malmö, to underscore our commitment to the policy of neutrality. I look forward to consultations with your leaders to promote that objective."

He stepped down, ignoring further questions from reporters and gave Erkko a sharp glance, warning him not to push any further.

Erkko, apparently understood his message, concluding the impromptu news conference after only a few more questions and turned toward Muller, preparing to depart.

"Well spoken," he said smiling and taking Muller by the elbow, leading him away from the press pack. "I probably should have asked if you wanted to make a statement," he added by way of an apology, which it was clear he didn't really mean.

"But all in a good cause".

Muller kicked himself; a Minister under heavy diplomatic and political pressure–of course he'd grasp at any chance to bolster his standing by invoking support–and not just from the results of the

Conference, but the visit of an important, a *neutral*, Swiss diplomat.

Well, the deed was done, and he'd responded on his own terms–reaffirming neutrality as a policy and Switzerland's commitment to embracing it. Nothing to be gained by complaining. But he let Erkko stride ahead, staff members surrounding him, already deep in conversation with them.

Two youngish men approached him.

"Ambassador Muller?" asked the taller of the two. He had dark hair parted on the side and a large lantern jaw.

Muller nodded.

"Sir," said the other, "we are assigned to accompany you to Viipuri and your tour of the front." He was a broad-shouldered, muscular man with short blond hair and bright blue eyes; he was wearing a military uniform which looked well-worn.

They stood before him at attention, deferentially.

Muller smiled and extended his arm to shake hands with the men.

The dark haired-man introduced himself as Vilho Venta, second secretary at the Ministry of Foreign Affairs; the other said he was 2nd Lieutenant Pekka Joleka, attached to the General Command staff.

"Welcome to Finland, sir," said Venta, as Joleka leaned down to take Muller's bag.

"We'll leave directly for the train station when you're ready."

"Let me have a word with the Minister and we can go," Muller said.

At the doorway to the terminal, before leaving, Erkko turned back toward Muller.

"Well, it's still tense, Ambassador Muller," he said. "The journalists were pressing me on how we'll respond if the Russians invade. I told them what I told you earlier; the Russians are bluffing.

"I hope I'm right," he added, "or you may have a livelier inspection tour than either of us is expecting.

"Good luck, I'm looking forward to speaking with you when you return from the front."

The man looked exhausted but was obviously determined to continue projecting an upbeat appearance. Muller grinned as they shook hands, trying to match Erkko's enthusiasm.

"You've assigned two stout young men who seem capable of looking out for me," he said, gesturing toward Venta and Joleka, who stood at attention before the Minister.

"Take good care of him," Erkko said, smiling at them and clapping Venta on the shoulder, "and bring him back to me safely, here in Helsinki, in a day or two."

With that, Erkko disappeared with his retinue.

His escorts directed Muller outside to a waiting staff car that drove them quickly along dark, largely deserted streets, depositing them at the railroad station, where Venta and Joleka led the way toward their boarding track.

Striding through the terminal Muller was amused to see signs for the mainline connections to Leningrad's famed Finland Station; it really *was* nearby, he said to himself, feeling a sense of anticipation for the trip that lay ahead.

The platform was bitterly cold, and snow drifted down from the vaulted overhead, but his escorts had reserved a compartment in the first car, and it was warm, so they could remove their heavy coats and shove them into the overheads.

As they took seats and rubbed their hands to warm them, a conductor slid open the compartment door and delivered a large wicker picnic basket with food and drink. Muller realized that he was ravenously hungry and helped lift the center table where they could lay out a spread of meats, still warm, along with potatoes and breads.

"I hope you like reindeer meat, Ambassador," said Joleka with a smile, "and the potatoes are our silli and mätti, topped with herring and fish roe; Finnish specialties–which I'm afraid you won't be eating at the front," he added.

Ventra took charge of a bottle of red table wine.

"Santé", they toasted one another, then dug into their meal.

Muller decided that he like reindeer meat and Finnish potatoes.

Afterward, he offered Gitanes from his cigarette case and fired his lighter for the three of them.

"I've never done a 'neutrality' inspection tour before," Muller said; "can you gentlemen enlighten me on the agenda you've organized for me?"

The two young men looked at one another uncertainly, hesitating before replying.

"We're not sure what you mean by 'a neutrality tour', sir," said Venta finally. "My instructions–which I was given only around noon today–were to organize a tour of the front right away for a high-ranking Swiss diplomat. As a foreign service officer, I don't have a way to do that, so I contacted Pekka–ah, excuse me, Lieutenant Joleka–as he's on the Army's General Command staff, to request his assistance."

Muller was beginning to see where this was going.

"And Lieutenant Joleka, when did you receive Mr. Venta's request?" he asked

"About 2 PM this afternoon, sir," Joleka replied.

"So, you two know one another, I take it."

"Oh yes sir," Venta replied brightly. "We met in the special high school French language program, and we've been best friends ever since."

Muller smiled. An order from the Minister to 'set up a program' for a visiting Swiss dignitary gets kicked down the bureaucracy to a second secretary, who has no solution and decides to contact his best friend, who's fortunately on the Army General Staff, to figure out how to get a tour to the front for the Swiss bigwig; they're giving it their best shot–but they really haven't any idea if they're going to succeed in pulling it off.

"So, we're winging it," he said, "am I right?"

The two young men looked at one another a little sheepishly, then smiled wanly and nodded.

"I'm afraid that's about it, sir," Joleka said, with a nervous chuckle, which sounded a lot like a giggle.

"I have a letter of authorization from my superior, but we haven't had time to make many arrangements."

Muller grinned.

"Then we'll have to make the best of it, won't we?" he said. "You got us something to eat–and to drink," he toasted them with his cup of wine, "so we're off to a good start at least.

"But Mr. Venta, maybe you can give me a little background on how Finland got itself into this predicament. What precipitated this crisis with the Soviets? I've certainly heard of Paavo Nurmi, your Olympic runner and Jean Sibelius' *Finlandia* is a favorite in my classical record collection. But Finland's dispute with the Soviets?" he shrugged; "I confess, I don't know much about it."

Venta nodded and sat forward on his seat in the compartment, obviously relieved at being asked about a subject he felt confident addressing.

"Well, sir, to begin, we Finns have a complicated history, being situated right between Sweden and Russia," he said, "and for a long time we were a kind of punching bag for both nations;

twelve major wars were fought between them on what we now claim as our territory.

"Then, in the redrawing of European boundaries during the Napoleonic Wars, we somehow found ourselves ceded to Russia as a self-governing Grand Duchy, which established the foundation for the current Finnish nation. We developed our own Finnish language and culture and carved out a more or less independent role for ourselves, albeit within Russia. But all that ended under Nicholas, the last Czar, who installed brutal administrators and destroyed nearly all of our separate institutions."

Joleka interrupted.

"A favorite sport of the Russian occupiers under Nicholas was to bull-whip Finnish agitators they'd arrested in Helsinki's Central Square," he said. "I had an uncle who bore the scars of a Russian whipping," he added.

"So, when the Great War broke out in 1914, thousands of Finnish nationalists–including my uncle–fled to Germany to fight the Russians. They were enrolled in a school in Lockstedt near Hamburg and formed what became known as the 27th[th] Royal Prussian Jaeger Battalion. Many of today's Finnish leaders trained under the Germans," he added; "they're no friends of Russia."

"Pekka's uncle is one of those leaders, Ambassador Muller," Venta said, interrupting his friend. "He served in the Jaegers and then was a senior commander in the Finnish military for many years."

"Tell him the story, Pekka," he said.

Joleka shot a dirty look at Venta but turned to Muller with a grin.

"He always does this to me, sir," he said. "My uncle was pretty well known as one of the leaders in securing Finnish independence and Venta regularly embarrasses me by telling people about him."

"So, what's the story, then?" asked Muller? "I'm interested."

"It's complicated, sir," replied Joleka, unsmiling, "like a lot of things in Finland."

He drew a deep breath, then, crossing one knee over the other on the compartment seat, he leaned forward, hands on one shin.

"My uncle was Bertel Joleka," he began. "He's dead now; died in a traffic accident two years ago. But he was a power in the Finnish military; second in command to Field Marshal Mannerheim, whom you've probably heard of."

"I've heard reference to 'the Mannerheim Line'," Muller replied," but I don't know anything about Mannerheim himself."

"Well, that's a good place to begin, then," said Joleka, "because Carl Gustav Mannerheim is today–and has been since the beginning–the most prominent leader in Finland's short history.

"He was born here in what's now Finland, but to a Swedish-speaking family and he didn't even learn to speak Finnish until he was in his fifties. During the period when Finnish relations with Russia were cordial, he became an officer in the Russian Imperial Army, fought in Manchuria and Korea during the Russo-Japanese War in 1905, served in Poland, then a Russian possession, and fought for the Czar in the Great War. He'd married the daughter of a powerful Russian nobleman and moved in the highest circles of the Romanov regime.

"He was–and remains–hostile to Bolshevism and he opposed both the overthrow of the Czar and Bolshevik revolution, but he was powerless to prevent what finally transpired. So, in the chaotic aftermath of those events, he returned to Finland, just about the time Finnish leaders–most of whom he didn't even know, and whom he had difficulty communicating with because of his lack of Finnish language skills–declared Finnish independence.

"The formal declaration was issued on December 6, 1917, so our celebration is next week." Joleka smiled at this diversion.

"But once the deed was done, the Finns realized they needed a military leader to defend the new state they'd established; Mannerheim was determined to mount a campaign to oust the Bolsheviks from the new state so, voila! Their interests coincided and Mannerheim became Commander of the Finnish Army."

"Except no Finnish Army existed," Venta interrupted with a laugh," and that's where Uncle Bertel enters the story.

"You go on with the story, Pekka," he said, rising to his feet, "I'll go fetch us another bottle of wine," and he slid open the compartment door, stepping into the corridor.

"Vilho's right," Joleka said, accepting Muller's light and exhaling. "That's also when leaders of the Jaeger Battalion in Germany resigned their commissions, returned to defend newly-independent Finland–and found a highly credentialed General who desperately needed to establish an Army to command, but who lacked both the local knowledge and the language skills to do so.

"So, I'm guessing your Uncle Bertil filled those needs," Muller said with a grin, thinking to himself how he'd played a similar role as Secretary to Sean Lester, the League of Nations High Commissioner in Danzig five years earlier.

Joleka nodded.

"Through a series of coincidences, that's precisely what happened," he said.

"When the Russian Empire was overthrown, the Czar's minions were still in charge of most of the institutions which Finnish leaders were determined to take over and there were 20,000 Russian soldiers stationed in the country. Most of them had become radicalized like the Russians troops that mutinied against the Czar, so they threw their support to leftist elements in what was now Finland, with the objective of establishing a Bolshevist state here.

"Mannerheim, the Jaeger veterans and their supporters were determined to prevent that from happening, forming military units that became known as the 'White Guards', which supported an independent, Finland. They secured vital assistance from Sweden, which also strenuously opposed Bolshevism and even persuaded Germany to send both troops and naval support to oppose what inevitably became known as the Bolshevik 'Red Guards' in the civil war that ensued.

"It's a long and, as I said earlier, a complicated tale," Joleka said as they both stubbed out their butts in the center table's ash tray.

"The Civil War was bloody and vicious, as those things tend always to be," he continued. "But in the end, the Whites prevailed, the Germans departed after they surrendered in the Great War and in October of 1920, the Finnish Government and Lenin's Soviet Union signed the Treaty of Tartu, which established the border between our two nations–the same border that defined the Grand Duchy of Finland before the War, by the way–and the same border that exists today, the one Stalin is demanding we surrender."

Venta returned with a bottle of wine.

"Have we won the Civil War yet?" he said teasingly to Joleka as he refilled their cups. "He can go for quite a while about the battles around Rautu and all that," he said to Muller with a grin.

"Kippis." They toasted.

"Finished," Joleka said grinning at his friend; "we won again in this telling."

"Good," replied Venta, "because now I can pick up the storyline.

"After the Treaty of Tartu–Pekka, you talked about that?" Joleka nodded.

"Well, after that treaty, both Finland and Russia–now the Soviet Union–retreated into their respective corners and, frankly, picked at the wounds they each believed they'd suffered. The Soviets deeply regretted losing what was now a stubbornly and aggressively independent Finland and we Finnish developed an almost pathological aversion to Soviet Communism which was right next to us–just across our border.

"We became, by virtue of hard work and our embrace of western values, a more prosperous and successful society than our Soviet neighbors and, while we have serious left-right differences among our political parties, there is an overwhelming popular consensus in favor of independence and aversion to the Russian-Soviets."

"And that is the rock upon which this crisis with Russia, as you correctly referred to it, Ambassador Muller is poised to shatter," Joleka added.

"Right," said Venta.

"Mannerheim has been Chairman of the Finnish Defense Council since the end of the civil war, but has always had strained relations with the elected politicians, who challenged his autocratic approach and, in particular, rejected his repeated demands for funds to modernize and equip a Finnish Army.

"So, they gave him the title of Field Marshal, then did their best to ignore his advice."

Joleka nodded.

"There's always been this peculiar tension between a national consensus that opposes the Soviets and the political divide on whether or not to arm ourselves," he said.

"And it's still on full display right now," he added.

"Go on, Pekka," Venta said, "tell the Ambassador what happened in August."

Joleka nodded.

"Tensions spiked here after the Soviets and Germans signed that so-called Non-Aggression Pact—which we all view as an alliance, by the way," he said. "So, there was broad support for a show of force to demonstrate Finnish commitment to our policy of independent neutrality."

"At least the contending interests could agree on that much," Venta interjected.

Joleka then continued.

"The Army mobilized 100,000 reservists from around the country to conduct maneuvers and stage a big parade in Viipuri. All the Finnish bigwigs were there and Marshal Mannerheim, the centerpiece of attention for most of the troops, sat on his horse for hours, saluting the men as they marched by."

"But then the politicians took over and our Prime Minister, delivered a speech that seemed to undercut the entire exercise," Venta again interrupted.

"Sorry, go ahead," he said to Joleka.

"Cajander—that's our Prime Minister—celebrated the fact that we lack a modern army and a strong defense," said Joleka.

"This isn't a direct quote, but he said something to the effect that Finns can be proud that we don't have a lot of rifles and uniforms and other equipment rotting away in warehouses since we're never going to need them. Instead, he said, we Finns have a high standard of living and a strong education system and that's our best defense."

Joleka shrugged.

"That's about as clear an illustration of the division over military readiness as I can offer, Ambassador Muller," he concluded.

"Where do the negotiations stand with the Soviets?" Muller asked. "Erkko certainly seemed to be concerned after that impromptu press conference today."

His two companions looked at one another.

Finally, Venta spoke up.

"Stalemated, so far as we know," he said. "We've steadily resisted Stalin's demands, which he keeps ratcheting up. The last negotiations were in mid-November; it's been a war of nerves since then."

"But there's a Mannerheim wrinkle to that issue too," Joleka added. "Whether it's because of his Russian history–or just his worldview…" he paused, then continued. "Mannerheim thinks Stalin sees this as an issue of Soviet survival and that he won't back down.

"Leningrad is vulnerable to attack from Finland," he went on; "it's only twenty miles or so East of where we are right now. Stalin knows perfectly well that he doesn't face a risk of invasion by Finland itself, but he fears either Germany or Britain could use Finland as a base for an attack."

"In other words, invade us, then just keep going and attack the Soviet Union via Leningrad," added Venta.

He paused.

"It's not a crazy idea," he added, "and Mannerheim is confident he's right. He's been urging the cabinet to begin negotiating terms for the concessions Stalin's demanding–ceding territory but hoping to get him to agree to arrangements like we had when we were a Russian Grand Duchy."

"The political leaders won't hear of it," Venta said. "Offering concessions to the Soviets would be a political kiss of death."

"Mannerheim keeps saying it's preferable to being attacked by a nation with 88 million citizens it can throw into a war against us," Joleka said. "So, he's threatening to resign."

He shrugged and shook his head.

"That would demoralize the Army," he said dolefully.

"But it might happen."

The men finished the last of the wine and, as they did so, the conductor slid open the compartment door and announced they were arriving in Viipuri.

"So, I guess we'll see, won't we," Muller said as they got to their feet and put on their heavy coats.

If War Should Come

CHAPTER 28

The train platform at Viipuri was snowy, and it seemed to have gotten even colder. Looking back on the platform after stepping down from the compartment, Muller could see dozens of men exiting the train dressed in what passed for Finnish Army uniforms: heavy coats and thick pants above study high boots, and they all wore warm fur hats of various kinds.

"It's the mobilization troops," muttered Joleka. "That'll make our plans even dicier. But at least it'll ensure there'll be buses to take us to the base.

"I'm afraid this isn't going to be very luxurious Ambassador," he added.

Muller waved off the remark. His outfit didn't seem as warm as the ones the soldiers were wearing, and he certainly didn't have one of those warm fur hats; his ears were already freezing.

"Let's find one of those buses," he said.

They walked through the small brightly lit station–no blackout here either–and exited to find at least a dozen buses–all painted in white camouflage, Muller noted–awaiting them. They boarded one, took seats, and when it was full, including soldiers standing in the aisle, the driver closed the door, and they took off into the night.

Twenty minutes later, they were waved through a well-guarded gate and pulled to a stop before a low L-shaped building. A soldier with a Suomi submachine gun strapped to his shoulder directed them inside to a large receiving hall with desks set up for processing the reservists. Joleka told Muller and Venta to line up while he strode to a doorway on the right, knocked once and entered.

Moments later, he emerged with a uniformed officer, who beckoned them to follow him. They mounted a staircase and walked down a corridor. The officer checked the room numbers then opened a doorway on their right, motioning them to enter. It was smallish dormitory room with four beds, a washstand two folding chairs.

The officer gestured to Joleka and they spoke in Finnish.

"Well, this is our billet, Ambassador. Sorry; you've got us for roommates, I'm afraid. But it's better than the enlisted men's quarters."

He saluted the officer, who retreated down the corridor.

"Leave everything here," Jokela said; "I'll lock up. But let's go directly to the dispensary and see what kind of outfits we can find to keep ourselves warm tomorrow. We'll try to avoid extended exposure but…" he shrugged. "It's supposed to drop to ten below tonight, so best to be prepared."

Muller smiled; well, you signed up for this, he reminded himself.

There were large stacks of heavy jackets and padded trousers and piles of heavy mittens and fur caps with earflaps, and it didn't take long to find what they needed. Joleka then led them across the room to where boots and gators were lined up.

"These are what we call *pieksu*," he said; "they're special padded boots we use for our ski troops.

"See?" he said, finding one and putting it on. "The turned-up toe fits right into the toe-binding on skis. Then this," he strapped on an insulated gator that covered his leg from the shoe nearly to the knee.

"And these," he picked out a couple of leather belts and handed them to Muller and Venta, "are what you attach to the skis, so you don't lose them if you have to crawl under fire.

"That's not our plan, tomorrow," Joleka said with a grin, "but better to be equipped than not."

They hauled their new paraphernalia back to their quarters and organized themselves for the next morning.

"Up before 6 and on the road by 7 tomorrow morning" Joleka announced cheerfully"

Muller slept soundly until awakened early the next morning. They went to the mess hall in civilian clothes for breakfast, then returned to their billet and donned their new winter equipment.

The snowy yard in front of the building was lit by bright spotlights and buses and other vehicles were drawn up.

"I've organized a van for us," Joleka told Muller and Venta; "We'll take some non-coms along as far as Summa, the last town before the border, then we can use it to approach the border itself, a few miles East."

They bundled themselves into the narrow van, which had a heater that failed to warm the interior, so they huddled into their greatcoats, as the convoy moved out.

It was still pitch dark when they left the lighted billet yard. Light snow was falling in the half-covered headlights ahead of the van, and Muller had the sense of forest on both sides, but he could only make out shadows in the darkness.

"When does it get light?" asked Muller.

"Sunrise is around 9 AM, and lasts until 3 in the afternoon," Joleka answered. "But it's very low on the horizon; you won't see much even at noon; we're used to it," he added.

Their van bumped along a road covered in snow and ice but traffic and the freezing cold had hardened it and there were no delays. A half hour later, they arrived in Summa, which consisted of a dozen or so low buildings. The Army had set up a canteen on outdoor stoves, so they were able to stretch their legs and enjoy a cup of hot coffee before boarding the van again, this time with a fresh set of soldiers hitching a ride up to the border, that Joleka told them was about five miles ahead.

By now, the first hints of grey light began to lift the darkness and Muller could see they were enveloped by thick pine forest on either side of the narrow track on which they were driving, trailed by motorized sledges on skis carrying supplies. Their driver doused his lights and soon they began to drive in the center of the track between formations of infantry on skis that moved to either side to make room for their van. Steep banks fell off on either side of the narrow track, and Muller looked down at sharp boulders that were scattered at the bottom of the ravines that had been created by engineers dynamiting through rocky formations to build this narrow track.

"Where is this Mannerheim Line that people talk about?" asked Muller, speaking softly to Joleka who was seated across the aisle from him on the driver's side of the van.

Joleka chuckled quietly and pointed out the van's window to the infantry skiers they were slowly passing.

"No Maginot concrete or gun emplacements here, sir," he responded. "Just fierce fighters and defensive terrain."

Joleka began to say more, when suddenly the horizon in front of them exploded in a sheet of blinding light and a sound louder than Muller had ever heard enveloped them; so loud he could feel it physically. Then, without warning, fiery explosions burst around them and the realization dawned on him; they were being shelled in a massive artillery attack.

Shit! Muller gripped the armrest of his seat and began to rise when suddenly the van was violently tossed in the air and the concussion from an exploding shell seemed to suck the air right out of Muller's lungs. He felt, more than he could see the van disintegrate and he heard screams of pain and fear before he landed hard on snow and rocks, banging his head and left side in a painful and awkward landing which knocked the breath out of him and left him prone and disoriented. Nearby explosions scattered debris on him, and his first involuntary movement was to curl up and try to burrow down into wherever he'd landed.

He couldn't see a thing, then realized his fur cap had come down over his eyes. Righting it and fumbling with tying it beneath his chin, his eyes suddenly focused, then squeezed shut again as more explosions on the road just above him rocked the steep embankment where he found himself pinned.

Gripping the embankment to avoid sliding or tumbling down the steep slope, he cautiously looked around him. Pine trees everywhere were aflame, casting shadowy light on scene, then another series of bright explosions sent him scratching still further into his burrow on the embankment. He shut his eyes tight and tried to make himself smaller, his heart pounding and his mouth clamped shut; he felt more afraid than he'd ever been in his life.

When there was a lull in the shelling, he tried to lift his head to orient himself, only to cringe back into his burrow when still another barrage of shells exploded nearby with blinding light and huge concussions that seemed to pound every part of his body.

Christ! Stop. Stop.

But still another barrage sent him shrinking again into his smallest body position, pulling his legs up to his torso and willing himself to hug the uneven ground beneath him. He kept his eyes shut, cringing as the shelling continued.

He had no idea how long the attack lasted; it seemed endless.

But finally, the shelling stopped, as suddenly as it had started, and there was a moment of eerie quiet, then shrieks and screams of pain from wounded men and shouts of men giving orders shattered the silence.

Muller willed himself to sit up, still braced on the embankment and ready to curl up again if the attack resumed. Somehow, he'd been thrown clear of the van and landed on this steep, snowy bank that was below the road and had provided him protection.

Then he looked below him to the bottom of the ravine where the embankment ended and he saw the twisted remains of the van, upside down, its walls blown off, impaled on sharp, rocky boulders.

Christ!

Muller scrambled to his feet, but then, overcome by dizziness, had to sit back down in his burrow and take stock of his own condition. His head hurt and his left shoulder was very sore–but he tried moving his left arm and found it worked, though painfully. He succeeded in getting up on all fours, his left knee sore, but apparently serviceable, then slowly rose to his feet, careful to keep one arm on the embankment for balance. He drew a deep breath then stood up, his head clearing. Finally getting himself oriented, he began slowly picking his way down the embankment toward the remains of the van.

He could see the driver's body, thrown half out of the van, the remains of his head impaled on a bloody ridge of rock. Sliding down the last few steps he steadied his arm on the shattered side of the van and bent to look at the interior. The grey light of early morning didn't offer much detail, but there was no need. The occupants had been flung against the rocks in the ravine and their bodies were piled against one another in a bloody tangle.

Good God, Muller said to himself in disbelief.

Good God!

Stepping around the wreck and trying to find places he could stand, Muller began the grisly business of attempting to remove the bodies to make sure none were still breathing. He stopped after pulling out the bodies on top, all of them dead. Beneath them he could see the remains of the others. Joleka's head was split in two and his brain matter was visible on the rock beneath him and Venta's neck was dangling at a ninety-degree angle from a strut of the van, his sightless eyes still open.

Muller sank into the snow next to the wrecked van and put his head in his hands, his mind unable to focus. He had no idea of how long he sat there, stunned and in shock.

But then he became aware of someone shouting from the road above. Turning, he saw a soldier pointing and waving at him, beckoning him back up the steep incline.

Responding, Muller got to his feet and slowly began clambering his way up on all fours, finally getting to the top where he could stand. The soldier looked at him, and said something which Muller didn't understand, then turned and began leading Muller along the roadway, where he could see more soldiers–a lot of them, fifty, maybe more–were gathering around the supply sledges that Muller recognized as having accompanied the van.

Two of the sledges were tipped on one side, but otherwise intact, and Muller saw the soldiers taking white, poncho-like, coverings out of a big sack that had been placed on the roadway and pulling them on over their heads as camouflage. Cross-country skis were being pulled from a sledge and passed to the men, along with ski poles, which the men were exchanging among themselves to get the right fits.

As Muller and the soldier leading him approached, they were both tossed camouflage outfits which they pulled on before stepping up to get a pair of skis. Muller was surprised how easily the tip of the boots Joleka had helped him pick out the night before clicked into the bindings; he tested a couple of the ski poles before finding two that were right, and he followed along to where the men were assembling. Another sledge must have contained weapons, as Muller saw disassembled machine guns being strapped to the backs of a half dozen of the bigger men. Rifles were passed around to the others–Muller didn't recognize what kind it was and didn't care. He took one, slung it over his shoulder, and shoved two pouches of ammunition in a pocket under his white cloak.

His mind was still reeling, and he simply followed instructions. There was no point in trying to explain his predicament; no one would care, even if he could have made himself understood; they were under attack and they were preparing to defend themselves. He might be Swiss and neutral, but all that mattered at the moment was that he was just another soldier.

Following shouted orders Muller couldn't understand, the men began skiing–in the direction the artillery barrage had come from. This was no retreat, Muller realized; this was a counterattack. Well, he would try to do as he was directed, following the lead of the soldiers around him.

As an experienced cross-country skier, Muller found he had no difficulty in keeping up as the soldiers deployed on a wide front, gliding silently through the snowy forest. Fires still blazed in some of the pine trees, but Muller could see that, while the barrage had felled trees and thrown up craters of sand and rocks in the snow, there hadn't been much damage–except, of course, when the explosives had found pockets of men, like the convoy and his van. He willed the image of crumpled bodies out of his mind as he plowed ahead.

He had to avoid felled trees and branches with his skis, but the snow wasn't deep, and it was slick in the cold, so he found he could make good time moving forward alongside the white-clad soldiers on either side of him.

After fifteen minutes or so, Muller found himself winded, and could see others laboring as well. Their leader called a halt and, as they caught their breath, plumes of frozen breath surrounding them, they heard what sounded like a dull roar.

Muller cocked his head to listen; it was evident that others had heard it too, and they began nodding and speaking softly to one another, grim-faced. There was no complaint when they resumed their pace and Muller could hear the sound–whatever it was–growing louder.

Then, at a command, the soldiers all stepped out of their skis and knelt to affix their skis to their leather belts. Muller fumbled with his, and the soldier on his left crawled over to show him how to do it, then clapped him on the shoulder with a grin, saying something Muller didn't understand.

The formation then crawled forward, literally, their skis trailing behind them. After a hundred meters or so crawling on his stomach, Muller thought his lungs would burst, when suddenly they found themselves at the end of the forest, on a ridge overlooking a snowy field. No, Muller realized, not a field; a frozen lake, and there, lumbering directly at them, were three Soviet tanks, their engines roaring as they labored through the snow–that was the noise he'd heard, Muller realized–and trailing the tanks were what looked like several hundred Soviet infantrymen, wearing brown uniforms, not even attempting camouflage, some of them Muller could see not even wearing heavy coats.

Orders were being issued in low voices in his formation. The machine guns were unstrapped and assembled and being set up behind rocks and fallen trees. Muller could see the camouflaged soldiers on either side of him crawling into depressions and other spaces where they could lie prone and fire, with at least some protection. Muller, doing the same, found himself directly behind a dead tree branch and worked the rifle strap off his shoulder so he could maneuver it into position to fire. As he did so, he discovered his mitten had a special wool trigger finger; smart, he thought as he readied himself.

Christ, those tanks were headed right at them.

The lead tank, bigger than the other two, began firing, it's turret gun belching flame and the other two smaller tanks behind it followed suit. But they were firing wildly, their shots passing harmlessly above the prone soldiers.

No one spoke as the tanks churned closer and closer to the ridgeline, the Soviet infantry packed behind them. As the tanks reached the edge of the ridgeline and began to climb, an order rang out and the Finnish machine guns began raking the Soviet soldiers. Muller and his camouflaged companions began firing at the enemy.

The snowy frozen lake suddenly turned blood red as Soviet soldiers were felled by the murderous fire at nearly point-blank range. Muller could see them throw up their hands in terror as they were cut down. A few lifted their rifles to fire, but their shots were wild, and men sank to their knees in terror or fell dead or wounded.

The big tank was only yards from the Finnish formation; it stopped as it mounted the ridge, its turret gun searching for targets; it's two side machine guns began firing, but again wildly.

Suddenly, Muller saw a camouflaged figure leap to the side of the tank. The Finn calmly used his lighter to fire a rag stuffed in a bottle, then hurled it into the tank's machine gun aperture where it burst into flame. Muller was close enough to hear the screams from the tank crew as the flames enveloped them. The turret opened and they tried to leap to safety, clothing ablaze, but were quickly shot by the Finns. The two smaller tanks stopped, and one circled back toward where it had been coming from. Two Finnish soldiers leaped down the short slope, firing to cover one another, then the first man slammed a spike into the tank tread, dislodging the track, and the tank stopped in its place, its motor racing, but unable to move. One of the Finns crumpled and fell, but the other threw himself over a nearby log and scrambled to safety among the rocks.

The surviving Soviet soldiers wavered, then began running back in the direction they'd come. Muller continued firing, as did the rest of the formation, cutting down the fleeing men. Sighting his rifle, Muller saw figures in the back of the retreating Soviet formation shooting at their own retreating men.

Christ! They were actually doing that.

He squeezed off a round at one of the men and missed, but then watched in satisfaction as another bullet–maybe from the retreating Soviet soldiers spun the man around and he fell.

At a signal, the Finnish soldiers stopped firing. The lakefront where the Soviets had attacked was a scene of carnage like nothing Muller had ever even imagined, a bloody tangle of men–dozens and dozens of them–lying in contorted heaps; Muller could hear screams and moans from wounded men, but his command paid them no heed.

Looking across the frozen lake, they could see–even as it began snowing harder–a new attack being mounted, as more tanks---he counted a half dozen or so–began crossing the frozen lake in their direction, trailed by even more brown-clad Soviet soldiers.

Following commands he couldn't understand, Muller left his skis in place and along with the others tried to run and stumble in the snow back in the direction they'd come. A sledge had somehow been driven to their rear and the men lined up alongside it. Each man took two objects, one in each mittened hand and began walking carefully back to where they'd left their skis.

Christ! They were mines, Muller realized. Each man was taking two mines back to build a minefield as a defense against the next attack.

When it was his turn, Muller took two of the round steel objects, one in each hand, and followed the lead of his companions as they trudged slowly and carefully back toward the ridgeline. He watched as the man next to him placed the first of his two mines in a snowy depression, flicked a metal handle from vertical to flat on the mine's surface, then carefully and gently covered it with snow and stray branches. Then he moved a few yards away and began doing the same with the second mine.

So that was how to activate the mine.

Muller rapidly, and carefully, followed suit, then pulled his skis and poles back away from the mines, stood up, buckled his bindings, and joined the others turning away and retreating from the lakefront. A sudden blast and screams of pain behind them made Muller pause and look back, but his companions put their heads down and continued to move away from the lakefront.

Muller had no idea how long they skied; they stopped occasionally to catch their breath, then pressed on silently, saving their breath. He was desperately thirsty, but canteens would have been useless in the freezing cold, so he just concentrated on putting one ski after the other, willing himself forward with the others, his mind blank and all of his energy directed to keeping up.

Then finally, they halted at a campsite. There were low, snow-covered huts and dozens of small, white canvas tents. By now it was nearly dark, but the men seemed to know how to divide up. Muller followed the soldier next to him as they planted their skis and poles in the deepening snow, then ducked after him into one of the tents. There was a small stove on a wood plank toward the front and it gave off enough heat so the men untied their ear flaps and removed their big mittens; a pot of stew was warming on the stove. The men–there were five of them–passed the pot from hand to hand, serving themselves with a single large spoon. Then they passed around a coffee pot and individual tin cups.

Muller ate his share gratefully. The hot coffee quenched his thirst and he lay back trying to relax, his mind mostly a blank.

The men began chatting in low tones, laughing softly with one another; they spoke to Muller and he tried replying in German, French and English; the men looked at him querulously, uncomprehending, but the two nearest him clapped him on the back in friendly fashion before returning to their own conversation.

We're all in this together, was the unspoken message. It was a feeling that Muller found reassuring and he fell into an exhausted sleep.

Sometime later, he had no idea what time it was, everyone was awakened by the sound of shrill whistles.

It was pitch dark and the only light was from a few lanterns set in the snow outside the tent. The men fumbled with their heavy gear to relieve themselves nearby, then retrieved their skis and poles. Orders were given by a man who was evidently the commander; Muller didn't understand a word, but he fell in along with the others as they began to ski off through the forest, each man scarcely able to see his neighbors as they made their way in the darkness.

After what Muller estimated was roughly 30 minutes, they halted, breathing heavily, but alert. Not far away, they saw campfires burning brightly and they could hear the sound of men yelling and singing–even the sound of some kind of musical instrument.

It was a Soviet encampment, Muller realized with a start.

If there were sentries, Finnish soldiers must have silenced them somehow. Muller followed the lead of the men around him as they once again resumed their prone positions and creeped toward the campfires. They halted only meters from their target, and Muller heard quiet voices and metallic clicks as the machine guns were assembled.

Then he heard a shouted order and the Finnish machine guns and riflemen opened fire, pouring deadly rounds into the Soviet camp. Some Finns must have crawled even closer, where they could hurl grenades–and a couple of the flaming bottles that Muller had seen them use against the tanks. They burst into flame– gasoline, Muller guessed–when they shattered on impact, making fiery explosions.

Pandemonium broke loose in the Soviet camp, the fires and muzzle flashes revealed Soviet soldiers racing away into the darkness and falling in heaps, their screams audible over the roar of the gunfire.

Tank motors started and searchlights sought out the Finns, but their attack had obviously wreaked havoc in the camp and there was no organized resistance and just a few wild shots as the Finns' deadly fire continued.

Then, as before, they were ordered to stop. The men slipped their weapons onto their backs then turned and began crawling, but not back; this time off to one side, as the Soviets, finally reacting, began firing at the place they'd occupied.

Their formation continued to crawl further, then finally got to their feet and onto their skis, silently gliding away further into the forest.

It was an even longer journey this time, made more difficult by the darkness, and men fell as their skis caught tree limbs and other obstacles under the snow, which was deeper by now and more tiring to traverse. Muller was about at the end of his rope when, suddenly the formation arrived at another Finnish camp–or maybe it was the same one; he couldn't tell and didn't care.

He stacked his gear at the entry to one of the low huts and he stooped to follow another soldier inside, lifting the heavy blanket that covered the entryway. The same kind of stove, this one larger, threw off welcome heat. Even as the snow had continued, the temperature had continued to drop, Muller was sure.

The dozen or so men in the hut once again shared a stew of some kind and something to quench their thirst. This time bottles of aquavit were passed around, and Muller savored the sharp bite of the liquor before rolling over and falling into another deep sleep.

Awakened again by whistles, Muller exited the hut, groggy and stiff; God, his legs were killing him. He took several deep breaths and then bent over at the waist, trying to touch his toes to stretch.

"OOOff." He must have groaned aloud, because the man beside him chuckled and made known that he too was suffering from yesterday's exertions. Muller looked about him and found he could see better, then glanced up and saw the skies had cleared and stars and a crescent moon threw off nocturnal light.

Muller spied a large white colored tent off to one side. The flaps were down, but traces of light escaped beneath it. Men lined up at the entry and he shuffled along with them; it was a mess tent, Muller realized. Once inside he saw low stoves and what resembled picnic tables where soldiers were serving up large bowls of what turned out to be hot mush of some kind along with large biscuits. He took his bowl and several biscuits over to an empty corner and began slurping the oatmeal from his bowl–no spoons– and gnawed at the bread.

God, it was good.

He put his empty bowl in a pile with others and took a tin cup, joining a line for hot coffee.

Sheer bliss, as he drank the hot dark coffee and continued to attack the hard biscuits.

Standing to the side, he saw a man bearing some kind of insignia approach him; an officer perhaps?

"Do you speak German?" the man asked.

"Yes," replied Muller, his mouth still full of biscuits. "Sorry," he apologized, putting his hand over his mouth as he swallowed the last of it.

"Yes, I speak German," he said.

The man smiled at him.

"Well, good. Maybe you can tell me who you are then," the man said. "Several of my men have told me about some guy in our ranks who doesn't speak or understand Finnish, but who's been a good soldier.

"So, who are you anyway?"

Muller told him the story.

The officer, if that's what he was, listened with a surprised, but friendly expression.

"So, you're a Swiss diplomat, you were touring the front and after the barrage you just joined up with us? Do I have that right?" he asked.

Muller drew a deep breath.

"My escorts, Lieutenant Joleka and Mr. Venta, from the Foreign Office were killed in the artillery attack," he said. "I was somehow thrown out of our van, but all the others were killed when it crashed down into a ravine.

"Did you say Lieutenant Joleka?" the officer asked. "Killed in the barrage? Good God, he was one of our best young officers. Damn!"

The officer stamped his foot in anger.

"Well, we're giving those Soviet bastards back a lot more than they bargained for. But....Damn!"

"I don't know how I survived the attack," Muller said, his mind finally beginning to function again. "But when it finally ended and I realized we were under attack, I just joined the other soldiers. There wasn't much other choice," he added, "no one would have cared if I was some kind of diplomat. I don't speak your language and, to be honest, my mind was still reeling from what had happened, so I just followed along."

"And managed to kill your fair share of Goddamned Soviets, I'm told," the officer said, clapping Muller on the shoulder, then extending his mittened hand to shake Muller's.

"My name's Hakala," he said.

"Muller," Muller replied, "Thank you for coming over to speak to me, what's the plan?"

Hakala looked at Muller and chuckled.

"Well, *our* plan is to go kill more Soviets. But we've got to get you back to Helsinki. I'd say you're a Helluva lot more valuable to us alive, telling the world what you've seen, than going back out with us to fight the Soviets."

Stepping away, he shouted at the group of men that were taking down the Mess. Beckoning one over, Hakala spoke to him, gesturing at Muller.

"Mr. Muller, this is Bolski, he's driving a truck back to Summa for supplies. You'll accompany him. I've instructed him to tell the Summa commander to get you out of here."

Hakala offered his hand in another vigorous handshake.

"You were a fine soldier, Mr. Muller. Thank you. Finland thanks you."

He turned to leave.

"You'd better take your gear and your weapon along for the ride; I hope you don't need them, but…" Hakala shrugged, then turned to leave them.

"Good luck," he said over his shoulder.

Muller stifled an impulse to object. Hakala was right; he had no business going back out to fight the Soviets–and he certainly did have a story to tell if he ever got back to civilization.

CHAPTER 29

The trip back to Summa was uneventful. The skies had cleared and Bolski had kept a wary eye out for Soviet fighters that might attack the slow-moving truck as it labored through the snow toward Summa; maybe it was the white paint camouflage, or more likely the Soviet pilots were busy elsewhere, but they didn't see any planes.

An officer in Summa listened as Bolski explained who Muller was, then nodded and quickly loaded him aboard a bus headed back to Viipuri.

Even without understanding the conversation, Muller could see that Summa, the small hamlet where his party had paused for a cup of hot coffee on its way to the border–how many days ago was it? It seemed long ago–had now grown busy, with a steady stream of reservists arriving from Viipuri, and another stream of wounded Finnish soldiers being loaded aboard the buses for the return trip.

Muller's bus had a half dozen wounded soldiers that medics loaded onto bus seats, using rope to tie them so they wouldn't fall into the aisle if they lost consciousness. The aisle itself was where they loaded the most seriously injured men so they could lie prone on the floor. Muller himself was seated at the very front of the vehicle. He was given to understand that was so he and the driver could flee the bus and take cover in the event of an attack by Soviet planes; nothing was said about what to do with the wounded if that were to happen.

The journey was mercifully short; wounded soldiers cried out as the bus bumped along and Muller felt guilty that there was nothing he could do to lessen their discomfort. Snow on the road had been hard packed by the shuttle operation, so the bus made good time and 30 minutes or so later, it pulled into the security gate at the Viipuri base camp. Muller could see the Finns had erected large white canopies above the roofs of the low buildings as camouflage, but there was a line of bomb craters off to one side that was evidence of near misses.

Muller found the locker where he'd stored the big canvas bags with his belongings, then lined up for the short shuttle ride to the railroad station. He turned in his rifle but followed the example of other men, keeping his heavy outer wear for the train ride back to Helsinki. Once he arrived, he saw nearly all the passengers—mainly older men and women with children—wearing cold weather gear too; Soviet planes probably also attacked the train, he assumed.

The platform was crowded, and it was evident that ticketing formalities had been waived, so people were simply boarding as soon as a train arrived, ready for it to resume the journey back to

Helsinki. No warm compartment with a picnic basket this time, Muller mused to himself; the train was packed, and he felt fortunate to find room to squeeze into a corner of the corridor at one end of a middle car with just enough room to sit on his bag and rest his back against the wall of the last compartment.

It turned out to be a long journey; no air attack, but delays and unexpected stops added time, so it was dark when they finally reached the terminal in Helsinki. Black-out rules were in effect, so the platform was hard to navigate for the crowd of de-training passengers. Looking up as he edged along with the others, Muller thought he saw a gaping hole in the vaulted roof he'd admired on the way out, where a bomb or shell had caused damage. And there was a smell–it was smoke, he suddenly realized, acrid and dirty; Helsinki must have been attacked by Soviet bombers.

Finally, the passengers worked their way into the terminal building, but it too was dark, with only a few hooded lights showing the way to the doorway. Muller was able to navigate the exit but as he did so, he saw the entire plaza in front of the station was crowded with people and there was no sign of any taxis.

What the Hell was he going to do? He'd figured he'd find a hotel to clean up and contact the Ministry of Foreign Affairs to reconnect with Erkko, or someone on his staff. But where was a hotel? There was no way to ask anyone.

Shit.

He'd also run out of cigarettes; a man nearby lit up and Muller pantomimed asking for a smoke, which the man offered from a crumpled pack and lit with his lighter. He said something with a smile and shake of his head, but Muller didn't understand and simply smiled, clapping the man on the shoulder.

Having no better idea of what to do, Muller worked his way across the crowded plaza away from the station. The only light came from a dozen or more flickering fires from bomb-damaged buildings nearby; the flames offered shadowy images, but enough for Muller to see there had been serious damage inflicted; probably bombs aimed at the terminal building or tracks that missed their mark and exploded in the surrounding neighborhood.

As Muller worked his way to the edge of the crowded plaza, he saw several big cars parked at the curb–and to his astonishment, saw that one of them bore British Union Jack flags on each fender. It had to be an embassy car.

Muller shouldered his bag and strode toward it. Moments later, a man with a peaked chauffer's cap approached the car and bent to unlock the driver's side door.

Muller put a mittened hand on the car door.

"Do you speak English?" he asked.

The man, surely the chauffer, looked at Muller with a start.

"Yes," he replied, looking Muller up and down in confusion, "some."

"Is Ambassador Snow at the residence?" Muller asked.

The chauffer looked even more perplexed, then, with a shrug of dismissal, began to slide into the car, but Muller held tight to the door.

He realized that he looked like a refugee of some kind, but no matter.

He yanked the chauffer back out and roughly stood him up against the car.

"I am Ambassador Paul Muller of Switzerland. I have been fighting Soviet invaders in the East."

Muller put his face inches from the chauffer's whose eyes widened.

"You will take me to Ambassador Snow at once or I'll see to it he has your *head*."

Muller than pushed the man aside, opened the rear door, threw his bag on the seat, and stepped in, shoving the chauffer toward his front seat.

"Now drive me to the Embassy," he said peremptorily.

"*Now*," he said again, loudly.

The chauffer, either cowed or persuaded–Muller didn't care which–did as he was told, and ten minutes later, the big car pulled into the circular drive of a large building, only dimly visible in the dark.

Muller followed him to the doorway and stepped inside, ignoring the chauffer's instructions to wait.

A butler in formal attire hurried to meet them, an expression of scorn on his face as he eyed Muller.

"I am Ambassador Paul Muller of Switzerland," Muller said, drawing himself to his full height and addressing the man in a commanding tone. "Kindly advise Ambassador Snow of my arrival."

Just then, Snow descended the center stairway, evidently coming to find out what was happening. Seeing Muller, he stopped on the stairway and gawked.

"Muller? Is that really you?

"My God, man," he said, with a start of recognition.

"What the Hell is going on? You look awful. But come in, come in."

Muller managed a wan smile.

"Dropping in on short notice I'm afraid," he said, swaying in exhaustion.

"Karl, take the Ambassador's things for goodness sakes," he directed the butler, descending the stairs and approaching Muller with a welcoming smile.

"A bit of a surprise, old boy," he said, as the butler helped Muller shed the heavy coat and he saw Muller's Finnish soldier's uniform.

"My goodness; you're a soldier now, Muller? Not neutral anymore? That must have been some tour to the front."

Snow was chortling, then he stopped as the realization hit him.

"My God, Muller," he said his face suddenly grim. "You were caught in the Soviet attack?

"My God," he repeated, "but you somehow got here. Well, thank goodness for that, at least.

"Karl," he gestured to the butler. "Take Ambassador Muller to the guest suite. Muller, get yourself cleaned up and come down when you're ready, so you can tell me everything."

Muller nodded; he didn't have the energy to do much more

"Thanks very much," he said and followed the butler.

Toweling off after a deliciously warm shower, Muller examined himself in the mirror. He had an ugly red bruise on his shoulder and left arm, doubtless from his fall after the van had been hit, and his legs were rapidly stiffening up, a reminder of his cross-country skiing exertions. And he badly needed a shave. But he was in one piece, he confirmed, with some satisfaction.

Though God knows it had been a near thing.

It was nearly an hour before he descended the staircase–gingerly, acknowledging his sore legs–to find Snow in a first-floor study, warmly lit, but with heavy blackout curtains drawn. A fire crackled in a large fireplace.

Snow rose from behind a desk where he'd been working and gestured to upholstered chairs beside the fire. He went to the sideboard and poured them both large whiskies, handing one to Muller and taking a matching chair.

"Cheers and welcome, Ambassador Muller," he said as they toasted one another. "You look much better."

Muller took a gulp of the whiskey and savored it.

"I've never enjoyed getting cleaned up more," he said with a smile. "Thanks very much."

"I want the whole story," Snow said. "Don't leave out a thing."

Muller proceeded to do so, but haltingly, as he tried to recreate for himself and put into words the hectic and confused set of events that had engulfed him.

Snow listened quietly, refilling their glasses and offering cigarettes as Muller unburdened himself.

When he'd finished, he asked,

"What's today's date Ambassador Snow?"

"Why, December 5," Snow replied.

Six days; they'd embarked on the tour of the front on November 30. Muller shook his head and took a deep breath; it seemed a lot longer.

As he spoke, the reality of what had happened had begun to sink in. It had been a blur of snow, forest, cold–and blood. Now as he tried to describe events for Ambassador Snow, he found his memory summoning up the helpless terror he'd felt during the bombardment and the awful discovery of the shattered van and broken bodies inside; he'd been in shock, he realized. He'd lined up obediently with other survivors to fight his attackers, his mind a fog, simply doing what he'd been told.

He recollected snatches of the events that had followed: confronting the huge, clanking Russian tank–God, what a fearsome weapon–and the violent firefight that turned the snowy frozen lake into a bloody killing field; laying a minefield; and trying to follow the lead of Finnish soldiers–not one of whom he knew or could communicate with. Sitting now in this warm study, the images he conjured up–the fear and the unremitting cold, the exertion of skiing to the very edge of his stamina; firing at the Soviet soldier–caused him to pause, to gaze down at his hands and try and gather himself, as he haltingly put his experience into words.

But then, he began to speak with renewed vigor and a growing sense of outrage.

Somehow, he'd survived unimaginable peril–a small, but deeply intense personal experience that had transformed the diplomatic effort that he'd embarked upon. The Soviet Union had unleashed a fierce, savage attack–it was waging war on its neutral neighbor in violation of every standard of lawful, civilized behavior. Germany had invaded Poland and brutally crushed it; he hadn't been in Danzig to witness what surely were terrible events. But he certainly was witness to the vicious attack the Soviets had just let loose. He'd instinctively fought back, and he was glad he'd been able to do so; in fact, reconstructing the events now, he wished he'd been able to do more.

As he got his bearings back and came to grips with what had happened, Muller came to a sudden realization: he had a stake in the outcome of this fight.

He fixed Snow with a crooked smile.

"Being attacked–and surviving–is a little disorienting," he said, "the events are still a little foggy, and somehow I'm still in one piece.

"But what happened here? The Soviets bombed Helsinki?"

"About the same time that they attacked you at the border," Snow replied, nodding.

"No warning," he said. "Bombers suddenly appeared overhead dropping incendiaries and high explosives. The air raid sirens didn't even go off till after they'd left. Then they came back about dusk for another run and killed a lot of rescue workers. At least that time the flak batteries got off a few shots at them. And they've come back every day since, too. Fortunately, they have terrible aim and damage isn't too bad; but the attacks have completely upended life here."

"Is the government resisting?" Muller asked. "Erkko's prediction that the Soviets were bluffing was certainly wrong."

Snow smiled.

"It literally blew up in his face, didn't it?" Snow smiled. "He and the rest of the government were sacked the next day."

"So, who's Foreign Minister now?" asked Muller.

His visit to Finland and the tour of what was supposed to be the neutral border with the Soviet Union were both completely Erkko's doing; if he was out of power, would his replacement know about them? Or even know about Muller's existence?

"Väinö Tanner," Snow replied. "He's head of the Social Democrats and took charge after the Soviet attacks. He took the Foreign Ministry for himself and got the Diet to appoint Risto Ryti, the Finnish Central Banker as the new Prime Minister.

"Good guys, both of them," Snow added. "Ryti's running the war effort, including getting aid from abroad and Tanner's working the diplomatic front.

"Oh, and most important," he added, "Marshal Mannerheim withdrew his resignation and has been installed as Commander in Chief of the Finnish Army. The Three of them are committed to defending every meter of Finnish territory and inflict maximum casualties on the Soviet invaders to force Stalin to offer terms. They're putting up a helluva fight too."

"Did you see troops using Molotov Cocktails, Ambassador Muller?" asked Snow excitedly, leaning forward and refilling their glasses.

Muller looked at him quizzically.

"The bottles they fire up to throw at Soviet tanks," Snow said, smiling. "That's what they're called; everyone's talking about them."

'Molotov Cocktails', Muller repeated to himself; well, why not?

"I did," he replied. "They're very effective weapons."

He didn't share the image of panicked Soviet tank crews desperately trying to escape their flaming vehicles and being cut down by Finnish gunfire.

"The State Liquor Board has gone into high gear to produce enough bottles for the soldiers to use," Snow said enthusiastically. "The image of tossing Molotov Cocktails has become a big morale booster here."

The butler, Karl, entered the study and announced that dinner was being served.

"I'm afraid, it's not going to be very haute cuisine," Snow said, leading Muller into a small dining room. "Strict rationing rules have been imposed, so the stalls aren't very well stocked. We're down to left-over reindeer sausage and potatoes–but a good claret to wash them down."

Snow was garrulous as they took seats at the table.

"The authorities are trying to force embassies to move out of town, to Grankulla, to avoid the Soviet bombs," Snow said, "But I'm determined to stay. My communications section is here and let me tell you, I've had plenty to say in messages I've sent to Whitehall about punishing the Soviets for their attack."

Snow's tone grew angry.

"Goddamit, I predicted this," he said; "I told them the bloody Soviets were worse than the Nazis and laid out a strategy for widening the war to take account of what was happening. But nothing! They just sat on their hands."

Snow put his elbows on the table and waved his knife and fork.

"It took a full-scale Soviet assault on Finland to finally get their attention–that fatuous Halifax and his bureaucratic minions."

Snow lowered his hands and sliced his sausage vigorously, as if to underscore his annoyance.

"But now, they've seen the light–at last. *This* is where we're going to have to fight," he said, slapping the table. "Right here, and the Soviets will be our main targets–it's finally all set in motion," he added confidently.

"They won't back me on bringing in the Japanese–though they should; the Japs could mount an attack in Siberia that would drain Soviet troops off to the East where they wouldn't bother us. But at least they're now at work creating a European bloc to fight both the Germans and the Soviets–including the Balkan states, and possibly even Mussolini and the Italians."

Snow paused to pour them each another glass of claret.

"You were skeptical of that approach when we met in Malmö, Ambassador Muller," he said, gazing at Muller across the table in a challenging way.

"I hope finding yourself on the receiving end of a Soviet calling card has caused you to reconsider."

Muller replied quickly and unequivocally.

"The Soviet attack is a disgrace," he said. "It's every bit as bad as Hitler's invasion of Poland. And you're right; I was a skeptic. But if the Allies were right to declare war on Germany then, there's every reason to do so against the Soviets now–maybe even more so, after they joined Germany in dismembering Poland, then occupied the Baltic states.

"I wasn't persuaded that so-called Non-Aggression Pact was a de facto alliance," Muller admitted. "But I'm convinced now."

"Ha!" Snow responded with a big grin. "One of the telegrams I received today quoted a leading Tory in Parliament as saying the same thing: 'the two gangsters will continue to cooperate as long as there's loot to be got.'

"Who knows where they'll stop?" he said, tipping his wine glass toward Muller's.

Then, placing his wine glass back on the table, Snow leaned toward Muller and spoke quietly.

"But we do have a pretty good idea where they'll *start*," he said. "They're aiming to conquer Finland, then head straight for the Northern coastlines of Sweden and Norway to seize bases there so they can directly threaten Britain and break the British embargo.

"That's their plan," Snow hissed, *"I'm sure of it!"*

Snow sat back, and fixed Muller with a penetrating gaze.

"We have to take the offensive, Ambassador Muller, and do it *now*. Britain has to seize Narvik on the Norwegian coast and the railroad South to Sweden; we need to deny them to the Soviets and to use them ourselves to reinforce the Finnish resistance.

"Oh, and by the way," he added, "that's how to cut off Swedish iron ore shipments to Germany too—so we get to kill two, well, actually *three* birds at once.

"Actually, *four* birds," he went on, sitting back with a satisfied grin. "It's also the way to avoid fighting the Germans again in France—something both we and the French desperately want.

"Fight it out in snowy Scandinavia," he said, lifting his wine glass. "A much better place to do it than Flanders."

"So, forget that 'neutrality' nonsense from Malmö, Ambassador Muller," he said, rather too loudly, Muller thought. "The Soviet invasion changed the entire chess board; they're our target now," he continued, "and high time too."

Karl, the butler, entered the dining room to clear the table and bring a bottle of cognac and snifters. Snow signaled to wait while Karl tidied up.

When he'd left, Snow bent closer to Muller.

"I shouldn't be telling you this," he said; "I'm not even supposed to know about it myself. But I do, and it's the key to solving everything.

Snow paused, gazing at the cognac in his snifter before looking directly at Muller.

"We're going to destroy the Soviet oil industry," he said quietly. He sat up a little straighter and continued, speaking intensely.

"We'll bomb their oil fields in the Caucuses and their refineries at Baku. There's spilled oil everywhere there; it'll all go up in flames once we hit them with incendiaries.

"Oil *burns* when it's set aflame, Ambassador Muller," he said; "oil *explodes* when it's bombed.

"BANG," he hissed, spreading his arms wide.

"It'll be a conflagration," he said.

"We've got aircraft to do the job–from Turkey and Iran; no issues there. It's something we can absolutely do."

Snow hunched even closer toward Muller.

"And here's the point, Ambassador Muller," he said. "Here's why this is the ultimate solution to our most vexing problems.

"Destroying the Soviet oil industry would cripple their military, so we'd instantly have the advantage on the battlefield.

But even more important, it would destroy their collective farm system. No more oil and gas for plows, tractors, harvesters, and all the rest of their farm equipment. They couldn't grow enough food to feed the nations; they'd face *starvation*!"

Snow clasped his hands on the table and hunched his shoulders.

"It would cause the collapse of the Soviet government," he said triumphantly. "The whole bloody Bolshevist apparatus would come crashing down and we'll finally be rid of them.

"Think of it, Ambassador Muller," Snow said, reaching across to grab Muller's arm. "We can destroy our worst enemy–and they'll take Germany and the Nazis down with them too.

"The West will win this war and dictate the future. It's all within our grasp," said Snow, sitting back and smiling broadly.

He took a large swallow of cognac and tipped his glass toward Muller's.

"Victory is at hand," he said, as they clinked snifters.

EPILOGUE

Ambassador Snow's prediction could not have been more mistaken.

But the real Ambassador Snow, a veteran and influential diplomat who was the British envoy to Finland in 1939–and is the inspiration for the fictional character of the same name in the novel–was in fact writing telegrams to the British Foreign from his beleaguered embassy in Helsinki around the same date- December 6, 1939–which articulated the very same prescriptions for British policy.

And they were being taken seriously in Whitehall.

It's what a lot of thoughtful people believed at the time.

In the immediate wake of the Soviet attack on Finland on November 30, 1939, Britain and France did in fact seriously consider declaring war on the Soviet Union. And they did in fact undertake planning and deployed forces to bomb the Soviet oil industry in the Caucuses. It was called Operation Pike.

This is not the end of the Paul Muller series.

There is a lot more history to cover and another good story to accompany it.

AUTHOR'S AFTERWORD

The book you have just completed reading is a work of fiction. As in my earlier novels in the Paul Muller series, I've tried to portray historical events accurately and in context. Still, a novelist takes fictional liberties, and I've done so here, perhaps even a bit more so than in my previous books. So, as in those works, I have added this Afterword, to share with the reader some further insights into both the history itself, in my telling of it, and the fictional embellishments I added.

* * *

Early chapters of the book portray the tortured delays preceding Britain's declaration of war against Germany in early September 1939. Readers will remember that Paul Muller was dispatched to Geneva to meet Jimmy West, the British agent, to find out what was happening and learned about Chamberlain's refusal to act promptly, even in the face of unmistakable evidence of Germany's invasion of Poland. West's description of Chamberlain's hesitancy, his support for efforts by French Foreign Minister Georges Bonnet to induce Italian Premier Mussolini to mediate a solution short of war and his search for other ways out, as related in the novel, are historically accurate and vividly described in Tom Schachtman's *The Phony War 1939-1940* at pp. 53-57.

According to Schachtman's account, leaders of the Tory Party, some in the formal wear they had donned for dinner, descended upon 10 Downing Street on the evening of September 2, 1939, and forced a dramatic showdown with Chamberlain, while outside, fierce thunderstorms engulfed London with rain so heavy as to cause local flooding.

"After a discussion lasting past midnight, it was agreed that Henderson [Britain's Ambassador in Berlin] should present an ultimatum to Hitler at nine [the next morning in Berlin]; if there was no satisfactory reply, England would be at war. Chamberlain, now icy cold in manner, said, "Right, gentlemen, this means war." There was an immediate echo from the heavens, a thunderclap that shook the building and nearly deafened the ministers. After a few moments, they went out into the night, determined, chastened and thoughtful."

I find the imagery striking.

Readers will recall that Muller returned to the Hotel d'Angleterre in Geneva that next morning where he learned about the ultimatum and then, with West, listened to Chamberlain's radio address to the nation. The novel quotes Chamberlain's actual text (though I did also add a paragraph from the address to the Commons that he delivered only a few minutes later). Muller found Chamberlain's remarks weak and uninspiring, an impression I think is entirely justified. West's observation in the novel that it "sounded more like the lament of a man deploring his own failures than a call of a nation to arms," captures the moment. The language is taken from a sentiment Schachtman ascribes to Anthony Eden.

In the novel, Muller criticizes Chamberlain's delivery as sounding "thin and reedy." If interested, the reader can do as I did and actually hear a recording of Chamberlain delivering his speech at https://www.history.com/speeches/chamberlain-declares-war-on-germany. After listening, I think readers would agree with Muller's characterization.

An air raid warning was in fact sounded in London almost immediately after Chamberlain's address to the nation ended, and, according to Schachtman, "*all London hurried to shelter. In one cubicle were Winston Churchill and his wife. Churchill had at last been called by Chamberlain to take a post in the new war cabinet. Mrs. Churchill commented favorably on German promptness and precision in scheduling a raid just as war was declared.*"

It was, as the novel accurately reports, a false alarm.

The air raid warning was not in fact broadcast by the BBC World Service as the novel recounts. That is a fictional flourish. But I thought it a fitting addendum to the very tawdry process by which Britain was able, finally, to bring itself to honor the commitment it had made (albeit in the passive tense) to Poland–

and to the world–in Chamberlain's Declaration issued in March 1939 in the wake of Hitler's brutal occupation of Czechoslovakia.

* * *

I wanted to add an observation here regarding Muller's dinner at the Turkish restaurant Scimitar (fictional) in Geneva, during the Swiss mobilization, with Alexandru Munteneau, the Romanian Chargé d'Affaires and Timur Sadek the Turkish Ambassador (also fictional characters).

The ensuing discussion over raki and Turkish *mezé* served two literary purposes. First, it introduced the subject (which, as the reader now knows, is a central theme of the novel) of the widespread conviction that the German-Soviet Non-Aggression Treaty was much more than that; that it was in fact an alliance between the two countries to conquer and carve up the region. Second, it introduced the reader to Romania's perceived vulnerability to potential invasion by both Germany and the Soviet Union and laid a foundation for its apprehension of German–and Soviet–retaliation in the wake of Poland's rapid defeat by both nations which, unbeknownst to everyone, lay just around the corner.

We all know now, of course, that Romania's fears were well-founded as, less than a year later, the Germans occupied Romania and the Soviet Union annexed what was then called Bessarabia (Bukovina), Romania's Northern-most territory.

The victorious post-war Soviet Union created what was (and remains) the nation of Moldova in that territory. Consequently, Romania and Poland no longer share a common border, and readers looking at a contemporary map will, understandably, be confused by descriptions in the novel, when that important 100-kilometer border did exist, and which fleeing Poles crossed to enter Romanian territory and escape German and Soviet invaders–along with the Polish gold reserves.

* * *

Ah, the Polish gold reserves. What an intriguing subject to be pursued.

I came across a random reference to the gold during research on Romania's role in the conflict. It struck a distant chord of memory and I Googled it. One of the first hits was a site describing the event, but which then went on, seemingly as a reference, to refer to "a fictional portrayal of the gold's evacuation…in the novel *A Polish Officer* by Alan Furst."

Of course! That's why it rang a bell. I promptly went to a cupboard in my living room and extracted a dog-eared paperback copy of *A Polish Officer* and re-read Furst's exciting account of the event, written in 1995.

I should digress here to explain to the reader that I was (and remain) an admirer of Alan Furst's inter-war espionage novels; in my estimation, he is the master of the genre. I marvel at his ability to transport the reader into the fraught atmosphere of the 1930's and to recreate the tense surroundings of the time. Indeed, when launching my own writing venture five years ago (which, in truth, was inspired in part by my admiration for Furst), it was my goal to try, at least, to emulate Furst's skills in capturing the atmospherics of the epoch. I lacked the imagination to fashion his fictional plot twists, so I opted instead to tether Paul Muller, my fictional protagonist, to historical events–first, the struggle for the Free City of Danzig (*Danzig*), then, Hitler's takeover of Austria (*A Spy in Vienna*), and last, the threat of economic warfare against Switzerland (*Target Switzerland*). The novel you have just finished continues the same theme of political intrigue, which has become my literary footprint.

Still, I aspire to Furst's incomparable skill at creating literary atmospherics of the time, and it has been a source of very considerable pride that several of the (so far) nearly 500 reviews of my three books have favorably compared my work to Furst's.

So, the reader can imagine my excitement when I put down *A Polish Officer* and discovered that Furst *took the Polish gold reserve only as far as the Romanian border*. At only page 35 of the novel, Captain De Milja, Furst's protagonist, looks with satisfaction upon his achievement and disappears back into Poland to pursue other adventures.

What happened next? Did the gold reserves somehow reach safety to support the Polish government in exile? I decided then and there that this was a mission for Paul Muller.

And that, dear reader, is how Muller came to travel to Romania.

The chapters dedicated to that tale are book-ended by actual events. Romania had in fact offered assurances to Polish requests for assistance in evacuating its gold reserves in the wake of the German invasion. But as the scale of the Polish collapse sank in, Romanian officials become apprehensive at the very real risk of German retaliation if they facilitated shipment of the Polish gold to safety. There was confusion and delay in deciding what to do with the train after the Polish gold had been loaded aboard a Romanian train at the border (which is as far as Furst took the story).

Romanian Prime Minister Armand Câlenescu was in fact assassinated at just this moment in time, and in the manner described in the novel–with the mutilated bodies of the Iron Guard perpetrators strung up for public viewing. That event did, in fact, have the effect of paralyzing the Romanian government, which contributed to the ensuing confusion. This was also the same moment in time when the Soviet Union attacked Poland from the East (before dawn on September 17, 1939). Within a matter of hours, Soviet forces occupied the territory in Southern Poland South of Lwow and North of the Romanian border–which was in fact known as 'the Romanian Bridgehead'–and which Polish forces had intended to use as a final defensive redoubt against the invading Germans. With the loss of this territory and the link-up between German and Soviet forces, the fate of Poland was sealed and retreating Polish soldiers and refugees poured across the border into Romania in vast numbers.

What happened to the gold in this chaotic situation?

There are conflicting accounts and rumors abound–still. The gold's evacuation was even the subject of a 1986 Polish-Romanian movie *Zloty Pociag Trenul de Aur (the Gold Train)* which incorporates dramatic episodes worthy of a Hollywood epic.

So, the stage was set for Paul Muller (and the reader) to have a Romanian adventure. But how to get him caught up in that business? Muller's a Swiss intelligence officer, sitting in Bern; what could take him to Bucharest and ultimately to Cernâuti in Northernmost Romania to play a starring role in saving the Polish gold reserves?

As the reader will remember, he accepts an assignment to be the Special Representative of the Bank of International Settlements–which was in fact, then, as now, a central bank for central banks situated in Basle, Switzerland–and he is charged with converting the Polish gold into the Bank's gold in order to minimize Romania's risk of German retaliation for transporting it to the Black Sea port of Constanta.

This, I must confess, is a wholly fictious plot invented by your author.

So, while, the narrative that unfolds once Muller flies into Bucharest is, as I declared earlier, bookended by actual historical events, the storyline of the novel is a fictional account.

The gold reserves were in fact somehow transported to the Port of Constanta, loaded aboard a vessel named the *Eocene*, and shipped off to Beirut and I feel confident that the contentious issues–financial, political and strategic–that the characters in the novel wrestled with in order to accomplish that feat were actually in play during the real-world events that unfolded.

For example, who was going to pay for transporting the gold to Constanta–and for the cost of resettling and expatriating retreating Polish forces, some 120,000 of them according to historical accounts, many of whom wound up fighting for the French and the British later in the war. Polish pilots, for example, are credited with having played a pivotal role in the success of the RAF success in the Battle for Britain against the Luftwaffe 1940. There are even conflicting stories about whether some of the Polish gold was diverted to the Romanian Central Bank during the evacuation and then later 'repaid' in 1947, during the Cold War when both nations were occupied by the Soviet Union.

The true historical record of the evacuation of the Polish gold is a tangled tale, even involving shipment off to Dakar after France (where it had been deposited after leaving Romania and Beirut) was itself occupied by the Germany in 1940. That is another story and the best reference I can offer any reader wishing to read further about this intriguing tale, is to refer them to the internet and a Special Issue of Bankoteka Magazine, published by Narodowy Bank Polski, "The Wartime Fate of the Polish Gold," September 2014.

So, there it is. I wanted in this Afterword to share with the reader the creative origins of Paul Muller's Romanian adventure.

Maybe Alan Furst will also find solace in learning that the gold's journey, the first stage of which he captured in his novel, ended successfully in mine.

* * *

I took the opportunity of Muller's arrival in Istanbul to revisit the theme of how confused policymakers were in 1939 about the array forces that confronted one another. Turkey is a prime example of the uncertainty that prevailed at that early stage of the war.

The reader will doubtless remember that Turkey's predecessor, the Ottoman Empire, had aligned itself with the Central Powers in World War I, and in the chaos of defeat, had found itself cast aside, and large swaths of territory occupied by Allied troops. The revolution that ensued, led by the legendary Mustafa Kemal Ataturk, established the new Republic of Turkey, which abolished the Caliphate and installed a secular democratic government that was recognized by the international community in the 1923 Treaty of Lausanne.

As war clouds gathered in the late 1930's, Ataturk's successors weighed the options available to Turkey as a new and poor nation, but which still occupied a vital geographic location at the juncture of Europe and Asia and controlled the Dardanelles, the maritime choke point between the Black Sea and the Mediterranean.

Under Attaurk's leadership, Turkey had decisively embraced the secular West. While elements of the Turkish military had been trained in Germany and had ties there, Nazi doctrine had little appeal in Turkey. Consequently, Turkey sought to align itself with Britain and France, though it also had always to contend with the Soviet Union–which was, like itself, a new entrant on the world stage, but also a successor to the territorial and geopolitical interests of Czarist Russia which Turkey had contended with for centuries.

Earlier in the novel, we'd seen Muller dining in Geneva with the Turkish ambassador to the League of Nations. Now we find him meeting with a Turkish Foreign Ministry leader at the Sublime Port itself in Istanbul. Several strands of the themes in the novel came together.

Germany had dispatched Franz Von Papen to Turkey as its Ambassador, and there's a certain satisfaction that we can share with Muller (and his Turkish hosts) at having successfully parried Von Papen's efforts to seize the Polish goal. His presence in Istanbul also enabled the fictional tete-a-tete between Muller and Marte Von Papen, which readers of *A Spy in Vienna* will relish.

So, one theme is Turkey wooing Britain and trying to fend off Germany. In the end, the Turks avoided being attacked or subjugated by Germany during the whole of World War II.

But another theme is recurring confusion over Soviet behavior and the deep suspicions held by the Turks (shared widely by others in the West) that the 1939 Ribbentrop-Molotov Non-Aggression

423

Pact was in fact a de-facto alliance to divide up territory–very possibly including Turkey, a long-standing Russian goal that, arguably, had been adopted by Stalin and the Communist regime in the USSR.

At the time of Muller's fictional arrival in Turkey (September 1939), two historically accurate events transpired that fed this suspicion (which I included as literary devices to expand upon this theme in the novel). The first was the release of the German propaganda film showing German and Soviet commanders strutting around a ceremonial stage in Brest and celebrating their joint victory over the Poles. There was in fact such a film and the images of German-Soviet friendship that it displayed were deeply unsettling to Western observers (including Turkish leaders, as the novel relates). Second, the Turkish Foreign Minister did in fact travel to Moscow for consultations at just this moment in time. And, as related to Muller, the Minister was given a diplomatic cold shoulder by Molotov and forced to twiddle his thumbs in the National Hotel for three days while Molotov and Ribbentrop wound up their second agreement, this one called the Soviet-German Friendship and Boundary Agreement, which, among other things formally divided up Poland between them.

Emin Unsal's drunken appearance at the end of Muller's dinner with the British Consul General in Istanbul, introduced the reader to the actual text of the communiqué issued by Ribbentrop and Molotov at the conclusion of their second meeting.

Even reading it today, the language seems redolent of shared ambitions to cooperate in future aggression. Emin Unsal read it as announcing a Soviet-German alliance likely aimed at Turkey and, in the novel, he proceeded to get drunk at the fearful prospect of a Soviet invasion.

The language was interpreted as an alliance elsewhere too, and it fed uneasiness in Western capitals, which began seriously considering the potential necessity of declaring war on Russia as the next step in the drama unfolding before them. This is a subject I returned to later in the novel. It serves as a reminder how our knowledge *now*–of what happened *then*–blinkers us from recognizing that, what *did* in fact happen wasn't pre-ordained in any way; events could have been very different–for example a Western decision in 1939 to attack and cripple the USSR. Now, *that* would have led to a very different outcome than the one we're accustomed to reading, wouldn't it?

I find it fascinating–and a reason to immerse myself and the reader–in a narrative, albeit a work of historical fiction, that rekindles the atmosphere of uncertain choices that men and women confronted at that time, without the perspective that we possess today, as we look back.

* * *

The novel's description of Muller's role in negotiating the secret defensive agreement between Switzerland and France as Minister Minger's representative is fictional, but based upon

historical events, as such an agreement was in fact negotiated and–
as readers of *Target Switzerland* will have immediately
recognized–was discovered by the Germans when a cache of Top-
Secret files belonging to French Commander-in-Chief, General
Gamelin, was seized from a train abandoned by French forces in
the town of La Charité-Sur-Loire during the French retreat in June
1940.

Having captured the Top-Secret documents, the Germans
immediately understood the value of the files relating to the Swiss-
French military agreement as a propaganda tool for undermining
Swiss claims to strict neutrality. They proceeded to publish the
contents of the file for the world to see and mounted a campaign to
impugn Swiss assertions of neutrality as being false and
hypocritical. Most important, the Swiss feared that Hitler would
use the discovery as a pretext for invasion.

All this occurred many months in the future from the time of
the current novel's narrative. But readers will, perhaps, understand
and appreciate the irony of Muller participating in this secretive
negotiation–which no one expected ever to be revealed–but which
was not only discovered but made public. In the event, Swiss
officials denied its existence and sought to distance themselves
from it, but the shadow of the event hung in the background,
especially over General Guisan, as the war progressed–and as we
may see in a future Paul Muller adventure.

There is very little information available concerning the actual
contents of the files that the Germans discovered. The Abwher

apparently destroyed the captured documents in the waning days of the war and the Swiss are presumed to have done the same with their copies. Excerpts from the minutes of a negotiating session in Paris at the War Office, which included General Gamelin himself and a French officer named André Garteiser, exist but are incomplete.

Consequently, my description of the negotiations in the novel are speculative. In my account, I created a fictional character André Garteiser and assigned him the role of key intermediary in my fictional narrative which I believe the real character of that name played in the actual event. I also introduced General Besson in my narrative. The real Besson was in fact appointed Commander of the French 8th Army in October 1939, but he had no known role in the Swiss-French agreement. I used the fictional Besson as a device to introduce the reader to divisions that did in fact exist among both the military and political leaders of France at the time. And yes, Daladier and Reynaud were both known to have ambitious and well-connected mistresses who intrigued for their rival lovers in the halls of power in France. The fictional, but fact-based, exchange between Besson and Muller serves as a reminder of the rot in French society that contributed to the nation's collapse when the Germans invaded in May 1940.

The exchange between Muller and Christian Francin, his brother-in-law, who was a Captain in the French Army, concerning the capabilities of the French Char 1B tank, had a similar goal of illustrating unsuspected French weakness on the eve of the German attack. I was struck at unexpectedly discovering, during routine research, that these powerful French tanks couldn't communicate with one another except via Morse Code. They weren't fitted with radios because they were thought to be too noisy. By contrast, German Panzers were all equipped with short wave radios that enabled them to communicate in real time and adapt their tactics to battlefield conditions as they occurred. As a consequence, in the Battle of France that was to be fought after the German invasion began in May 1940, there are myriad tales of German Panzers simply by-passing and isolating French Char 1B tanks, using their Blitzkrieg tactics to overwhelm largely static French defenders.

Incidentally, the term 'Blitzkrieg' ('lightning war' in German) only came into use following the German invasion of Poland, as Francin tells Muller in the novel. While today we think of the term as defining German warfare at that time, it appears to have been popularized only in autumn 1939 by journalists seeking a colorful term to describe German battlefield success in Poland.

* * *

The Chapter describing the failed assassination attempt by Georg Elser at the annual Nazi Party celebration at Bürgerbräukeller on November 8, 1939, is an accurate summary of the events that took place. Hitler did in fact unexpectedly–and uncharacteristically–cut short his remarks and was aboard his private train returning to Berlin when the time bomb that Elser had painstakingly built and placed in the column behind the podium exploded at 9:20 PM.

The explosion certainly would have killed Hitler and his entourage had he been speaking when it detonated. Photos available online confirm that the bomb destroyed the podium area and show that the overhanging balcony did, in fact, collapse, leaving only a pile of rubble where Hitler and his entourage were meant to be gathered.

How different history would surely have turned out had Hitler not decided to end his remarks and depart the doomed premises.

It is cause for reflection and I decided the incident was worth adding to the narrative.

But the assassination also coincided with the collapse of what seems to have been a very real, if not very professional, conspiracy by senior German generals to mount a coup against Hitler, driven by their desperate opposition to his insistence on ordering an invasion of France and the Low Countries on November 12, 1939.

Haussamann's fictional account of those events in the novel is based on contemporary accounts described by Tom Schachtman in *The Phony War,* cited earlier.

That such an invasion was being seriously considered–indeed, had apparently been ordered to take place, even in the face of determined opposition by the German Army command–is another cause for reflection. What if the Battle of France had begun in the rain and mud of November 1939 instead of May 1940? How different history surely would have been. The autumn of 1939 remains among the wettest on record for that region, and it was followed by the brutal winter of 1939-1940 that remains among the coldest and snowiest on record. What would have happened?

The events serve as another reminder of how differently events might have turned out, had other decisions been made–equally plausible, and in fact actually seriously entertained–than those we read about in our history books.

* * *

A few words are in order on the sections of the book treating Finland and The Winter War.

First, I've tried to offer an historically accurate description of the events that took place and their antecedents. I suspect most readers–if they were aware of the Winter War at all–aren't familiar with the tangled diplomatic disputes that preceded it, or with the ferocity of the conflict itself. This was the period of 'the Phony War', after all, when not much was supposed to be going on.

Well, as Paul Muller found out firsthand, the Winter War wasn't 'phony' in any way.

The Malmö Three Kings Conference in 1914 took place, much as I described it in the novel and photos of the three monarchs can readily be found online, preserving their awkward pose as they peer expressionless at the camera. The (then) three Scandinavian nations remained neutral in the Great War and, presumably, the Conference contributed to that outcome.

But the 1939 Malmö Conference described in the novel, is entirely fictional; nothing like it occurred, so far as I am aware.

At that point in the narrative, I was seeking a plot device for sending Paul Muller to Scandinavia so he could experience the Russian attack on Finland and the start of the Winter War. After learning about the 1914 Conference, I thought to myself, why not create a fictional Malmö event in November 1939 and have Paul Muller attend it as a way to set the table for his adventures in Finland.

I decided it was a plausible storyline. Certainly, at that time, the Scandinavian nations (four of them now, including Finland) were, in fact, desperately trying to preserve their status as neutral nations and to avoid being drawn into the new conflict by the belligerents–or by the Soviet Union, which, most of them–perhaps all of them–perceived as allied with Nazi Germany.

So, I created the fictional conference, decided to situate it in Malmö, appointed Muller as the Swiss delegate and invented what I hope the reader accepts as a realistic and credible conference event. I endeavored to incorporate the elements of what such a conference might have looked like, situating it in the historic Wallenberg Bank Building and describing the agenda and sequence of proceedings that such a conference would likely have included.

I decided, as well, to incorporate a fictional pre-conference dinner at the Kramer Hotel (which was the leading hotel in Malmö at the time, and still exists, as part of a modern hotel chain) in which Muller is invited to join the two British 'observers.' P. I. (Jim) Wilson, an assistant to Anthony Eden, will be familiar to readers of *A Spy in Vienna*, an earlier Paul Muller novel. I decided to revive him as the mouthpiece for the mandarins at Whitehall in London. The John Snow character is new, and my character is a fictional version of the actual British Ambassador to Finland at the time, who was a dedicated anti-Communist and the prolific author of fiery messages to the Foreign Office encouraging the government to declare war on the Soviet Union. The real Ambassador Snow did in fact actively advocate not just war with the Soviets but also a British alliance with Imperial Japan as a counterweight to Soviet influence, and his ideas were in fact actively debated at the highest levels of the British government. After the Soviet attack on Finland, as the novel describes, he re-doubled his efforts to encourage a British (and French) declaration of war against the Soviet Union.

I put the term "Teutoslavia" in the mouth of the John Snow character to capture an attitude that assumed an alliance between the Germans and the Russians. It is a term that was in fact bandied about in Whitehall at the time.

We now know, of course, the agitation ultimately came to naught. But, as related in the novel, it was a policy option that was in fact seriously considered at the time by both British and the French leaders. I hadn't been previously aware of this little-known, but historically accurate agitation to declare war on the Soviet Union, and I hope readers find it as fascinating as I do.

Having created the fictional neutrality conference in Malmö, I went on to add a fictional proposal for Muller to be invited to lead a delegation of representatives from the conference to visit Finland and lend support to Finland's assertion of its neutral stance. This would be the way to get Muller into the line of fire in the Winter War.

But before getting to that point, I created the fictional episodes where other delegates refused to join him in a symbolic journey to the Soviet border to warn the belligerents to respect neutral Finland–and, by extension, other neutrals too. It seemed to me a good way to illustrate the timidity of nations at that point in time and their fear of offending Germany–and the Soviet Union, its putative ally.

The panicky Dutch-Belgian reaction to the realization that Hitler fully intended to attack them on November 12, 1939–related to Muller in the novel by the Belgian delegate–is largely accurate. King Leopold did in fact drive to the Hague and meet through the night with Queen Wilhelmina, desperately trying to stave off the threat. And their note to Hitler, offering mediation in the conflict, was in fact delivered to the German Chancellery on November 7, 1939, the very date Hitler delivered his speech at the Bürgerbräukeller in Munich only minutes before the bomb went off attempting to assassinate him.

I hadn't previously been aware of this late-night Dutch-Belgian drama and decided to incorporate it as the excuse used by those delegations not to travel to Finland with Muller.

As we know, the German attack–which Hitler did in fact insist should begin on November 12, 1939, and which was vehemently opposed by the German Army leadership, almost to the point of mutiny–was postponed at the last minute.

To this day, Hitler's decision to postpone the November 12 invasion order, remains wrapped in mystery. Observers ascribe it to some combination of the awful weather and the aftermath of the assassination attempt. What scholars do agree upon is that the security crackdown by the Gestapo in the wake of the failed bomb plot terrified the Generals who were, in fact, actively discussing a military coup to prevent Hitler from issuing the invasion order; they abandoned it entirely and, relieved that the November invasion orders had been shelved, returned to planning the invasion that in fact ultimately took place the following May.

* * *

The Chapter describing Muller's travel to Finland and finding himself caught in the ferocious Soviet attack is entirely fictional. But once again, I tried to capture a historically valid description of the events that did in fact transpire. For example, the attack began with a fearsome Soviet artillery barrage along virtually the entire length of the Finnish-Soviet border–and was at its most intense along the border with the Karelian Isthmus where Muller and his two unlucky (fictional) escorts were visiting.

My accounts of the fighting are also intended to be historically valid. The so-called Mannerheim Line was, as Muller was told, largely a combination of defensive terrain and fierce Finnish fighters. The Finnish Army employed the kinds of guerrilla warfare tactics I describe and for months fought the Soviet Army to a draw, exacting fearful losses from the Soviets' ill-prepared and badly led forces. The images of snowy, frozen lakes turned red by the blood of Soviet soldiers being gunned down are harrowing but realistic.

And the Winter War did see the invention of what was called the Molotov Cocktail, a bottle of flammable liquid with a cloth top that was lit and tossed at tanks and Soviet personnel with devastating results. They're weapons still used today–and still called Molotov cocktails.

I used Muller's introduction to the fictional Lieutenant Joleka and foreign service officer Venta as a device for exploring, again I hope historically accurately, the tangled diplomatic disputes that preceded the Winter War.

I was particularly taken by the bitter disagreements that existed between the political leadership of Finland and Field Marshal Mannerheim, its military commander. He turned out to be on the right side of the argument; Stalin wasn't bluffing. Soviet determination to take control of Finnish territory bordering Leningrad and Western Russia trumped the risk of international condemnation and Stalin unleashed his forces. The war lasted until March 1940 and gained Stalin less than he'd sought–and at a fearsome cost; but he achieved his objective, and the events that occurred only eighteen months later, when Germany invaded the

Soviet Union and laid siege to Leningrad, would very likely have turned out differently had he not proceeded as he did.

Readers wishing to learn more about this subject may wish to consult *The Winter War* by Eloise Engle and Lauri Paananen, which I found to be a very helpful source.

Incidentally, readers searching to locate Viipuri on a current map of Finland should know that in the wake of World War II, the Finnish-Russian border was moved fifty miles or so to the West; consequently, most of Karelian Isthmus today lies within Russia (providing added territorial protection for Leningrad, now St. Petersburg) and what was Viipuri in Finland is now Vyborg in Russia.

The End

REQUEST TO REVIEW

Dear Reader,

If you enjoyed *If WAR Should Come,* please go to the book's page on the Amazon/books website and scroll down to **write a review.** It only needs to be a brief comment on the book and/or your reaction to it. This is my most important link to you, other readers, and potential readers.

As an independent author publishing on Amazon, I am dependent upon Amazon to market and distribute my books, and strong reviews are an indispensable part of its sales promotion process.

I am greatly complimented and honored by the wonderful reviews for my first three books–over 600 so far–which I like to think is only a small percentage of the readers I have been able to touch.

I would be grateful if you'd take a moment to add your reactions in a review.

THANK YOU.

WILLIAM WALKER BOOKS

The Paul Muller Series (in order)

Danzig

A Spy in Vienna

Target Switzerland

If WAR Should Come

ABOUT THE AUTHOR

William N. Walker brings to his series of Paul Muller novels a lifetime of experience as a diplomat, government official and international businessman.

Mr. Walker was Ambassador and Chief Trade Negotiator for the United States in the Tokyo Round of Multilateral Trade negotiations conducted under the auspices of the General Agreement on Tariffs and Trade in Geneva. He lived in Geneva for more than two years and brings first-hand diplomatic knowledge to the story. While the GATT was hardly the League of Nations, international organizations now, as then, are unwieldly and susceptible to the kinds of infighting and manipulation that we witness in the book.

As a member of the Nixon Administration, Mr. Walker was also a close observer of the political intrigue that destroyed Nixon's presidency. Later, he served as Director of the Presidential Personnel Office for President Ford. After leaving government, he became a partner in a large Wall Street law firm, running a successful international law practice. Later, he established a company, which he continues to operate, devoted to international business that has included transactions in the Europe, the former Soviet Union, Turkey, Central Asia, and the Middle East. He describes himself as a recovering attorney.

As a young man, Mr. Walker was a professional baseball player. He is a founder of the Virginia Rugby Club and the Chicago Lions RFC (both of which remain flourishing organizations all these years later) and was inducted into the Virginia Rugby Hall of Fame in 2013. He is a long-time member of Winged Foot Golf Club and Larchmont Yacht Club.

He also remains an active commentator on national and world events and is the author of Op Ed articles published during 2021 in *The Wall Street Journal* and *The Washington Post*. (Texts are available in the News section of http://www.authorwilliamwalker.com)

Mr. Walker is a winner of the Distinguished Alumnus Award from Wesleyan University. He is the father of three grown children and lives with his wife on Cape Cod in Massachusetts.